The Secret of the Silver Serpent

Serpent

A Cozy Mystery

L.L. Gray

Heroic Rose Publishing

For my readers

*Thank you for stepping into this world with me.
Whether you're here for the mysteries,
the magic,
or just to escape the chaos for a while,
I'm endlessly grateful for every moment you spend here in Havenwood.*

*So curl up, get cozy, and let's go on an adventure together.
This book—and all the ones to come—are for you.*

Contents

Grab your FREE novella now!

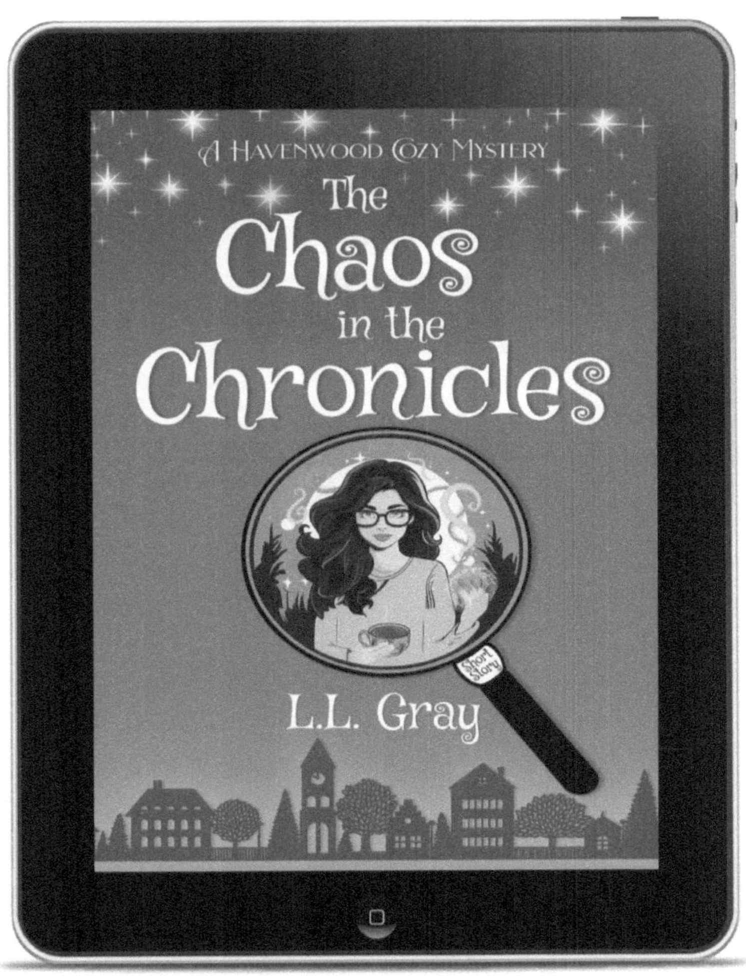

Want a free book?

Of course you do, what madness could possess someone to **not** want free books?
There's no catch - you do sign-up for my mailing list but you can unsubscribe at any time.
There's also no spam.
Ever.
Sign up here to get your free book!
https://www.subscribepage.io/havenwood

To Ask or Not to Ask

DELICATE SNOWFLAKES DRIFTED LAZILY from the heavens, blanketing the quaint streets of Havenwood in a soft, shimmering veil of white. The bell above the door jangled as my customer left, clutching the latest Kristen Painter book close to her chest. I waved goodbye, thankful for the cozy warmth of my bookshop as an icy breeze blew her down the street. The air that gusted into Spellbooks as she hurried out into the wintery scene was filled with the crisp scent of frost-covered pines and the faint hint of wood smoke from nearby chimneys. The door swung shut, cutting off the snow and chilly wind, leaving behind just the snug embrace of my shop.

I breathed deeply, savoring the tranquility and warmth of a momentarily quiet bookshop. This enchanted space was mine, and while I relished sharing it with fellow lovers of the written word, I cherished these peaceful moments. Gradually, the shop's cozy ambiance enveloped me, chasing away the chill of the December day. I smiled as I glanced around the bookshop, comforted by the familiar scent of good stories, freshly brewed coffee, and toffee nut cookies dusted with cinnamon and sugar.

I gave into temptation, plucking one of the decadent cookies from the plate, savoring its warm, nostalgic flavor as it melted on my tongue. The strains of classic Christmas songs floated through the air, playing softly on the small Bluetooth speaker that looked like a vintage radio nestled on a nearby shelf.

As I nibbled on my cookie, I looked around my shop with pride. I'd inherited Sullivan's Spellbooks from my great-granny nearly three months ago, and, except for an unexpected and narrowly avoided imp-related catastrophe during the Halloween season, I felt like I was really settling into life here in Havenwood. I'd even made sure to get my holiday decorations up in time for all the town events leading up to Christmas with no magical mishaps. Things had been running smoothly since then, and I'd just completed the first of my online business courses. All in all, it felt like I had my act together and was thriving as a shop owner in Havenwood.

Inside Spellbooks, the atmosphere was cozy and inviting, illuminated by the soft glow of twinkling Christmas lights that adorned the windows and shelves. Mr. Wigglesworth, the Maine Coon cat who deigned to grace us with his presence as Spellbooks' shop mascot, lounged on his bed that I'd covered in a cheerful fabric featuring Christmas trees and Santa hats. In the other window snoozed our resident rabbit on her own festive bed. With her sharp eyes and snowy white fur, Luna offered sage—and often snarky—advice to the locals who knew enough to ask her, and most days, even those who didn't. Her cantankerous demeanor was well-known in Havenwood, but her wisdom was undeniable, making her a revered, albeit grumpy, presence in the shop.

Lost in the comforting embrace of the season and a quiet moment in the day-to-day business of running Spellbooks, I reflected on how far I had come. From uncertain beginnings, I was gradually becoming a more capable business owner. Business was steady, and I was finally finding my footing, feeling more confident each day. For the first time in my life, I felt like I was putting down roots in a place where I could enjoy being for a very long time.

My gaze drifted to the elegant invitation that lay open on the counter before me—an invitation to the illustrious annual ball hosted by the wealthy Silverthorne family, who basically owned most of Havenwood. The delicate gold script shimmered in the soft light, beckoning me to step into a world of holiday festivities unlike anything I'd ever experienced.

*You are cordially invited to join us for an unfor-
gettable evening of enchantment
at the Silverthorne's annual Christmas Eve Ball.
Dress Code: Formal Black Tie
The theme of this year's ball is "Enchanted Elegance."
We encourage you to don your most elegant holiday-inspired attire
as we celebrate the season.
Please Note:
In adherence to the hostess' express wishes,
no jewelry is permitted at this year's celebra-
tions.
Rest assured, the night's festivities will provide
ample opportunities for you to shine.*

As I traced the intricately embossed holly pattern, a thrill of anticipation coursed through me. The Silverthorne Ball held almost legendary status in Havenwood. It promised to be a night of enchantment and revelry. Never in a million years had I imagined receiving an invitation to such an exclusive event, especially in my first year as a full-time resident in Havenwood. However, I had helped the youngest Silverthorne, Isadora, out of a rather difficult situation with some quick thinking and even quicker action. She'd initially invited me as a thank-you, but over the past couple of months, we'd become friends even though she'd gone back to her private magic academy after Halloween. To me, the invitation to the ball was a testament to the unexpected twists and turns life could take. For one, six months ago, I couldn't have predicted that I would now live in Havenwood, running a magical bookshop, and talking to an irritable rabbit daily. But here I was.

Luna, the white rabbit in question, had been my granny's closest companion before she passed. She hopped up onto the counter, carefully selecting a cookie for herself. I never understood how she could occasionally eat human food without getting sick, but I supposed it was one of the perks of being a magical, talking rabbit.

"What are you looking at?" Luna asked as she delicately nibbled at the cookie, her pink nose twitching with curiosity.

I showed her the invitation. "I'm just thinking about the Silverthorne Ball. It's a good thing Isadora promised to take me dress shopping because I don't think I have a thing to wear to an event like this," I said, mentally reviewing my stock of jeans, sweaters, and heavy boots. They were great for battling the winter cold in Connecticut but wouldn't even be close to appropriate for a Christmas Eve Ball.

"I suppose it depends on the theme Vivienne picked this year. Your granny has quite a few costumes and dresses tucked away. I'm sure you could alter one if you really needed to. You are a sight taller than she was."

I thought of the massive, dusty attic I'd discovered back in October. Not only was Spellbooks a magical, sentient bookshop that could and did communicate with me regularly, but it was apparently not constrained by the same laws of physics and space as the rest of the buildings in Havenwood. Or the world, for that matter. I had a feeling I'd only uncovered the smallest fraction of the secrets Spellbooks held, which was both thrilling and slightly nerve-wracking.

Luna cleared her throat loudly. "Fluff and furballs, you're more distracted than an elf in a candy cane forest. What is going on with you?"

I shook my head to clear my thoughts and chuckled as the song on the radio shifted to one of my favorite carols. "Just excited, I guess. I've never been to anything this fancy before. Sure, there was the occasional event or gala on the bases where my dad was stationed that we attended as a family, but nothing like this." Speaking of dad reminded me I hadn't talked to either of my parents recently. I made a mental note to call them.

"Well, the Silverthorne Ball is a rather exclusive event. I've always enjoyed it when Beatrice and I were invited," Luna said.

"You've gone to the Silverthorne Ball?" I asked, astonished.

Luna smirked, her whiskers twitching. "Of course, I have. They rotate the invitations around so the locals of Havenwood get invited every so often. Why, the last time I went, it was a Winter Wonderland theme. I had crystals put in my fur and Elowen Wispdale made me the most darling little snowflake tiara."

I nodded, my mind flashing back to Elowen's jewelry shop. She was a gifted jeweler who crafted unique and gorgeous pieces. It didn't surprise me in the least that Luna had worn something made by Elowen to the Silverthorne Ball, although I would've given anything to see Luna hopping around in a tiara.

Luna asked, "What is the theme this year? It's usually something with snow or ice."

I tapped the invitation and then slid it over to her. "Enchanted Elegance. But look here, they specifically said no jewelry."

"Hoppy horrors! No jewelry? The audacity! Jewelry is the best part of any ball! What is Vivienne thinking?" Luna exclaimed.

Luna's opinion didn't surprise me. Personally, I was looking forward to the dress, but I imagined it was fairly hard to fit a ballgown on a bunny, let alone hop efficiently in one. When she'd attended the ball, maybe she wore a jumpsuit with a skirt train? Although if I mentioned something about a jumpsuit to her, she'd probably go off on a thirty-minute tangent on how rabbits should be influencing more of the fashion world today, including jump-suits. Knowing Luna, she'd probably rename them to leporine leapwear or hop couture.

Rather than go down that rabbit hole, I said mildly, "This is my first ball, so I won't know the difference."

Luna's nose twitched. "I suppose, but you are missing out on at least half the fun. Well, you've got the dress and lack of jewelry sorted. Now, let's talk about your plus one. Who's it going to be?" she pressed eagerly.

As Luna leaned forward, her eyes sparkling with curiosity, I couldn't help but feel a pang of uncertainty. I'd originally planned to go with Bella, my best friend. She'd been so welcoming and kind since I returned to Havenwood. Spending a magical Christmas ball with her seemed like a perfect way to say a small thank you for all she'd done to support me, but as luck would have it, she received her own invitation when the Silverthornes sent the town invites out. Unsurprisingly, since I was already going, Bella asked her new/old boyfriend, Alex, to be her plus one. He'd recently returned from a culinary course overseas and was now working in the poshest restaurant in town. It hadn't taken long for him to ask Bella out officially, especially because they used to be an item years ago. They'd called it quits because of the long-distance thing, but now that Alex had moved back to Havenwood, they were giving the relationship another try. They were so cute to-gether. I was thrilled they'd reignited a relationship that seemed to be straight out of a fairy tale. They were really perfect for each other.

However, now that Bella and Alex were attending the ball together, I needed to find my own date. Something, if I was being completely truthful with myself, I'd been putting off for far too long. I really wanted to ask Finnegan Oakheart to accompany me. He was the druid who owned the tattoo shop next to Spellbooks.

I'd been toying with the notion of inviting Finn as my date to the ball ever since Bella asked Alex. However, given the timing, I didn't want him to think that he was a backup plan. Maybe he wouldn't. But every day I stalled, my anxiety over asking him grew incrementally. I think my insecurity came from our casual dating arrangement, which was probably my fault. I was hesitant to jump into a relationship after having so recently moved to town and made so many big life changes. Especially since that potential relationship was with my very handsome next-door neighbor. What happened if things didn't work out between us? Would that make things awkward around town? It's not like I could avoid him completely in a town this size. I sighed, running my hand through my wavy hair. Currently, our relationship lacked definition. Would asking him to the ball change things between us? Would he see it as a sign of commitment, or would it just be another enjoyable evening together? More to the point, which one did *I* want?

I hesitated, torn between confiding in Luna and keeping my internal dilemma private. But as her expectant gaze bore into mine, I knew she wouldn't let the matter drop until she had an answer.

As if to prove my point, Luna thumped her back foot expectantly. "Well, who are you going to invite? Surely you aren't going alone?" Her tone drifted toward slightly horrified.

"I've been considering asking Finn," I finally admitted, my voice tinged with uncertainty. I paused, unsure of how to articulate my concerns.

Luna's ears perked up with interest. "Ah, the charming neighbor with the gorgeous smile and twinkling eyes," she remarked, her tone playful yet perceptive.

"Yeah. We've been out a few times, and I always enjoy spending time with him. But..."

"You haven't spoken about where you stand," Luna finished for me when I trailed off.

"Exactly. Asking him to the ball feels like a big step. He and I would be an item. In front of all of Havenwood. I'm not sure if I'm ready for that, but I'm not sure I'm *not* ready for that either. Does that make any sense?"

"Fluff and furballs! Do you like this boy or not?" Luna exclaimed.

"I wouldn't call him a boy," I murmured, sipping from my coffee cup to hide my smile. Luna was opinionated, to say the least.

"At my age, every male your age is a boy. Sometimes a child. Occasionally infantile." She sniffed and added. "Perhaps more than occasionally. However, that's not the point. Put on your big girl ears and ask the man."

"I thought he was a boy."

"Radish ruckus! Talking to you is almost as infuriating as watching that monstrosity you call a cat eat. Food is meant to be savored!" she said, shooting a dark glare at Mr. Wigglesworth.

The decision to ask Finn to the ball marked a potentially pivotal moment in our relationship. Maybe I was overthinking this, and I should just go for it.

Or not.

Okay, I was definitely overthinking this. I should just ask him. A sense of anticipation settled over me like a blanket of snow, tinged with both the tingle of excitement and the icy chill of uncertainty. I felt much the same way I had when I first moved to Havenwood, and that had turned out better than I could have ever expected. Besides, what was I so nervous about? Luna was right. I should just ask him. Worst-case scenario, he said no.

Little did I know then how wrong I was.

Pink Hair, Don't Care

THE NEXT DAY WAS Saturday, and I closed Spellbooks early so I could meet Bella and Isadora to shop for dresses for the ball. We'd set up the date ages ago, and I'd been looking forward to it almost as much as attending the ball itself. As I hurried down the street, the air was filled with the tantalizing scent of freshly brewed, spiced cider mingling with the subtle fragrance of evergreen boughs adorning the windowsills. Snowflakes danced a graceful ballet through the chilly air, adding to the picturesque scene of a small town caught in the midst of a winter wonderland. For a moment, I just stopped and stared, entranced by the beauty of Havenwood. The town looked like it was the epitome of a Christmas card scene.

With Jack Frost nipping at my nose, I crunched over a layer of freshly fallen snow towards the boutique. As I turned down Emperor's Way, I saw Bella and Isadora walking towards me along the snowy street. At least the sidewalks had been cleared, but at the rate the snow was falling, they would have to be shoveled again soon. Isadora waved a mittened hand enthusiastically as I hurried towards them.

"I'm so glad you could make it," Isadora said, giving me a warm hug.

"Of course! I'm very excited about the ball," I said, squeezing her back.

"And I'm excited about visiting the Silver Needle," Bella said, pointing at the preeminent boutique in Havenwood.

"Have you ever been before?" Isadora asked.

Bella and I both shook our heads. "I haven't attended any super formal events since I moved back after college," Bella said.

"And the fanciest Havenwood event I've been to was the Pumpkin Parade," I said, referencing the culminating town event leading up to Halloween.

"That's not fancy!" Isadora exclaimed with a laugh.

"Maybe not," I said with a shrug.

"Besides, I've never been able to afford anything Elliot Ashford makes," Bella said wistfully, looking at the gorgeous dresses displayed in the window.

"Well, don't you worry about that. Like I told you both before, your dresses are on me. It's the least I can do to say thank you for all the help Harper gave me when I was home for Halloween."

"Please, I was just doing what anyone would," I protested.

Isadora snorted and flicked a strand of light pink hair out of her eyes. Last time I'd seen her, she'd had bright pink tips. Before coming home, she'd lightened the color to a pretty pastel that complimented her eyes beautifully. "Not everyone. But ever since you put me in touch with Mason and he made that emberite and lavastone steel ring for me, I've been able to control my fire magic so much better. Even my professors noticed when I went back to the academy." Isadora was an elemental mage, but struggled with controlling her powerful gifts, which is why she attended a special, swanky magic school.

"Speaking of, are you here through the new year?" Bella asked, hopefully.

"Yeah, classes don't start again until the second week of January," Isadora said.

"Oh good!" Bella exclaimed.

Isadora arched an eyebrow curiously. "Why do you ask?"

"My parents host a small New Year's Eve party at the Oasis every year and are letting me organize it this year. I thought planning it might be fun and give the three of us a chance to hang out," Bella explained.

"Sounds awesome. I'm in!" I said enthusiastically.

"Me too. I've never really had girlfriends in Havenwood be-fore. Everyone either wants something from my family or is scared of my mom," Isadora said.

I shivered, and it wasn't from the cold. To say Vivienne Silver-thorne was intimidating was like saying a blizzard was a tiny bit nippy. I tried to hide my response to Vivienne by nudging Isadora with my shoulder. In contrast to her mother, she'd always been warm and welcoming to me. "You've got us now. I bet the three of us could plan an amazing party."

Bella nodded vigorously. "One hundred percent. We'd be like the three musketeers but with better snacks."

"Much better," I said, my mind flashing to Bella's mother, Honey DeLuca. She was famous in town for her baking abilities. There wasn't anything that she could set in front of me I wouldn't enjoy.

"Well then, I guess you could say this is a first for all of us," Isadora said, steering us towards the boutique's door.

"You've never been here either? I thought you said you knew the owner," I said, perplexed.

"Oh, I do. Elliot Ashford's been dressing my family for the ball for ages. What I meant was I've never done the whole shop-ping-with-girlfriends thing."

"Like, ever?" Bella asked in disbelief.

Isadora shrugged. "It wasn't easy growing up here with my family being who and what they are. The kids I was allowed to socialize with were either jerks or just wanted to get close to me because their parents told them to. Whether it was for the perceived power my family has or our money, I never knew. Anyway, I suppose you could say it jaded me. I had one good friend in high school, but she moved away our junior year. And this special magic academy my mother sends me to isn't much better. Thank goodness, the term between Halloween and Christmas was so short or I might've gone crazy. I'll be glad when I finish my studies and can put all those insincere sycophants in my rearview mirror."

"It must've been hard," I said. My own childhood hadn't been full of friends because we'd moved so much, but I was never as miserable as Isadora sounded. "Well, now you have us, and we're not going anywhere," I said, looping my arm through hers.

"Except into that boutique," Bella added with a grin.

Isadora laughed brightly. "Precisely! These are the holidays! And I'm determined to make this the best ball ever, now that you two are coming. We've got dresses to try on and champagne to drink! Let's go!" Isadora marched confidently into the boutique, propelling us on her wave of enthusiasm.

Inside, the boutique was decorated to the nines with a tasteful abundance of Yuletide charm. Twinkling fairy lights cast a soft, ethereal glow over racks of sumptuous fabrics in hues of emerald green, ruby red, and shimmering gold. Glittering decorations hung from the ceiling, catching the light and scattering prismatic reflections across the room. A magnificent Christmas tree stood proudly in the corner, adorned with delicate ornaments and cascading ribbons in hues of silver and blue, casting a spellbinding aura of purely mundane holiday enchantment.

A man behind the counter handed over a large garment bag to an elderly woman with blue-tinted silver hair I didn't recognize, but Isadora apparently did. She waved and smiled as the man, who I assumed was Elliot Ashford, walked the older woman to the door. It gave me a chance to admire his excellently tailored suit. It was a masterpiece of holiday-inspired elegance and something I'd never have the confidence or the fashion sense to pull off. The suit was a rich burgundy hue, reminiscent of mulled wine, with subtle accents of gold thread that shimmered like Christmas lights against the deep velvety fabric. Intricate embroidery adorned the lapels, depicting delicate snowflakes and holly leaves, adding a touch of festive charm to his ensemble. A red velvet bow tie complemented his crisp white shirt and a sprig of fresh holly peeked out from the pocket of his jacket, nestled against an excellently folded, creamy white pocket square. It was a subtle yet striking nod to the season. Suddenly, I felt very under-dressed in my jeans and sweater. I tried to brush my wavy hat-hair into a semblance of order, but only succeeded in stroking more static electricity into it, making it rise from my head as if possessed.

The man turned from the door, his warm smile and twinkling blue eyes welcoming. He threw his arms wide and cried, "Isadora, darling! It has been much too long! What have you done with your hair?" he asked as he clasped her hands and gave her air kisses on either cheek.

"Like it?" Isadora said, fluffing her pink locks that somehow still looked stunning despite the winter hat she wore.

"Like it? I *love* it! It suits you down to a tee. But it is going to make it a little hard to choose a color palette for your gown this year," he said, tipping his head to the side contemplatively.

"I trust you, Elliot," Isadora said, patting his hand.

"Of course you do, darling. That's why you always look fabulous! Now, who are these lovely ladies with you, and do I get to dress them?" he said, shooting a charming smile our way.

Isadora introduced us. "Harper Sullivan and Bella DeLuca, meet Elliot Ashford who has the best eye for fashion in all of Connecticut. Maybe even the entire Eastern Seaboard."

"Isadora, darling, you'll make me blush," Elliot said, fanning his face with a hand. He winked at us. "She's not wrong though." The soft chime of the clock next to the door interrupted them, causing Elliot to glance up. "Ah, I see you are as punctual as ever," he remarked to Isadora.

She smirked. "I remember your rules. 'Show up on time or fashion leaves you behind.'"

"Elliot! I need your opinion on the chiffon over the satin," a shrill voice called from the hall, leading to what looked like dressing rooms.

"Speaking of someone who needs a refresher on the rules," Elliot said under his breath with a roll of his eyes. "Why don't you three start with my lookbooks, and I will be with you in a moment?" He gestured at a cozy arrangement of chairs around a table neatly stacked with books. As Elliot swept back to the dressing rooms, Isadora handed us each a slim book.

I opened mine to see an exquisite selection of hand-drawn gowns and dresses, each more enchanting than the last. With Isadora's expert guidance, Bella and I reveled in the joy of choosing the perfect attire for the Silverthorne Ball, our soft laughter and excitement blending seamlessly with the festive melodies of classic carols playing softly in the background.

A whiney, nasal voice that sounded vaguely familiar rang out from the back of the shop, growing suddenly louder. "But *why* won't you give those others to Thomas? Don't you know what this is for? It's for the *Silverthorne* Ball."An aggrieved-looking Elliot strode back into the main room of the shop, followed closely by none other than Oswald and Hortense Puddleton. I had to work hard not to grimace. The Puddletons owned the Dusty Tome, the other bookshop in town. Ever since I officially moved to Havenwood and took over Spellbooks, they'd convinced themselves that being competitors in business meant I was their nemesis. At first, I thought it was personal, until I saw them interact with other people. Then I realized they applied their disagreeable attitude liberally to anyone not buying books from them. Which explained why Oswald's pudgy face looked like a tomato ready to burst, and

Hortense was vibrating with outrage as she clutched an armful of colorful fabric swatches to her chest.

"Oh no, it's the Puddletons," Bella whispered to us as the odious pair accosted Elliot.

"Really, Ashford! This is too much! My wife needs a dress as we have been invited to the Silverthorne Ball this year. You're the best. As such, you are the only one we will accept to create the masterpiece to show off my wife's beauty to the fullest," Oswald declared, putting his hands on his hips and striking an indignant pose that set his jowls to quivering.

Hortense nodded emphatically, her pinched face somehow becoming even more fraught as she glared at Elliot. "I absolutely refuse to be dressed by Thomas! I demand you finish our appointment as you promised."

Elliot set his shoulders and forced a professional smile as he turned back to the Puddletons. "And I would have been able to, had you shown up on time. As it is, I've given you several suggestions, all of which you have turned down by the way. I have clients waiting who scheduled and arrived early for their own appointments. If you'll excuse me, Mr. Puddleton. Mrs. Puddleton," he said crisply, performing a slight bow in each of their directions before turning towards us.

"Here! Wait a moment!" Oswald called, hurrying after Elliot and grabbing him by the arm. "It's imperative that we have you." He leaned in conspiratorially, but somehow his voice got louder. "I wasn't supposed to say anything, but the Silverthornes have requested us personally. I wouldn't go so far as to say we are guests of honor, but that is what the invitation said, isn't it, sweetheart?" He forced the last out through a gritted smile that bordered on terrifying.

"Oh, yes, of course!" Hortense nodded like a bobble head. "Guests. Of honor."

"You wouldn't want to disappoint the *Silverthornes*, now, would you?" Oswald said. He clucked and shook his head. "Think of what kind of damage that might do to your business. To your *reputation*?"

Isadora stood suddenly and walked over to Elliot with a book in hand. "I think I found something I like. I can't wait to get started," she said with a bright smile.

Oswald glared at her. "Wait your turn. Can't you see we're talking with Ashford?"

"And we're guests of honor at the Silverthorne Ball," Hortense added in her shrill voice.

"I bet *you're* not even invited," Oswald said with a sniff, obviously not recognizing Isadora, possibly because of her new lightened pink locks.

"Which means our needs for Elliot's expert eye are far greater than yours," Hortense said haughtily.

I could see the side of Isadora's face, and, although her smile didn't falter, it did take on an edge that would've sent warning bells clanging in my head had I been the Puddletons. Unfortunately, they didn't seem to notice.

"You're right," Isadora admitted. "I don't have an invitation to *my own ball*. It's more that my mother *requires* her children's presence rather than offering an invitation. We're working on her, but I'm afraid she is very set in her ways." She shrugged and tossed her hair. "Now, let me see if I can remember the guests of honor this year. Oh, what did you say your names were again?"

Oswald's face went the color of puce and Hortense's drained to a ghostly pallor. When neither answered, Elliot smoothly supplied, "This is Oswald and Hortense Puddleton. They own the Dusty Tome." I would've been hard-pressed not to sound overly smug in his position, but he walked the social tightrope between professionalism and showing his satisfaction that the Puddletons were getting their comeuppance.

"And I'm Isadora Silverthorne. I just arrived back from university. You'll have to forgive me for not remembering you. It's hard with such an extensive list this year," Isadora said with a laugh. She snapped her fingers. "I've just remembered! Our guests of honor this year are Seraphina Everbright and Dominic Umbra. I'm so excited for the special surprise they are bringing. I do hope you'll enjoy it," she said, linking her arm through Elliot's, gesturing at us, and sweeping towards the back of the shop. She paused as if a thought had just occurred and turned back to them, a concerned expression on her face. "Do make sure you bring your invitation with you. My mother is being quite strict, and all invites will have to be presented at the door. You know. For security purposes," she said with a little flip of her hair before disappearing with Elliot towards the dressing rooms. We followed her, but not before I saw the Puddletons whispering angrily at each other and shooting dark looks in our direction. I tried not to let their Grinch-like attitude impact my experience, but their appearance certainly had put a damper on dress shopping.

That is, until I entered the magical dressing room run by Elliot Ashford.

Fairy Godfather

WHEN I SAY MAGICAL, I meant it in every sense of the word. His working space was like *Harry Potter* met *Bridgerton* rolled into one with a sprinkle of the fabulous fairy godmother. Godfather. But without the mafia connotations. The next hour passed in a whirl of silk, satin, and velvet as Elliot draped color after color around each of us. Using his gift for manipulating fabric, he whipped up a mockup for each of us using what I could only imagine were enchanted trial dresses so we could get an idea of each gown would look like.

By the time he and Isadora settled on the specifics, I was feeling more than a little like the Christmas version of Cinderella, content to hold my tongue and let someone else create an incredible dress for me. True to form, Bella found her confidence sooner than I did and started offering her opinions almost immediately, discussing options in depth with Elliott.

After much deliberation, we each left the workshop with colors and fabric choices selected, and our measurements taken, but I still didn't have a clear picture in my head of what each gown would look like. Isadora's had taken the longest, but eventually, she and Elliot settled on an ombre lavender look, complete with color changing lights embedded in the layered skirt. I couldn't even imagine what that might look like, but the prospect excited both of them. Bella had picked a deep cranberry red velvet that Elliot suggested, pairing with some gorgeous gold lace. They agreed on a fitted bodice with a flowing skirt and a slight train for drama.

For my dress, Elliot seemed to have an idea in his head I couldn't quite envision. He spread his hands wide, exclaiming, "Picture it! Layers of navy chiffon, dancing with all the colors of the night sky, adorned with a sprinkle of crystals to mimic the stars themselves. It will be breathtaking from afar, but simply enchanting up close. Absolutely stunning, I promise you."

I nodded in silent acceptance, willing to take him at his word, even though my imagined version looked quite dull next to Isadora and Bella's gowns. However, I didn't want to say anything to upset Elliot or seem ungrateful to Isadora as she was picking up the bill for my dress. Besides, I was still getting to wear a bespoke gown. That should be enough excitement for me.

Elliot led us back out into the front room of his boutique. He shook each of our hands warmly, saying, "It has been an absolute joy working with you, and I honestly cannot wait to get started on your gowns. You will be the belles of the ball. I just know it."

"This is why I come to you, Elliot," Isadora said with a radiant smile. "You know how to make a girl feel like a princess even on her worst days."

"I aim to please, but you can hardly expect me to believe that any of you have less than perfect days," Elliot said chivalrously.

Isadora shot me a knowing glance, toying with the emberite ring on her finger. "Good friends help, but there's certainly been at least a couple of less than perfect days this year."

"Oh, I've had my share," I said, thinking back on my recent escapades at the Halloween Harvest Festival.

"Well, not when you're wearing one of my creations, you won't. Everything will work out just the way it's supposed to, and you will get your happily ever after. If you don't, I'll lose my fairy godmother wings," he said with a little shimmy.

"Are you..." I trailed off, not wanting to ask something that might be impolite, but my curiosity was piqued. Given that this was Havenwood, was it possible Elliot really was part fairy godparent?

He waved a hand in front of his chest, negating my unasked question. "Oh, no, darling. I'm a witch through and through. But I do like making dreams come true. Speaking of, pop back around the shop in a week. That will give me a day or two to make any adjustments or alterations you might need."

"As if," Isadora snorted. "Your measurements are always perfect."

"There's always a first time, darling," Elliot said with a wink and a little faux-hair flip.

"Forgive my ignorance, but a week doesn't give you much time to complete three gowns," I said, concerned we would be like the infamous emperor with nothing to wear. Although the locals of Havenwood were not nearly as gullible as the fictional ruler had been.

"Darling, I dress most of those attending the ball. Trust me, you don't have to worry about a thing." He leaned in and wiggled his fingers. "Because magic works faster than any sewing machine I know of," he said, conspiratorially.

Bella's phone jangled in her purse, and she pulled it out, glancing at the screen. "It's Alex," she said as a little blush colored her cheeks. "Excuse me a moment." She answered the call as she headed back towards the dressing rooms for a little privacy.

The bell above the door tinkled musically, and a young woman, perhaps slightly older than the three of us, glided in on a swirl of snowflakes. She was an ethereal beauty with loosely cascading blonde curls that framed a delicate porcelain face, flushed from the cold. Though of moderate stature, she carried an air of unmistakable grace, each movement a testament to her poise. Dressed impeccably for the chill of a Connecticut winter, she wore a sophisticated ensemble that married elegance with practicality. A tailored coat of rich, camel color hugged her frame, its collar just high enough to suggest the embrace of warmth against the cold. Beneath it, glimpses of a fine woolen dress hinted at a seamless blend of style and comfort, its evergreen color a soft contrast to the starkness of winter. Her eyes, reminiscent of polished emeralds, were nearly a perfect match for her dress. They sparkled with warmth as she recognized Isadora.

"Oh! I didn't expect to see you here, Isadora. What a pleasant surprise!" she exclaimed, reaching out to squeeze Isadora's hands with sincere affection.

"You know Mother. Always efficient. I was meeting my friends for a fitting so she made a call to Elliot to see if he could squeeze you in after us so I could take you back up to the manor if you need some more time to go over party logistics," Isadora said, with a genuinely warm smile.

"That was ever so kind of her. And of you," the newcomer said with a gracious dip of her head toward Elliot.

"I'm always happy to assist Vivienne in any way that I can. And if that means that I get to create an exquisite gown for one such as yourself, then I will endeavor to rise to the occasion. Elliot Ashford, at your service," Elliot said with a flourish and bow that somehow didn't seem over the top coming from him.

"Seraphina Everbright," the blonde woman said with an elegant little curtsey.

The name tickled at my memory as one of the guests of honor Isadora had slapped the Puddletons with. I'd assumed that she'd just made it up on the spot, but apparently there really was a Seraphina Everbright. It made me wonder who the other guest of honor was. What was his name again?

"Seraphina is our special guest this year. This is the remarkable woman behind Starlight Treasures. She, along with her business partner Dominic Umbra, are the premier providers of magical artifacts and rare jewels on the Eastern seaboard. Not only is she a visionary in her field, creating a network of magical artisans, but she's also an enchanter elf, known for her captivating charm and unmatched proficiency in enchantment," Isadora said.

Seraphina blushed prettily and shrugged out of her coat. "I should make you my head of PR. You'd do great," she murmured to Isadora.

"Well, it's not often I actually like the person Mother honors at one of her balls. Besides, you lived in Havenwood for a while, so you're practically family."

"It was almost three years ago and only for a short time," Seraphina demurred.

"Still. It's good to have you back," Isadora said, giving her an impulsive hug.

"It's good to be back," Seraphina said, returning the squeeze.

"Oh, let me introduce you to my friend. This is Harper Sullivan. She runs Sullivan's Spellbooks over on Arcadia Avenue."

Seraphina's brows rose as she shook my hand warmly. "Sullivan? Any relation to Beatrice Sullivan by chance?"

I nodded. "I'm her great-granddaughter."

Seraphina's eyes went sad. "I was so sorry to hear about her passing. You have my deepest condolences," she said sincerely, her words like soft summer rain in her musical voice.

"Thank you," I murmured.

Isadora jumped in before the conversation turned too maudlin. "Seraphina here is the reason for that no jewelry clause on the invitation."

"Oh? I've been so curious. Why is that?" I asked.

Isadora's eyes darted around, ensuring our conversation remained private, even though the boutique was empty. She leaned in, her voice dropping to a conspiratorial whisper, tinged with excitement. "This is still top secret, but Seraphina's company, Starlight Treasures, works closely with some of the most talented magical jewelry artisans in the world—think of talents like Elowen Wispdale, but from every corner of the globe. For the ball this year, she's orchestrating something truly special. All the jewelry for the event is being supplied by jewelers she represents. It's going to be an unparalleled showcase of enchantment and craftsmanship. Best of all, we get to wear some exquisite pieces!" Isadora finished with a little squeal and a happy dance. From the look on Elliot's face, it didn't seem like this was news to him. Although as the town's premier dressmaker, I imagined Vivienne probably informed him of the situation so he would not create a dress that clashed with her theme. He moved away, straightening up the counter and giving us a moment to chat.

Seraphina, with a gentle nod, confirmed Isadora's words. "It was an honor to be asked to come back to Havenwood to contribute to this distinguished event in such a significant way." A shadow of concern passed over her features.

"Is everything okay?" I asked, unable to ignore the worry etched on her face.

Seraphina hesitated, glancing at Isadora. "It's nothing, really. I don't want to worry anyone."

Isadora smiled reassuringly. "It's cool, we can keep a secret." Again, she twirled the emberite ring Mason had made for her to help control her fire, sharing a knowing look with me.

Seraphina sighed, the weight of her thoughts clear. "There's been some...concerns lately in the jewelry world. Nothing to trouble any of you, but it is causing me some headaches."

I leaned in, feeling a surge of empathy. I knew how hard it could be to run a business, even though operating Spellbooks was probably on a much smaller scale than what Seraphina did with her business. "In Havenwood, we look out for each other. Maybe we can help?"

Seraphina looked thoughtful. "Thank you, but the magical jewelry business can be quite a tricky one to navigate, what with all the high society clients and artists. Securing and transporting that much jewelry can be...problematic."

Before I could respond, Elliot, who had been rearranging fabric swatches nearby, overheard and joined the conversation. "Are you talking about the thefts that have been plaguing high society magical events recently?"

"Has everyone heard?" Seraphina asked, looking distressed.

Isadora shrugged. "It's a secret so naturally everyone's whispering about it and pretending not to." She turned to Seraphina and nodded encouragingly, "But Harper is right. We look after each other here in Havenwood."

Seraphina looked nervous but cleared her throat and said, "Yes, someone has been targeting several society parties, stealing jewelry from the guests before or after the events. Starlight Treasures hasn't been immune to the thieves' exploits, although we've only been hit once."

My eyes widened. "A jewel thief? Targeting high society events?"

Elliot nodded gravely. "It's becoming quite the gossip lately. The thieves are not only audacious, but professional. No one knows who's behind it."

Seraphina sighed again. "I didn't mean to alarm anyone, but it's been a real issue. I'm just trying to stay vigilant, which is why Vivienne and I are spending such a lot of time on party logistics."

"Well, we'll all be at the ball. Let us know if you want an extra set of eyes or three," Isadora said.

I offered the lovely jeweler a reassuring smile. "That's the Havenwood spirit I was talking about. We're here for you. If there's anything we can do, just let us know."

Seraphina gave a small, grateful nod. "Thank you. That's very kind."

Isadora's eyes sparkled with empathy as she reached out, placing a comforting hand on Seraphina's arm. Her voice was soft but filled with determination. "Havenwood hasn't been the same without you and your incredible talent. If this jewel thief knows what's good for him, he'll steer clear of Havenwood and leave you in peace. Remember, Havenwood is more than just a place; it's a community that looks out for others. Regardless of whether you decided to take a little three-year holiday or not, you're still part of that community in my mind."

"Thank you, Isadora. Your support means the world to me." Seraphina, visibly moved by Isadora's words, took a moment to compose herself, her posture straightening as she adopted a more resolute expression. With a deep breath, she shifted the conversation towards a lighter topic, her professional demeanor shining through. "Now, let's not dwell on these troubles any longer. I'd love to see the sketches Elliot has created for your gowns. It's important to me that I select the ideal pieces to complement your looks perfectly for the ball. After all, if I'm part of the Havenwood community, there's no time like the present to start participating in town events again."

Elliot handed over his rough sketches of our gowns with a flourish. Seraphina meticulously examined each sketch, asking insightful questions that let me know this was not just a façade. She truly cared about making the night magical by matching our gowns with her exquisite jewelry. Finally satisfied with Elliot's answers, Seraphina snapped some photos of both the sketches and of each of us with her phone in order to select the perfect pieces to match our gowns.

After that, Elliot led Seraphina away for her fitting. Bella returned shortly thereafter, having wrapped up her phone call with Alex. We bid farewell to Isadora, who was waiting for the elf to finish her dress appointment. The air was filled with holiday cheer as we exchanged warm wishes and festive goodbyes.

As Bella and I braved the snowy cold once more, I couldn't help but feel a thrill of anticipation coursing through my veins. My dress might not have been everything I wanted, but now I could see how keeping the gown simple would enhance the enchanted jewelry Seraphina's artists were bringing to lend all the ball attendees. Not only that, but the talk of stolen jewels lent an air of mystery to the holiday enchantment. I wondered if the jewel thief would be audacious enough to show up to the Silverthorne Ball. Part of me hoped not. It was mostly for Seraphina's sake, although I didn't want to be embroiled in another drama, especially when I'd be in Vivienne Silverthorne's home. Not that I'd ever say it to Isadora, but her mother intimidated me. However, Seraphina seemed genuinely upset by the whole affair and, although I'd only just met her, she came across as such a kind and sincere person that I didn't want anything bad to happen to her or her business.

As Bella and I made our way through the thickening snow, our steps crunching softly beneath us, my excitement about the upcoming ball continued to mingle with a growing sense of unease. Bella chatted away, but it was hard for me to focus on her words. The revelation of a potential jewel thief targeting events like the Silverthorne Ball cast a shadow over my festive spirit. It might have been my overactive imagination, but it seemed that each whisper of the wind was a harbinger of possible misfortune. I hoped these thieves, emboldened by past successes, wouldn't consider the Silverthorne's exclusive ball their next target.

Just as we reached the end of the road where Bella turned left to go back to the Enchanted Oasis and I turned right to head back to Spellbooks, Bella grabbed my arm, her eyes sparkling with excitement. "Oh! And I can't wait to tell Alex about my outfit! Do you think he'll be able to find a tux that matches my dress?"

I mentally pulled myself away from thoughts of jewel thieves and grinned at her. "Knowing Alex, he'll probably insist on renting the most extravagant tuxedo he can find. Maybe with tails and a top hat? What do you think?"

Bella laughed. "Oh, I can totally see him in a top hat! Do you think he'll try to sneak in some culinary accents? Like a bow tie shaped like a spoon or a piece of pasta?"

"Absolutely," I chuckled. "And maybe cufflinks shaped like tiny frying pans."

"Hey, that's not a bad idea! He'd probably love that," Bella said, her laughter ringing through the snowy street. "But seriously, I'm so glad we're doing this. It's going to be an amazing Christmas; I just know it."

"Definitely," I agreed.

"Speaking of dates, have you asked Finn yet? He's going to need time to find a tux too, you know," Bella pointed out, her eyes twinkling.

I blushed slightly. "I've been meaning to. I...just want to make sure it's the right time."

Bella gave me a playful nudge. "Well, the ball is coming up fast. Don't wait too long, or he might end up wearing his customary jeans instead of a tux. If he tried that, I'm not sure Vivienne would let him in, even if he was your plus one."

I laughed. "You're right. I'll ask him soon, promise."

"Good!" Bella said with a grin. "Now, I've got to go convince Alex to wear something that doesn't clash with my dress. I'm not sure I approve of pasta bow ties unless they are cooked to perfection and served in a delectable cream sauce, but I'd be okay with culinary-themed cufflinks. Wish me luck!"

"Good luck!" I called after her as she turned towards the Enchanted Oasis. "And if he refuses, just remind him you have two very persuasive friends!"

"You could say the same thing to Finn," Bella shouted back to me as she waved, leaving me with a smile on my face. I made my way back to Spellbooks, the earlier tension melting away, replaced by the warmth of friendship and the anticipation of a magical night at the ball. I just hoped that jewel thieves would stay far, far away from Havenwood.

Push-ups and Peppermint Mochas

SUNDAY MORNING DAWNED CRISP and cold. Frost decorated my windows with elegant fractal patterns and downstairs I could hear Michael Bublé croon over the speakers. He was Luna's third favorite, after Frank Sinatra and Bing Crosby, of course. Waking up to music drifting through the floorboards had become a regular occurrence since I'd showed her how to use the remote. She'd been thrilled it didn't require thumbs and often spent a great deal of energy finding the perfect tune. Luckily, neither Mr. Wigglesworth nor Spellbooks ever seemed bothered by the rabbit's taste in Christmas music.

I glanced at the clock on the wall. Michael's unforeseen serenade had kicked off nearly two hours before I normally woke. I contemplated rolling over and going back to sleep. After all, Sunday was the day I usually opened late, so there was no rush to get downstairs. But then I remembered Pixie Pastries had been running a special all month. You could have your choice of specialty-flavored coffee paired with either a holiday-themed muffin that changed weekly or a breakfast sandwich. Despite being known for their sweets, people had been raving about the Christmas Dinner for Breakfast Sandwich. Apparently, it came with generous cuts of juicy smoked turkey, savory stuffing, and a dollop of cranberry sauce with a side of gravy for dipping. At first, I thought it was too heavy for breakfast, but by the way people were talking about it, I knew I would regret not tasting it at least once before the promotion ended. The only problem was the sandwich usually sold out before I got there. Maybe there was a silver lining to being woken at the crack of way too early by a festive bunny. Not that I'd ever tell her that.

I dragged myself out of my cozy nest of blankets, almost instantly regretting my choice. However, with the promise of a breakfast I didn't have to cook floating on the horizon, I decided braving the cold would be worth it. Five steps into my snowy journey outside Spellbooks, I nearly changed my mind despite being bundled up with multiple layers. However, I told myself it was too late to turn back. Rather than thinking about the cold, I pulled out my phone and used voice command to dial my mom. There was no way I was taking off my gloves to dial, but I owed Mom a call.

She answered on the second ring. "Harper! Honey! How are you? Wait. It's early there. What's wrong?"

I chuckled. "I own a business now, Mom. Remember? I can get up early."

"And I lived with you for most of your life. I remember exactly three occasions when you woke up before us and those all involved presents."

"Well, maybe responsibility is changing me for the better," I said loftily.

"Edward!" my mom called. "Harper says she's a morning person now!"

My dad's voice sounded in the background, but I could still understand him. "I know *that's* not true. Isn't that her distress phrase? Should we send reinforcements? I could make a call to my buddy in the Air Force."

"Dad," I groaned, rolling my eyes.

"Don't be so silly, Edward," my mom replied, clearly intending me to overhear her. "It would be a better idea to call those paratroopers you were helping train. Remember, the snow in Connecticut can get pretty brutal."

Dad's voice sounded closer. "I don't know. It might take them a while to get to her."

"Why? Where are they?" Mom asked.

"Australia. If she can hold out for another twenty-four hours, tell her to slip 'emu' casually into the conversation. If she can't, then I'll have to call in a favor with the cavalry scouts up at Fort Drum. They're the only folks I know who are trained to handle that kind of snow and crazy enough to pull Harper out of whatever she's gotten herself into."

"Oh, good. The literal cavalry. Even better," Mom said.

"Yeah, if she needs them, tell her to work 'horse' into the conversation. Or is that too on the nose? What about 'hoof polish' instead? Is that subtle enough?" Dad asked.

"And you think 'hoof polish' is easier to casually slip into conversation than 'emu'?" Mom asked skeptically.

"You guys are hilarious. You should quit the military and take your show on the road," I said dryly.

"What'd she say? Was there an emu?" Dad asked.

"No, but I believe she volunteered to drop and give you twenty push-ups," Mom said.

I looked down at the snow I was crunching through. No way I was doing push-ups here. My dad interrupted my knee-jerk reaction, "Ah, she's giving you lip again? Tell her to make it thirty. As it's nearly Christmas."

"See? You're both hilarious!" I said sarcastically.

"For that you can drop and make it a nice round fifty," Dad said, his voice a mock-stern tone I'd learned to recognize early in life.

"I love you too, Dad," I called loudly into the phone with a laugh.

Mom chuckled and dropped her voice to a reasonable volume once more. "All teasing aside, how are things over there, honey?" she asked.

As quickly as I could, I caught her up on the highlights of everything that had happened since the last time we talked. It was probably just nostalgic recall from my childhood, but the magic of her soothing aura seemed to pour through the phone, making me feel more relaxed. By the time I turned onto the street where Pixie Pastries was located, I'd nearly answered all of her questions about the gowns and the ball.

"Hey Mom...," I started to say as I hurried down the street.

"I know, I know. You're busy and have things to do. Just one more quick question. Now that Bella's going with Alex, are you going to ask anyone to go with you?" my mom asked. I could almost imagine her eyes sparkling with excitement.

"I don't know—"

"Oh, come on. There must be someone. What about your neighbor? Didn't you say the two of you had gone out a few times? What was his name again?"

"Finn. Finnegan Oakheart. And yes, we've gone out, but it's nothing serious."

"Well, do you want to ask him?"

"Mom!"

"What?" My mom sounded completely unrepentant for her prying.

I sighed, my breath forming a cloud of steam in the air. "It's complicated. Everything's been very casual up until now. This ball is a big deal here in Havenwood. If we go together to it, it will change our relationship."

"And is that a bad thing?" I heard the gentle smile in my mom's voice.

"No. Yes. I don't know," I groaned.

"Look, in the worst case, he says no, and you don't waste any more time on a relationship that isn't going anywhere anyway. But let's not focus on the negative. I bet you're not giving him the benefit of the doubt. Why, if you asked me to a ball, I'd say yes."

"You're my mom. You have to say that. It's in the contract," I said dryly.

Mom chuckled. "Maybe, but I still think you should ask him. The ball is what? A week away?"

"A week from Tuesday," I said.

"So, he'll still have time to rent a tux. Ask him," Mom urged.

I bit my lip, holding open the door of Pixie Pastries as a woman balancing two trays of coffees shot me a grateful look. "I'll think about it. But I just got to Pixie Pastries and that turkey sandwich is calling my name."

"Perfect. Get him a coffee and a muffin and ask him to the ball," my mom said.

"Is that really the food of a formal ball invitation?" I teased.

"Fine. Get him a scone and a tea. I don't care. Just stop sitting on the fence!"

"I hear you, Mom."

"I love you, honey. Have a good morning!"

Dad's voice rang out in the background. "Is she going to ask him?"

"Hush, Edward. Stop pushing the girl."

"And what precisely have you been doing?"

"I've been *encouraging* her. It's different."

"Sounds the same to me," my dad grumbled.

"Okay, okay!" I laughed. "I'll do it."

"See! Encouragement works," my mom cheered.

"*Badgering* works. I should know. After all, I've lived with you for over thirty years," my dad replied, speaking to my mom.

I cut them off before their gentle teasing dragged on and left me standing out in the cold. "You both win. I've got to go. Love you!"

"Love you too, honey!" they chorused.

I headed inside. The warmth of Pixie Pastries was both physical and emotional. I wouldn't go so far as to say spiritual, but there were fresh croissants and coffee, so it was a near thing. A delightful shade of pink adorned the walls, invoking the charm of a Parisian bakery with a whimsical twist. Elegant pastries were displayed in glass cases against this rosy backdrop, and the air was thick with the irresistible aroma of baking bread, melting sugar, and the rich, robust smell of freshly brewed coffee. The symphony of scents beckoned me further inside, and resistance was simply not an option.

The display case that lined the entire right-hand side of the bakery was a treasure trove of culinary delights—flaky croissants, decadent chocolate eclairs, and, in a nod to the season, gingerbread cookies shaped like stars and snowflakes, dusted with sugar that sparkled under the twinkling fairy lights strung from the ceiling.

Despite the early hour on a Sunday, the breakfast rush was in full swing. Locals and tourists alike were drawn by the bakery's reputation for the finest coffee and pastries in town. I didn't agree with that particular sentiment out of loyalty to Bella's mother's baking, but in my mind, Pixie Pastries was a close second to whatever Honey DeLuca pulled out of her oven.

Behind the counter, the staff moved with practiced ease, their aprons crisply pressed and faces bright with smiles as they took orders and served up plates of steaming, freshly baked goods. The clink of cups, the hiss of the espresso machine, and the murmur of contented customers created a bustling, yet surprisingly comforting, cacophony.

I joined the line, scanning the menu. In addition to their normal yet excellent selection of baked goods, the featured holiday items today were a gingerbread spice muffin, a peppermint mocha that sounded like coffee heaven, and the turkey sandwich that had given me the courage to brave the Connecticut cold.

Looking at the displays behind the glass, I couldn't make up my mind. There were too many good options! However, maybe Mom was on to something. I could easily order an extra coffee for Finn and a muffin. Wildwood Ink, his tattoo shop right next to Spellbooks, was usually closed on a Sunday, but I could swing by his apartment. It was a little out of the way, but Mom was right. Sitting on the fence would get me nowhere.

But first, I needed that turkey sandwich and a large peppermint mocha with whipped cream and candy cane sprinkles. For courage.

Unexpected Encounter

As I MADE MY way to Finn's apartment, my heart was aflutter with anticipation. I carefully balanced the gingerbread spice muffin and peppermint mocha, unwilling for an accidental slip on the ice to spill my tokens of invitation. I just hoped the coffee would stay warm long enough, so he didn't think I'd bought it for him iced in this weather. The winter chill kissed my cheeks, but the thought of asking Finn to the ball filled me with an inner warmth. Mom was right. I should've done this ages ago. Why had I been so worried in the first place?

Rounding the corner, my steps faltered at the unexpected sight of Finn standing on the stoop of his apartment building next to Seraphina, the elven beauty from the dress shop. They were deep in conversation. Seraphina laid her hand on Finn's arm and threw her head back, her silvery laugh tinkling merrily through the frosty air. He smiled warmly in return. Their interaction seemed so natural and with an underlying familiarity that caught me off guard. Suddenly, Seraphina leaned in to give Finn a hug and brushed his cheek with a kiss as she retreated with a casual intimacy that left me with a storm of questions swirling through my mind. How did Finn and Seraphina know each other? Their ease with one another suggested a closeness that went beyond mere acquaintances, igniting a mix of curiosity, unease, and, yes, perhaps a twinge of jealousy within me.

From a distance, I hesitated, torn over how to proceed. The sight of them together, at this early hour on his doorstep, made me second-guess my decision to ask Finn to the ball. Was there something between them? No, that couldn't be it. Could it? Was I overthinking a simple, friendly gesture? But why the kiss? That wasn't merely friendly, was it?

Before I could decide what to do, Finn caught a glimpse of me standing on the corner watching them. His eyes widened in surprise. I couldn't very well turn and walk away now, so I put on a smile and waved with the coffee cup as I approached.

Seraphina smiled brightly as they walked down the steps to greet me. "Harper! How good to see you again," she said, giving me a hug, which was strange to me as we'd only just met. I awkwardly returned it while still holding the coffee and muffin.

"Umm, hi. Good to see you too," I said, trying not to spill mocha all over her pristine white wool coat.

"You two know each other?" Finn asked, surprised.

"Yes, Harper and I met yesterday at the Silver Needle. Elliot Ashford is making both of our gowns for the Christmas Eve Ball," Seraphina explained.

"Oh?" Finn glanced at me.

I opened my mouth, unsure of what to say. I didn't want to ask him out with Seraphina standing right there.

Before I could formulate the words though, she jumped in. "Harper is a special guest of the Silverthorne's. Isadora took her to the Silver Needle personally, and I got a sneak peek at Elliot's ideas for both their dresses. They are divine, by the way, and I'm so excited to complement them with some gorgeous pieces from the collection. For Harper's, I've picked out the most stunning silver—" A merry chiming melody interrupted her, and she held up a finger, plucking her phone out of a dainty little purse. "Oh dear. I really must take this. Business, you know. I'm dealing with all the details about relocating Starlight Treasures back to Havenwood." She shot a look at Finn that seemed laden with unspoken meaning, but I didn't fully comprehend. It only lasted a heartbeat before she shot a brilliant smile at me, saying, "Harper, it was so lovely seeing you again, and Finn, don't forget about tomorrow."

She reached out with her free hand and squeezed his arm through his coat.

"I'll remember," he said.

"Great! It's a date then. See you both soon!" she said, answering her phone as she walked towards a sleek silver sedan parked at the curb. "Hello...No, take a breath. It's all going to be fine. I promise." Seraphina beeped a key fob and her car flashed, allowing her entry. Rather than drive away, she seemed content to sit in the warming car and continue her conversation. I couldn't think of a worse time to practice safe driving skills. Not for her, of course, but for me.

"So...Seraphina," I said, trying to keep my tone light. Was my smile forced? It felt forced.

Finn stuck his hands in his jacket pockets, hunching his shoulders up as a brisk breeze gusted down the street, nipping at our noses. He nodded toward where Seraphina had stood moments before. "Yeah, Seraphina..." he echoed, his voice trailing off.

"She seems...umm...nice. Do you know each other well?" I asked, unable to help myself. The image of her kissing his cheek was still fresh in my mind's eye.

Finn sighed, the weight of his words palpable in the cold air. "Seraphina...she's my ex," he started, hesitating as if finding the right words was a struggle. "I would've mentioned it earlier, really, if I thought it was relevant, but with her living in New York and constantly flying around the world for her business, the chances of her turning up in Havenwood after three years seemed pretty slim. However, now I realize not mentioning her might have been a mistake."

A sarcastic retort danced on the tip of my tongue — "ya think?" — but I swallowed it down, choosing the high road despite the turmoil swirling inside me. We had promised to be open and honest with each other, yet here Finn was, hiding things from me. Or was he? Was this a genuine oversight and perhaps poor judgement on his part, or was it a red flag? It's not like I had shared everything about my past either, but if we couldn't be honest with each other now, what hope did we have for the future?

"We all have a past," I said, going for easy breezy. Either I pulled it off or Finn was distracted as Seraphina eased the car out into the sparse Sunday morning traffic.

"I suppose so," Finn murmured as the sedan turned the corner. "I just didn't want you to get the wrong idea."

"What kind of idea would that be?" I asked cautiously.

"That I was trying to hide my previous relationship. Things between you and me have just been so easy. Casual. It's a nice change."

"Change from..." I trailed off, not sure I wanted him to finish that sentence.

Finn ran a gloved hand over his knitted hat. "Seraphina and I were pretty serious when we were together. We even moved to Havenwood together."

Unable to help myself, I said, "I thought you moved here because you met Thandor." At least, that's what he'd told me while on a magical picnic in a beautiful garden while we'd been enjoying Thandor's delicious gourmet finger foods.

"I did. Thandor told me about Havenwood when I met him while camping."

"So how does Seraphina fit in?" I asked, my mouth running away before I could get it under control.

Finn looked away, scuffing a toe in the snow. "In hindsight, I should've mentioned we were dating at that time. It just didn't seem relevant, I guess. As far as I was concerned, she was in my past. *Is* in my past."

Remembering the scene I'd just observed, it very much seemed like things weren't firmly in the past, but I didn't want to come across as judgey, so I kept my mouth shut and just nodded.

Finn sighed, looking down the road where Seraphina's car had disappeared. "Meeting Thandor seemed like serendipity. Seraphina and I were looking for a place far away from my arch-druid, but somewhere we could still be us, you know? Havenwood seemed perfect. When we moved here, I thought we wanted the same thing. A small-town life where we could each run our own businesses and not have to hide our magic from the world all the time. Then her company really took off. We're talking meteoric rise. But she couldn't manage the business from Havenwood, so she moved to New York. We gave the long-distance thing a try, but it was hard when she was constantly taking calls from Italy or flying to Japan. Communication was difficult. We grew apart and eventually ended things, but that was nearly three years ago."

"Oh." It wasn't very elucidatory, but it was all I could manage.

He sighed and looked at me, meeting my eyes. "I swear I didn't mean to keep it from you. We've just never had that talk, and with her all over the world, there didn't seem to be a pressure to bring it up. We've kept in touch on birthdays over the years, but ultimately neither one of us was willing to budge. I wanted more than just a phone call relationship, and she wanted to pursue her business."

"And now she's back," I murmured.

Finn took a deep breath, glancing back down the road where Seraphina's car had disappeared. "Yeah. She's back."

Part of me wanted to ask him if they were getting back together, what was going on between them, and most of all, what Seraphina meant by "It's a date," but all of that would make me sound like a jealous girlfriend.

Which I wasn't.

Finn's girlfriend, that is.

I was more than a little jealous of the beautiful and successful Seraphina. I looked down at the snow covering the sidewalk, realizing I was standing exactly where she had been. In that moment, standing in Seraphina's footprints—both literally and figuratively—I couldn't help but wonder, next to her brilliance, her success, what did I have to offer? I shifted to the side, not wanting to consider the somewhat depressing answers that floated to the forefront of my mind.

Finn took a deep breath, his gaze lingering on the empty street corner long after Seraphina's car had turned out of sight, as if he could still see her there. It left me with an uneasy feeling, a premonition that Seraphina's return to Havenwood was going to complicate things far more than I had initially feared.

Swallowing the torrent of questions threatening to spill over, I forced myself to focus on the less tumultuous, though no less pressing, matter at hand. "Well, I should really head back before my muffin succumbs to the cold," I said, the words feeling as brittle as the ice beneath our feet. My smile felt as forced as the cheerfulness I tried to inject into my voice, a poor mask for the whirlwind of emotions churning inside me.

Finn's expression shifted, a mixture of concern and something else—regret, perhaps—flitting across his features. "Yeah, of course. It's cold out here, and this is out of your way home, isn't it?" he asked.

"I like the cold," I lied, my voice a little too bright. "It's nice to get a breath of fresh air before starting the day, don't you think?"

"I suppose. Well, enjoy your coffee. I hope it's still warm. And Harper..." He paused, as if searching for the right words, but then seemed to change his mind. "Take care," he finished, leaving a galaxy of unspoken words hanging between us.

Turning away, I started back down the path I had come, each step feeling heavier than the last. The snowy sidewalk, now marred by the imprints of our brief encounter, seemed to mock my solitary retreat. Behind me, I left unanswered questions and unasked invitations, the cold shadow of what might have been creeping in, settling around me like the insidious winter chill.

A Distress Call

THE NEXT WEEK SWEPT me up in a festive tempest, the air rich with the scent of cinnamon and pine, while holiday tunes hummed in the background. The last week leading up to Christmas was the busiest shopping time of the year, and Spellbooks was bustling with customers.

Each book sold, destined for a spot under someone's tree, was a reminder of the season's cheer that I couldn't fully embrace. As I gift wrapped another book, my mind wandered, tangled in thoughts of Finn and Seraphina, each ribbon twisted, mirroring the knot in my stomach. With every passing day, the puzzle of Finn and his ex loomed larger, casting a shadow over my festive spirit. I knew I should go talk to Finn, but by the end of each day, I was so exhausted that tumbling into bed was all I could manage—though I had to admit; I was partly putting off the conversation as well.

One evening, after closing up Spellbooks, I couldn't take it anymore. I texted Bella, asking if she could meet me at the shop. "Need to talk. Bring ice cream?"

She replied almost instantly, "Ice cream? Uh oh. On my way."

Bella arrived with two tubs of our favorite ice cream. One was a rich chocolate with a decadent fudge swirl, and the other a refreshing mint chocolate chip, studded with chunks of dark chocolate. She'd even included a small homemade pot of hot fudge that we warmed up in the microwave. Once we were settled on the cushion filled window seat in my apartment above Spellbooks with blankets, spoons, and ice cream, she said, "Okay, I recognize a distress call when I hear one. Tell me everything."

I took a deep breath and recounted the whole mess—meeting Seraphina, Finn's revelation, my own hesitation. Bella listened, her expression shifting from shock to sympathy to thoughtful determination.

"So, let me get this straight," Bella said, putting down her spoon. "You've been stewing over this all week and didn't think to call me sooner?"

"I didn't want to bother you," I mumbled, feeling a bit foolish.

"Harper, you're my best friend. You're *supposed* to bother me with this stuff," Bella said firmly. "Besides, this is what ice cream and late-night chats are for. Now, do you even want to be with Finn if you're stalling this much?"

I hesitated, then sighed. "I do. I think. No, I do. For sure. I'm just scared. And seeing Seraphina really threw me for a loop."

"I can't believe she's back," Bella said.

"Yeah, she is. Did you know about her?" I asked, hoping for some insight.

Bella licked her spoon and nodded. "Yeah. I wasn't close to them or anything, but I used to see her around town before she moved away, and they broke up. He never told you about her?"

I shook my head. "Nope, never mentioned her. Not once. Do you know why they broke up?" I asked, hoping for more clarity.

"Not really. Like I said, I didn't really hang out with either of them much. All I know for sure is that Seraphina left town, and they ended things. I think it was mutual? Anyway, as far as I was aware, Finn hasn't dated anyone else seriously since. Sure, there's been some flirting or maybe a first date here or there, but nothing that's lasted," Bella explained.

I felt a pang of uncertainty. Was that all I was to Finn? Just fleeting interest as he pined over Seraphina?

Bella noticed my expression and quickly added, "Harper, you're different. I've seen the way he looks at you. But you need to talk to him and find out where you both stand. Sitting here eating ice cream might be delicious, but it won't get you the answers you want."

"You're right," I agreed. "I've probably been overthinking everything. Tomorrow, after the fitting at the Silver Needle, I'll go talk to him."

"That's the spirit," Bella said, raising her spoon in a mock toast. "And if you need me to cover the shop while you talk, just say the word."

Bella's support warmed me from the inside out. "Thanks, Bella. I really appreciate it." Changing the subject, I scooped up a spoonful of mint chocolate chip. "So, enough about me. How are things going with Alex? Tell me everything."

Bella blushed and smiled. "Things are going really well. He's been super thoughtful and sweet. We've been cooking together a lot, and he surprised me with a homemade dinner last night."

"Wow, that sounds amazing," I said, genuinely happy for her. "He's really raising the bar for all the other guys out there."

Bella laughed. "He is. And we've even been talking about our future, like planning trips we want to take and things like that. I suggested camping, but he's got his heart set on taking me to Italy to show me all the places he visited while he lived there. Not to mention taking me to all his favorite foodie spots."

"That's fantastic, Bella. You deserve someone who treats you like a queen," I said warmly. "And if you need any help planning those trips, you know I'm always here. I might not have lived in Italy, but it seems like I lived almost everywhere else. Happy to help you plan an amazing itinerary that'll blow both your socks right off!"

"Thanks, Harper. You're the best," Bella said, giving me a hug. "But don't think that just because I'm with Alex, I'm letting him steal all my time. Ice cream nights with you are still a top priority."

"Good to know," I said, laughing. "Because ice cream buddies are hard to find."

"And ice cream buddies are sacred," she said seriously, raising her spoon towards me.

I chuckled and tapped mine against hers. "Absolutely. I mean, who else is going to appreciate my artistic drizzle of hot fudge? It really is an underappreciated art form"

Bella grinned. "Exactly. For the record, I've never met a better hot fudge drizzler."

"Nor will you." I said, striking a pose with my spoon in the air. "And he better not even try to replace me as your mint chocolate chip consultant," I teased.

"Don't worry, you're irreplaceable," Bella said with a wink. "Plus, he doesn't appreciate the art of eating straight from the tub."

"Well, that's his loss," I said, taking a big spoonful. "More for us."

We both laughed and continued chatting, making jokes and sharing stories until the ice cream tubs were nearly empty. By the time Bella left, the earlier tension had dissolved, replaced by the warmth of our friendship.

As I climbed into bed that night, a sense of calm settled over me. With friends like Bella by my side, I knew I could handle anything—even a difficult conversation with Finn that I'd been putting off for far too long.

Galaxy Gown

THE NEXT MORNING DAWNED overcast and gray. Spellbooks basically had to shake me out of bed. As soon as my feet hit the floor, I started shivering. I looked around, rubbing at my arms and wondering why I was so cold. Across the room, I saw I'd left a window cracked. It had been so stuffy in the apartment after Bella left last night that I'd needed some fresh air but must've forgotten to close it before going to bed.

"Sorry," I murmured to Spellbooks as I hurried to close the window. I didn't know if the spirit of the bookshop could feel chill, but it seemed like the polite thing to say. Instantly, the floorboards under my feet warmed, making my toes curl with pleasure and halting my shivering almost instantly.

"Hey, thanks! That was nice of you," I said, laying a hand on the wall. There was a slight vibration of pleasure under my fingertips. I continued talking to my building, something I'd grown accustomed to doing in the past few months of living here. "I have to go to this dress fitting this morning, and then I'll be back to open up for any last-minute Christmas shoppers. Keep an eye on Luna and Mr. Wigglesworth for me? Don't let Luna start anything with him, okay?" Another vibration I took for a chuckle met my words.

With warmth flooding up from the floorboards, I hurried through my morning routine, adding another layer of clothing to combat the cold front that seemed to have descended upon Havenwood overnight. I even took an extra ten minutes with my hair and make-up. Although I was sure my gown wasn't going to hold a candle to Isadora's or Bella's, I at least wanted to feel good about myself when I looked in the mirror, wearing Elliot's creation for the first time.

I clattered down the stairs and gave Mr. Wigglesworth a quick scratch behind the ears, and the enormous cat rumbled loud enough to wake Luna, who promptly started grumbling.

"Do you have to be so loud this early?" Luna muttered, her nose twitching irritably.

"Good morning to you too, Luna," I replied cheerfully, feeling much better after my late-night ice cream session with Bella. "Did you sleep well?"

"I was, until someone decided to turn the cat into a vibrating alarm clock," she huffed. "If I didn't know any better, I'd say there was a rogue lawnmower loose in the shop," she muttered.

"Well, consider it payback for last week when you woke me up at the crack of dawn blasting Christmas music," I said with a grin.

"I was getting into the festive spirit," Luna sniffed, looking decidedly unapologetic. "And you're the one who left the speakers on."

"Uh-huh, sure," I replied, raising an eyebrow. "And you just 'accidentally' turned up the volume to max."

"Maybe if you appreciated good music, I wouldn't have to educate you," Luna shot back, but her eyes twinkled with mischief.

"Touché, Luna. Touché," I laughed. "How about I make it up to you with some breakfast?"

"Only if it's something festive and delicious," Luna sniffed, looking pointedly at her bowl.

"You drive a hard bargain, but fine," I said, shaking my head with amusement. As quickly as I could, I dumped some dry cat food into Mr. Wigglesworth's bowl and arranged her morning vegetables into a wreath, complete with carrot ornaments.

"You call that festive? I've seen more impressive decorations in a toddler's play kitchen," Luna quipped.

"If you think you can do better, you're welcome to try," I offered.

"I would, but the lack of thumbs is a perpetual problem."

Rather than stay and listen, I switched on the music, opting for some Bing Crosby this morning. I slipped into my coat as Luna's grumpy mutterings faded in the face of Bing's smooth baritone. Not even she could stay upset when Bing was crooning away. Foregoing a hat so I didn't mash my hair, I grabbed a scarf and some earmuffs before heading out into the cold.

I was the first one to arrive at the Silver Needle. Elliot greeted me warmly, ushering me into the empty boutique from the cold bite of the winter wind. Elliot's attire for the day was a masterclass in festive sophistication: a tailored, navy velvet blazer adorned with a discreet, holiday-themed brooch in the shape of a snowflake on the lapel, paired with a silvery silk shirt. His look was completed with polished oxblood leather boots, featuring subtle festive embossing. His accessories were minimal, while his coiffed hair added a polished finish to his ensemble.

"Darling, I do hope the walk wasn't too much. It's getting colder, isn't it? Make sure you stay warm and hydrated. Catching a cold at this time of year is absolutely no fun. Speaking of, I'm going to make you a cup of lemon and ginger tea with loads of honey in it. That will help you shake off the chill!" he exclaimed, settling me in a chair as he eased the coat from my shoulders and hung it neatly on the waiting coat stand before hurrying to make the tea. I unwrapped the scarf and eased the earmuffs off, trying to keep my hair in order so I wouldn't look like a windblown mess when I tried on my dress.

Bella and Isadora arrived a few minutes later. Elliot bustled around, making sure we were all settled and comfortable with steaming cups of fragrant tea. I was already relaxing into the festive ambiance but couldn't suppress the excited butterflies fluttering in my stomach. After all, this was my first time having a custom dress made for me, and I couldn't wait to try it on!

Elliot clapped his hands. "I'm so glad you ladies didn't mind coming in early this morning. It gives me time to make any adjustments I need to before I'm inundated with last-minute festive requests. Now, I rarely do this, but if you are very careful, you can bring your tea to the back while I do the final fittings. Just don't tell anyone," he said with a conspiratorial wink.

We all murmured our assent and followed the charismatic designer towards the back. Elliot beckoned for Isadora to go first. While Isadora changed, Bella and I relaxed on comfy chairs in the lounge area, complete with a three-piece mirror and a small pedestal, presumably to make the pinning and hemming process easier. Elliot disappeared into the depths of the boutique, where I could hear a constant rustling of fabric. I wondered if he had help or if he could control all the fabric and sewing with his magic. If the latter was true, that was still no small feat. Juggling my metal magic always demanded my full focus, making the casual mastery Elliot showed over his fabrics seem even more extraordinary if he was doing this all himself.

Bella leaned over and whispered. "Did you ask him yet?"

"Huh?" I grunted, startled by the question. Why would I ask Elliot about his gifts? In the world of magic users, probing into another's magical prowess uninvited was a faux pas as glaring as asking a stranger their age at a first meeting—a breach of an unspoken code of privacy and respect. I always appreciated that unwritten rule because it kept people from finding out that I could open any lock I wanted and assuming I was some sort of international bank robber.

"Finn," Bella pressed. "Did you talk to him? Text him? You know, ask him to the ball yet?"

I couldn't help but chuckle, though the humor barely masked my underlying nervousness. "What are we, in high school?" My attempt at lightness felt thin, even to my own ears.

"No. High schoolers couldn't afford Elliot Ashford's prices. Remind me to thank Isadora for footing the bill, or on Christmas eve, I'd be wearing something off the rack," Bella said.

I pressed a hand to my chest and widened my eyes. "Heavens! Not off the *rack*!"

Bella waved a finger at me. "Don't try to distract me. Why haven't you asked Finn? The ball is only a couple of days away."

I sighed, toying with my teacup. "Yeah, I know. I planned to go over after the fitting. Wildwood Ink is normally open today, and I was hoping to catch him between clients, but I still can't get that image of him and Seraphina out of my head."

Bella fixed me with a look that brooked no argument, her determination igniting a spark of resolve in me. "You're driving yourself crazy. You know what you have to do," she insisted, her voice firm. "Talk to him. Figure out what's going on, and if he's not with her, ask him to the ball. But do it today. No more delays."

I opened my mouth to respond, but Elliot re-entered the room, knocking softly on the dressing room door. "Are you ready?" he asked.

"Absolutely! You've outdone yourself," Isadora answered enthusiastically.

Elliot smiled and grandly gestured for her to enter the mirrored lounge area. The moment Elliot stepped aside, revealing Isadora in her gown, it was as if the room itself exhaled, captivated. There she was, not just draped in lavender but embodying beauty itself, her every movement a testament to Elliot's wizardry with fabric and light. Isadora exited the dressing room, and all thoughts of my personal dilemmas vanished as I saw Elliot's sketch brought to life.

Elliot followed her as Isadora floated towards the pedestal on a cloud of lavender and our appreciative applause. Her dress was a vision of delicate beauty, embodying the essence of a feminine grace. The gown featured a delicate transition from a soft lavender bodice to a deeper violet hue at the hem, achieved through expert ombré technique. The bodice itself was adorned with intricate beading that caught the light, enhancing the expert craftsmanship of the designer. What made the dress truly stand out, however, was the innovative addition of color-changing lights delicately embedded within the layers of the skirt. These lights shifted through a spectrum of pastel colors so gently that you really had to watch to catch it happening. The effect was mesmerizing, casting a soft, enchanting glow around Isadora as she moved. She twisted on the pedestal, viewing her reflection from all angles in the large mirrors. "It's gorgeous, Elliot," she said, doing a little pirouette.

Elliot strode forward, a pleased expression on his face. "I have to admit, I took a risk with this one. But when dressing one as lovely as you, it's hard to make a gown that can compare to your natural beauty."

"And this is why I'll never shop anywhere else. They can never measure up to your skill with a needle. Or smooth flattery. You've truly outdone yourself."

"I merely follow where the muse leads," Elliot murmured, his humility belying the passion and precision evident in every stitch and bead. "Now, spin for me once more please, but slower."

Isadora complied. From what I could tell, the dress fit perfectly. Both she and Elliot seemed pleased with the results. While she went to change, Elliot ushered Bella into a separate room so she could dress. In the few minutes I was left on my own, I thought about Bella's words. She was right. I needed to talk to Finn, but Seraphina's sudden reappearance had really stirred a whirlpool of doubts I hadn't realized I was capable of feeling. Was I just a placeholder until someone from his past decided to return? It might have been easier if she'd been awful or petty, but she seemed so genuinely nice that it was hard to dislike her even though her reappearance complicated my own relationship with Finn.

Before I could settle my thoughts enough to actually call Finn, Isadora reemerged in her black jeans and oversized sweater, plopping on the seat next to me.

"Elliot is a genius, isn't he?" she gushed. "I can't believe the things he's able to do. Are you excited to see your dress?"

"Yes, so excited," I said, even though his sketch for my dress was rather plain compared to Isadora's masterpiece. However, she was a Silverthorne and also picking up the tab for my gown, so I didn't really have a right to complain. "And again, thank you for the dress. It was very generous of you to arrange all of this," I said, waving at the boutique.

Isadora brushed my words aside. "Think nothing of it. Besides, it can hardly repay the favor you did for me at the Harvest Festival," she said, toying with the emberite ring Mason Forham had made for her.

She noticed me looking and dropped her hand to her side. "I don't know what I'd do without it. Probably set the town on fire again. But I'm getting better at controlling my magic. I've even successfully experimented not wearing it a few times and haven't lost control," she said. With the help from Mason's ring, it seemed like her confidence in her ability to control her magic grew daily.

"Is it going to be a problem? I mean, keeping the ring on at the ball? Didn't the invitation say no jewelry allowed?" I asked as the sudden thought occurred to me. What would happen if Isadora lost control and set the drapes or the punch on fire? I didn't think Vivienne Silverthorne would look favorably on either of those interruptions to her ball.

Isadora shrugged. "Who's going to tell me no? It's my family's ball after all, and the only one who would comment is Mother. If she says something, I'll slip it off and then back on again when she's not looking. But, speaking of the ball," Isadora said, her eyes glittering with excitement as she leaned forward and dropped her voice. "Have you asked anyone yet? If so, I need to add their name to the place cards for dinner."

"Well, no. Not yet, but—"

"Oh good, I was hoping you'd say that," Isadora said, bouncing in her seat and clapping her hands.

I chuckled awkwardly, taken aback by the unexpected response. "Most people are pushing me to have a date. My mom. Bella. My rabbit. Why are you happy I *don't* have one?"

Isadora leaned forward. "Because my brother Gabriel keeps asking about you. You remember him, don't you? Curly hair, kind of quiet, good with illusion magic?"

I raised my eyebrows, surprised. Of course, I remembered Gabriel, but I hadn't run into him since Halloween, so hadn't given him much thought since then. Now that she mentioned his name though, his image, both from the festival and in quieter moments when I'd hung out with Isadora, flickered through my mind, a calm contrast to the stormy emotions Finn stirred within me. He and Lucas, the oldest of the Silverthorne siblings, had been instrumental in protecting the town's magical secret from the oodles of tourists that visited during Harvest Festival, which was also when I'd accidentally set loose a pair of mischief-loving imps on the town. It all worked out. Eventually. But it could have easily tipped into disaster if it hadn't been for Gabriel's quick thinking and concealment illusion spells.

"Yes, I remember Gabriel," I said hesitantly, not sure of how to tell her about my intention, however wavering it had been in the past week, to ask Finn to the ball.

"Well, he's mentioned you a few times. By *name*. He even said he admired your bravery, especially after I told him what happened during the Harvest Festival." My brow furrowed, and she hurriedly added. "Don't worry. No one keeps a secret better than Gabriel. And I thought, since he's single and you're amazing, why not play matchmaker? If you like, I could give him your number? I know he doesn't have a date yet either. Maybe the two of you could get to know each other better at the ball? It could be fun!" Isadora's eagerness was tinged with excitement.

A wave of shock washed over me. Gabriel's interest, if sincere, was flattering, but I couldn't shake the feeling that Isadora might be exaggerating. After all, I had only met Gabriel a handful of times and barely spoken more than a few sentences to him. The last thing I wanted was to be set up on what turned out to be a pity date.

I opened my mouth to respond, but all that came out was a stammer. "Uh, I—um, I don't know..."

Before I could gather my thoughts further, a knock at the door interrupted us. Elliot asked Bella if she was ready. When she answered she was, he opened the dressing room door with a flourish for her grand entrance. Bella emerged, her gown a fiery declaration of strength and elegance, a mirror of her unwavering spirit and the warmth of her friendship. Bella's choice of a deep cranberry red velvet complemented her coloring well and gave her gown a regal, luxurious feel. Rich velvet caught the light with a subtle sheen, its inundating color providing a stunning contrast to the intricate gold lace detailing that adorned the fitted bodice. The lace was gorgeously stitched with precision, featured delicate poinsettia patterns. The skirt flowed gracefully from the bodice, moving with a life of its own, and the slight train added a dramatic flair that left a lasting impression. The combination of the plush velvet and the shimmering lace embodied a perfect blend of opulence and elegance, making Bella look like royalty. Watching Bella, regal and radiant in the mirrors, I couldn't help but wonder if Seraphina might choose a crown or tiara for Bella's jewelry at the ball. It certainly would be in the right style for her stunning dress.

Elliot turned to me. "Your turn, darling," he said, leading me to my dressing room. Before he opened the door, he lowered his voice and said, "I believe each woman should feel like a princess in the gown I design for her, but if I may be so bold, I've truly outdone myself with yours. Please let me know if you need any help with the lacing in the back."

The moment the gown came into view, I was unable to suppress the gasp of astonishment and delight. It was as if Elliot had reached into my very dreams to craft this masterpiece. Elliot had envisioned a gown that captured the mystique of the night sky. What had seemed plain and drab in his sketch was nothing of the sort in real life. The skirt, a cascade of chiffon, whispered against my skin as it shifted through hues of midnight blue to cosmic purple. Scattered across the fabric and through the layers were shimmering crystals that mimicked the stars, each one catching the light to sparkle like a true celestial body. The bodice was laced into a corset at the back with a strapless sweetheart neckline that also had a dusting of crystal embellishments. With Elliot's skilled hands securing the laces, the gown hugged my form. As the fabric settled, I felt myself stepping into a role I never knew I was destined to play. That of a princess worthy of not only this dress, but the enchanted evening to accompany it. Bella and Isadora applauded loudly as I stepped out of the dressing room, Elliot escorting me to the small pedestal by the mirrors.

"It's incredible, Elliot. Simply breathtaking. I've never worn anything so magical before," I said honestly. "I'm glad you like it, but you haven't even seen the best part yet. Give me a spin," Elliot said, fluffing my skirt twice before stepping out of the way.

I did as instructed. I twirled, the multicolored skirt billowed around me, creating the illusion of moving through the night sky, surrounded by a constellation of my own making. I gasped again when I realized it was much more than that. Upon spinning, the gown came *alive*. I don't know how else to describe it. The skirt swirled in a cosmic dance around me, each crystal flaring to life like a star being born in the velvet embrace of the night sky. It wasn't just fabric and crystal; it was magic, woven and spun, enveloping me in its celestial embrace. Reflecting on the transformation of the girl in the mirror before me, a realization dawned, washing over me with the warmth of a thousand starlit nights.

This dress was a reminder of my own worth, a visual cue that I, too, possessed a light deserving of being seen and celebrated. At that moment, I realized Elliot had given me a gift with this dress. It was like he recognized and highlighted my own inner strength and independence. In that moment, any trepidation about inviting Finn to the ball transformed into an exhilarating challenge. This ball was an opportunity not just to be seen, but to shine in front of the community of Havenwood.

Another round of applause erupted from behind me, but it sounded louder this time. I slowed my spin, halting, facing my friends and only slightly dizzy. To my astonishment, Bella, Elliot, and Isadora weren't the only people in the room. Standing in the doorway, her face shining with delight, was Seraphina.

And right behind her, with his jaw hanging open, was Finn.

Tangled Web

SERAPHINA STEPPED FORWARD, HER eyes sparkling with excitement. "Harper, that gown is absolutely gorgeous," she exclaimed, her tone brimming with sincerity. "Oh, now I really can't wait to pick out the perfect piece of jewelry for you! Something this stunning deserves an impeccable match. Now that I've seen you in this, I have to pull the most incredible piece I can find to do both the gown and you justice."

"Thank you," I murmured, not knowing what else to say as compliments about the dress flowed freely. Elliot seemed to shine under the praise as the women exclaimed over his genius.

Finn, recovering from his initial shock, added his own voice to the chorus, his eyes never leaving mine. "I've never seen anything quite like it. You look...incredible," he said, the depth of his words hinting at more than mere admiration for the dress. But he'd shown up here with Seraphina when he was supposed to be running his shop. What did *that* mean?

I didn't have time to ponder the implications of them arriving together, let alone ask any questions as Isadora hustled me off to the dressing room, exclaiming over the shoes that would fit each dress. As soon as she'd unlaced me, she headed back out to speak to Elliot about hem length and heel height.

When I slipped out of the dressing room, voices drifted from the main boutique. Based on the sound, Finn was chatting with Bella and Isadora. To my amazement, I saw Seraphina, already wearing her gown and standing before the mirror with Elliot by her side.

Her gown was a tailored, emerald green silk that hugged her figure, gracefully flaring slightly at the knees to allow for an easy freedom of movement. The fabric had a subtle sheen, catching the light with every motion, reminiscent of a forest under the first light of dawn. The sleeves were sheer, billowing gently to cinched cuffs at her wrists, adding a touch of whimsy to her otherwise sleek silhouette. A modest V-neckline was tastefully accented with delicate silver embroidery, looking like glistening dewdrops on morning leaves.

Seraphina turned to Elliot. "Thank you so much! This is a dream. I'm used to being cinched up so tight I can't breathe or in a sack that does nothing for me. This dress is stunning, but somehow also thoughtfully designed for both practicality and ease of movement so I can work."

"It is my absolute pleasure, and might I add that you have exquisite taste. The emerald silk was an excellent selection," Elliot said.

"Elliot, could you possibly fashion something for Finn that matches my ensemble?" In a moment that seemed to freeze time, Seraphina's hopeful words to Elliot cut through the air. "I'd really like to surprise him with something special to wear to the ball." Her request sent a wave of icy dread through me. I immediately jumped to a heart-wrenching conclusion: Finn was going with Seraphina.

My delayed invitation had left an opening I hadn't fully anticipated, despite Bella's warning. The thought that Finn might see hesitation as indifference gnawed at me, planting seeds of doubt about possible signals I'd been sending. Maybe he thought I wasn't serious about our relationship because I hadn't asked him. Maybe they were rekindling their old flame. My head spun, and I slipped out without a word.

In the other room, Bella and Isadora buzzed with anticipation for the ball, but a cold knot of realization settled in my stomach. Amidst the warmth of their chatter, a chill of doubt and jealousy crept in, clouding the joy of the moment for me. Finn stared at me questioningly as I walked up, but I refused to meet his eyes.

When he opened his mouth, Isadora jumped in, linking her arm through mine.

"We really must sort this shoe situation. Elliot says he can adjust the hems in a flash, but we have to get him the heel heights today. Then he will have the gowns delivered to the manor, and you both can come over and get ready with me."

"That sounds great," Bella said excitedly. "I think I have the perfect pair at home." Bella's enthusiasm offered a brief respite from my spiraling thoughts, her excitement a reminder of the friendship that grounded me even in moments of turmoil.

"I don't have anything that will work with that dress," I said, thinking of my collection of sneakers and boots back at Spellbooks. Heels weren't really my thing, and I rarely had an occasion to wear them.

"Don't worry. We're the same size, aren't we?" Isadora asked.

I nodded, remembering the night we went to the Vault for welcome home drinks and Isadora broke a heel. I had lent her a pair of my shoes because my house was closer.

"Then you don't have to worry. I have the perfect pair for your dress. Do you trust me?"

"Absolutely," I said honestly and gratefully. I wasn't a fantastic dancer at the best of times and adding heels on top of the massive skirts of the gown had every potential of me ending the night like a baby giraffe wearing ice skates.

"Great! I know you need to get back to Spellbooks this morning, so I'll bring them in when I bring mine. Elliot is a whiz at these types of things and will be able to work out the measurements in his sleep. Oh, you're going to look so gorgeous!" Isadora finished with an excited little squeal.

"Seriously, these dresses are incredible," I said. "I feel like a princess when I put it on. Thank you so much for arranging everything with Elliot."

"You're more than welcome. You look like one too. A princess, that is," Isadora agreed. "I can't wait to see everyone's faces at the ball. We're going to be the talk of the town."

We both laughed, the excitement bubbling between us. I patted my jeans pocket, suddenly remembering I'd left my phone in the dressing room. "Oh no. I forgot my phone. Just a second."

As I dashed back into the fitting room, Seraphina was still in her dress, talking on the phone.

"Don't worry. Nothing is set in stone yet. Yes, I'm sure that..." she trailed off as soon as she saw me, waving brightly as I entered.

I gave her a double thumbs up and indicated the dress as I hurried towards the fitting room. She shot me a gracious smile before continuing her conversation. Despite my best intentions not to eavesdrop, it was hard not to overhear snippets of Seraphina's conversation.

"We'll navigate this together, ...No...Yes...No, you don't have to worry about that. It's all taken care of. No...No, the business shouldn't take a hit...We'll be fine. I promise..." The conversation, even if it was one-sided, offered a glimpse into her world, one where professional challenges were met with the same grace she seemed to apply to everything.

I grabbed my phone and waved it at her as I left. She shot me a charming smile before turning her attention back to her conversation. "More threats? No, that's crazy. Vivienne Silverthorne was on the mage council, remember? Yes, we've increased security...I promise, nothing is going to happen...No, I'm sure that won't be a problem, but..."

Her voice faded as I headed back out to the main room of the boutique. It sounded like whoever was on the other end of Seraphina's phone call was much more concerned about this event than she was. However, she might also be distracted. Namely, by the handsome druid she was taking to the ball. Speaking of Finn, he was standing with Elliot across the room, looking at a vibrant display of ties. He looked up as I exited the dressing area, our eyes locking in a brief, intense moment.

Rather than engage in conversation with him here, I hurried across the room to my friends, wrapping up tight against the cold before I made my escape. Braving the winter chill suddenly seemed a veritable sanctuary compared to the warmth of the boutique, now thick with my unspoken feelings for Finn and the tangled web of emotions that seemed to constrict around my heart.

I decided then and there that the next move was his to make. If he truly cared, he would reach out with explanations or apologies. As I walked away, the cold air biting at my cheeks, I felt the sting of disappointment and yet a flicker of hope that maybe, just maybe, he would fight for us.

Becoming Cinderella

IT SHOCKED ME THAT Finn never texted or called in the days since I'd last seen him. His silence spoke louder than any words could. No matter what was going on with Seraphina, it was clear he was done with me. I resolved to put all my unsettled feelings aside, ignore Finn if I saw him, and just have an amazing time at the ball with the girls.

The chill of the winter evening had nothing on the icy knot of disappointment lodged in my chest as I approached the Silverthorne mansion the day of the ball. Isadora's invitation to get ready together for the evening was a welcome distraction, a glimmer of warmth against the backdrop of my unresolved feelings regarding Finn. The grandeur of the mansion loomed large as I crossed the threshold, its opulent halls so lavish they bordered on uncomfortable, like stepping into a world where I didn't quite belong. The formality of the space felt almost stifling, more like a museum than a home, each room meticulously decorated to perfection. It was beautiful, yet suffocating, the weight of its opulence pressing down on me, making me feel even more ill at ease.

Isadora's excitement was palpable, her energy infectious as she led Bella and me to her suite of rooms which, despite their size, felt like a cozy enclave within the vastness of her family home, brimming with personal touches that spoke to her vibrant personality. Her suite was a revelation, a blend of elegance and rebellion against the expected, mingled in such a way that left Bella and me in awe. An eclectic mix of classical art and modern graffiti adorned the walls, a bold statement that married the past with the present in an unexpected dance of creativity. Rich, velvet drapes framed the large windows while a chandelier made of what appeared to be shimmering, delicate glass butterflies cast a soft, enchanting light throughout the room. That is until I recognized the face of a famous heavy metal musician in one of the butter-fly's wings. Then I realized the chandelier illuminated Isadora's personal space with a touch of whimsical defiance that made me feel more at ease than the opulent perfection in the rest of the mansion.

Her wardrobe, an impressive collection of fabrics, colors, and designs, unfolded like the pages of a high-fashion magazine come to life. We couldn't help but exclaim over each piece. As we admired Isadora's dresses, Bella noticed my bummed-out expression.

"Hey, what's wrong?" Bella asked, concern clear in her eyes.

I sighed, feeling the need to explain. "It's Finn. I overheard Seraphina asking Elliot to make something for Finn that would match her dress. It's why I didn't ask him in the end. I assumed he was going to the ball with her and didn't want to make a fool of myself. It's over between us, but I don't think I've quite come to terms with it yet."

Isadora's eyes widened. "Wow, that's rough. I didn't know they were... rekindling things."

Bella squeezed my hand. "You don't need him to have a good time tonight. Besides, we've got each other. What you need is a distraction, and what better than a fabulous ball? You have a stunning dress and fantastic friends. Sounds like the perfect recipe for an amazing night to me."

I managed a small smile. "You're right. I just need to focus on having fun with you guys."

Isadora suddenly perked up. "I have a great idea! Remember those rumors about jewel thieves?"

Bella's eyes widened with curiosity. "Jewel thieves? What rumors?"

I quickly filled Bella in on what Seraphina had told us earlier. "Apparently, there's been a jewel thief targeting high-society events," I finished.

Isadora chimed in. "We don't think anyone would dare try anything at my mother's party, but we'll keep a lookout. See if we can spot anyone who might be a daring jewel thief? We could even have code names or something. It could be a fun game to keep your mind off Finn."

"Great idea," Bella agreed. "We'll be like undercover agents."

"I'll be Lavender Butterfly," Isadora said immediately.

"I think you might have already had that name picked out," I said with a surprised chuckle.

"What? Every girl should always have a fabulous alias at her fingertips, don't you think?" Isadora said, striking a pose that was half-martial-arts and half-butterfly-caught-mid-flight.

"Okay, Lavender Butterfly," Bella said with a laugh. "I'll be Scarlet Raven."

They both turned to me expectantly. I hesitated, then grinned, leaning into the fun. "How about...Midnight Fox?"

Isadora clapped her hands together. "Perfect! Lavender Butterfly, Scarlet Raven, and Midnight Fox. The most stylish undercover agents ever."

"We'll be unstoppable," Bella agreed, linking her arm through mine.

I couldn't help but smile. "Alright, ladies. Let's be on the lookout for some jewel thieves."

"And if it turns out my mother's reputation has frightened them all away and there aren't any in attendance tonight, then we'll just have to make sure we're the life of the party." Isadora added with a playful glint in her eye, "Deal?"

"Deal!" Bella and I said in unison, laughing as we prepared for the evening ahead.

With a newfound sense of camaraderie and excitement, we decided to try on some clothes from Isadora's extensive wardrobe. Each piece we tried led to exaggerated poses and hilarious faux-fashion show impressions, complete with impromptu runway walks and mock-serious expressions. The room was soon filled with laughter and playful banter between friends. My worries about Finn were forgotten for the moment amid the joyous chaos.

Eventually, we settled down just as a platter of Christmas treats was delivered to Isadora's sitting room. The silver tray was filled with miniature gingerbread houses, peppermint bark, cranberry and Brie tartlets, and petite roasted turkey sliders. The scent of festive food filled the air with comforting Christmasy aromas. I made it a point to taste at least one of everything on the platter, the nostalgic flavors serving as a perfect prelude to the evening's festivities. We all nibbled on the delicacies while putting the finishing touches on our hair and makeup. Finally, we slipped into our custom dresses, transforming from casual camaraderie to ball-ready elegance. It was a testament to the magic of friendship and fine tailoring.

As the final adjustments were made and we stood together, reflections of grace and beauty mirrored back at us, a sense of solidarity settled over me. The weight of not attending the ball with Finn still pressed heavily, but in this moment, surrounded by the support and joy of my friends, it felt lighter. Isadora's suite, with its laughter and shared anticipation, became a haven, a reminder that the night was still ripe with possibilities.

"The Lavender Butterfly is ready for flight," Isadora declared.

"As is the Scarlet Raven," Bella added.

They both looked at me expectantly. I cleared my throat. "The, um, Midnight Fox is...um...feeling foxy?"

Isadora nudged me. "Girl, you need to work on your undercover lingo."

Bella chuckled. "Maybe stick to just being mysteriously alluring for now."

I shot Bella a playful glare, but before I could retort, a knock on the door interrupted us.

"Who is it?" Isadora called.

"Your handsome brothers here to escort you and your friends to the ball!" a male voice exclaimed through the heavy wooden door.

"Oh?" Isadora called back. "I'll admit I have brothers, but I wouldn't go so far as to call either of them handsome."

The retort was immediate. "You prefer charming? Debonair, perhaps?"

"Annoying and usually in need of a grooming is more like it," Isadora teased as she swept across the room to open the door.

"Just wait until you see us in the tuxes Elliot designed," a new male voice chimed in. "I bet we put your dress to shame!"

"I'll take that bet," Isadora said instantly.

"Deal!" came the response from two voices.

Isadora shot us a wink and whispered, "Oh, I've got this in the bag." She faced the door again and raised her voice. "On three? One, two, three!" She swung the door wide to reveal her brothers, Lucas and Gabriel Silverthorne.

Both looked incredibly dashing, in my opinion. Lucas wore the traditional tailored tuxedo well, the crisp black and white cut elegantly. The only color in his otherwise simple palette was a burgundy tie embroidered with poinsettias. Gabriel's tux was more unique than his brother's, which I found intriguing. Based on the few times we'd met, I had always considered Gabriel the quieter and more subdued of the two. His jacket was a deep midnight blue shot through with abstract silver designs and lined in black satin, which he wore over a silver shirt and dark trousers with shoes that had been polished to a high shine.

"You win," all three Silverthorne siblings said in unison. Laughter filled the room.

Lucas peered around Isadora. "Are those roasted turkey sliders I see?" he said, plucking one from the plate.

"Hey! Those are for us!" Isadora protested good-naturedly.

Lucas moaned in pleasure as he bit into one. "Don't blame me, blame Gabriel. Ours were all gone before I even knew they had been delivered."

"That's only because you take an hour to do your hair," Gabriel said with an unrepentant grin. He nodded a greeting at us. "Good to see you again, Bella. Harper."

Was it my imagination, or did his gaze linger on mine for a moment longer than anyone else's? Maybe Isadora hadn't been exaggerating his interest. Or she had, and I was reading far too much into the situation. Confused, I looked away, focusing on his jacket instead. Upon closer inspection, I saw the abstract designs also held a sprinkling of delicately stitched silver snowflakes, adding a touch of winter wonder to his ensemble.

"Brie tartlets! How come we didn't get any of these? Really, I think the cook likes you best, Isadora," Lucas exclaimed, turning to shake a mock stern finger in her direction.

Isadora grinned mischievously. "Maybe it's because I'm the favorite," she teased, reaching up to muss Lucas' hair.

He dodged out of the way just in time, snagging a tartlet from the tray as he did. "You wish!" he shot back, popping the tartlet into his mouth with a satisfied grin.

Isadora darted up behind him, but just as her hand was about to make contact, Lucas caught her wrist with a swift, practiced motion. "Nice try, sis," he said, chuckling as he held her at bay and grabbed another tartlet from the tray with his free hand. "Really! I can't imagine why we didn't get any of these. The cook knows I love them."

Gabriel caught my eye and winked unrepentantly, pointing a finger at his chest. *"My fault,"* he mouthed. Then he flicked his head, miming a pretentious slide along his head. *"Hair,"* he mouthed again.

I hid my smile behind a hand as Lucas extended his arm to Isadora. "Mother insists that we are fitted with our holiday sparkle before the guests arrive. Care to accompany me, sister dear?"

Isadora, her eyes twinkling with mirth, accepted gracefully. "Lead the way, oh brother mine."

Lucas turned his attention to Bella with the polished charm of a gentleman. "And Miss Bella, may I have the pleasure of escorting you downstairs to see what sort of holiday cheer awaits? Although I don't know what Starlight Treasures might have that could enhance your radiant beauty."

Isadora swatted at her brother. "Stop that."

Lucas feigned a wince. "Ow! Surely, a little flattery is permissible among friends?"

"Laying it on a little thick, aren't you?" Isadora said.

"Is it a crime to let a lady know when she looks fabulous?" Lucas said innocently.

Bella chuckled, adjusting her gown before taking Lucas' other arm. "Certainly not, but just so we're clear, I'll be meeting up with Alex, my *boyfriend*, later."

"Ah, you wound me," Lucas said, clutching at his heart dramatically. "But until he arrives, I'd be happy to keep the rest of the eager young men of Havenwood at bay."

Isadora, feigning a dramatic huff, interjected. "What about me?"

Lucas winked at her, patting her hand. "I trust that you are more than capable of correcting any young man who sets even a toe out of line. But in the meantime, I have two arms and am fully capable of escorting two dazzling ladies." And with that, he swept them both out, their laughter trailing behind them like a melody.

In the newfound quiet, Gabriel's eyes found mine. "Harper, might I offer to escort you?" He paused, then said in a rush, "To the jewelry stand, I mean. The stairs can be tricky in a formal gown. I understand if you're waiting for someone else to accompany you."

"I don't have a date," I admitted, the words tumbling out softer and more vulnerable than I'd planned, the echo of Seraphina's laughter with Finn haunting the edges of my confession. Did the unexpected confession make me sound lame? I hurried to explain.

"I mean, thought I had a date, but...apparently I...umm, I was wrong."

Gabriel's smile was gentle, almost shy, and tinged with a comforting sadness that drew me back to the present. He didn't dwell on my confession or press for more details. Instead, he offered me his arm. "In that case, would you allow me the pleasure of showing you around? I assure you, I'm quite familiar with the evening's most intriguing attendees—and those worthy of avoidance. Besides, if the festivities grow too overwhelming, I know the fastest path to the kitchen's freezer which is always stocked with an impressive selection of ice cream." Gabriel's words were laced with a genuine warmth that starkly contrasted the practiced charm of his brother.

I laughed; the sound more natural than I expected. "An ice cream escape plan? I'm sold."

As he led me from the room, an unexpected, errant thought danced through my mind—retreating to a quiet corner to share ice cream with Gabriel could be one of the evening's highlights and just what I needed to put the thought of Finn and Seraphina together out of my mind.

Enchanting Possibilities

I SLOWLY NAVIGATED THE staircase, grateful for Gabriel's muscular arm under my hand. As we descended, I focused on each step, thankful for his slow pace and the fact I wasn't wearing heels. But as we reached the bottom, I lifted my gaze and the sheer magic of the scene stopped me in my tracks.

I caught my breath. The grandeur of the Silverthorne ballroom was a sight to behold, resplendent in its vastness and holiday adornment. Enormous sparkling chandeliers dangling with crystals shaped like snowflakes hung from the high ceiling, their light reflecting off the polished marble floors that gleamed like the surface of a frozen lake under a winter moon. Towering Christmas trees stood at strategic points, bedecked with twinkling lights, silver tinsel, and gorgeously coordinated ornaments that sparkled in the light. Lush garlands of holly and mistletoe draped elegantly over the grand staircase's balustrade, spiraling down into the heart of the festivities.

Around the ballroom, familiar faces from Havenwood mingled and busied themselves with final preparations. On one side, the baking artisans of Pixie Pastries were arranging a spectacular dessert buffet. Towers of delicate macarons in shades of red and green, platters of frosted sugar cookies shaped like holly leaves and snowflakes, and a majestic gingerbread house centerpiece infused the air with the scents of sugar and spice. Near the immense windows looking out onto a frosty night, a small ensemble of musicians was tuning their instruments, their notes blending into the soft hum of anticipation that filled the space.

The entire scene was like stepping into a dream, the surreal beauty enveloping me and melting away my earlier worries. Gabriel guided me gently, his presence a comforting anchor amidst the enchantment surrounding us.

"Welcome to our Christmas Eve Ball," he said softly, his voice breaking through my reverie.

I turned to him, a genuine smile spreading across my face. "It's...breathtaking," I whispered.

Gabriel nodded, his eyes twinkling with the reflection of the lights. "I'm glad you like it. Shall we?"

I took a deep breath, feeling a newfound excitement bubbling within me. "Yes," I said, my voice steady.

Gabriel guided me around the ballroom, his gentle presence making the grand space feel less overwhelming. As we moved, he pointed out various enchanting details, each one more magical than the last.

"Look over there," Gabriel said softly, gesturing to an open doorway draped with twinkling fairy lights. Inside, an indoor garden bloomed with winter flowers, illuminated by soft, floating orbs that gave the space an otherworldly glow. The scent of fresh pine and delicate blooms filled the air, adding to the dreamlike atmosphere.

"Wow," I whispered, feeling as if I had stepped into a fairy tale.

Gabriel smiled, leading me to another area. "And here," he continued, "is the ice sculpture gallery. Each piece is enchanted to never melt." I marveled at the intricate sculptures, each one depicting scenes from beloved winter tales. One sculpture, a magnificent reindeer, was carved in mid-leap as if ready to soar into the night.

We wandered further, and Gabriel pointed out a cozy library off the ballroom, complete with a roaring fireplace. The flickering flames cast a golden glow, and plush armchairs invited guests to sit and relax. "For those needing a bit of warmth or a quiet place to compose themselves. This is one of my favorite rooms in the house," he said.

"I can see why!" I exclaimed, my childhood dream of having floor to ceiling bookshelves with rolling ladders come to life before my eyes.

"One of my earliest memories was my mother reading to me as I played on the carpet. I loved everything she picked from *Treasure Island* to family histories. We have an entire shelf of journals and books about our family, right there next to the Silverthorne family crest," he said, pointing to the large medieval style crest painted on an enormous display shield prominently hung in a place of honor.

"It must be fascinating to read about your family's exploits. I don't think I know my family tree back beyond Granny Bea," I said.

Gabriel shrugged. "Some of them are interesting, but most are fairly dull. However, from what I knew of your granny, she lived a life full of excitement. I believe her exploits have become something of town legend, especially the one involving feathers, magnets, and peanut butter."

"I keep hearing about that, but no one ever elaborates. Can you tell me what happened?"

Gabriel chuckled and shook his head. "Let's just say that the pranks from Halloween paled compared to what your granny could devise. I'm just glad she never truly set her mind to causing mischief or we all would've been in trouble."

"Now that I can believe," I said earnestly.

The ballroom, still absent of guests, was alive with the promise of the night's enchantment and the merriment soon to unfold. Gabriel's gentle guidance made everything feel even more surreal, his quiet presence adding to the enchantment of the evening. Each new discovery was more magical than the last, and for a while, I forgot all about Finn and the worries that had plagued me.

He led me past the small ensemble of musicians softly practicing a holiday tune, their notes blending into the soft hum of anticipation that filled the ballroom. In the opposite corner from the musicians, a small stage had been erected. The rest of the décor had been so overwhelming that I'd completely missed it the first time.

"What is this?" I asked curiously, examining the black velvet curtain that cut off the stage from whatever was behind it. A woman in a sequined suit pushed through the curtain and gave us a courteous, professional smile as she set a small table on the left-hand side of the stage. A lithe woman with platinum blonde hair passed her a top hat from backstage, and the first lady stuck her arm up to the shoulder inside the hat, rummaging around with a frustrated expression.

"What's going on?" I asked in disbelief.

"This is Mystique," Gabriel explained softly. "She is a world-renowned illusionist. We've met professionally a few times over the years, but I never thought she'd actually take me up on my invitation to perform at our annual ball. Her illusions are incredible! I know I'm decent with illusions, but she makes me look like I am a kid pretending to pull a coin from behind your ear."

I'd seen some of Gabriel's illusions up close, and he wasn't giving himself enough credit. His control of his magic was excellent, but his description of Mystique's abilities made me excited to see her perform.

"Incredible! I can't wait!" I said, taking in the duo's final preparations.

"Do you like it?" Gabriel asked, gesturing at the entire ballroom.

"Like it? It's amazing! I feel so lucky to be here tonight. I've already thanked Isadora but thank you for the invitation and taking the time to show me around," I said softly, my voice filled with genuine gratitude. "This is...it's all so beautiful."

Gabriel's eyes sparkled with warmth. "I'm glad you're enjoying it. But I have one more thing to show you before the guests arrive."

His words touched me deeply, and I felt a rush of emotion. In that moment, I realized that tonight was about more than just the ball. It was about finding joy and beauty in the unexpected, and perhaps even finding a bit of magic in myself. The night stretched ahead, filled with endless possibilities.

Bejeweled

Isadora approached, nearly bouncing with excitement. "It's time! Come on, you two!"

"Time for what?" I asked, my imagination already stretched to its limits by the enchanting beauty of the ballroom.

"You'll see," Gabriel said, a twinkle in his eyes.

Unable to contain herself, Isadora had already dashed away, corralling Lucas and Bella and leading them toward a large foyer to the right of the ballroom that Gabriel hadn't shown me yet.

"What's over there?" I asked.

"Allow me to escort you, and we'll discover what has Isa so thrilled," Gabriel said, offering his arm once more.

I accepted it, feeling even more like a princess as he guided me across the ballroom floor toward the mysterious doorway. "Whatever it is must be sensational if Isadora is more excited for that than all of this," I said, gesturing broadly at the grand, magical expanse of the ballroom.

"I'd love to hear your opinion once you see it, you know, to see if her excitement is warranted," Gabriel said as we followed Isadora, Bella, and Lucas into the foyer.

The atmosphere here was markedly calmer than the last-minute bustle in the ballroom. Burly looking security men with curling plastic earpieces wearing jackets that emphasized their bulk stood at the doorway with their arms folded. However, it was what was inside that made me gasp in surprise and delight.

The room before us unfolded into a treasure trove that rivalled Aladdin's cave. Seraphina, resplendent in her emerald gown, was deep in discussion with a darkly handsome man who exuded an aura of sophistication. At first guess, I assumed it was probably her business partner. What had Isadora said his name was? Oh, that's right. Dominic Umbra.

My conjecture seemed to be confirmed as the pair turned in unison and began directing the assembled jewelers with the precision of experienced conductors leading an orchestra. The sparkle on the tables captured my attention and for a moment, I forgot how to breathe. The tables around the room were adorned with a breathtaking array of holiday-themed gems and jewelry that captured the light and the imagination. To my surprise, I even recognized one of the jewelers. Elowen Wispdale, the lavender-haired fairy who owned a local jewelry shop, stood by a display that gleamed with the ethereal glow of radiant moonstones, sparkling sapphires, and dazzling diamonds, her delicate fingers arranging the pieces carefully to catch the light to the fullest.

A stern woman in a formal dress of deep evergreen swept into the foyer, clapping her hands to get everyone's attention. I recognized her instantly as Vivienne Silverthorne, the powerful mage and hostess of the ball. Other than the five of us and Seraphina's assembled coterie, the only other person in the room was an older woman dressed in a silver gown that perfectly matched her hair.

Vivienne looked up as we entered, her stern expression softening slightly at the sight of her children. "Ah, well done Isadora. It seems we are all here now," she said as the five of us drew in closer. "As you know, these exquisite pieces, courtesy of Starlight Treasures and crafted by our most talented jewelers, are inspired by the holiday season. Each guest tonight will be matched with a piece of enchanted jewelry to wear for the duration of the ball."

Bella nudged me. "The invitation!" she whispered.

I nodded numbly, still entranced by the sparkling treasures. Vivienne's words gradually penetrated the haze of awe surrounding me. "I don't remember anything about *enchanted* jewelry," I whispered back. Bella and I exchanged a confused look, and she shrugged.

Gabriel must've caught at least part of our whispered exchange because he leaned over and whispered, "With an enchanter elf like Seraphina and some magical gems, the sky's the limit for what a piece of jewelry can do for the wearer. Although, knowing Mother, she's probably requested that the enchantments be kept fairly low-key."

Vivienne turned towards us, her eyes sharpening. Perhaps she realized we were confused because she offered further explanation. "Gabriel is correct. I have no wish for any mayhem to occur at the ball." Was it my imagination, or did her gaze linger on me longer than anyone else? Before I could make up my mind, she continued. "Each item has been given a touch of magic by the jeweler to elevate the night's revelry. Every guest tonight will have the privilege of donning these magnificent creations for the duration of the ball in return for their phones and car keys. I don't know if Isadora has told you, but I prefer to keep these events private, even from social media. But there is a professional photographer on site. Although you will have to return the jewelry, we'll provide photos as keepsakes for this event."

Bella recovered herself before I did. "That's very thoughtful of you."

I hurriedly added. "Yes, thank you very much. This is such a wonderful treat."

Vivienne smiled, but it didn't quite seem to reach her eyes. "It's my pleasure. Now, why don't we allow Ms. Everbright and Mr. Umbra to select our pieces for us before the rest of the guests arrive?"

A murmur of assent rippled around our small circle. Bella grabbed one of my hands excitedly, and Isadora took the other, leading the way towards the nearest table. Seraphina and her business partner stepped forward, attending to Vivienne and the elderly lady in silver first. That suited me just fine because it allowed me a moment to examine some of the exquisite pieces of jewelry. Vivienne's revelation of the jewelry's magical aspect sent a shiver of delight through the room. The promise of experiencing a ball where magic was not just a backdrop but woven into the very fabric of the evening sent my heart racing with anticipation. As I looked upon the displays, I wondered what piece I would get to wear and what its hidden enchantment was. Would I be able to dance with unparalleled grace? Or fly as if Peter Pan sprinkled fairy dust on my head? Maybe not. Vivienne might deem that magic too flashy for her tastes. However, the possibilities unfurled before me, and I had to make a conscious effort to focus.

The foyer was a flurry of activity for a few minutes as Seraphina and Dominic selected items for each of the Silverthornes to wear before moving on to Bella and me. In the hubbub, I discovered that the lady in silver was Isadora's great-aunt, Elara, who was not only a staple at the Silverthorne balls but also very opinionated when it came to jewelry.

I lingered by Elowen's table displaying a stunning array of gems, my fingers hovering over the moonstones that seemed to glow with a light all their own. I was lost in thought, imagining the lovely lavender-haired jeweler bending over her workbench to create such beauty, when Seraphina approached.

Seraphina smiled winningly at me. "That dress is just exquisite. You look truly lovely tonight," she said, her sincerity making it very difficult to maintain any animosity I was still carrying from seeing her with Finn.

"Thanks," I murmured, looking around awkwardly. I realized I was the only one who was not yet wearing a stunning piece of jewelry. A delicate diamond tiara sat atop Vivienne's expertly coiffed hair. Isadora toyed with a stunning amethyst pendant that perfectly matched the deepest shades of purple in her gown. Sparkling earrings dangled from Bella's ears as she bent to help Lucas with the ruby cufflinks he'd been given. As everyone crowded around, comparing items and chatting excitedly, I noticed Gabriel watching me out of the corner of my eye and almost blushed.

"Come with me," Seraphina said excitedly, taking my hand and leading me to the table at the end of the row. I didn't want to appear rude, so I followed without a word. "I knew your outfit was crying out for something dramatic, and I didn't want to disappoint." Her emerald eyes sparkled with excitement as she grandly presented me a silver necklace with an intricate snake design coiled around a sizable, luminescent opal.

My heart sank. The symbol of a snake carried connotations with it that weren't altogether flattering. Deceptive, treacherous, venomous. What was Seraphina implying here? That *I* was a snake? Maybe she'd somehow sensed that there was something between me and Finn and her niceness was a cover for her underlying feelings of jealousy?

"Umm, thanks," I mumbled. I hesitated, my gaze drifting toward Elowen's moonstone display. "Would it be possible to wear one of those instead? Perhaps that lovely silver cuff bracelet?"

Seraphina's voice softened. "I know it isn't as expensive as many of the other pieces, but this isn't just a snake, Harper. The silver serpent is a symbol of transformation and growth among my people. I enchanted this necklace myself. I rarely pull it out of the safe, but when I saw your dress, I knew it was meant for you tonight. The enhancement enchantment I laid on the necklace is a special one. Utterly unique. It is designed to make your night an unforgettable one." She held it out, a sincere expression on her beautiful face. "Please take it. I picked it out especially for you to ensure that your first Silverthorne Ball is a wonderful experience." She seemed so earnest, and though a small part of me harbored doubts, her sincerity shone through. Could anyone be that kind without an ulterior motive? But no matter how hard I looked, I couldn't see even the smallest crack in her kind expression.

As Gabriel passed by, he caught the tail end of the conversation. A curious expression crossed his face, and he paused, his interest piqued. "What an interesting enchantment," he said, joining us. I noticed a small, shining, star-shaped pin now sparkled on his lapel. Gabriel's item was more subtle than some of the others, but I thought the less ostentatious item suited his personality.

Seraphina turned to him, but her encouraging words were directed at me. "I was rather proud of the enchantment when I came up with it. It's all about enhancing your evening. And who knows? It might just give Harper the extra nudge to truly shine tonight, to stand out as a radiant star," she said, her tone innocent and gentle. Heat flooded my cheeks.

Now what did THAT mean?

Was that a dig at me? That she was with Finn, and I wasn't?

Gabriel took the necklace out of Seraphina's hands and held it up to me, considering it intently. Finally, he nodded. "It suits you," he said. There was something undeniably genuine in his tone that made me want to believe his words, even though I doubted Seraphina's intentions. "You should wear it," Gabriel added.

"Here, let me help you," Seraphina said solicitously.

Trapped between the enchanter elf and a host of the ball, there didn't seem to be a graceful way for me to demur, so I turned and allowed Seraphina to drape it around my throat. It was heavier than it looked, but as soon as it settled against my collarbones, the weight seemed to ease slightly.

"Gabriel? Come here a sec," Lucas called from the other side of the room. Gabriel shot me an encouraging smile before moving to join his brother.

Now that my body was turned, I saw Isadora's great-aunt arguing in hushed tones with Seraphina's partner, who held a sapphire and diamond snowflake pin in his hand. The silver-haired lady raised her voice, "No, I do not wish to wear a mere brooch. I don't care how many diamonds you've encrusted it with."

The smile never left Dominic's face, and the words he uttered were too soft for me to catch. A moment later, though, he was pinning the brooch to the lady's dress while she smiled with pleasure at the sparkling snowflake.

Behind me, I heard Seraphina suck in a breath. "I'm so sorry. Please excuse me," she said in a rush, gliding swiftly over to her partner and firmly steering him away from the tables while whispering urgently up at him. She did not look pleased.

"What's going on?" Gabriel asked as he returned to my side.

"Not sure," I replied, "But it looks like Seraphina is upset."

Gabriel sighed. "Must be Aunt Elara causing trouble again. She does that. Quite the stubborn lady when she sets her mind on something."

Curious, I asked, "She's your great-aunt, right? I've never met her before tonight. Does she spend much time in Havenwood?"

Gabriel hesitated, clearly not used to sharing too much about his family. He tipped his head to the side, obviously weighing his words before saying in a hushed whisper, "She's very opinionated and seems to enjoy causing a stir. She's...quite a character. But Dominic must be an excellent salesman to smooth things over that quickly."

I glanced over to see everyone was smiling at each other once more. Was it my imagination, or did Seraphina's expression look a little too tense? Why would that be? Was there a reason she didn't want Elara to wear the brooch?

A sudden thought occurred to me. I wondered if Elara was related to Hank, the book thief who had broken into Spellbooks the week I arrived in Havenwood and had stolen what he thought to be a rare book. They'd have to be related if they were both Silverthornes, right? I caught my breath. What if she was married to him? Could she want revenge on me? After all, my uncovering his theft was the reason Hank no longer owned a shop in Havenwood. Although what exactly had happened to the mad mage turned pirate treasure hunter was a mystery unto itself. After he barged into Spellbooks, the rumors claimed that Vivienne Silverthorne brought her incredible influence to bear. All anyone knew was Hank had never spent a night in jail, but hadn't been seen anywhere in Havenwood since.

Gabriel noticed my distraction. "Is everything okay? You look like you've seen a ghost." He made a show of looking around. "I thought I gave them all strict instructions to stay away this evening."

I smiled anemically at his joke, too distracted by thoughts of what kind of revenge his seemingly sweet great-aunt might rain down upon my head. Not wanting to cause any more family drama, I quickly searched for a diversion. My eyes caught on the sparkling star on his lapel and words tumbled out before I could stop them. "All the jewels are enchanted. What's the power in your pin?"

Gabriel's face brightened. "It's quite a piece, isn't it?" he said, touching the pin on his own lapel. "The star is enchanted to enhance the wearer's natural charm. Although, they should've given it to Lucas. I'm afraid I might be a bit of a hopeless case." He shook his head with a rueful chuckle, glancing over at his older brother, who was obviously charming the nearby jewelers with flattering small talk.

"I disagree. You're just as charming as Lucas. More so even, because you're so genuine," I said, reaching out to straighten the pin. "I think it suits you. It's subtle but striking. Just like...you," I blushed when I realized just how much my mouth had run away with me, my eyes sliding away from the star pin and refusing to meet Gabriel's.

He caught my hand, giving my fingertips a little squeeze. "That's kind of you to say. I don't think I've ever been called subtle or striking before. Normally, I'm just the Silverthorne sibling everyone overlooks. I can't really blame them with Lucas on one side and Isadora on the other."

"Well, I think you're selling yourself short," I said stubbornly, feeling like I needed to explain my answer, lest he misinterpret what I'd meant. The only problem was, what did I mean exactly? I stuttered to a halt, trying to think of something that wouldn't make me sound strange.

Gabriel saved me from embarrassing myself further by tucking my hand into the crook of his arm. "Why do I get the feeling nothing slips by you?"

"I...umm...well..." I searched for the right words to say, but somehow my extensive vocabulary from the multitudes of books

I'd read throughout my life completely eluded me precisely when I needed them most.

"With you to keep things interesting, I think I'm going to enjoy this ball more than I'd anticipated," Gabriel said with an amiable smile. "And if Aunt Elara causes problems, there's always the promise of ice cream. Shall we?" he asked, gesturing towards the ballroom.

I nodded mutely for fear my tongue would betray me again and allowed him to lead me from the foyer. Seraphina smiled brightly and waved as we left. Unsettling questions tangled with my excitement. Could the necklace she chose with such care truly be an act of kindness on her part, or was there an edge to her charm, a hidden barb I had yet to discover? Could Elara bear a grudge against me over the Hank situation? None of the other Silverthornes did, but she could be the anomaly. If so, surely she wouldn't do anything to disrupt her family's ball, would she? With each step I took beside Gabriel, I felt the necklace's weight seem to grow—a symbol of transformation, perhaps, but into what?

It's All Magic

As I re-entered the ballroom, a world of grandeur and unseen intrigues unfolded before me, promising an enchanting night. Over the next hour, guests arrived, and were ushered toward the jewelry before being allowed to enter the ballroom. The air was thick with anticipation and the quiet hum of excited conversations blending with the soft strains of festive music from the string quartet. Fairy lights twinkled like stars overhead, casting a magical glow over the room. The polished marble floors gleamed, reflecting the opulent decor and the shimmering gowns of the guests. Bella and I tried our best to stay out of the way as Gabriel and Isadora, along with the rest of the Silverthornes, played their roles as gracious hosts.

Bella tipped her head towards the buffet tables. "Come on! We should definitely try some treats before they're all eaten," she said, making a beeline towards the impressive displays of enticing macarons provided by Pixie Pastries.

I chuckled at her eagerness but allowed her to pull me along without much resistance. "The Scarlet Raven has sighted her prey!" I teased.

"And I have to try every one. You know, for posterity or whatever," she said, examining the confections.

"I don't think that means what you think it means," I said skeptically.

"What it means is this one is delicious. But I wonder which one is the best," Bella whispered around a mouthful of raspberry and vanilla cream. She looked down the line of cookies, her borrowed ruby earrings sparkling in the light as she turned her head back and forth. "There are too many here. We must divide and conquer, Midnight Fox! Quick! Try the blue one with silver filling," she said, plucking one from the tray for me.

"I don't think undercover spies are supposed to be spending their time taste testing macarons," I said with a laugh even as I accepted it.

"Why not?" Bella made a point of spinning in a slow circle, scanning the room. "I don't see any jewel thieves here. Besides, with all the security the Silverthornes have, there's no way anyone is going to be stupid enough to rob the ball. Even if they do, where are they going to go? Everyone has to turn over their keys, and the Silverthorne estate is on the outskirts of Havenwood. If I were a jewel thief, I wouldn't want to make my getaway through the snow in a ballgown."

"Maybe they have a sleigh," I suggested.

Bella put her hands on her hips. "Are you suggesting Santa is moonlighting as a jewel thief now?"

I laughed. "Hey, he knows when you're sleeping and when you're awake. Maybe he has a side hustle we don't know about."

"You bite your tongue! I can't believe you'd even suggest such a thing. Eat your macaron," Bella ordered with a mock stern look.

"Which is it? Bite my tongue or eat the macaron?" I teased.

"You'd better eat it quickly or I'm going to taste test them all on my own while standing far away from you, just in case your badmouthing Santa gets back to him. I don't want to get put on the naughty list just because I was standing too close to you," Bella said.

"Okay, okay! You win, Scarlet Raven."

"I always do," she said with a sniff.

I took a bite of the blue macaron, and a burst of flavors danced on my tongue. The silver filling was a blend of enchanted peppermint and creamy white chocolate, with a hint of nutmeg that left a subtle, magical warmth lingering in my mouth. "Mmm, it's like tasting a winter wonderland," I said, savoring the delightful combination.

"And that is just the start of our magical evening," Bella said, immediately handing me a green macaron with a scarlet red filling.

"Speaking of magic, those earrings are amazing! What enchantment is woven into them?" I asked curiously, taking advantage of the opportunity for a little gossip with my best friend.

"They are meant to enhance my natural grace, but honestly, I'd wear them even without the enchantment. They're gorgeous, aren't they?" Bella asked, tossing her head.

"Stunning," I said honestly, nibbling at the holiday macaron in my hand. The flavors of spiced cranberry and pistachio danced across my tongue. The filling had a delightful tartness balanced by a touch of sweet orange zest, creating a flavor combination that was both rich and refreshing, like a perfect holiday symphony on my taste buds.

"Speaking of stunning, that is a statement necklace if ever I saw one. What enchantment does it have? Because if it's the ability to weave through crowds, we might have to swap," Bella said.

"Why?" I asked, distracted from the conversation by finding a third macaron to sample. This one was a deep brown with a golden filling. As I bit into it, the unexpected yet delightful combination of caramelized apple and cinnamon greeted me. The filling had a buttery smoothness, with a hint of clove that lingered on the palate, evoking the warmth and comfort of a crackling fireplace on a cold winter night.

"Once people get a taste of these macarons, there won't be enough space around the table to get even one," Bella said, plucking yet another from the tray and biting into the delicious treat. Her eyes went wide as she looked over my shoulder and she muttered, "Uh oh."

I swallowed my bite of apple and cinnamon. "What?" I asked.

"Look," she said, jerking her chin towards the door.

Posing in the entryway to the ballroom as if they were waiting for their photograph to be taken on a red carpet were none other than the Puddletons. Their clothing was impeccably tailored, no doubt because of Elliot Ashford's skill, but the color combinations were all wrong. Hortense's green dress was three shades too bright, erring closer to lime than the more seasonably appropriate kelly green. There were also too many ruffles for my taste. I didn't want to be uncharitable, but the dress made her look like a fancy string bean with heels. Oswald, on the other hand, had gone for an unexpected purple. Perhaps he thought it would make him look royal. However, the combination of the cane, the aggressively purple top hat, and — was that a monocle? — made him look like a pompous plum.

I glanced at the macaron in my hand. Perhaps I should stop eating the delicious treats before all of my thoughts turned to food analogies.

"The Puddletons?" I whispered to Bella as I set the macaron aside. "We knew they were coming. But in a room this size, they should be easy enough to avoid. Although maybe we should have a secret signal or call. What sort of sound would a Midnight Fox make?" I asked.

Bella nudged me, jerking her chin past the Puddletons. "Not them. Him."

The ballroom's bustle seemed to pause for a heartbeat as Finn emerged from behind the Puddletons, his black suit with emerald green accents a perfect complement to his fiery red hair. Our eyes locked across the room, and, for an instant, the world stilled. But the moment shattered as Seraphina, graceful as ever, reached Finn with an affectionate embrace and a kiss that left a mark of lipstick upon his cheek. She laughed and wiped it away with her fingertips.

Heat raced up to my cheeks, and I looked away as she led him towards the foyer. The weight of the serpent necklace Seraphina had draped around my neck pressed down on me. The enchantment woven into my necklace was supposed to make my night a memorable one, but I wondered if it might be memorable for all the wrong reasons.

Being the amazing friend she was, Bella not only noticed my silent interaction with Finn but also my reaction. "I don't know about you, but I'd like to get a better look at that photographer. I need a picture to remember this evening," Bella said firmly, taking my arm and steering me in the opposite direction towards the photo booth. A small sign proclaimed that the photographer was offering free pictures for the evening. I didn't recognize the dark-haired man and wondered if he was a Havenwood local or hired especially for this event.

Regardless, he seemed to know his craft well. He was already commanding the attention of a small crowd of partygoers. With a graceful wave of his hand, he invited a couple onto the set created by a backdrop that shimmered with an almost ethereal glow. As they posed, he whispered a few words, and a soft, golden light enveloped them, enhancing their features in the most flattering way. He snapped several shots, the flash capturing their radiant smiles and the magical aura around them.

Next, he took a single rose from a table of props nearby and handed it to a guest, instructing them to hold it close. As the camera clicked, the petals began to sparkle and emit a faint, enchanting glow, mesmerizing the audience, who clapped politely. His assistant, a woman dressed in a stylish but efficient black pantsuit, whisked the used prop away with a practiced smile, disappearing behind the curtain framing the backdrop as the next couple approached. With each click of the camera, subtle bursts of magic danced around the guests, making each photograph a unique piece of art.

Bella seemed enthralled by the photographic artistry, but my thoughts distracted me. My mind drifted back to Finn. Why did he have to look so handsome? Why had I squandered my chance to ask him to the ball? More importantly, what was going on between him and Seraphina? I shook my head slightly, trying to clear my thoughts.

I shifted my body, keeping half an eye on the photographer's performance while really scanning the room. The ballroom was filling up quickly, guests streaming in, their laughter and chatter creating a lively atmosphere. The jewelry of every new arrival seemed to sparkle brighter than anything I'd seen. Perhaps that was because I knew each one was enchanted with a subtle magic. Yet none felt as ostentatious or as heavy as the coiled serpent around my neck. I yearned for the simplicity of a tennis bracelet or the understated elegance of stud earrings, anything that didn't feel like a noose around my throat.

Through the open door, I saw Finn and Seraphina chatting as she returned to the foyer, presumably to oversee the jewelers. She squeezed his hand and laughed at something I couldn't hear from the other side of the ballroom. I looked away, not wanting to be caught staring at the pair. That's when I noticed Dominic. He leaned in, murmuring into the ear of a guest. The gesture sparked my curiosity. I couldn't help but wonder what secrets passed between them, and, for a fleeting moment, I wished I could command his ability for salesmanship—whispers that could, perhaps, suggest Seraphina find a different companion for the evening.

Bella nudged me. "Harper? It's our turn."

I shook myself out of my thoughts and smiled at her. The last thing I wanted to do was ruin her night with whining about Finn. "Let's do it!"

We stepped onto the set, and the photographer greeted us with a warm smile. "Just relax and be yourselves," he said, positioning us expertly in front of the shimmering backdrop. Bella wrapped an arm around my shoulders, and I managed a smile as the flash went off.

The photographer snapped a few more pictures before tipping his head to the side, considering us thoughtfully. He spoke to his assistant. "I think the masquerade masks," he said.

"Exactly what I was thinking," she said, stepping forward with two elaborate half masks on convenient sticks to avoid mussing hairdos. We held the masks in front of our faces, posing as the photographer snapped several more pictures. Finally, he nodded in satisfaction and his assistant ushered us away from the backdrop.

"The photographs will be emailed directly to you once Johann has a chance to make some final edits. Please, enter your addresses here," she said, passing us a small tablet. I handed her the masks as Bella started typing.

The assistant whisked them away behind the backdrop, giving me a momentary glimpse behind the curtain. The private area was full of neatly organized props and boxes of equipment. I wondered if Vivienne had made a request that all her guests have individualized photos or perhaps it was Johann the photographer's choice to change the props with every new picture taken. Either way, the number of items behind the backdrop was impressive. No wonder there was a curtain separating the staging area from the rest of the ballroom. Otherwise, guests might have helped themselves or, horror of horrors, the props could've clashed with Vivienne's aesthetic for the magical ball.

Bella passed the tablet to me, and I quickly typed in my email address. As I looked up, Alex, Bella's boyfriend, suddenly materialized through the crowd, making a beeline for us while I returned the tablet to the assistant. The string ensemble seemed to seize the moment, their music swelling into a lively melody that beckoned the guests to the dance floor.

With a beaming smile, Alex extended his hand to Bella. "That dress was made for showing off, and I know the perfect way to do it," he said, his tone an impeccable blend of teasing and charm.

Bella grinned up at him and then shot me a worried look. I gave her a little nudge, urging them both towards the dance floor. "Go on, enjoy your evening. I'll catch up with you later," I said.

Isadora appeared just as Bella twirled away, her color-shifting gown glittering and glistening. Pulling me aside to a quieter corner, Isadora's brow creased with curiosity. "Harper, have you seen Finn and Seraphina?" she inquired, snatching a canapé from a server who happened to be passing by. Behind her back, he shot her a scowl which seemed at odds with the surrounding merriment.

"Oh, those are good," Isadora said, turning and plucking another from the tray, completely oblivious to the darkening expression the waiter directed at her as she looked back at me. "So, what gives?"

"What do you mean?"

"Well, whenever we talked, I got the impression you and Finn were, you know, into each other. But you didn't invite him to the ball, so I figured maybe you weren't ready to go public yet or maybe you had a falling out? I don't know. But then he turns up here with his ex? Was that why you didn't ask him? You found out he still had feelings for Seraphina?" Her eyes were full of concern, and perhaps a hint of mischief—typical Isadora, never one to shy away from the heart of the drama.

Surprised, I stammered, "Um, I was...I mean, I didn't know...about Seraphina, until recently. As for Finn, well...it's complicated."

"Isn't it always with men? What are you going to do?"

"I don't know," I admitted. "We haven't talked since we bumped into each other at the Silver Needle."

"I thought you looked a little tense when we were there," Isadora said. She shot me a commiserating look. "I'm sorry things are difficult with him, but if there's anything to get your mind off your troubles, it's got to be a magical Christmasy ball, right?

"I guess so, but—shh! He's heading this way!" I hissed at Isadora.

Before Isadora could say anything else, Vivienne swept over from the opposite direction, her borrowed tiara sparkling against her dark hair. "Isadora, I need your assistance, please. Aunt Elara seems to have misplaced her reading glasses again, and she needs them to review the details of her speech tonight. You know how to calm her down better than anyone. Do you suppose you could help her?" Vivienne asked, as she gestured towards the elderly aunt, who was peering at her notes with a furrowed brow. "Now, please."

"Of course," Isadora said, stuffing the last of the canape in her mouth as she followed her mother. She shot me an apologetic look as she departed.

My gaze caught on Finn once more. The Puddletons had intercepted him, and they were conversing in low tones but with very large gesticulations. Finn looked as though he'd like to make an escape, but it was two on one, and, for the moment, he was trapped in conversation. It was probably for the best. I didn't want to have the discussion I needed to with Finn in such a public setting, anyway. I wheeled, intending to slip away before he could notice me, only to collide with someone standing right behind me. Strong arms steadied me as I nearly lost my balance.

"Whoa. Are you alright?" Gabriel asked, genuine concern in his dark eyes.

"Yes. No. I don't—" I took a deep breath. "What I mean to say is 'thank you,'" I said, trying to inch past him.

Gabriel wasn't about to be brushed aside so easily. "You look like you've seen another ghost, and I thought we banished all of them after Halloween," he teased. When I didn't laugh, he tipped his head to the side. "What's bothering you?"

"It's...nothing. Don't worry about me. I think I overindulged on the macarons, but they were delicious," I said, trying to force some holiday cheer into my words.

He seemed to sense I wasn't telling the whole truth and completely ignored my dessert-based conversational decoy. "You're a guest in my house. Of course, I will worry about you." The quartet suddenly shifted songs, playing a slow, sweet melody. Gabriel offered me his hand. "Maybe a dance will cheer you up?" he suggested.

Unwilling to make a scene, and with no other way to extricate myself from Finn's line of sight gracefully, I laid my hand on his. Gabriel swirled me out onto the dance floor, and I nearly lost my footing as my shoe caught the hem of my full skirt. In an instant, Gabriel was there, steadying me with both hands at my waist as we gently swayed in time to the music.

"Sorry," I whispered, my cheeks heating. "I've never really been a dancer and definitely never tried it in a ballgown before."

Gabriel shifted his grip on my waist, inching us closer together and holding the small of my back gently but firmly as he lifted my hand with his free one. "Don't worry. Just keep your eyes on me. I won't let you fall." Before I could protest further, he swept us off into the rhythm of the dance.

To my surprise, I found my steps matching his with an elegance I didn't know I possessed. Was it his skill on the dance floor or the enchantment of the silver serpent that made me move with such poise? As the music swelled around us, Gabriel matched it with an effortless ease that I found both comforting and almost exhilarating. I wasn't making a fool of myself. A small giggle escaped me as Gabriel twirled us in a circle, and I found myself actually *enjoying* the dance, much to my surprise. I decided for the duration of the song, I would allow myself to forget the complications awaiting me off the dance floor and just live in this glorious moment. My spirits lifted with joy for the first time all evening, feeling almost as light as my feet did under Gabriel's expert guidance.

As the final sweet notes of the dance faded, Gabriel spun me in one last graceful twirl, and I came to a gentle stop. I smiled up at him in silent gratitude before turning to applaud the musicians.

Across the room, Finn met my eyes over Seraphina's head, obviously concluding a dance of their own. Finn's gaze carried a complexity of emotions I couldn't decipher from this distance—a mixture of questions, hurt, and perhaps disappointment. The swell of positive emotions within me faded with the last echo of the music. The urge to flee from Finn's look was overwhelming.

I mumbled a hasty thanks to Gabriel and turned away, only to collide with the couple standing behind us, nearly sending everyone into a brief and clumsy tangle.

"I'm so sorry," I stammered, steadying myself.

The woman in a simple, high-necked, green dress with dazzling diamond chandelier earrings wore a tight smile that barely seemed to hide her impatience. "Don't worry about it."

Her companion, a dark-haired man in an all-black tux, leaned down and whispered in her ear. She nodded, and he spun on his heel, weaving through the crowd with a swift, almost practiced ease. As she moved to follow him, Vivienne stepped into view onto the small stage, the Silverthorne matriarch's tiara glinting like a beacon of authority and drawing everyone's attention. I hesitated, realizing that slipping away now would be impossible without drawing attention to myself. I turned towards the front and found myself pressed against Gabriel's side as the surrounding guests shifted to face the stage, closing ranks and effectively blocking my escape.

"Ladies and gentlemen, esteemed guests, I invite you to turn your attention to the stage for an interlude of enchantment. This evening, we are privileged to host a renowned illusionist who is here to bewitch your senses and challenge your perception of reality. Prepare to be dazzled by her mesmerizing feats of magic that will make the impossible seem possible, right before your very eyes. Please join me in welcoming...the incomparable Mystique!"

She stepped to the side, leading the applause as the illusionist in the sequined suit stepped forward, raising her hands and casting what appeared to be a handful of snow out into the audience. It shimmered as it fell, vanishing completely before it could ruin the fancy clothes of the guests below.

"I thought we were supposed to keep our magical powers under wraps in Havenwood?" I whispered to Gabriel.

"Everyone likes a good show," Gabriel whispered back. "Besides, who's going to tell? Even if they do, without proof, anyone who isn't here will just assume that the magic is just stage magic. Anyway, Mystique is one of the best. Just watch, and then tell me at the end if you don't find the show thrilling."

I recognized her as the woman in the sequined suit I'd observed setting up the stage earlier. She was already commanding the attention of many the partygoers. With a graceful wave of her hand, she conjured a bouquet of white lilies from thin air, their petals unfurling one by one in slow motion, enchanting the audience, who clapped politely. Next, she took a single pearl from a velvet pouch and tossed it into the air where it multiplied, a shower of pearls cascading around her before they disappeared just before touching the ground. This was met with a chorus of "ooo's" and "ahh's" from all around me. Her assistant, a lithe woman I saw before, whisked the bag away with a practiced smile, disappearing behind the black velvet curtains.

Mystique stepped forward with a playful grin. "Ladies and gentlemen, I am Mystique," the illusionist proclaimed from the stage. Enthusiastic applause met her words, and she waited with a patient smile until it died down. "It is an honor to be here to entertain you tonight. Together with my assistant, Selene, we hope to thrill and intrigue you in equal measure this evening. Now, I promise you, no doves were harmed in the making of this next illusion. In fact, they demanded a raise afterward."

Mystique lifted the top hat from the small table with a flourish and made a point of showing the audience the empty interior before reaching inside and pulling out not one, but two doves. Her assistant reappeared from behind the curtain and took the hat back as Mystique held up the birds for all to see and then threw them into the air. The crowd let out a delighted gasp as the doves flew, trailing rose petals and golden coins.

Gabriel plucked one out of the air and held it out to me. "Now tell me this isn't worth it for the free chocolate," he said with a wink. I accepted it, peeling the gold foil away easily to reveal the dark chocolate disk. I bit into it, surprised by the quality of the chocolate. Normally, the chocolate in gold coin wrappers was fairly pedestrian stuff.

"This is delicious!" I exclaimed.

"I can see why the doves wanted a raise," Gabriel teased.

"How did she do that?" I whispered in awe, looking from the chocolate to the doves fluttering to land on Mystique's outstretched hands.

"Magic," Gabriel whispered back with a knowing smile.

"If this is her opener, I can't wait to see the finale," I said, looking around to see the surprised delight on the faces of those around me. Off to my left, I saw Bella and Alex enjoying their own chocolate coins, and, just beyond them, at the edge of the room, I caught a glimpse of Finn and Seraphina. He looked concerned, as she whispered urgently to her business partner in what seemed like a heated argument.

Mystique waved her hands, and the doves seemed to magically turn into matching bouquets of red roses, which she graciously handed to Vivienne and Elara Silverthorne, accompanied by another round of applause.

Mystique nodded graciously and held up her hands. "For my next trick, I will require some aid. Don't worry. I won't make you disappear," she said with a wink. Chuckles rolled around the room. "If you will..." she trailed off, raising her hands to the ceiling. Everyone, including me, looked upward, waiting for the illusionist's next elaborate trick.

Which is precisely when the lights went out.

There was a collective pause, as if the room held its breath, waiting to see what happened next.

A moment of silence ... then screams started, followed by something tugging forcefully at the serpent necklace around my throat.

Mounting Suspicions

INSTINCTIVELY, MY HANDS SHOT to my collarbone, grasping the necklace as the unexpected tug pulled tighter, threatening to choke off my breath. I felt the necklace start to slip wide and twist around my neck. Whoever was behind me, lurking in the shadows, had undone the clasp! I wasn't about to let the expensive, enchanted necklace be stolen right out from under my nose, even if I couldn't see anything at the moment, given the complete and utter blackness that engulfed me.

Gasping for air and unable to shout a warning, let alone be heard amid the chaos which had descended upon the ballroom, I did the only thing I could think of. I reached out with my magic, latching onto the necklace with my talent and my hands. Power shot through me and the slip and slide of the silver against my skin halted instantly. My eyes widened in surprise. My gift with metal was relatively small in the world of magic. Typically, I could pop a dent out of a bumper, but not much else. Now? Now it felt like I could lift the entire car without breaking a sweat.

The assailant behind me yanked with such force that I nearly toppled over, yet my grasp on the necklace, bolstered by my magic, held unyielding and firm. It was like my will fused with the jewelry. Beside me, I felt Gabriel grab for my hand in the darkness, apparently startled by my sudden movement. For a moment, I was the rope in an unexpected game of tug-o-war. Whoever had a hold on my necklace suddenly released it, sending me crashing forward into Gabriel's arms. He caught me with a surprised "oomph" and a moment later, a silver light sprang to life in the palm of his hand, barely beating back the all-encompassing darkness surrounding just us.

"Are you okay? What happened?" Gabriel asked, holding me tightly to his chest as the confusion and chaos reigned in the dark around us. Unfortunately, even his illusionary light wasn't enough to combat the unexpected shadows. The weak illumination barely lit his concerned face as he looked down at me.

Still in the process of catching my breath, I nodded while focusing my attention and magic on the serpent necklace. I felt the clasp snap back into place with a touch of my talent. "Someone tried to steal my necklace," I finally rasped, rubbing at my tender throat. Seraphina's enchantment on the necklace was the only thing that had kept the thief from succeeding. I'm sure my power alone wouldn't have held the necklace in place.

Gabriel clutched me tighter, turning with his light outstretched against the darkness to try to catch a glimpse of the thief, but it was no use. The shadows were oppressive. A sudden shout of surprise rolled through the room. I couldn't figure out what was causing it until a wave of light spilled across us, beating back the shadows slowly. I blinked and squinted as the sudden light felt blinding after the inky blackness. Across the room, Lucas and Vivienne stood together with hands outstretched, obviously combating whatever spell had descended on the ballroom.

Confusion reigned supreme as people gasped and exclaimed. However, it didn't take much for me to put two and two together. The jewel thief, who Seraphina mentioned was plaguing high society events, had just struck again, and the assailant was likely still in the room. Instantly, I started scanning the visible crowd for anyone fleeing the scene, but it was hard because the shadows were retreating sluggishly.

Vivienne and Lucas stood alone on the stage. A quick scan revealed an ominous vacancy; Mystique and her assistant had vanished, as mysteriously as any of her illusions. Were they behind this? Someone jostled me, and a wave of uneasy murmurs rippled through the crowd. The gasps and exclamations grew louder, but it was still possible to hear individual voices over the rising din. The crowd was a mass of movement and confusion as people tried to make sense of what had just happened. As the shadows pulled back, I saw Finn standing protectively in front of Seraphina and her partner. Seraphina looked like she was about to cry, and Dominic's expression was one of fury.

After two previous mysteries around this town, my thoughts immediately turned to suspects and who had the opportunity. Neither one of them could have been the thief who attempted to steal my necklace. Not from that distance. As quickly as I thought about it, I amended my assumption. In a room of magic users with unknown gifts, anyone could be a suspect. For all I knew, Seraphina had enchanted super speed into her gown and could zip around the room in an instant, snatching jewels. Looking at her face, I thought it was unlikely, but the idea bore consideration.

The shadows pulled back further and were almost at the edge of the ballroom when the first shout of dismay rose above the hubbub.

"My bracelet! It's gone!" a woman's voice called from nearby.

"My earrings too!" I recognized the woman in the high-necked dress I'd bumped into, looking around in distress as she tugged on her empty lobes.

"And my watch!" a man in a tuxedo a little further away called.

The roar of the crowd increased as more and more guests realized the valuable jewels that had been lent to them had vanished. Everyone was shouting in confusion except Vivienne Silverthorne, who was attempting to regain control of the situation.

Knowing I was one of the thief's intended victims and possibly his last target before the lights came up, I twisted in Gabriel's arms, ignoring the chaos in the hopes of seeing the thief flee the scene. There! At the back of the ballroom, a flash of movement caught my eye as the retreating shadows revealed someone running through a doorway the catering staff had been using all evening. Whoever it was disappeared down the hall and out of sight. The only glimpse I caught before he or she vanished was of a black sleeve and something that glittered. In that instant, there wasn't doubt in my mind. The thief was getting away! I didn't hesitate. I shoved through the crowd, not caring about the gasps and shouts of anger as I rushed toward where the thief was making an escape.

"Harper! What are you doing?" I heard Gabriel shout from behind me, but I didn't dare pause to explain. Who knew what kind of escape plan the thief had? There wasn't a moment to spare in explanations or the culprit might get away. Instead, I hoped

Gabriel was following me as I shoved through the crowd toward the exit. I lifted my voluminous skirts so I could make better time, and I broke through the last of the crowd, sprinting towards the door. Behind me, I heard Gabriel calling for me to wait. Over the noise of the crowd, Vivienne's commanding voice rang out, but I ignored it all. I wasn't going to let the thief ruin this perfectly lovely evening.

I dashed down a plain hallway that led me to a huge kitchen area, efficiently laid out with trays of food. This was obviously the caterer's prepping area. Surprisingly, there were only two people in the room, but from the way they were glaring at each other, I could tell I'd stumbled onto some drama. I just didn't think it was the one I'd been looking for.

Gabriel appeared a moment later, half-stepping in front of me. I think he meant to protect me, which was sweet, but unnecessary, as the two only had eyes for each other.

"Jasper! I can't believe you would try to ruin Mystique's show!" the slim woman in the glittering black gown stormed, stomping her foot and putting her hands on her hips. I recognized her as Selene, Mystique's assistant.

"What are you talking about?" the waiter said, scowling at her.

His expression jarred my memory. It was the same waiter who had glared at Isadora earlier in the evening. What was this guy's problem?

"Don't give me that!" The assistant strode forward, actually quivering with barely contained rage, sending her long blonde hair rippling down her back. "I *saw* you! I know what you did."

"And what did I do?"

"You're still on this insane crusade, aren't you? Admit it!" Her voice was tight with anger.

Jasper gave a mocking little bow. "With pride. Mystique is a fraud, and your little act is a total sham."

"You're just bitter," Selene snapped.

"Oh yeah? Prove it," he sneered.

"You think I can't?! I'll show you—" the assistant said, tossing back her hair. Sparkles of magic gathered in her palm.

"What are you going to do?" sneered the server. "Drop a glitter bomb on my head? News flash, a long hot shower is all I need to wash away any of your so-called magic."

"Just you wait!" the assistant yelled, her voice rising as she drew back her arm.

"Whoa, hang on a minute," Gabriel said, dashing forward and grabbing her wrist before she could hurl the contents of whatever was in her hand directly in the waiter's arrogant face. Not that I blamed her at the moment. Part of me wanted to join her in hurling glitter at him for the way he'd spoken. Possibly preceded with a good deal of super glue. But the thought of ruining all the delightfully prepared food halted any of my glitter-related schemes in their infancy.

"She started it," Jasper, the waiter, said petulantly.

"I did not!" the assistant yelled, a flush of red racing up her cheeks all the way to her slightly pointed ears.

"Okay," Gabriel said, lowering his voice to something calm yet authoritative. "Jasper, was it? You sit down. Selene, take a deep breath, and tell me what's going on."

"Who are you to boss me around?" Jasper said belligerently.

"Gabriel Silverthorne. Sit. Down. Now." The room seemed to darken slightly, and lightning crackled around Gabriel. I could even smell burned ozone in the air. I knew he was good at illusions, but this was next level.

For a moment, I wondered just what Gabriel was capable of. Coming from a powerful mage family, his talents likely extended far beyond mere illusions. What other gifts did he possess? How dangerous could he truly be? The thought sent a shiver down my spine, and I realized I knew very little about the full extent of his abilities.

Jasper sat. I would've too if I'd been in his position.

Selene, the assistant, kept her eyes locked on Jasper, but spoke to Gabriel. "I knew there'd be trouble as soon as I saw him here. I just expected him to make a snide comment or, you know, try to accidentally-on-purpose spill red wine all over Mystique. Something like that."

Jasper snorted, but before he could jump in, Gabriel snapped at him and held up a finger without ever looking away from Selene. "I'm missing something. Why would Jasper want to do anything to you or to Mystique?"

"Because we're not just partners on the stage," Selene said, shooting Jasper a dark glare. "He decided he was the world's gift to women, and when Mystique turned him down, he swore he'd get revenge on her. And that's what he did tonight by ruining our show."

"That's not true!" Jasper exclaimed, half-rising from his seat. Gabriel shot him a look that made the waiter wilt back into the chair.

"Tell me what you saw," Gabriel said gently to Selene.

The illusionist's assistant pointed at Jasper. "He's got electromancy. An affinity to electricity. He can't do more than turn off the lights without touching a switch, but he likes to use that to pull pranks. I've seen him do it more than once. He was standing at the back of the room watching us with this awful sneer on his face. Then I saw him smirk and gather his power like I've seen him do before. The next thing I knew, everything went dark. It's his fault! He's trying to undermine us just because of his grudge against Mystique!"

"You little..." Jasper growled, standing up once more. A look from Gabriel halted him in his tracks, but he didn't sit back down.

I caught my breath. Could Jasper the waiter be behind the missing jewels? Part of me didn't believe that this guy could mastermind anything more complicated than tying his own shoes, but I'd been wrong before. However, what had happened in the ballroom wasn't merely turning off the lights; it was *magical* darkness. Maybe he was working with an accomplice, who had stronger powers and was the brains behind the situation. As soon as that thought occurred, it made more sense to me than Jasper the creep working alone.

Gabriel patted Selene on the shoulder. "I've got it from here. Why don't you go check on Mystique?"

Selene huffed and shot one more pointed glare at Jasper before flouncing out the door with a toss of her platinum hair. "She ran off the stage as soon as the lights came up. I think she was embarrassed. I'll check the dressing room and bathrooms for her," she muttered as she left.

Gabriel nodded and turned his attention back to Jasper. "Care to tell me your side of the story before I turn you over to my mother? You know, Vivienne Silverthorne? The most powerful mage in town. Maybe even on the Eastern Seaboard. If you want to avoid her wrath, start talking."

The anger dropped from Jasper's eyes, and a sheen of sweat sprang up on his now pale face. "Look, dude. I didn't mean any harm."

"Tell me what you did. *Dude.*" Gabriel's voice was soft, but there was more than a hint of steel in it.

Jasper fumbled in his jacket pocket, withdrawing a phone. "I swear I had nothing to do with the lights going out. Just look at the footage! I was right at the edge of the ballroom, filming," he said, his thumb flicking across the screen. "I was going to prove Mystique is a fraud. Look!" He thrust the phone at Gabriel. "See? If I'd used my magic to short out the lights, it would have also killed my phone. My powers are kind of an all or nothing situation."

I leaned in, peering at the small screen as Gabriel commandeered the phone, his fingers scrolling back to play the video again.

"Look, the only reason I ran in the first place was because we were told no phones were allowed. I didn't want to get fired, man. I need this job. That's the honest truth. I panicked and I ran. Nothing more, I swear," Jasper said in a rush.

Gabriel held up a finger, commanding silence in that one slight gesture. Jasper gulped and went even more pale but shut his mouth. We watched the figures on the screen, small and moving at high speed, as Gabriel scrubbed through the video. It showed Jasper holding the phone, then flipping the camera at the beginning so it was directed out at Mystique. When the lights went out, Gabriel slowed the video back to normal speed. On the playback, we heard Jasper curse and stumble down the hallway until he appeared back on screen in the middle of the brightly lit kitchen before the video cut out.

Something snagged at my attention, and I took the phone from Gabriel, running the video back to the beginning as he looked back at Jasper. "So, I'm guessing this means you have nothing to do with the missing jewels?" Gabriel demanded.

"M-m-missing jewels? Me?" Jasper swallowed audibly as I dragged my finger across the playback bar and slowed down the speed. "Nah, man. I wouldn't do that."

"Just mess with a lady who had no interest in you. Yeah, you're a real stand-up guy," Gabriel said sarcastically.

"It was just a prank. No one was gonna get hurt," Jasper whined.

I ignored him, focusing my attention on the video. Then I saw it again. The thing that had caught my attention the first time. A blur of darkness darting across the screen and emanating from the stage's direction just before the ballroom was plunged into shadow.

"Gabriel," I interrupted, tugging on his sleeve and pulling him to the side. "Look at this," I whispered. I re-started the video just before the strange shadow descended. "He might be a jerk, but I don't think he's responsible for the lights going out."

Gabriel and I exchanged a glance, the same realization dawning on both of us. "The blackout...it came from Mystique's performance area," I murmured. Doubt crept into my voice as the pieces began to fall into an unsettling pattern. "Was she...could she be involved in this?"

"I need to show this to my brother," Gabriel murmured.

Jasper, who had been sulking nearby, overheard us. "You can't just take my phone!" he whined.

Gabriel turned to him, his eyes cold and unyielding. "None of the staff were supposed to have phones. What would your supervisor say if I reported this?"

Jasper blanched, his bravado crumbling. "Please, don't tell him," he pleaded, voice trembling.

Gabriel stepped closer, his presence intimidating. "Here's the deal. I won't report you, but I'm keeping the phone."

Jasper's eyes darted around nervously. "But that's not fair!"

Gabriel's voice dropped to a dangerously soft tone. "It's the phone or your job. Make your choice."

Jasper swallowed hard, his resolve breaking. "Fine, take the stupid phone," he muttered reluctantly, his shoulders slumping. "But I'm telling you, Mystique's probably responsible for all this anyway."

Gabriel's gaze didn't waver, making Jasper squirm even more. "Watch your mouth," he warned.

Curious at the intensity of his vitriol, I couldn't stop myself from jumping into the conversation. "Why do you think that?" I asked.

Jasper sneered, apparently having rediscovered some of his bravado. "Of course, she was. She's the illusionist, isn't she? Who better to slip into these fancy parties and steal from all the rich fat cats?"

Gabriel narrowed his eyes, but all he said was, "Don't leave the premises." Jasper opened his mouth to protest, but Gabriel cut him off with a piercing stare. "You're lucky I'm not reporting you. Don't push me."

Jasper wilted under Gabriel's intense gaze, muttering a weak, "Fine," before slinking away to the opposite side of the kitchen and making a show of grabbing a fresh tray of canapes.

Gabriel turned to me, his grip firm but gentle as he took my hand. I followed him from the kitchen, neither of us speaking until we were sure Jasper was out of earshot.

"What do you think?" I asked in a whisper.

"That you're right. He didn't cause the blackout, but we need to find out who did. We also need to find Mystique, my brother, and my mother."

"Your mother?" I asked in surprise. The thought of Vivienne Silverthorne's anger still filled me with an existential dread I couldn't quite verbalize. Even though I'd done nothing wrong. I didn't want to be too close to her impending wrath.

"Absolutely. I need to tell her to double check security protocols with the catering staff," Gabriel said with a grim expression.

"I thought you said you wouldn't tell his supervisor," I whispered.

"And I'm not. I'm telling my mother. Believe me, that is exponentially worse. But I'm not a complete jerk. I'll keep his name out of it as long as he doesn't cause any more problems."

I nodded thoughtfully, but my mind was already racing past Jasper and his petty dramas. Instead, it was filled with questions and suspicions. Could the esteemed illusionist, Mystique, be the mastermind behind a heist at her own show? It seemed almost too bold, too blatant. And yet, here was circumstantial evidence that suggested she had played a part in the chaos.

"Hey, can I see that video again?" I asked on impulse, hoping I might spot a clue before the phone was turned over to Vivienne. Gabriel handed it over, watching me curiously.

As I re-watched the video, something caught my eye. Just before the blackout, Mystique seemed to glance directly at the shadowy form that barely entered the edge of the frame. I'd missed it completely the first few times, but now that I was examining Mystique, I saw the shift in her gaze. It was subtle, almost imperceptible, but there was a brief moment where her eyes locked onto the darkness, and her head jerked. Was that a nod? Of recognition, perhaps? My heart raced as I replayed the segment, confirming what I had seen.

"Gabriel, look at this," I said, tugging on his sleeve and showing him the screen. "Watch Mystique's eyes just before the blackout."

Gabriel leaned in, his expression darkening as he watched the footage. "She saw something. It looks like she recognized that figure. This can't be a coincidence. Too bad the rest of him or her is out of frame."

My suspicions deepened with Gabriel's confirmation. The moment of recognition between Mystique and the shadowy form was definitely more than just an innocent glance. It suggested a level of awareness and possibly even collaboration.

"We need to find her," Gabriel said, his voice low and resolute. "Now."

Rumors and Riffraff

As we reentered the grand ballroom, the enchanting spell of the evening seemed to have shattered like fragile glass. The atmosphere, once vibrant and filled with laughter, now felt heavy with suspicion and unease. The ballroom's glittering lights, which had earlier cast a warm and welcoming glow, now seemed harsh and unforgiving, throwing long, ominous shadows that crept into every corner.

A palpable wave of frustration and anxiety from the crowd washed over us. My heart pounded as I scanned the surrounding faces. Each one was a potential suspect, and every whisper was a possible clue. The air was thick with tension, and the jovial chatter had given way to hushed conversations and furtive glances.

A sudden realization hit me with startling clarity: beneath the facade of charm and sophistication, an audacious jewel thief was likely hiding, blending seamlessly into the crowd. The ballroom, which had seemed so enchanting, now felt like a place where secrets festered, and danger loomed just out of sight.

Guests were milling about, their earlier gaiety replaced by furrowed brows and concerned murmurs. In the midst of it all, Vivienne and Seraphina were beacons of calm and order, directing guests towards a growing line where people were returning their borrowed jewels, piece by sparkling piece, and the jewelers were compiling lists of both returned and missing pieces. Serious-looking security guards blocked the ballroom's exits, scanning each party goer for any sign of threat or non-compliance.

Suddenly, Lucas appeared at Gabriel's side, his expression urgent. "Gabriel. Where'd you disappear to? Mother wants us both right now," he said, pulling his brother away. Gabriel shot me a concerned look.

"I'll be okay," I murmured.

"And I'll be back soon," he promised, before disappearing into the crowd with his brother.

I stood there for a moment, feeling adrift on a tide of unrest. I wanted to help, but what could I do? Just as I was about to go find Bella, she and Alex emerged from the crowd, their faces filled with concern.

"Harper!" Bella exclaimed, rushing to my side. "We've been looking everywhere for you!"

"Are you alright?" Alex asked, his brow furrowed in worry as he looked at my throat.

"Oh, my goodness! What happened?" Bella asked, her hand flying to cover her mouth. I wouldn't be surprised if there was an ugly red line across my neck from where the necklace dug in. By now, there might even be some bruising.

I lifted a hand to my throat, fingers grazing over the tender skin. "It... got a little rough," I admitted, feeling the slight sting where the necklace had dug in. "But it's nothing serious." I could tell Bella wasn't entirely convinced, her gaze lingering on my neck with a flash of worry. I managed a smile. "I'm fine. Really. Just a bit shaken. There's so much happening."

Bella pulled me into a tight hug. "I'm so glad we found you and you're okay. It's chaotic! Can you imagine? The jewel thief actually struck right here in Havenwood and in the middle of the Silverthorne Ball, no less!"

"So much for the Scarlet Raven and the Midnight Fox," I said with a wan smile as I rubbed at my throat. The skin was tender to the touch, and I tried not to wince.

Bella noticed my reaction, and her mouth firmed in determination. "I think this is just the time for the Scarlet Raven and the Midnight Fox. There's no way I'm going to let them get away with hurting my best friend."

I squeezed her hand. "Thanks, Bella."

Alex cleared his throat. "I don't know what's going on with the ravens and the foxes, but I agree with Bells. We should stick together until the thief is caught."

"Speaking of, have you heard anything about what's going on?" I asked.

Bella shook her head. "Not much apart from the gossip. If you believed everything people have been saying, the culprits are somewhere between an evil Batman, a shadow mage, a klepto-maniac ghost, or possibly someone with an invisibility cloak."

"Do those really exist?" I asked.

Alex shook his head. "Not that I've ever heard of, which is why I'm leaning towards the ghost theory."

Bella swatted at him good-naturedly. "You're trying to make that happen, and I keep telling you it doesn't make any sense."

"None of it makes any sense," Alex said, easily dodging her.

Bella turned back to me. "What have you heard?"

I shrugged. "Not much. Gabriel thinks there's more to this than just a simple blackout. Mystique might be involved."

Bella's eyes widened. "Mystique? The illusionist? That's wild."

"I know," I sighed. "It's hard to know who to trust right now."

"Well, you can trust us," Bella said firmly. "We're in this togeth-er."

Alex nodded in agreement. "Absolutely. We'll figure this out."

Their support buoyed my spirits. "Thanks, guys. I'm so glad you're here."

"But I'd like to advocate for a cool name of my own," Alex added. "I'm thinking Disco Platypus."

"No!" Bella and I said in unison and then grinned at each other.

As we were talking, Oswald and Hortense Puddleton, the odi-ous couple who owned the only other bookstore in town, drifted over. They began a very loud conversation, clearly meant for me to overhear.

"I just can't believe such a dreadful thing could happen here," Oswald said, his cutting, nasal voice carrying to everyone nearby.

"Absolutely," Hortense agreed, her tone dripping with disdain. "It must be a newcomer. A Havenwood local would *never* act in such a reprehensible way."

I could feel my cheeks burning as I overheard their con-versation. Tourists were common enough in Havenwood, but no tourists would be invited to the Silverthorne Ball. It was well-known that I was one of the most recent additions to Haven-wood. Despite realizing that they derived their only joy from stirring up other people, I couldn't control my reaction. I blushed fiercely, feeling the sting of their words.

Bella noticed the effect their comments had and turned towards the Puddleton couple, her eyes flashing with anger. "Why don't you take your baseless accusations somewhere else? You're not helping."

Hortense smiled meanly in satisfaction, her eyes glinting. "Oh, we're just concerned citizens who want the best for Havenwood."

Oswald nodded vigorously in agreement, sending his jowls wobbling. "Yes, it's best to address these issues swiftly. Clean up the riffraff before they can cause more of a ruckus."

Bella's reaction was immediate and fierce. She moved to storm over and give them a piece of her mind, but Alex restrained her, whispering calming words in her ear. "Bella, it's not worth it. Don't give them the satisfaction."

Oswald spoke up again, this time louder. "You know, I think you may be right, Hortense. There's no way an established local would commit such a horrible crime. And on Christmas Eve, no less!"

"Do you think we should share our theory with the powers that be? Do our part to put an end to this total fiasco?" Hortense suggested, her thin lips twisting into a tight smile.

Oswald nodded, meeting my eyes directly. "I do. Yes, absolutely. And I know exactly who is at the top of my suspect list."

Hortense chimed in, her voice dripping with false sweetness, "We should make sure to mention this to the powers that be, Oswald. Before she causes more trouble in our lovely town." As one, the Puddletons shot me matching triumphant stares. They didn't need to say my name to get their point across. Everyone within earshot knew *exactly* who they were talking about. With a haughty sniff, the pair turned and swept away without another word.

I was dumbfounded, my cheeks burning with embarrassment and anger. Bella immediately stormed after the Puddletons, her temper flaring.

"You have no right to talk about Harper like that!" Bella cried, attracting the attention of more nearby guests.

Alex rushed to stop her, grabbing her arm just in time. "Bella, don't. They're not worth it," he whispered urgently, trying to calm her down.

Bella struggled for a moment before relenting, glaring daggers at the retreating figures of Oswald and Hortense. Meanwhile, a whispering crowd left me standing in the middle, making me feel exposed and vulnerable as everyone seemed to have their eyes on me.

The whispers grew around me, and people turned away, their hushed conversations prickling my skin. Were they whispering about me? Surely, they couldn't believe I was responsible. Could they?

A figure suddenly loomed out of the crowd, approaching me with an outstretched hand. I flinched away instinctively, not recognizing Dominic Umbra, Seraphina's partner, until he was close enough to touch.

"Ah, I'm glad to see the silver serpent wasn't lost to the thieves," Dominic said, reaching towards the necklace with a look of intense relief on his face. "It's a precious piece, and I'd hate to see it vanish. Let me help you with that, and I'll see it gets back to its rightful place," he offered. His uninvited touch near my throat made me flinch back, remembering the jolt of someone grabbing at the necklace.

For a moment, I was back in that instant, scared and confused as the serpent necklace was tightening around my throat and cutting off my airway. In the darkness. All alone. Someone tugging hard on the necklace and it digging into my skin, pulling me back.

I looked at his outstretched hand. Something was wrong. It took me only a second to realize what it was. Dominic was significantly taller than I was. If he'd been tugging on the serpent necklace, it would've dug up under my jaw instead of straight across my throat. Which meant whoever had grabbed it must've been my height. Possibly shorter and wearing heels, if I was going to account for every possibility. A clue! It wasn't much, but it was something. Wasn't it?

A sudden memory of Dominic standing across the ballroom with Seraphina and Finn surfaced. Unless he had super speed that rivaled the Flash, and did it all while crouching down, it probably wasn't Dominic who'd attacked me. But I couldn't dismiss him entirely. The improbability of his involvement didn't mean it was impossible. Starlight Treasures was his company, after all. A spate of jewel heists had to be bad for business. And yet, maybe his eagerness was just about securing all the remaining jewels.

I automatically began listing and ranking his means, motive, and opportunity to commit the crime. Means? He had access to magical jewelry. Motive? Protecting his business, but that didn't quite add up as a reason to steal from his own event. Opportunity?

He had been across the room, making it difficult, but not impossible, for him to have been involved directly.

Perhaps I was getting into a bad habit from the other adventures I'd had since moving to Havenwood. I'd gotten used to putting suspicious people onto suspect lists as I tried to figure out who was behind the theft of rare books at the shop or was responsible for the pranks around town. It almost felt like second nature now to evaluate means, motive, and opportunity. As I analyzed, it didn't make sense that Dominic was responsible or realistically could've committed the theft.

Amidst my contemplation of suspects and creating lists, my hands naturally reached for the back of my neck to release the clasp and hand it back to him.

Isadora appeared out of the crowd and grabbed me by the elbow. "Harper! I need you. Come with me."

Dominic's nostrils flared and the skin around his eyes tightened momentarily, but he quickly composed himself, offering a charming smile. "Wait a minute, please. I must ask you to return your jewelry before leaving. We're making a list to ensure we have a proper inventory of what's missing."

Isadora shot him a look she must've learned from her intimidating mother. "And she will. But for now, I need Harper and her necklace. You can write down in your little book that the pendant is safe. Trust me, I'll vouch for her."

Isadora turned in a swirl of lavender and dragged me towards a large double door blocked by a bulky security guard. He shifted immediately to the side, and we slipped into the room beyond. The library loomed before us, its floor-to-ceiling bookshelves casting long, shadowy fingers across the room. Rolling ladders creaked eerily as we passed them and under the large medieval-style crest painted on an enormous display shield. It glinted menacingly in the dim light. The room felt darker, more oppressive, as if the very walls were closing in, harboring secrets within their ancient tomes.

Lucas and Gabriel stood to one side, talking in low tones to Vivienne and the elderly aunt in silver. Aunt Elara, I remembered her name was. Their hushed voices barely penetrated the heavy air, which seemed to absorb sound and light alike. The rich wood and leather-bound volumes, once a source of wonder, now felt like silent witnesses to the night's unsettling events. The grand manor, which had been so full of Christmas magic earlier, now felt like a labyrinth of shadows, each turn and corridor cloaked in an unsettling darkness.

"I have the solution to our problem," Isadora announced grandly, stopping in the middle of the room with me by her side.

Four sets of eyes turned toward me, and just for a moment, it looked like Vivienne suspected me of ruining her evening. It might have only been a millisecond of an icy glare, but I knew then I never, *ever* wanted to be on the wrong side of the Silverthorne matriarchal mage. Ever. I shrunk back. What had Isadora just dragged me into?

"What do you mean, Isa?" Gabriel asked.

"You caught the thief?" Lucas said, striding aggressively forward, his eyes locked on me.

He couldn't mean...no...he thought I *was the thief?!?*

Gabriel was faster than his brother, darting forward and positioning himself in front of me. "What? No way could it be Harper. I was with her the whole time," Gabriel protested firmly. He looked in confusion at Isadora and then at me.

I felt a wave of panic. "Wait, what? I didn't steal anything!" I stammered.

Isadora winked at Gabriel. "The whole time, huh?"

Lucas interrupted, frowning. "Your friend stole the jewels, Isa?"

"What?" she exclaimed.

"What is going on?" Vivienne's authoritative tone cut through the overlapping questions, her eyes narrowing dangerously.

"You're giving me a headache, that's what!" Elara said, sinking into a chair with a dramatic sigh. "Can't you all just talk one at a time like normal people instead of shouting all higgledy-piggledy at once? Goodness gracious me!"

The room fell into a tense silence, the urgency and confusion hanging thick in the air. My heart pounded in my chest as Gabriel stood protectively in front of me, his jaw clenched while he awaited Isadora's explanation.

It was Lucas who broke the sudden silence first, shattering it like brittle glass. "Your friend stole the jewels, Isa?" he repeated, his voice dangerously quiet.

"What? No!" Isadora waved her hands dramatically in negation, and I sighed silently in relief. Considering what the Puddletons had not so subtly alluded to, I wouldn't have been surprised if I was a suspect.

Oblivious to my thoughts, Isadora continued. "I overheard Seraphina when she was explaining the enchantments on the jewelry before the party. I was curious and asked her about each of ours in more detail. Harper's necklace has an enhancement charm that not only augments the wearer's experience, but also enhances magic. You just said we need to keep the thief here, and Harper's necklace could be the key," Isadora said, pointing at my necklace triumphantly.

My mind whirled. How did she know about my metal magic? Had I let it slip somehow? No, I would remember that. But what if she had overheard something? And even if she did know, how was this necklace supposed to help? Could it really enhance my power enough to lock all the doors in the mansion and keep the thief inside until we could identify him or her? That seemed impossible. What were the limits on the enchantment, anyway? Did it come with a user manual or was this more of a trial-and-error situation? Doubts and questions swirled around me, each one adding to the confusion and chaos in my mind.

"Explain. What is your plan, Isadora?" Vivienne demanded, her voice slicing through the tension, her gaze piercing.

Isadora spoke excitedly. "This place is enormous. Even with your beefy security men, a determined thief could sneak out of here without too much difficulty. We did it easily enough after all when we were teenagers."

"What?" Vivienne said, her tone dangerously sharp.

Isadora waved a dismissive hand. "Not the point, Mother. We need to do something to keep *everyone* inside until we can get to the bottom of this, and I think Harper has the key. Well, Harper and Aunt Elara." All eyes turned to the silver haired older lady.

"Me?" she squeaked, looking surprised. "What can I do?"

Isadora laid a hand on her arm, her voice gentle as she addressed the elderly lady. "You have weather magic, Aunt Elara. Do you think you could magic up a deterrent to keep the thief inside? Like some icy rain to shut down the streets or something?"

"A little bit of cold won't stop a determined and audacious thief," Lucas protested.

"So, make it bigger," Isadora replied instantly. "Our own mini-snowstorm right here on the Silverthorne grounds."

Elara raised a wrinkled hand. "Sorry to burst your bubble, darling, but my talents for magic have always been limited. I don't command the power that your mother has in her little finger, let alone enough to magic up some weather event that could keep a thief trapped in the manor."

Lucas glanced at Isadora and then stepped forward. "You might not have the weather magic to conjure one, but what about repositioning one?"

Gabriel nodded eagerly, clearly following his brother's logic. "That's right, there's a massive snowstorm passing just north of us. It was supposed to miss us."

"But what if it doesn't?" Isadora finished, her eyes gleaming with excitement.

Elara stroked her chin thoughtfully. "I suppose it's possible. With a little luck, it just might work."

"Which is why you need Harper's necklace," Isadora said, turning towards me with her eyes shining.

I blinked, taken aback. What was she talking about? Then it hit me like a bolt of lightning. If the necklace could enhance my magic enough to withstand the determined efforts of a thief, maybe Elara could use it in combination with her weather magic to pull the incoming snowstorm to Havenwood and, in so doing, keep the thief on the grounds. The realization sent a jolt through me. If we were going to pull this off, we needed to work quickly. I fumbled with the clasp, flicking it open and holding the necklace out to Elara.

"Here. Let's see if it works," I said, draping the necklace gently around her throat.

"I don't know...Oh my! That's heavy. However did you manage to wear this without tipping over?" Elara tittered.

"It is substantial, that's for sure," I murmured, clasping it.

"But do you think you can use it to keep the thief trapped in the manor?" Vivienne asked urgently. "Time is of the essence. If the thief slips away, then all we will have accomplished is locking everyone else in the manor. Along with hitting this entire part of the state with a snowstorm they don't expect."

"It's the East Coast in December," Lucas reassured his mother. "It's not like we're in Florida and the state shuts down if they see a snowflake. Trust me, it'll be fine." Vivienne didn't look convinced, but there also didn't seem to be any better options, so she didn't argue either.

"Only one way to find out," Elara said, closing her eyes. When she opened them, they were stunningly bright blue. She flung her hands outward. I don't know what I expected to happen next. Maybe storm clouds to gather in the library or lightning to shoot out of her eyes. The real occurrence was slightly underwhelming. I think the wind might have picked up a little outside. That was it. However, the bright blue faded from Elara's eyes, returning them once more to a chocolatey brown.

"Well?" Vivienne asked.

"I've done my best. I just hope it is enough," Elara said and moved to take off the silver serpent. I hurried to help her. "That's quite an enchantment that is woven into your necklace. Whoever made it was powerful and knew what they were doing."

"Yes," I murmured, running a finger down the engraved scales of the undulating serpent. Elara's words reminded me that Seraphina had enchanted the necklace. She was not only brilliant and charming but also incredibly powerful. And possibly stood the most to gain from jewels going missing. After all, she wanted to move back to Havenwood, an idea her partner might not support. Her business's future depended on the stability of Starlight Treasures, especially if she was contemplating a big move.

Could she have staged this heist to finance her move? If there'd been a recent spate of jewel heists, Seraphina might've orchestrated this one to throw off suspicion while building up her bank account.

Dominic, on the other hand, still seemed to lack a solid motive in my mind. Besides, I had serious doubts he was the thief purely because of his height. But Seraphina was about the right size to pull the necklace directly across my throat.

Could she really be responsible?

She'd been standing next to Finn when the lights went out, but I couldn't remember her being there when they came back on. However, I'd been distracted by chasing Selene into the kitchen. Had Seraphina still been with Finn? Maybe. Another thought occurred to me. Could Seraphina have enchanted a piece of jewelry to give her super speed? The chances were high, which meant she could've dashed around in the darkness. Who knows? She might've even had an enchantment to *cause* the magical darkness in the first place.

In that moment, Seraphina jumped to the top of my suspect list with Dominic as a distant second. But would Elara's weather magic be enough to keep her from getting away with it?

To Catch a Thief

WITH THE EFFICIENCY OF a general, Vivienne deployed her family back into the ballroom. "Isadora, I want you to ensure the return of all the jewelry continues to go smoothly. Talk to Seraphina and Dominic. Bring me the detailed list of the stolen items along with the names of the guests affected. Lucas, coordinate tightly with our security team to ensure every inch of this estate is sealed off. No one leaves until I say so. Gabriel, deploy your illusion magic and conduct discrete surveillance of the crowd. Listen for any scrap of information that could lead us to the perpetrator. Elara, you're with me. Our priority is to maintain order and reassure our guests. The Silverthorne name will not be tarnished by this audacious act of thievery. Rest assured; we will not stand idly by while someone attempts to undermine us."

Vivienne ignored me completely, sweeping out of the room with Elara close on her heels. Being left out of the instructions, I hesitated and was unsure of what to do. Lucas followed the two women, but paused at the door, looking back. Gabriel and Isadora had started to leave as well, but Isadora, seeing my lost look, took my hand.

"Here Harper, why don't you come with me? We can return your necklace at the same time," she suggested. She paused, leaning closer to get a look at my throat. "Hey! Are you sure you're okay? Your neck looks really painful."

Instinctively, I rubbed at the tender skin on my throat. "The thief tried to take the necklace when the lights went out. Whoever it was pulled pretty hard," I said.

Gabriel's brow furrowed in concern, and he reached out, his hand hovering just shy of touching my neck. "That does look painful." he agreed with Isadora. "Are you okay?"

"How did you keep it on?" Lucas asked. I couldn't tell if his tone was strictly curious or if there was a hint of suspicion in it. I supposed it was natural for him to suspect everyone, given the current situation. If I'd been in his shoes, I probably would've added 'Harper Sullivan' to my short list of suspects too.

I shrugged, trying to play it off, my old instincts about keeping my magic a secret resurfacing. "I guess the clasp must've been harder to open than they expected. Even I had a little trouble getting it off just now."

"You must've put up a fight. Can I get you some salve or something?" Gabriel asked.

I shook my head, not wanting to make a big deal out of it. "It's not that bad. I think it might look worse than it feels."

"Well, if that changes, let me know. We have first aid supplies in the house if you decide you need them," Gabriel offered. He ran his hand through his hair. "I didn't even realize it was happening, and I was standing right next to you."

"How could you not notice?" Lucas asked, his eyes narrowing with suspicion.

Gabriel sighed, shooting his brother a look. "It was chaos, Lucas. The lights went out, everyone was screaming, and people were panicking."

"It all happened so fast," I added. Lucas considered me thoughtfully, but didn't seem convinced.

"Why would they go for Harper's necklace?" Isadora asked. "Surely, after it didn't come off right away, they had to realize there were easier pieces to steal."

"Maybe they didn't know about the clasp. Or they thought it was one of the more valuable items. It looks fairly impressive after all," I said, running a finger along the silver serpent in my hands.

"Maybe," Gabriel mused, looking at it.

I paused, thinking through the details. "I don't know, but the thief had to be fairly strong to pull this hard," I said, rubbing my neck again. "That likely rules out anyone with an injury or the elderly. Oh, and they had to be about my height to reach the necklace comfortably."

Gabriel's eyes widened slightly, a mix of admiration and surprise in his gaze. "You kept your cool enough to recognize all that? That's impressive, Harper. Not many people would be able to think clearly in a situation like that."

"To be honest, it was only afterwards that I started putting the pieces together. However, any little clue could help solve the mystery, right?" I said.

Isadora reached to give my hand a squeeze. "You're turning into quite the detective."

"Not really," I blushed, looking down and trying to hide my embarrassment. "Just...observant or something."

"Or *something*," Lucas said. Gabriel nudged him, shooting him another look laden with silent meaning. However, it didn't take a genius to realize Lucas' suspicions of me were only growing, but what could I do about that now?

Suddenly, the wind outside picked up, blowing so strongly that it rattled the windows and whined around the corner of the building. All of us looked up.

"It looks like Aunt Elara didn't give herself enough credit," Isadora said appreciatively, moving towards the glass French doors that opened onto a balcony and then the gardens beyond. She cupped her hands around her eyes, peering out at the start of what sounded to be a fierce winter storm.

"Or the enchantment on the necklace is stronger than we thought," Gabriel said. "You know what? I don't think we should return it. Not yet at least."

"What are you talking about?" Isadora asked.

Gabriel pointed at the necklace. "Look at how handy it was just now. Besides, if the thief wants it, having it in our possession might prove to be the wiser move. Having Harper wear it would keep it away from the thief."

Lucas spoke up. "Or we could use it to lay a trap, lure the thief in," he said, keeping eye contact with me. I shivered at the intensity in his gaze. He obviously hadn't ruled me out as the thief.

"Lucas!" Gabriel exclaimed.

Lucas refused to back down. "We need to find the thief and return all the jewels as quickly as possible. Can you imagine what people are saying right now? That Silverthornes can't even keep their own home safe?"

"Okay, keeping the necklace away from the thief and setting a trap both sound like great ideas, but how do we do it? And what do we tell Starlight Treasures?" Isadora asked, obviously trying to redirect Lucas.

"Let's start with the illusion," Gabriel said, gesturing for me to give him the necklace. Without a word, I handed it over, earning me a brief nod of approval from Lucas. Gabriel carefully draped it back around my throat, snicked the clasp into place, and then waved his hand across my collarbones. I looked down in surprise, only to find the necklace had vanished. I could still feel the weight of it, but if it hadn't been so heavy, I would've said it was gone.

"Nice touch," Lucas said, his voice edged with tension. "But I think we should add an extra security measure."

"What?" Gabriel asked, his tone sharp.

"Why?" Isadora added. A twisting knot of anxiety formed in my stomach as Lucas glanced at me, tightening uncomfortably at the suspicion in his eyes.

"Something like that hex we used to put on our bedroom doors when we were kids," Lucas said, staring his brother down. "You remember the one? Only the person who laid the hex can open the door? Or in this case, the clasp."

"What?!" I exclaimed, unable to help myself. My hands flew to the invisible necklace. I wasn't about to let Lucas cast any sort of hex on me.

"Nothing lethal," he said. "Just...uncomfortable. If someone other than Gabriel tries to remove it, that is." The way he held my gaze, I knew what he was implying. If *I* tried to remove it.

"Lucas!" Gabriel's voice was dangerously soft.

"What? Trust but verify," Lucas said firmly.

Gabriel's eyes narrowed. "I trust her, Lucas. That should be verification enough."

The two brothers stood rigid, their postures tense, glaring at each other. I held my breath, uncertain if any intercession on my part would help the situation or send it spiraling. Gabriel's jaw tightened and Lucas' fists clenched at his sides.

Isadora unexpectedly broke in, stepping between the brothers. "I trust Harper too." She said firmly. "After all, remember what happened at the Pumpkin Parade?" She met Lucas' eyes directly, and I wondered how much she'd told him about my intercession at that parade when she'd lost control of her fire magic. Now wasn't the time to ask, however.

Lucas narrowed his eyes, trying to stare his younger sister down, but she refused to budge. Finally, he grunted but said nothing more as he left the room to attend to his assigned duties. Gabriel moved to my side, his presence a steadying force in the face of his brother's suspicion.

Isadora offered me an apologetic smile. "Sorry for that. Lucas can be...overly protective of the family reputation at times."

"True," Gabriel said with a tight smile. "Now, Harper, you should go with Isadora to report the necklace 'missing.' The thief obviously wants it. Maybe its sudden disappearance will lead to confusion and a mistake that might reveal the culprit's identity."

"And in the meantime, the necklace stays safe," Isadora crowed. "Brilliant work, Gabriel!"

He nodded, but his eyes flicked from my throat back to my face, looking a little sad. "I left the bruising visible though, so you might get some questions about it. Just so you are prepared."

I touched my throat again and winced, wondering who might be responsible for all of this mayhem. Perhaps it was someone who had a grudge against the Silverthornes? My mind flashed back to the waiter, Jasper. Unlikely that it was him. He seemed like the kind to hold a grudge, but not one to mastermind a series of untraceable jewel heists. Thinking of him reminded me of Selene. I gasped and my eyes went wide. How could I have forgotten?

"Someone needs to check in with Mystique!" I said urgently.

"You think she's responsible for the theft?" Isadora asked in surprise.

I quickly explained what we'd seen on Jasper's phone. "The angle wasn't great, but it looked like the blackout came from the same area as the stage," I said in conclusion.

"You really think she'd set up a theft in the middle of a show? Wouldn't she, as an illusionist, be one of the first people suspected?" Isadora said.

I hesitated, reticent to cast suspicion on people, given that I'd just been on the receiving end of such treatment from Lucas. At the moment, Seraphina was still at the top of my personal suspect list. However, based on the video, Mystique had seen something. Maybe that could be the clue that helped solve the case, especially since we were likely now locked in the Silverthorne mansion with the thief.

"From what we could see on the video, she definitely saw something, but I don't want to go pointing fingers at anyone until we have more information," I said tactfully. "However, the faster we solve this, the better. We don't know how long the weather will keep everyone from leaving."

As if responding to my words, the wind outside gusted, rattling the windows, but even that couldn't dim the excitement in Isadora's eyes. "Then let's go get her! If she *is* responsible, maybe when we find her, we find the jewels!"

"Maybe. Or maybe she saw something. Or maybe she was just responding to an audience member," I cautioned. "We won't know until we talk to her."

Gabriel interjected, his tone serious. "I agree. We don't know if she's involved at all, but if she is behind this, she's now been backed into a corner and might respond like a trapped animal. I'll go find her. At least I'll be able to use my magic if it comes to that. For now, you both need to stay safe and follow Mother's plan. If you see Mystique, don't jump to accusing her just yet," he said, heading towards the door.

"But she might be the thief!" Isadora exclaimed.

"And therefore possibly dangerous. Remember, she is a powerful illusionist and not just in the stage magic way," Gabriel replied. "But if she's an innocent woman, you'd be accusing her in front of a lot of powerful people."

I nodded, agreeing with Gabriel. "We wouldn't want to ruin her reputation and livelihood if we're not one hundred percent sure. False accusations can have lasting impacts," I said, unable to stop myself from glancing at the door where Lucas had disappeared.

"Fine. I'll admit you may have a point," Isadora muttered, rolling her eyes in a way that said she was humoring her big brother.

"Exactly. You never know what a desperate magic user is capable of," Gabriel warned.

"We'll do it your way. But we should still search for other clues," Isadora said, her eyes sparkling with more excitement than I thought was appropriate, given the circumstances. "There must be something we're missing." She turned to me, her enthusiasm undiminished. "C'mon, Harper. Let's see if we can find anything that points us in the right direction."

Given little choice, I allowed her to drag me out of the library, but something about Gabriel's wording made my stomach churn. Perhaps locking ourselves in the manor with the thief hadn't been the best idea. It might make them more desperate, and desperate people with few morals and forceful magic were capable of unimaginably dangerous things.

Could we stop them before a bad situation turned even worse? I could only hope.

Suspects in the Snowstorm

ELARA'S WEATHER-WORKING SURPASSED ALL expectations, escalating the storm swiftly from a gusting wind to a howling symphony outside the mansion walls. Within fifteen minutes, a curtain of snowflakes had ensnared the estate, transforming the manor into a stronghold against the winter elements. The growing fury of the snowstorm soon silenced the guests' murmurs for departure, replacing the earlier festive chatter with uneasy conversations. The manor seemed to shrink inward, its vast halls and ornate rooms feeling more like a labyrinthine trap than a place of celebration. Shadows danced in the flickering candlelight, and the once warm and inviting atmosphere took on a more sinister air as the full-scale blizzard descended.

Isadora nudged me, drawing my attention away from the snowstorm pounding its fury against the windows.

"So, Midnight Fox, who do you think did it?" she asked, keeping her voice low.

"What? I...well, I'm not..." I stammered, uncertain whether to voice my suspicions of Seraphina just yet.

"C'mon. I could tell you were holding something back. Spill," Isadora whispered.

"There you are!"

I turned to see Bella weaving her way through the edge of the crowd, with Alex following close behind her. "Where were you? Is everything okay?" she asked.

"Yeah, we were...," I trailed off and shot Isadora a look, unsure of how much I should say about her family's planning session. She gave me a subtle go-ahead gesture. As quickly as I could, I filled Bella and Alex in.

"Ah, that makes so much more sense," Alex said, his face relaxing.

"What does?" I asked.

"The weather," he explained. "My gifts are in weather prediction and, until recently, the forecast was cold and clear all week."

"Alex was afraid that the thief had called up the blizzard, attempting to hide an escape, which is why we were trying to find you," Bella explained.

I suddenly noticed that her sparkling earrings were gone. "What happened? Your earrings are gone!" I exclaimed. "Did the thief strike again?"

Bella shook her head as she sadly touched her bare lobes. "No, we had to return all the borrowed jewelry to the foyer. They are doing an inventory to see what's missing."

"That's where we were headed, hoping we could uncover any clues, right Midnight Fox?" Isadora said.

"Umm, right," I murmured.

"What do you want us to do? Come along? See if we notice anything?" Bella asked.

I looked from one to the other, thinking how sad it was that their romantic Christmas Eve Ball had been ruined. A thought occurred, and I shook my head, saying, "You know what would be more helpful? Splitting up. What if the two of you go enjoy the food, and go to dinner when it's time? You know, do the whole mingling thing? You can talk to people and try to find out if anyone looks shady. After all, we know the thief is very likely trapped in here with us."

"Great idea!" Isadora enthused.

"Are you sure?" Bella asked, shooting me a look that was half concern and half thanks.

I nodded firmly. "Absolutely. The more people we have watching for anyone to slip up and give themselves away, the better off we'll be. You two handle dinner and the guests while Isadora and I investigate the jewelry angle."

"Alright! The Scarlet Raven is on the case!" Bella said, thrusting a hand out. I grinned and placed mine on top as did Isadora.

"As are the Midnight Fox and the Lavender Butterfly!" she crowed.

Alex enthusiastically added his hand. "And the Disco Platypus!"

Bella shot him a look. "Oh, honey...no. Just...no." Her smile robbed her words of any sting.

"It's a good name!" he protested.

"It's a name," she said, wide eyed and smiling.

He caught her hand, tucking it into the crook of his arm. "It'll grow on you, I just know it." I could hear him explaining the unique undercover properties a Disco Platypus could bring to this situation as he led her away. Bella glanced over her shoulder at me, but I gave her an encouraging nod.

As Bella and Alex moved off, Isadora turned to me. "Ready, Midnight Fox?"

A small smile formed despite the tension, "Let's go, Lavender Butterfly," I said.

We moved through the crowd, keeping our eyes and ears open for anything suspicious. Guests filled the grand ballroom, attempting to enjoy the evening despite the underlying tension. The clink of glasses and soft murmur of conversations created a backdrop for our investigation.

As Isadora and I delved into the task of obtaining a complete catalogue of the returned and missing jewelry, a thought struck me. We needed to chronicle not just the names and missing pieces but also map out each guest's location at the moment darkness engulfed us. That might provide us with an insight into who might have been behind the missing jewelry or potentially where it was hidden if it was still on the Silverthorne estate. After all, the smallest detail might just unravel the mystery of the night. As Seraphina and Dominic scribbled the list of the missing pieces, Isadora and I gently questioned the victims who'd had their jewelry snatched. By the time everyone else had returned their jewelry and the final tally of items had been triple-checked, tensions in the ballroom were rising.

Vivienne appeared on the small stage, raising her hands to draw the attention of the crowd. Her voice soared above the unsettled murmurs, a beacon of calm authority. "My dear friends, thank you so much for your cooperation. I know this is not how you intended to spend the evening, especially with what looks to be an incoming blizzard arriving," she said, waving at the window. "However, we are all safe and warm. Not only that, but I am also told that dinner will be served within the hour."

A small cheer from the assembled crowd greeted her words. Vivienne smiled faintly and held up her hands again, calming the whispering once more. "My staff has also been busy organizing different activities in the adjacent rooms. There will be Christmas movies showing in the Blue Parlor in the East Wing. The library is open for anyone who would like to help themselves to our extensive collection. In the West Wing, the Billiards Room offers several games. Additionally, there are decorating stations set up in the North Wing for both Christmas cards and cookies if you are a little behind on your Christmas cheer."

Vivienne's announcement settled over the guests like a soothing balm. Her promise of warm festivities within the manor's protective embrace was a welcome reprieve from the blizzard's increasingly violent wrath outside and the unsettled nerves inside. She raised her hands and clapped loudly twice. Serving staff balancing trays loaded with cups of eggnog and plates of cookies appeared at the edges of the room. The growing tension in the room eased even more with the liberal application of sugary treats and holiday drinks.

Isadora tapped on her phone, which she'd reclaimed after returning her jewelry. She glanced up and caught my eye, silently tipping her head to the side, indicating I should follow her. Even though the delicious-looking gingerbread men on the nearest server's tray were practically screaming my name, I followed her to a small, secluded room where Gabriel and Lucas were already waiting.

Lucas' tone was edged with urgency as we slipped into the empty room. "Isa, I said to come alone. Don't you ever listen?" he demanded, his glance at me laden with a mix of confusion and wariness. My stomach dropped. It was obvious from his expression that he didn't want me here. I thought his suspicion would have eased, given the circumstances, but it only seemed to have grown.

Before I could mutter an excuse and extricate myself, Isadora put her hands on her hips. "Don't be so stuck up, Lucas. Harper has been nothing but helpful since this whole thing happened. It was even her idea to make a map of where each person was when the jewels were taken."

"Smart," Gabriel murmured, glancing at me appreciatively.

"I still think this should be a family affair," Lucas grumbled.

"And I think we should catch the thief before Aunt Elara's weather magic fades away," Isadora snapped.

Gabriel intervened in the brewing argument between his siblings, his voice a steady calm. I had a feeling this wasn't the first time he'd played peacemaker. "Lucas, Isa makes a valid point. Extra hands could make all the difference. But Lucas is also right, Isa. We must tread carefully, avoiding any unwarranted suspicions. We don't want to tip our hand and possibly bring the thief into our circle of trust. Not that anyone is calling you a thief, by the way, Harper."

Lucas' eyes narrowed. "We've already had this conversation, Gabriel. I think we should only trust family."

"And we've also discussed that baseless accusations won't help us catch the thief," Gabriel replied, his voice firm.

"I agree with Gabriel, but what do I know? I'm just the little sister," Isadora said heatedly.

Isadora and Lucas continued to glare at each other, but I could see that Gabriel's sensible words and calm tone were having an effect. Finally, Lucas huffed out a breath. "Fine. She can stay. But we each need to be on high alert, circulating around the other guests and staff to make sure we catch anyone acting shady."

"Um...," I murmured before I could stop myself. I wasn't sure that was the best way to catch the thief but didn't want to do anything more to upset the eldest Silverthorne sibling.

Lucas turned his glare on me, but before he could speak, Gabriel stepped in once more. "It sounds like you have an idea, Harper. We're open to any suggestion that might help us catch the person responsible for the mess more quickly.

I tried to ignore Lucas. He didn't look like he enjoyed me upstaging him, but Gabriel's voice was so calm and rational that I couldn't help myself.

"Suspects," I blurted out, trying not to wither before Lucas' glare. "We should make a list of suspects. That might help focus our efforts." I'd done something similar when I'd been trying to solve the mystery of the missing books back in September. Admittedly, it meant I suspected people who were completely innocent, but the process had helped me focus my efforts.

Isadora snapped her fingers and pointed at me. "That's a good idea. It would help us narrow down who could reasonably be behind this. We won't be able to keep an eye on everyone all the time. Especially with just the three, sorry, now four, of us." She shot an annoyed look at Lucas.

"Okay, anyone have any suspects?" Gabriel asked.

Lucas pointedly glared at me, but thankfully didn't say anything.

I shifted uncomfortably as I tried to decide if I should voice my thoughts about Seraphina. I didn't want to pull a Lucas and accuse an innocent woman, but she seemed to be the most likely suspect, given the information I currently had.

Isadora noticed my discomfort. "Harper? Do you have someone in mind?"

"Well, I think we should start with Seraphina Everbright," I admitted. "After all, she stood to gain the most."

"What about Seraphina's boyfriend? The one who runs the tattoo parlor? He could be in on it somehow," Lucas suggested.

The mention of Finn as Seraphina's boyfriend felt like a punch to the gut. I tried to keep my expression neutral, but Isadora must have noticed the flicker of pain in my eyes. She gave my hand a gentle squeeze.

Isadora rolled her eyes, exasperation evident in her tone. "Lucas, these thefts have been happening for longer than just tonight. It rules out most of the guests, including Finn."

Gabriel, ever perceptive, glanced between us, his brow furrowing slightly as if he were trying to piece together the dynamics at play. "Let's focus on what we know for sure. The thief is still here, and we need to work together to catch the miscreant," he said slowly.

I took a deep breath, nodding in agreement. "Right. Good idea."

"What about her partner, Dominic?" Isadora asked.

I hesitated and then shrugged. "I suppose he has a similar motive, but I saw him just after the heist, and he didn't seem like he'd just robbed a bunch of people. In fact, he seemed more set on security and retrieving all the jewels," I said, the invisible necklace heavy on my collarbones.

Gabriel scratched his head. "I'm not sure either is responsible. The bad press about the continued jewel heists has to be hurting their business, not helping it."

"But it works fine if you get a double source of income from insurance policies and by selling the gems you stole," Isadora interjected, echoing my own thoughts.

Lucas' tone held a note of expertise. "Insurance payouts typically go to the business, not individuals. Besides, wouldn't the individual jewelers hold their own policies for their own collections? Remember, they are just on loan to us through Starlight Treasures. Seraphina and Dominic, as astute as they are, essentially are just the middlemen. In this case, I assume any insurance payout would go to the jewelers' businesses, not to Starlight Treasures or specifically Seraphina and Dominic. We need to consider who actually stands to benefit financially from such a crime."

I found myself nodding unconsciously. His logic made sense to me.

"But aren't the most obvious suspects usually to blame?" Isadora asked skeptically.

Lucas shook his head. "I doubt Seraphina and Dominic are responsible for this mess. My money is on one of the jewelers themselves."

"An inside job? A jeweler robbing themselves to make it look like they're the victim while really grabbing as much of their competitor's loot as possible?" Isadora asked, her eyes sparkling. She seemed more excited about the prospect of tracking down the thief than upset that there was a theft in the first place.

Lucas nodded. "Exactly. Any one of the jewelers would have the expertise to recognize the most expensive pieces. They could easily target the highest priced items and then break down the jewelry quickly into something that wouldn't be recognized amid their own inventory. They would have the necessary skills after all."

"Good idea. I hadn't thought of that," I admitted. Lucas looked slightly mollified by my words.

Gabriel leaned in; his tone laced with conviction. "Consider the caterers—constantly on the move, easily overlooked. A perfect cover for theft, don't you think? It would be easy for one of them to slip a couple of bracelets or a necklace into their pocket. Once it was out of the ballroom, there are many ways to get it out of the house. We know that all too well."

He was right. My mind flashed back to my race through the empty hallway to the nearly deserted kitchen. Which reminded me of our encounter with Jasper and the strange shadows I'd seen on his phone. "What about someone like Mystique? She was walking through the crowd earlier, wasn't she? Has anyone seen her?"

Everyone shook their heads.

"She doesn't exactly blend in, not with all those sequins," Lucas pointed out.

"So where is she?" I pressed. When none of the three Silverthornes offered any insights, I bulled forward. "If Seraphina robbing her own event wouldn't give her a financial or a business boost, then we need to look at other suspects. One of the jewelers is a good idea, but what about Mystique? I don't want to be presumptuous, but she is an illusionist, and her show was just starting when all the jewels went missing. We already know that her illusions are more than the average stage performer's. She has real magic. Maybe she used it to steal the jewels."

Isadora held up the map we had made, pointing out the obvious flaw in my logic. "Maybe, but as you can see, most of the jewels vanished from this center left section of the ballroom. The lights weren't off that long. Could she have really zipped over there and disappeared before they came back on?"

"If she had a talent for speed, it's a possibility," Gabriel mused.

"I'm not sure speed is in her wheelhouse as an illusionist," Lucas said skeptically.

"Even if it is, why didn't she steal some items along the way? Why just target this one spot?" Isadora chimed in.

"Maybe she was working with someone," I said softly. "An accomplice who complements her powers. She turns off the lights and someone else grabs the jewels."

"Like her assistant!" Isadora exclaimed.

Gabriel shook his head at once. "I doubt it. Selene looked mad when she tracked down Jasper. If she was stealing jewels, why initiate a confrontation instead of searching for either an exit or hiding place?"

"All good points." Lucas shot me a look of grudging approval. "But I'm inclined to agree with Harper. If Mystique was involved, then she likely had an accomplice."

"Playing devil's advocate, maybe she wasn't involved at all. Or someone is trying to frame her," Gabriel said.

"None of those scenarios answer the question of where she is," I pointed out.

Lucas squared his shoulders, a determined glint in his eye. "We've got a list of potential suspects to scrutinize," he declared with a note of command. "I'll start with the jewelers, Seraphina, and Dominic. Isadora, you take the catering staff. Gabriel, see if you can find Mystique."

Gabriel raised his index finger to forestall his brother. "I'm not sure that it's such a good idea to go off on our own. If someone is audacious enough to target our family and rob our guests in the middle of a party full of magical beings, then who knows what they might be capable of?"

Lucas' expression tightened. "Agreed. We don't want this situation to escalate any more than it already has. Isadora, come with me. We'll confront the caterers first, then talk to the jewelers and Seraphina and Dominic. Gabriel, take Harper. Delve into Mystique's whereabouts but stay vigilant. We have to find this thief. The sooner the better."

As we split to undertake our tasks, the mansion felt larger; the corridors stretching out in all directions. I imagined them capable of hiding any number of secrets—or dangers. The storm's howl intensified, a fierce wail that seemed to echo the urgency of our quest. As Gabriel and I set off, the blizzard's crescendo was a chilling reminder we needed to unravel this mystery before Elara's icy barricade melted away.

The Missing Magician

AS THE STORM OUTSIDE raged on, Gabriel and I made our way across the ballroom towards the small stage area. Selene, Mystique's assistant, appeared from behind the small curtained off backstage area.

"What are you doing here?" Selene's reception was icy as the gale outside, her tone sharp. It might have been guilt, but I didn't think so. Mostly because of Selene's red and puffy eyes. She'd been crying. If I had to guess, I'd say she was genuinely concerned for Mystique's well-being, not plotting to smuggle a small fortune of jewels out of the manor. I reminded myself not to get distracted. Selene was used to being on stage. Perhaps the tears were just an act to throw off suspicion.

"Could we talk somewhere a little more private?" Gabriel asked, keeping his voice low. Despite his attempt at discretion, a few guests nearby shot curious glances our way as we huddled together on the stage. I spotted Hortense and Oswald Puddleton across the room, their glares boring into me. I could almost hear the malicious whispers they were likely spreading, but I forced myself to stay focused.

Selene followed Gabriel's gaze and nodded silently, holding the curtain aside so we could slip backstage.

Once the curtain fell back into place, cutting off the prying eyes of the guests, Gabriel turned to Selene. "Do you know where Mystique is? We really need to speak with her."

"What do you want with her?" the assistant snapped, her gaze darting around nervously.

"Just to talk," Gabriel said, his tone soothing but firm. "We think she might've seen something just before the lights went out. Anything she can tell us could help us figure out who's behind this and where the jewels might be. We're not accusing her of anything. We just need her help. Where is she?"

I had to give him credit—Gabriel was remarkably good at winning people over. Despite our recent discussion about Mystique possibly being involved in the theft, there wasn't the slightest hint of suspicion in his tone. It was clear Mystique's absence had Selene on edge, but Gabriel's sincerity was almost palpable, his tone that same peaceful calm he'd used to deescalate the conflict between his brother and sister. I was starting to realize not all of his gifts were magical.

"Well, if I knew, I would tell you," Selene snapped.

"Mystique is still missing?" I asked in disbelief.

"Yes!" Selene exclaimed, her voice spiraling upwards. Her lower lip trembled, and she took a shaky breath. "I've looked everywhere, but I can't find her."

Despite Selene's apparent distress, Mystique's disappearance pushed her to the top of my suspect list. As an illusionist, she certainly had the skills to orchestrate a robbery. Had the other high society heists also employed Mystique? It was something I needed to investigate further.

"Where could she have gone? Did you check the bathrooms? Her car perhaps? She wouldn't have left you here, would she?" Gabriel asked.

"She's not anywhere, but her car is still here. Wait." Selene's eyes flashed and a crackling sparkle gathered near her hands. "You're not implying she had anything to do with the theft, are you? Because she didn't. Did you even look into that creep, Jasper?" Selene demanded, her voice shaking as she clenched her hands into fists.

Somehow, Gabriel maintained his poise. "I have someone looking into him now, but I'm worried about Mystique. Aren't you? If you're sure she isn't involved in the theft, then where is she? Maybe she stepped outside to have a smoke or to chat with someone? I'd hate to think she somehow got caught out in the storm. Think, Selene. Where could she be?"

"I don't know!" Selene's voice trailed up into a despairing wail, and tears welled up in her eyes. She released her hold on her magic, covering her eyes as she tried to hold back sobs. I had to hand it to her. If she was faking, this was the most believable performance I'd ever witnessed.

Gabriel reached out, his voice gentle. "We just want to make sure she's safe, Selene. Help us find her."

She'd do us no good in the hunt for Mystique if she completely broke down now. Looking for something to distract her, a clutter of stage props caught my eye, glinting in the dim backstage lighting. "What's all this? Could something here explain her disappearance?" I inquired, pointing to the collection.

Selene stepped in front of the props protectively, declaring, "These are off-limits. They're part of our act. Nothing here would have made her vanish. Not for real anyway. Even if she uses real magic, her powers are still just illusions."

A large, cumbersome box on wheels caught my eye. It was the only thing that looked like it was large enough to conceal a person, if the person was flexible and not claustrophobic in the slightest. The rest of the items were a mishmash of glittering fabrics and various stage paraphernalia. Flowers, stacks of cards, interlocking rings, and even a couple of bowling pins. I wondered if they were part of an illusion or if Mystique used them in some sort of juggling display to distract her audience. Something small in the corner and half under a pile of scarves caught my eye. It was a chest about the size of a breadbox. From the casual way the colorful fabric had been tossed, I could see a large padlock glinting in the dim light. I sucked in a breath. The chest was the ideal size for hastily stowing away a small amount of stolen jewelry. Could we have uncovered the thief's hiding place already? If so, the location would imply either Mystique or Selene was involved. Possibly both.

"See? She's not here," Selene said, wringing her hands and looking caught between anger and fear.

I looked at the large box again, wondering if it might not have made for a convenient hiding place for an illusionist-turned-jewel-thief.

Gabriel caught my intrigued look and turned back to Selene. "The box on wheels, could we take a quick look inside? For peace of mind," he coaxed, his eyes searching hers for a flicker of consent.

"You're wasting your time." After a moment of hesitation, marked by a sigh that seemed to carry all her frustrations, Selene relented. "Fine, but when you find nothing but more scarves, trick cards, and a pile of costumes, I expect an apology and some real help trying to find Mystique," she grumbled, pulling the box into the open.

With a theatrical flourish that the illusionist herself probably would've appreciated, Selene unlatched the box. The hinged door swung open, but the chest didn't contain the expected array of an illusionist's tools. I gasped, my heart leaping into my throat. Inside the box was a crumpled body. My heart pounded in my chest as the reality of what I was seeing hit me like a freight train.

"Oh no," I whispered, my voice barely audible.

Selene's eyes widened, her face draining of color. "Mystique!" she gasped, stumbling back and nearly falling. Her hands flew to her mouth, trembling violently.

Gabriel immediately knelt beside the box, his fingers seeking a pulse. For a tense moment, the world seemed to hold its breath. Then he nodded. "She's alive," he said, his voice steady. "Her breathing is shallow, but she's breathing."

Selene's relief was unmistakable, but it quickly turned to frantic urgency. "We need to get her out of here! Now!" she cried, her voice high-pitched and desperate.

I was thankful Mystique was okay, but my mind started racing again. The discovery of Mystique sparked a cascade of new questions. I couldn't help but wonder whether her disappearance was her part in the night's foul play, or if she was merely another victim. Was this all an act from two seasoned stage professionals? Could Mystique be involved, or did she witness something incriminating, and the thief tried to ensure she couldn't share it?

Gabriel crouched down, slipping his hands under her shoulders. "Harper, grab her legs and help me lift her out of here. Selene, get her a blanket. She's cold." His commanding tone spurred us both into action.

We carefully lifted Mystique from the box, trying to make her more comfortable. Selene grabbed a nearby blanket and spread it on the floor, and we gently laid Mystique on it. Selene draped a large sequined jacket over the illusionist for warmth. The movement must have roused her, as Mystique's eyelids fluttered open, revealing a glint of confusion.

"What—what's going on? Why aren't you on stage, Selene?" the illusionist said weakly.

"Forget about the show! Are you okay?" Selene asked, tears streaming down her face as she grabbed Mystique's hand.

"Forget about the show? Never! Especially not when we are in the middle of it!" Mystique exclaimed.

Gabriel and I exchanged perplexed looks. "Mystique, the show ended abruptly over an hour ago," Gabriel said, his voice soft and gentle.

"An hour ago? No. You're wrong. The show just started! Why are we backstage? What's going on?" Mystique said, shaking her head.

Selene grabbed her hand. "He's telling the truth. You were just getting started, and then the room went dark. When the lights came back on, you were gone." Mystique's jaw hung open, and her eyes went glassy. She shook her head weakly.

"Mystique, can you tell us what happened?" I asked gently, trying not to overwhelm her.

She blinked up at us, her expression a blend of bewilderment and disbelief. "I...I was starting the show. The usual routine—I step into the box, the curtain falls, and then...then the darkness came. I waited for Selene's cue, but it never came. This was supposed to be the grand surprise of my act," she murmured, her voice trailing off.

Selene reeled backward slightly. "What are you talking about? That's not how the show opens. We do the trick with the doves and the chocolate. It's how we've opened for months now."

Gabriel exchanged a puzzled look with me before turning back to Mystique and Selene. "She wasn't supposed to be in the box at all?"

"No!" Selene exclaimed, wringing her hands. "We use it for storage and then in the second act."

Mystique's confusion was growing as she ran her fingers over the box's edges, her memory clashing with Selene's account. "I remember Vivienne's voice, the curtain of shadows, and then...nothing until you opened the box. Someone should have released me right after, to reveal the surprise," she insisted, her gaze pleading for understanding. Her hands trembled slightly as she spoke, a physical echo of her inner turmoil.

Gabriel knelt beside her, his voice reassuring. "We'll get to the bottom of this, Mystique, but for now, we need to make sure you're okay. Why don't you come with me, and we'll find out if there is someone on site with more than basic medical training who can check you out."

As Mystique nodded weakly, she stood, leaning on Gabriel and Selene as they pushed past the curtain in search of help, leaving me alone backstage for the moment. As they left, Mystique's gaze lingered on the large box that had become her temporary prison. I couldn't help but feel a surge of resolve. It seemed like Mystique was just a pawn in the thief's game. My eyes drifted towards the locked chest under the scarves. Unless she wasn't. Maybe she was a very talented actress on top of being an excellent illusionist. After all, what better way to dispel suspicion than by casting yourself as a victim?

Before I could second-guess myself, I brushed the scarves off the small chest and grabbed the lock, focusing inward on my magic. A nudge of my magic, and the lock gave way as if eager to reveal its secrets to me.

Wow. The enchantment on this necklace really works! I thought to myself.

I shouldn't have been surprised. The blizzard raging outside was a testament to Elara's enhanced magic, after all. It also explained why I had been able to keep the serpent necklace when the very determined thief tried to tear it from my throat. Understanding that the necklace's magic wasn't just for having a fun night, but actually enhanced one's own power, was one thing. Experiencing the full force of that enchantment woven into the silver serpent necklace—especially while trying to use my own magic intentionally rather than in a blind panic—was something else entirely.

My heart hammered in my throat as I glanced over my shoulder at the empty backstage space, just in case Selene or Mystique decided to return abruptly for some unknown reason. Seeing that the small backstage space was empty, I took a deep breath and opened the chest.

As it creaked open, the lack of jewels was almost anticlimactic—only a slim journal lay nestled among the innocuous props. Puzzled, I plucked the notebook from the chest and flicked through the pages. Although my examination was only cursory, the journal appeared to be Mystique's notes about her tricks. What worked, what didn't, sketches for new ideas. But there were no gems. Given where and how we'd found Mystique, I had assumed she was involved somehow, but now, I wasn't so sure.

"Where did you say it was?" Gabriel's voice sounded just on the other side of the curtain, startling me.

"She thinks her inhaler might have fallen out of her pocket in the box," Selene replied, her tone urgent. "Stress is a trigger for her, and we need to find it!"

I froze, holding Mystique's trick journal next to the open chest. There was nowhere for me to go. If I couldn't hide, how could I explain what I was doing back here with the illusionist's private possessions?

My heart skipped as the curtain rustled and Gabriel appeared. His eyes went wide, taking in my incriminating expression while standing beside the open chest. Relief and panic warred within me. At least it was Gabriel and not Selene, but would he think less of me because I was snooping? His gaze immediately locked onto mine, and he arched an eyebrow, a silent question in his eyes. I saw curiosity there, but not a flicker of recrimination, letting me know he was on my side. I shook my head subtly, conveying that I hadn't found anything. He shot me a warning look and held a hand in front of his body in the universal sign to stop. The severity in Gabriel's eyes was a clear signal—we were in a game far more dangerous than any parlor trick. Then, his lips moved swiftly, and he brushed that hand through the air like he was swiping an app off a screen.

"Well?" Selene's impatience broke the tense silence as she barged through the curtain and past Gabriel.

With bated breath, I watched as Selene's gaze swept over the space where I stood concealed by Gabriel's magic. "No sign of it," Gabriel replied with calculated slowness, watching the assistant intently without appearing to. Her gaze didn't flicker an iota. She hadn't seen me.

Selene swung the lid to the box open, scooping out a blue inhaler from the bottom. "Oh, here it is!" she called triumphantly, hurrying back the way she'd come.

I let out a silent breath of relief as Gabriel turned to face me, reversing the direction of his swipe from a moment before. "What are you doing?" he demanded in a low tone as he dissolved the illusion spell.

I glanced at Gabriel, feeling the need to explain myself. "I'm sorry. When I saw the chest, I thought it was the perfect size to hide stolen jewels. I didn't want to come right out and accuse Mystique after, well, all she's been through, but ignoring a potential lead seemed...irresponsible."

He nodded, his gaze softening. "We'll figure this out together. Just keep me in the loop next time, okay?"

I gave a small, appreciative smile. "Deal. Is Mystique okay?"

"I think she'll be okay. Luckily, there was a doctor attending the ball. She's in a private room with Doctor Stone and one of the security team, just in case whoever was behind this comes back. What did you find?" he asked.

I gestured towards the empty chest with the slim volume. "Just this, but it looks like notes on magic tricks rather than any nefarious plans for a jewel heist," I said, handing it over.

Gabriel's expression shifted to impressed curiosity. "You're good at this Sherlock Holmes-ing thing." A blush at the unexpected compliment crept up my cheeks as Gabriel paged through the journal quickly. "I'm inclined to agree. I don't think this proves she's involved."

"No, but..." I trailed off.

"But what?" Gabriel asked encouragingly.

"Based on what we know so far, I think we're dealing with more than one perpetrator," I reflected aloud as I knelt to examine the box that had held Mystique. "Someone skilled in some sort of darkness inducing magic, another person swift-footed enough to take stolen goods across the ballroom from this stage."

"Then you don't think Mystique is involved at all?" Gabriel asked.

I shook my head. "Unless her acting skills are the best I've ever seen, no. She was genuinely confused when we pulled her out of that box. Any idea what might have caused that type of response?"

Gabriel scratched his cheek. "Mundane means? No. But magically? Yeah, I've got a couple of ideas. A disorientation hex would definitely do the trick. Possibly a memory fog spell, which can temporarily cloud a person's mind, or even a confusion curse. Whisper magic would work too, I suppose."

"And are any of those common?" I asked, hoping the answer would be no.

Gabriel clicked his tongue and nodded regretfully. "Unfortunately, yes. I'd say most witches, wizards, and mages with enough power could pull off the first three fairly easily. Whisper magic is pretty rare and is an inherent ability versus a learned spell. I've only ever met one person who was gifted with that ability. However, unless we can narrow down what spell was used, it will be nearly impossible to track down the perpetrator with this information."

"So, anyone could be behind this?" My heart sank.

"Unfortunately, yes." He hesitated, glancing at the box where we'd discovered Mystique. "As much as I don't want to say this, we can't discount the possibility that she's faking. Your theory makes sense that there were at least two people working together. Maybe she concocted this entire scheme with Selene, and they staged this whole thing to appear innocent."

"Or it's somebody setting her up and this is a frame job," I countered. "She'd be the perfect patsy. Think about it. Mystique, a known illusionist suddenly disappears just after the robbery took place? If it hadn't been for Elara's snowstorm, I bet the thief would've been long gone before we even discovered Mystique."

Gabriel nodded, a furrow of concentration between his brows. "Casting blame on Mystique could be a clever diversion. But how do we know if it's someone else or Mystique and Selene trying to pull a fast one?"

I crouched down by the box, giving it one more inspection to make sure there were no hidden compartments full of jewels. Unfortunately, the only things I discovered were dust and some broken sequins.

"What are you doing now?" Gabriel asked.

"Searching for more clues. We have to consider every angle. Selene and Mystique seem like the perfect suspects. They had access to most of the ballroom while they were setting up. Maybe they rigged something."

"By that logic, so could any of the catering staff, the jewelers, or the security guards," Gabriel pointed out.

I replaced the notebook and locked the chest, feeling the serpent necklace's weight as a reminder of the magic already at play. "You're right. There're just too many suspects with opportunity, and Selene and Mystique seem almost *too* perfect. However, that doesn't mean we should discount them."

"We just need to narrow down the suspects," Gabriel said.

"Exactly. Let's go back and look at the spread of stolen items," I mused, pushing the scarves back over the chest to hide our tampering.

"And possibly the enchantments on the items."

"And the value," I added.

"It's a good place to start." Gabriel's eyes met mine, his gaze sharp with the thrill of the hunt. "The more I think about it, the more I'm sure you're right. This whole thing was clearly premeditated and well-planned, but are we searching for an individual or a team? A team would require coordination along with the planning.

An individual acting alone, with the ability to do all of this, would be powerful. Either way, the person or people responsible are very clever, incredibly well-prepared, and skilled. They could be quite dangerous."

I frowned, considering his words. "I think you're right. It's hard to know for sure without more proof. But I agree. We need to be careful and stay open to all possibilities."

The small backstage area seemed to contract with the gravity of his words, the Gordian Knot-like situation seemingly impossible to untangle. As we stepped back into the bustle of the ballroom, the reality of our challenge settled over us like the heavy fall of snow blanketing the estate. The thief or thieves were hidden among the glittering crowd, their secrets as shrouded as the mansion in the blizzard's embrace. Questions loomed in the air, thick as the snowflakes falling outside, and every passing moment was an opportunity for the culprit to slip further from our grasp.

Echoes of Betrayal

GABRIEL AND I MOVED through the crowded ballroom, our senses heightened, alert to any sign of suspicious behavior. The festive atmosphere had turned brittle, a veneer of celebration masking the underlying tension. The guests, once carefree and joyous, now cast wary glances around the room, whispering in hushed tones.

We had barely made it halfway across the room when Vivienne announced that dinner was ready. The trickle of guests turned into a flood as those in the adjoining rooms heard the news about not only food, but something new to alleviate the strain and discomfort setting in from being locked in a house that was not their own during a blizzard.

It might be a good thing that dinner was being served. It would clear out the ballroom and give us a chance to examine the space as well as talk with Seraphina, Dominic, and the jewelers without being overheard. Gabriel must've reached the same conclusion because he extended his arm. I slipped my hand into the crook of his elbow, allowing him to lead me in the opposite direction from the hungry guests and towards the foyer area.

Across the ballroom, I spotted Bella and Alex. Bella's face lit up with relief when she saw us, while Alex's brow furrowed with concern. The pair adjusted course to seemingly cross our path naturally.

"Any news?" Bella asked, her voice low.

"We found Mystique," I said. "She was unconscious, locked in a box backstage. She's okay now, but we need to keep our eyes and ears open. Gabriel and I think there's more to this than we initially thought. Maybe a team or maybe someone really powerful."

Bella nodded, her expression serious. "What can we do to help?"

"The same thing as before, I think. Just act normal and mingle," I said. "Listen for anything suspicious. We need to gather as much information as we can without drawing attention to ourselves."

"And we need to figure out who's behind this before the blizzard blows over. Once that happens, we won't be able to detain guests without getting the police involved. Knowing my mother, she'd prefer to keep things as close to the vest as possible," Gabriel said.

Alex glanced out a nearby window, where the snowstorm raged on. "Based on what I can sense, you probably have another couple of hours at least. This weather is insane!"

Gabriel nodded. "Good to know. But we're on a clock, and we need to use this time wisely."

Bella gave me a quick hug. "We'll keep an ear out. Please make sure you stay safe. No unnecessary risks, okay?"

"Do I look like someone who would take risks?" I said, trying to reassure her.

She pulled back and shot me a look. "You really don't want me to answer that. Just be safe, okay?"

"I'll do my best," I said, squeezing her hand.

"And I'll look out for her," Gabriel said.

Bella looked between us. It might have been my imagination, but I thought her eyebrow crept upwards in surprise. If I knew my best friend, she'd have questions later.

Gabriel's eyes flicked up to the side, and he nodded to someone behind me. "Excuse me for a moment, please. My brother is requesting my presence." He gave me a warm smile and lifted my hand to his lips, brushing a light kiss against the back of my hand before dipping his head in a slight bow to Bella and Alex. He disappeared into the throng of hungry guests just as Finn strode over.

Bella took one look at Finn's face and froze. I didn't blame her. His expression was a mix of confusion, pain, and more than a little anger.

"Can I speak to you please?" he asked, his voice quiet but rough, with barely contained emotions.

"Harper, do you want us to..." Bella trailed off, apparently not sure of how to end her sentence and so leaving it up to me to interpret.

I waved her and Alex towards where the guests were lining up for dinner. "You guys go ahead. Finn is right. We need to talk."

Bella shot me a concerned look as Alex put his hand on her waist. They soon got lost in the crowd.

Finn cupped a hand around my elbow, steering me towards an alcove framed by two potted plants, giving us the semblance of privacy. "Are you okay? What happened?" he asked, reaching out towards my neck. His fingers froze mere inches away from the bruising, his face a mask of rage and concern.

"I'm fine. I promise. The thief tugged on my necklace, but it just looks bad now."

"Are you sure? The thief was right next to you. I don't like the idea of that at all."

"I'm fine," I repeated. "Besides, Gabriel was right there." I hesitated, sensing my mistake instantly as Finn's face darkened.

"Speaking of, care to explain what's going on with you and Gabriel Silverthorne? When did you start seeing him?" Finn asked, his voice low, but it couldn't hide the undercurrent of jealousy.

I pulled away, my own hurt rising to the surface. "I'm not. At least not in the way you mean. He's my friend's brother, not that it's any of your business, since you're here with Seraphina."

Finn's eyes were full of hurt. "Why does it matter to you who I came with? You never asked me despite having the invitation for ages."

His words caught me off guard. I hadn't realized he knew I'd been holding onto the invitation, waiting to ask him. The air between us was charged, fraught with misunderstandings and what-ifs.

"I was going to ask you," I admitted, my voice barely a whisper amid the festive clamor around us. "That morning, when I saw you outside your building. I went to Pixie Pastries and bought you—well it doesn't matter now. But then I saw you with her, and I just...I assumed she was trying to win you back. Then she said you two had a date, and the way you spoke about your relationship with her, it seemed you were considering reigniting something with her. I didn't want to be a placeholder in your life and so...I chickened out."

Finn's expression softened, a hint of regret seeping through. "Harper, I didn't come here with Seraphina. At least, not in the way you think. She said she needed an extra hand with setting up and monitoring the event. When you didn't ask me to come with you, I figured it was a better way to spend the evening than sitting home alone. There's no one else I'd rather be here with than you."

My heart skipped a beat at his words, and for a moment, memories of happier times flooded my mind. Finn looked so handsome, standing there in his tux with the green accents that matched his eyes. And also matched Seraphina's dress. He had a right to wonder why I hadn't invited him. I might have chickened out about talking to him, but he never called or even texted after he saw me at the Silver Needle. My heart clenched and my stomach churned at the memory. Apparently, the pain of the last week wasn't so easily banished. "Well, it's too late now for us both now, isn't it?" The words were bitter, laced with a cocktail of feelings I couldn't quite name.

He stepped closer, lowering his voice. "It's not too late. It's just...complicated."

Complicated was an understatement. With each passing second, the tension swelled, the room itself seeming to pause in anticipation of our next words. Finn's gaze held mine, searching, questioning, yearning for something more than what we had, something we weren't quite sure how to define.

I was tired of being confused when it came to him. "What does...what does that mean?" I asked finally.

Finn ran his hand through his hair. "It means I didn't expect any of this. You and me. Her coming back. Any of it."

My heart softened a little, feeling a twinge of empathy for the position Finn found himself in. "It seems a little out of the blue, doesn't it? Her turning up here and announcing that she's moving back to Havenwood. Then all of this happens."

"What's that supposed to mean?" Finn asked sharply.

I winced internally. I hadn't meant to say it like that. Not to him, at least. "Just that, she might have had an ulterior motive, that's all."

"What? Like grand larceny? You really think she's behind the theft tonight?" Finn asked, his tone incredulous. "I can't believe you would even suggest that!"

"It's just a possibility. And let's face it, Finn, you said yourself it's been years. People change and not always for the better."

"Not that much. The Seraphina I knew was as honest as the day was long. She wouldn't do something unkind, let alone illegal. Besides, her family is at least as wealthy as the Silverthornes. Maybe even more so. Why would she do something like rob herself and put her business in jeopardy when she's already rich?"

"But you can't be sure, can you? Maybe it's not about the money. What if she did it for the attention? To stir up some buzz around her business? Notoriety can be just as valuable as wealth, especially if she's looking to make a big move like relocating," I pressed, the doubt gnawing at me refused to be silenced. "Something could've happened. Just because you knew her once, doesn't mean—"

He cut me off, a flash of irritation crossing his features. "No, Harper, I can't be certain. But neither can you. You're willing to cast blame based on what? A hunch? Again?"

I felt my breath catch, the accusation stinging more than I expected. He was right. I'd let my suspicions get the better of me—yes, again. "I'm sorry," I murmured, forcing myself to meet his gaze. "You're right, and Seraphina has been nothing but kind to me. If you believe in her so much, then help me prove her innocence. Where was she when the lights went out? Anywhere near where the jewels went missing?"

Finn's discomfort was palpable, a physical thing that hung heavy between us. "Dominic pulled her away. They were arguing about Seraphina's relocation idea. That's all I know. Seraphina isn't capable of...this," he insisted, though his voice lacked its usual conviction.

"According to Isadora, they were very close to where some of the jewels were stolen," I pointed out softly.

"But I was basically next to her the whole time," Finn insisted.

"Except when Dominic pulled her away, right? Could you see her when the lights went out?" The next words almost stuck in my throat. "Were you...umm...holding her hand maybe?"

Finn frowned, but shook his head. "No, but let's not jump to conclusions," he said. "There's enough chaos without adding to it with baseless suspicions."

His accusation that I was contributing to the turmoil stung, especially when I was just trying to help, but before I could respond, Isadora's voice carried across the nearly empty ballroom room, urgent and insistent. "Harper! Could you come here please? Now."

I turned towards her, relieved at the interruption despite the unresolved tension with Finn. I glimpsed his conflicted expression as I moved away, both of us caught in a tangle of what could have been and the reality of what was.

As I approached, Isadora's mouth was set in a firm line, and her brow was furrowed. A chill ran down my spine. Something had happened, and it was clear from her tone that this was more than a simple update. I just hoped I could handle her news more easily than the drama with Finn.

A Pawn in the Game

ISADORA'S HAND GRIPPED MINE with urgency as she whisked me into a small, secluded room. Just as we rounded the corner, we nearly bumped into Alex and Bella, who were heading in the opposite direction, looking equally determined.

"Alex, Bella!" I exclaimed, surprised to see them here.

"Harper! Isadora! We were just looking for you," Bella said in a rush.

"Why? What's going on?" I asked.

"We've been mingling and trying to find some clues, just like you asked. We might have something, but it's not enough to go on yet," Alex said, his expression serious.

Bella glanced around to make sure no one was eavesdropping and then leaned in closer. "Yeah, we overheard some musicians whispering about a 'drop' that's happening at midnight. We thought it might be connected to the stolen jewels. They have those massive cases after all. There'd be plenty of space in there to hide the stolen jewels."

Alex picked up the story. "We tried to move closer, but they clammed up right away and refused to say anything else."

"We think the whole group might be working together," Bella said, her words tumbling out in a rush. "After all, a crew working together would be way more likely in this situation, don't you think?"

Isadora held up a hand. "I agree with you on the crew thing, but I don't think the musicians had anything to do with it. The 'drop' you overheard was probably referring to the surprise my mother planned. She was going to have an actor dressed as Santa, complete with his sleigh, magically drop into the center of the ballroom in a swirl of snowflakes, courtesy of yours truly, and pass out gifts to guests at midnight. The musicians were instructed to play 'Here Comes Santa Claus' as soon as she gave the cue. Besides, we've used these musicians at several events over the years. I can't imagine they're jewel thieves on the side."

Alex and Bella's faces fell. "I was so sure we'd cracked the case," she said.

I patted her shoulder. "It did sound like a solid lead."

"Have you discovered anything more useful?" Alex asked hopefully.

I glanced at Isadora, who seemed to be fairly bursting with pent-up energy. "Nothing concrete on my end," I said.

"But I may have something," Isadora said. She suddenly paused, her eyes narrowing as a new idea struck her. "Hey, speaking of, this is actually perfect that we ran into you. I was going to ask Harper to stand guard, but you two will be so much better."

"Thanks? I think..." I said, confused.

Isadora waved her hands in negation. "Nothing against you, Harper, but two people guarding the door are better than one."

Bella and Alex exchanged glances, then shrugged in agreement. "We can do that," Bella said, nodding. "We'll keep an eye out."

"Don't let anyone in," Isadora cautioned.

"You've got it," Alex said with a small salute.

I stepped back, ready to join them. "I'll wait with you guys—"

"No, no, three people standing around would just draw too much attention," Isadora interrupted, shaking her head. "Besides, if anything happens, Bella and Alex can always pretend they're making out or something. Public displays of affection always make people at Mother's events uncomfortable."

Bella let out a short laugh of surprise. Alex shot her a wink and said, "She's not wrong."

"No, she isn't," Bella murmured, a slight blush coloring her cheeks. For a moment, the theft wasn't the biggest mystery on my mind.

Unsure of what to do, I turned away. "Okay, well, I'll just go—"

"Don't be ridiculous," Isadora said, grabbing my hand before I could retreat. "You leaving right after I dragged you over here would just draw more attention. You'd better come inside." She stared Bella and Alex down. "No one gets in, right?"

"Absolutely," Bella said.

"You got it," Alex replied, folding his arms and leaning against the doorjamb.

"Good." Without another word, Isadora pulled me inside a dimly lit room, shutting the door firmly behind us.

Lucas and Gabriel were already there, locked in what appeared to be an intense interrogation. The atmosphere was thick with accusation and skepticism. Jasper, standing with his back against the wall, looked like a cornered animal—desperate and snarling.

"You must've thought you were really clever, getting your friend to film an alibi for you," Gabriel said, his tone deceptively calm as he brandished Jasper's phone like a piece of incriminating evidence.

"I don't know what you're talking about," Jasper sneered, but there was a tremor of fear beneath the bravado, belying his denial.

"You were right. If you had used your electromancy to short the lights, it would've messed with your phone too...if you'd been holding it. But you weren't, were you?" Lucas' question cut through the room like a scalpel, precise and revealing.

"What are you talking about? It's all right there," Jasper spluttered.

"No, Jasper. What I see is someone holding the phone. But it isn't you," Gabriel chimed in, his voice a deep rumble of certainty.

Jasper's defiance was crumbling around the edges. "How can you be so sure? You see my face right there at the beginning. What more proof do you need?"

Lucas tapped the phone's screen, drawing attention to a paused frame. "You're right. We do see your face. More than once actually. I had to slow down the playback, but if you watch carefully, right...there." Lucas' finger pointed at a reflection on the screen—a face caught in the darkened window that might have been a mirror for how clearly it showed Jasper's face. "That's you, isn't it, Jasper? Walking right across the screen. And mere moments later, the lights go out."

I stepped closer, curiosity piquing as the evidence unfolded before us. I hadn't seen the glimpse of the waiter in the video, but it was a testament to Lucas' observational skills that he had noticed such a small detail. Jasper's face had drained of color, and a bead of sweat traced a path down his temple. The confidence he wore like armor was cracking, revealing the panic-stricken man beneath.

"Nu-uh. No. I didn't do nothing," Jasper said, his eyes flicking back and forth between the brothers.

Lucas and Gabriel shared a long look. Gabriel nodded to his brother's unasked question, and stepped forward, a dark shimmer of magic coiling around his fingers—a silent warning that he was ready to take things further if necessary.

"Gabriel, you don't want to do that," Lucas warned.

"No, I really think I do," Gabriel said, his eyes locked on Jasper. The coiling magic around his hands snapped and twisted like a writhing snake. If I didn't know it was probably one of his hyper-realistic illusions, I would've been terrified.

Unfortunately for him, Jasper didn't seem to share my knowledge of Gabriel's magic. "Get him away from me!" he cried, cowering backwards.

"I would, but he's stubborn when it comes to things like this," Lucas said. "Remember the last guy, Isa?" he asked, directing his words to his sister.

"Do I ever. Although, there wasn't much left of him in the end to be remembered, was there?" she said, shaking her head regretfully.

"No there was not," Lucas replied.

The magic around Gabriel's hand crackled with electricity and Jasper whimpered, cringing further away. The illusion was so real, my heart started to pound, and I was standing on the sidelines.

Lucas, now playing the good cop, leaned in slightly, his voice deceptively calm. "Jasper, just tell us what happened, and Gabriel will put his magic away. We can pretend this never occurred. But only if you tell us everything."

Jasper's eyes darted between the two of them, the weight of their combined presence and the threat of magic breaking his resolve. "Alright, alright, I'll tell you what you want to know." Gabriel gave him a hard stare, but let go of his magic, the writhing coils disappearing with a crack that made Jasper jump. He swallowed hard, his voice trembling as he spoke. "I'm a DJ, okay? Or at least, I'm trying to be. But it's hard. An expensive business to break into if you don't have the connections," Jasper said, jiggling a leg as he spoke. "One day, this note appears on my doorstep. Just like that.

Says there's easy cash to be made for a flicker of lights. All I had to do was meet a dude at the park for details."

I frowned. The lights hadn't been off very long, but it had been way more than a 'flicker' as Jasper put it.

"And you just went?" Gabriel's tone was flat, skeptical.

"Hey, five hundred bucks for a flicker? I'm no genius, but I'm not an idiot either," Jasper retorted with a shrug. "So, I played it safe. I went to the park early and stashed my backup phone recording a voice note, just so I would have evidence of anything that went down. I left and came back later for the meeting. Pretty smart, right?"

The Silverthorne brothers exchanged a glance, both clearly weighing Jasper's version of smart.

The waiter rushed on. "Anyway, this guy shows up and starts talking to me about this job. All he wants me to do is flicker the lights right as Mystique is starting her show."

"What did he look like?" Isadora asked, pouncing on the opportunity.

"Never saw his face. It was too dark, and all the park lights were out. Odd, huh? I swear it wasn't me. I could've done it though. You know? I just...didn't want to, you feel me?" Jasper added with a cocky lift of his eyebrow.

"And this mystery man, he just asked for a flicker?" Lucas prodded, his voice sharp.

"Yeah, just a flicker. Exactly. I swear. A flicker, nothing more. Don't touch the system itself, just a simple command to the lights all at once, then back to business as usual. Easy as pie, that's what I told him. So, we struck a deal. I took the cash up front, half of it anyway, and bolted."

"And what about the other half?" Gabriel asked.

"It was waiting for me, in the kitchen under the sink. Just like the guy promised. You can check, it's all still there, in my jacket pocket," Jasper said, tipping his head towards his jacket.

Lucas roughly patted him down, reaching inside his right lapel and withdrawing three bills, two hundreds and a fifty. He held the money up for us to see.

A thought occurred. "You said you recorded something on your phone, right? Can we listen to it" I asked, my voice sounding loud in the tense room.

Jasper's smirk dissolved. "Yeah, but I must've set it up wrong. Pressed my mic into the dirt or something 'cause all I heard was some muttering, like he was talking quiet into his phone. I tried to make out what he was saying, but none of it made sense. I swear the guy said something about a snake, but this ain't no zoo. No way these rich folks come to a fancy house like this just to hang around with snakes all day, am I right? So, I deleted my recording."

Lucas shot him a disdainful look that made Jasper visibly shrink away. My fingers twitched, and I had to force them into fists to keep them at my sides instead of flying to the invisible necklace around my throat. Gabriel must've had a similar idea because he leaned in, interest lighting up his eyes. "The snake? What's this about a snake?"

"Who knows? I never liked reptiles myself, but whatever their thing was with snakes, I didn't want nothing to do with it. But I might've misheard. After all, the recording wasn't too clear. Who would go after a snake anyway?" Jasper said with a nonchalant shrug.

"What happened next? Did you hear anything else?" Lucas pressed.

"Not much. Maybe something about needing a big score and quick getaway to keep it going. Keep what going? The snake? Didn't make any sense. Then the guy hung up or walked out of my phone's range. Seemed like they had an entire operation going."

"Any names? Did you hear or see anything else? Anything useful?" Lucas demanded.

Jasper spread his hands wide. "Couldn't catch hardly anything. It was a one-sided conversation, and like I said, the recording was bad. Phone mics aren't nearly as good as some of the gear I got. Now, if you really want to see some quality sound equipment, I got it all. You know, maybe I could come around sometime? Like an audition or something?"

"Not interested," Lucas said coldly.

I chewed on my lip thoughtfully as Gabriel shared a look with his brother. Both their faces were set in determination. They had a voice without a name, a plan without a face, and a heist that seemed bigger than they initially suspected. Worst of all, even though it felt like we were making progress, we hadn't really uncovered any information that would lead us to apprehending the culprits.

The brothers continued questioning Jasper, their voices growing more intense as they pressed him for answers, but it soon became apparent that he knew nothing more. His responses were increasingly vague, his bravado fading into frustration. I tuned them out, focusing instead on what we'd uncovered so far. Maybe, if I could just put the pieces together...

A chilling realization hit me. Jasper wasn't the only pawn in the game. Maybe Mystique really was behind it, but my gut told me she had been framed as an unwitting scapegoat. Whoever was behind this had planned it all out, and, to make matters worse, they were smart, a chess player moving pieces with the ease of a master, and the Silverthorne Ball had been their game board all along. Worst of all, it seemed like the invisible necklace I still wore around my throat was the ultimate prize. The thieves hadn't secured it, which might explain the lack of an immediate or obvious escape. And as the thought settled, I touched my neck subconsciously, feeling the weight of the necklace. Why was it so vital to them? What did they plan to do with it? And how safe was I, still wearing it around the house, illusion spell or not?

Shadows and Whispers

As Lucas called the head of security and whispered in his ear, I quickly filled Bella and Alex in on what had happened. The burly, bald man who practically rippled with muscle nodded before leading Jasper away without another word. Lucas insisted on keeping the waiter isolated until the storm broke. Then they could turn him over to the police for his part in what had gone on tonight. I didn't envy Jasper. He'd pitted himself against the Silverthornes and lost. I had a feeling life was about to get very difficult for him.

"Where are you going?" Isadora asked when Lucas started walking toward the door that led to the dining room.

"Mother told us not to make a scene. All three of us failing to be present for dinner at our own ball will certainly draw attention," Lucas said, pointing at his siblings.

"While everyone is distracted by dinner, this might be the best opportunity we have to search for the jewels," Gabriel said. His logic was undeniable, but Lucas also had a point.

"That's true," I said, surprising myself as much as the others. "Someone will notice your absence as the hosts of the ball, but not the three of us. Bella, Alex, and I won't be missed. We could search the manor. I also think someone needs to check on Mystique. Maybe she saw something that could help us figure out who the thieves are," I suggested, remembering the video from Jasper's phone.

Everyone considered this for a moment, then Lucas finally nodded grudgingly. "It's a good idea but everyone needs to stay in pairs. For safety's sake." His eyes met mine and then slid away. I couldn't tell if that meant he still suspected I was involved and wanted someone to keep an eye on me or if he was beginning to believe I had nothing to do with the heist.

Alex and Bella exchanged a glance, and she spoke up. "While you guys make an appearance at dinner, Alex and I will search the ballroom and the other common areas where guests have been. Maybe we can discover a clue or, better yet, the place the thief stashed the jewels."

"I still think someone needs to talk to Mystique. I don't mind doing it if someone will show me which room she's recovering in."

Gabriel stepped forward, his expression thoughtful. "I'll take you. Afterwards, we can help Bella and Alex search."

Lucas shook his head. "That won't work. Someone will notice your absence at dinner. Remember, we're trying not to arouse any more suspicions. We don't want to spook the thief or thieves. They could be dangerous."

"Okay, after I drop off Harper, I'll swing by and make an illusion of myself at dinner. It'll buy us time to search without anyone noticing my absence. Then I'll join the others once the illusion is set." He looked at his siblings. "However, the two of you are going to have to run interference. My illusion won't be able to carry on full conversations. Simple stuff will be fine, but anything more than that..." he trailed off with a shake of his head.

Isadora fluffed her pink hair, a confident smile spreading across her face. "If anyone was born to dazzle and distract a crowd, it's me."

Lucas grinned at his sister. "Absolutely, little sis. Let's make sure no one has a reason to suspect anything more is off."

With the plan set, everyone moved into action. Gabriel and I hurried through the hallways towards Mystique's room. If the circumstances were different, I might have enjoyed the unfettered access to explore the grandeur of the Silverthorne mansion. But tonight, it felt more like a labyrinth designed to conceal secrets rather than to showcase wealth.

As we reached the door to the room where Mystique was resting, Gabriel paused and turned to me, his eyes locking onto mine with a mix of concern and something deeper, something that made my heart skip a beat. "I'll be back to pick you up after I get the illusion spell set in the dining area," he said, his voice warm but firm. "Don't leave without me, okay? I don't like the idea that the scoundrel could be hiding somewhere just waiting to pounce. This place is full of hidden corners and shadows where someone could be lurking. I'd feel better knowing you're safe."

"I can take care of myself," I said, suddenly grateful for the self-defense skills my father demanded I master.

Gabriel flashed me a brief, confident smile, the kind that made it hard not to smile back. "I don't doubt it, but I couldn't live with myself if something happened to you while you were in my home. Just... stay put and wait for me. We'll figure this out together."

For a moment, I considered ignoring his request and doing some searching of my own once I'd finished talking with Mystique. But the way he looked at me, a blend of trust in my abilities and genuine concern for my safety, made me reconsider. There was something about Gabriel that made it impossible to brush off his words. Instead, I found myself nodding, watching as he gave me one last lingering look before turning and disappearing down the hallway, leaving me to face whatever memories Mystique could recall.

I knocked softly on the door before slipping into the dimly lit room where Mystique was resting. Selene sat next to the bed, holding her stage partner's hand. They both looked up as soon as I entered. I noticed Mystique's eyes still clouded with the aftereffects of whatever had happened to her, whereas Selene's were puffy and red, a look of deep concern etched on her face. When Mystique looked at me, a faint smile tugged at her lips, but it didn't reach her eyes.

"Hi," I said, feeling awkward now that I was here alone. How did one conduct an interrogation with such a frail-looking witness, especially without any sort of authority? Probably best to start by building a rapport, right? "Umm, how are you feeling?"

"Better," Mystique replied, though her voice was a soft rasp. She coughed, pressing a trembling hand to her chest. Selene, who had been sitting tensely beside her, immediately grabbed a glass of water from the nightstand and helped her take a sip.

"This whole thing is ridiculous," Selene muttered, her voice a mix of fear and frustration. "Whoever did this..."

"Selene," Mystique said gently, reaching out to touch her arm. "It's okay. I'm okay."

"It's not okay," Selene insisted, her eyes flashing as she looked at me. "Do you know what Doctor Stone said? She said it was almost certainly a spell. But being shut up in that small, dusty box didn't help with her asthma at all. If you hadn't found her when you did, she could've had an attack or something worse. Things could've gone really wrong."

I nodded, feeling the weight of Selene's words. "I'm glad we found her in time. We're doing everything we can to figure out who's behind this, but I was wondering if you would be up to answering a few questions?"

Mystique gave a tired smile. "I'll do my best, but I'm not sure how much help I'll be," she said, her voice soft, almost fragile. "Everything's so... hazy."

I pulled up a chair beside her. "I understand, Mystique. But anything you can remember could be crucial. Can you tell me what happened before you were...spelled?"

Mystique furrowed her brow, her hand absently playing with the edge of the blanket covering her. "I remember the lights coming up. The crowd was making a ton of noise. I went backstage, feeling good. Like the show was going really well. Then... someone came up to me. I think they were congratulating me." She paused, her eyes narrowing as if trying to pull the memory from the fog.

"That's not what happened at all," Selene murmured.

"Do you remember what this person looked like?" I asked gently, leaning in a little closer.

Mystique shook her head slowly, her exhaustion evident. "It's so strange... All I can remember is a man. His back was to me, but I could tell he wore a nice tux. I always liked a well-tailored jacket. He turned towards me... I think he had dark eyes, but... then nothing. Just a void."

Selene's eyes filled with frustration and concern, her free hand clenching into a fist. "This isn't right. She should be resting, not trying to remember some... some shadow."

Mystique squeezed her hand, attempting to offer comfort despite her own weariness. "It's okay, Selene. I want to help. I just... I wish I could remember more."

I spoke gently, hoping to offer some reassurance. "Even the smallest detail can help. We'll piece this together."

Selene nodded, but the tension in her posture remained, a testament to how deeply she cared for Mystique and how helpless she felt in the face of what had happened.

I glanced back at Mystique, remembering her reaction in Jasper's video. "Just before the lights went out, did you see anything unusual? Maybe in the crowd?"

Mystique's expression grew more troubled. "Now that you mention it, maybe. I think so. There was something... maybe someone? It felt so familiar. But it's all shadows, just fleeting images."

"Close your eyes," I suggested. "Take yourself back there. Can you describe what you see?"

Mystique did as instructed. "I see...a person. Yes, I'm sure now. Someone I knew from...oh, I can't place it."

"Is it a man or a woman? What do they look like?" I pressed.

Mystique's brow furrowed, and she bit her lip. Finally, she opened her eyes and shook her head. "It's nothing but shadows."

I reached out and placed a comforting hand on Mystique's arm. "You've been through a lot. But, like I said, the smallest thing can be a big help. Could you try again? Anything you can remember might guide us to find whoever did this to you."

Mystique nodded, but the frustration in her eyes was clear. "I understand, and I wish I could give you more, but that's all I remember."

"Shadows," Selene said, surprising both of us.

Mystique blinked and looked at her partner. "What?"

"You said shadows," the assistant repeated. "Not darkness or a figure or even a silhouette. Shadows." She looked at Mystique earnestly.

Mystique clicked her tongue, tipping her head to the side. "It's a stretch, don't you think?"

"But *shadows*. It would explain it all, wouldn't it?" Selene said, leaning forward urgently.

I raised a hand, feeling a little foolish. "Sorry, but I'm completely lost. Why would shadows make a difference here?"

Mystique sighed, but Selene was nodding encouragingly. "When I was studying and perfecting my illusion magic, there were many other students with a variety of uncommon gifts. One of the rarest types of magic is that of shadow magic, but it is extremely useful for people in my line of work."

I hesitated because it felt wrong to pry into someone else's magic when I usually kept my own so private, but I had to know. "And is that the type of magic you have?" I asked.

Mystique shook her head. "No. I cannot do shadow magic of any kind," she said, but didn't elaborate further.

Although part of me wanted to press her to discover what kind of magic she had, I restrained myself. Barely. After all, I wasn't an officer of the law to demand answers from her. Instead, I tried a different tack. "What about this shadow that you saw in the crowd? Do you think it was cast by someone with shadow magic?"

Mystique lifted a shoulder and dropped it. "Maybe. From that point on, my memory becomes very fuzzy."

"But you said something seemed familiar. Could you have recognized the person using shadow magic?" I asked, unable to help myself.

"Maybe? Or I might have recognized the spell perhaps. Or it might have just been the lights going out, and whoever did this to me messed with my memory. It's hard to say." Mystique's voice faded near the end and her eyelids fluttered like she was struggling to stay awake. "I'm sorry. I think I need to rest."

"Yes, of course," I said. "But if you remember anything else, please let me know."

"I will," she murmured before turning on her side and facing the wall.

Selene stood silently and walked me to the door. In my heart, I now doubted that Mystique was involved at all. My gut seconded the notion. Either she'd witnessed something or possibly this was all a frame job, but either way, I believed her story that she'd been spelled and put in that box against her will.

At the door, Selene put a hand on my arm. I looked up at her in surprise. "I hope you find the guy responsible for this and put him away for a very long time," she said, her voice filled with quiet intensity.

Her words made me pause, and I realized I hadn't heard Selene's version of events. "Do you have anything to add? Did you see anything that might help us catch this guy?" I asked, curiosity piqued.

Selene glanced back at Mystique, who appeared to have drifted off to sleep, and then lowered her voice. "I didn't see anything. I was preparing the next trick. But if one of the shadow magicians she used to run around with is involved, you need to be very careful."

"It seems like you think they might be. Can you tell me why?"

"The sudden onset of darkness, for one. But the memory fog for another. Although shadow magic is a very uncommon gift, it has many esoteric uses. Most of which I'd never heard of before I met Mystique, but one of the scarier uses is whisper magic."

"Whisper magic? I've never heard of that before tonight."

Selene nodded. "Most people haven't. In simple terms, it's a compulsion magic. Someone gifted with whispers can get anyone to do anything. Give them all their money. Tell them their social security number."

"Get into a box?" I guessed.

Selene's expression turned grim. "And forget the whole thing. To be honest, it's so rare that I'd forgotten about it until she mentioned shadows and her studies."

"Was there someone in the crowd that she knew with this magic?" I asked, my mind racing.

"Maybe," Selene shrugged. "It was before I knew her. But since she knew people with shadow magic, there's a chance she knew someone who could whisper."

"Why have I never heard about this before? Wouldn't that be a really dangerous gift?"

"One, it's incredibly rare. And two, most people need to be very close to make it work. Like, they have to have a magical focus, eye contact, or even skin-to-skin contact. I don't know, exactly. Every magic user is different, but if she was whispered into the box, the person must have been backstage. If only I hadn't been off chasing that stupid waiter." She angrily brushed the back of her hand against her eyes, smudging her mascara.

"But if you had also been backstage, you could've been shoved into that box with Mystique and there's a very good chance we wouldn't have found either of you until much later," I pointed out.

"I hadn't thought of it like that," Selene admitted.

"So, you think Mystique might've recognized the thief from her school days, and then he approached her to make sure she couldn't reveal his identity?"

"Maybe. I can't be sure, but it fits, doesn't it?"

Selene's unanswered question hung in the air between us as my mind raced with the possibilities—if someone with shadow magic and whispering abilities was involved, then we were dealing with a much more dangerous opponent than I'd anticipated. And if Mystique had recognized the thief, that meant she knew more than she realized, which could put her in even more danger.

But with so many lingering questions and so little time, I needed to find answers as quickly as possible. The blizzard wouldn't last forever, and the longer we took to piece together the clues, the more time the thief had to slip away into the shadows—where the culprit clearly thrived. I needed to act fast, but with every step forward, the path seemed to grow darker, more uncertain. And somewhere in that darkness, a dangerous magician was waiting.

Crash of Accusation

WITH A SOFT CLICK, I closed the door to Mystique's room behind me, feeling more confused than when I'd entered. But one thing I was fairly confident about was that she wasn't involved in the heist. I looked down the long, dimly lit hallway, the ornate sconces casting flickering shadows on the walls.

At the beginning of the evening, I would have loved to explore the vast mansion, uncovering its secrets, and admiring its grandeur. But now? The last thing I wanted was to give the thief a chance to whisper me into a tiny box. I shuddered, the thought sending a chill down my spine as I contemplated my options.

I didn't want to be alone, which meant I could head to the dining room and find Gabriel or go to the ballroom and look for Alex and Bella. The ballroom was closer, but what if they weren't there? I hesitated, the silence of the mansion pressing in on me, every shadow seeming to shift and move in the wake of the Selene's suppositions. Before I could make up my mind, I heard the soft tread of approaching footsteps and froze. My heart leaped into my throat. Was it the shadow magic user, coming back to whisper Mystique into forgetfulness again? Should I warn her? Make a run for it? But how far would I get in this ballgown?

My pulse quickened, and just as I was about to bolt, Gabriel came around the corner. Relief flooded through me, and before I could stop myself, I let out a shaky sigh and practically threw myself into his arms. It wasn't until I felt his muscular arms wrap around me, grounding me, that I realized what I'd done.

I pulled back slightly, looking up at him, a handsome man I barely knew. My cheeks flushing with embarrassment. A *very* handsome man, and I'd just flung myself at him like a damsel in distress.

Gabriel's eyes met mine, a mix of surprise and warmth in his gaze. He didn't seem to mind, and for a brief moment, the world outside those hallway walls disappeared, leaving just the two of us standing in the quiet shadows.

"Is everything okay?" Gabriel asked, his voice soft yet strong.

I nervously pushed a strand of hair behind one ear as I took a step backwards. "Umm, yes. I mean, no, not exactly. I mean, that is, well, I think I may have discovered a lead, but I'm not sure how much it will help." As quickly as I could, I filled him in on what I'd learned.

Gabriel nodded thoughtfully. "I see what you mean. If Mystique has been whispered into compliance, it will be nearly impossible to prove it unless the perpetrator admits it. However, with so many branches of magic, virtually anything is possible if you have the right training. Like I said earlier, what happened to Mystique could've been attributed to any number of different spells."

"But what about the shadows she saw in the crowd?"

"Unfortunately, her memory is compromised." He shot me an apologetic look. "Look, it's a good idea, and it might very well be that someone whispered her into the box. However, it could just be her brain trying to make sense of the images she saw while also being influenced by the spell. We can't know for sure."

My heart sank. Part of me had hoped that Gabriel, with his more nuanced understanding of magic, would have a cure for Mystique. Or at least an idea of where to get her some help. If we could help her recover her memories, maybe she could identify the person responsible.

Gabriel must've sensed my disappointment because he touched my hand. "Don't worry. We'll figure this out. We just need to come at it from a different angle."

I sighed, forcing myself to set aside my disappointment. "Okay. What do you suggest?"

"For now, we need to let my family know about the possible use of shadow magic. One of them might know a guest who has that gift and can narrow down our suspect list. It's probably best to put them on alert," Gabriel said, his tone steady and reassuring.

"Same with Bella and Alex," I added quickly. The thought of my best friend and her boyfriend stumbling upon this doubly dangerous thief while searching the mansion made my stomach twist.

"Good idea," Gabriel agreed, nodding. "After that, we stick to the plan—search the mansion and see if we can discover where the jewels are being stashed. Unless you have a better idea?"

It was flattering that he asked for my opinion, but unfortunately, I didn't have a better plan. "Lead the way," I said, with a little wave towards the hall. He caught my hand and, tucking it into the crook of his arm like an old-fashioned gentleman, did just that.

Together, we moved swiftly through the mansion, heading toward the dining room first, where Isadora and Lucas were playing their parts as entertaining hosts. Gabriel called his illusioned doppelgänger over to the door, waiting until it was completely out of sight of the diners before re-entering the room as himself. He headed straight for his brother, whispering urgently in Lucas' ear. Through the cracked door, I caught a glimpse of Finn and Seraphina seated at one of the tables. My heart did a little jittery dance in my chest at the sight of the pair of them. Was jealousy rearing its ugly head again? However, they were sitting next to the odious Puddletons, who looked to be monopolizing the conversation. No, definitely not jealousy. Between making small talk with the Puddletons and hunting down a potentially dangerous magical thief in the bowels of the Silverthorne mansion, I'd take the latter any day of the week.

Gabriel returned swiftly, taking my hand once more and leading me down the hall. "Right, now to warn Bella and Alex."

"We also need to make sure we know where they've searched so we don't waste time covering the same ground," I suggested.

"Agreed," Gabriel said.

Finding them turned out to be harder than I'd anticipated. I'd assumed they'd still be in the ballroom, but they weren't. After a cursory look in several of the adjoining rooms, Gabriel and I decided to expand our search and hope we ran into them soon. Between the blizzard and dinner nearing its end, we didn't have time to waste. Besides, our friends had to be somewhere close. I just hoped we'd run into them before the thief did.

Gabriel led me to the door just off the ballroom. "We have to be methodical and quick. You take the left side of the room, and I'll take the right. Look for anything that might have been used as a handy hiding place for the jewels," Gabriel said as he opened the wooden door. We peered into a dimly lit study filled with relics and antiquities that could easily hide stolen valuables. I nodded, my pulse quickening with the thrill of the hunt. Each empty vase, each hollow statue, and every unlocked drawer that revealed nothing but mundane contents added to the growing frustration. Time was slipping through our fingers, and with it, the chance to catch the thief.

"Gabriel," I said after we searched the second room with no results. "If we don't find anything—"

"We will," he interrupted, determination etching his features. "We have to."

"Can you sense anything with your magic?" I asked hopefully.

He shook his head. "The sensing of illusions is more difficult than creating them. For me at least. Can you use your gifts?" he asked.

I bit my lip, still hesitant to reveal my affinity for metal magic. It was an old hang up from my childhood, but I hadn't yet come to terms with how easily people in Havenwood spoke about their magical abilities. However, this was important. I crafted a carefully vague answer. "I can try. With the enchantment on the necklace, I might be of some minor help." With a deep breath, I tapped into my magic, expecting the familiar whisper of my power.

But what I received was a shout.

The metal sang to me, an ethereal chorus not pulling but present, like a vivid overlay on reality. An augmented view that showed me the bones of the building and the whisper of wires within the walls. It was intoxicating yet dizzying, and I leaned against the wall for support as my head spun at the onslaught of information.

Gabriel was by my side in an instant, steadying me. "Are you okay? What happened?" he asked, concern washing over his face.

With effort, I focused past the tumult pulling at my senses. "It's more intense than ever," I admitted, the words a shadow of the storm inside me.

The realization dawned bright and clear; the silver serpent necklace was amplifying my senses, transforming me into a living metal detector. It was empowering, but daunting too. Could it lead me to the stolen jewels? And if the necklace boosted my abilities, perhaps it could amplify Gabriel's talents as well.

I lifted my hand to the invisible necklace, undoing the clasp with a brush of magic. As soon as it fell away from my neck, the illusion spell flickered, trying to hold on despite the abrupt movement. "I have an idea. Give me your hand," I said to Gabriel, offering my free one.

His hand met mine, his expression a blend of intrigue and trust. I looped the necklace around our joined hands, feeling the weighty chain link us together. The illusion spell wavered and disintegrated completely, exposing the silver serpent once more in all its glory.

"The enchantment is enhancing my magic," I explained as I worked. "Maybe it will strengthen yours too, which might help us find what we're looking for."

"It's worth a try," Gabriel said, giving my hand a squeeze.

Gabriel suggested examining the space where the catering staff was set up first, as it would be harder to sweep once they returned from the dinner service. I agreed, and we set off. As quickly and methodically as we could, we moved from room to room, prioritizing those closest to the ballroom.

Even though I could sense more with my magic than I'd ever been able to before, would it be enough? I hoped so, but with every room we cleared, my once buoyed spirits sagged. We hadn't heard from Bella and Alex yet so I guess they hadn't discovered anything. Had we all somehow missed the jewels? Or were they hidden in a different room we had yet to search? Perhaps the thief was cleverer than we were and had picked a hiding place we'd never find.

My heart hit rock bottom, and my stomach growled as the sound of laughter and the clink of cutlery drifted through an open door. Guests were spilling out of the dining area back into the ballroom, which meant our search just became infinitely more complex.

Gabriel gave my fingers a gentle squeeze before disentangling himself from the necklace wrapped around our joined hands. "It was a good idea. I wish we'd uncovered something, but we need to regroup with Lucas and make a plan now that the guests are no longer at dinner. We need to move quickly before the thief or thieves have time to move the jewels."

"I suppose you're right," I said regretfully, refastening the necklace around my throat. Gabriel looked at it critically and then waved his hand through the air, presumably reconfiguring the illusion spell to obscure the silver serpent again.

I let go of my magic after holding it active for far longer than I'd ever done before. The sensation that swept over me was similar to running for an hour at slightly over your comfortable speed, then sprinting another five minutes before stopping abruptly. My muscles felt wobbly and on fire all at once. My legs nearly gave out, and I would've crashed to the ground had it not been for Gabriel catching me.

"Are you okay?" he whispered, concern dancing in his dark eyes.

"I...I think so. Just overextended myself," I said under my breath as I realized we'd attracted a small audience of curious guests.

"You need to sit down and get something to eat," Gabriel said firmly.

"But, what about Lucas?" I asked. "You said time was of the essence, didn't you?"

"Harper? Is everything okay?" a familiar voice cut through the whispers of the small group of onlookers.

I glanced up to see Bella and Alex striding towards us, matching worried expressions on their faces. I must really look worn out to warrant that kind of attention.

"Hey! I'm fine. I promise. How about you guys? Find anything?"

"Nada," Alex said, shaking his head dejectedly.

Bella laid a hand on my arm. "Are you sure you're okay? You look like a snowball would knock you over."

"Yeah, all good. Just a little tired. I missed dinner," I said by way of explanation, not wanting to go into further detail with so many listening ears approaching.

Before they could press further, an all-too-familiar nasal voice cut through the air, dripping with condescension. "Well, well, if it isn't the drama queen herself, seeking all the attention, as always."

I turned to see Oswald and Hortense Puddleton approaching, their expressions as unpleasant as ever. Hortense's lips were curled into a sneer, and Oswald's bulbous nose twitched with disdain as he looked me up and down, which was impressive given that he was so much shorter than I was.

"Really, you've done nothing but stir up trouble since you came to Havenwood. And now you're trying to fling yourself at one of the Silverthornes in the middle of this catastrophe?" Hortense said with a sniff. "Some people never did learn manners, did they?"

All the remaining color drained from my face, and I stuttered, "I wouldn't...I mean, I didn't fling...why would I..."

"Young lady," Oswald began, his nasal voice took on a lecturing tone that grated on my nerves, "it's one thing to be the center of attention, but to fake an illness just to have the host fawn over you? That's a new low."

Hortense nodded vigorously, her overly styled hair bobbing with each motion. "Skipping a meal like this just to make a scene—honestly, it's shameful. Poor Seraphina has been distraught all evening, and here you are, playing the victim and dragging poor Gabriel away from all of his other guests."

Their words stung, even though I knew better than to take them seriously. But the real blow came when I caught a sudden jerk of movement behind Bella's head. Finn. He was standing with his arm around Seraphina, who looked like she'd been crying. His eyes went wide when he saw me, and an unspoken question radiated from him.

What had I been doing with Gabriel Silverthorne to cause me to miss dinner?

As I watched, Finn's expression shuttered, and he turned away. An unexpected wave of guilt rose up, nearly choking me. I hadn't been doing anything wrong. Quite the opposite! I'd been trying to help. But I could see from Finn's expression that the Puddletons' insinuations had clearly planted seeds of doubt in his mind. I needed to finish my conversation with him to clear the air. But this wasn't the time or place, especially now that Bella was on mother-hen alert.

Gabriel smiled winningly at Bella, but spoke loudly enough for the surrounding people, including the Puddletons, to overhear easily. "I fear it was my fault. Harper graciously was lending me her assistance, and we lost track of time. Unfortunately, I need to find my brother urgently. I don't suppose you could help her...?" he trailed off, raising a questioning eyebrow.

Bella jumped in, just as I knew she would. "Of course! You come with us, Harper. I think I saw where they were taking the plates. I bet we can find something more than cookies and eggnog for you," she said briskly. Gabriel squeezed my hand once more before hurrying off to find Lucas and adjust their plans. Bella shot Alex a look, and he hurried to place himself between me and the Puddletons, gently nudging Oswald out of the way as we passed.

Faster than I would've thought possible, Bella wrangled a plate of food I could eat with my fingers and Alex commandeered a relatively quiet corner for us to have a conversation while I ate. She always claimed to not have much magic, aside from a small gift for baking that paled in comparison to her mother's. However, with the speed at which she arranged for the food, I wasn't convinced. She had to be holding out on me.

Bella's leg jiggled as she watched me eat, her gaze narrowing with concern. After just two bites, she couldn't hold back any longer. "Okay, Harper, what's really going on? You look like you haven't slept in days. Something's off. You're more than just tired. Did something happen? Spill."

Her questions were direct, her tone a mix of worry and impatience. I looked around cautiously. There were clumps of people scattered all over the ballroom, but none except Alex were close enough to overhear us. I dropped my voice to a hushed murmur and filled her in on everything. Lucas Silverthorne might not want more people to know all the details, but this was *Bella.* She was as trustworthy as they came. Besides, the storm wouldn't last forever. We needed all the help we could get if we had even the slightest chance of recovering the jewels. Bella's jaw dropped when I explained about Mystique and the possibility of the shadow mage.

"So do you think she was involved?" Bella asked.

I shook my head, swallowing my hastily chewed bite of sandwich. "I'm not sure. She definitely has a few tricks up her sleeve, but if you pushed me for an answer right now, I'd say it's more likely she was framed. You didn't see her, but she looked so weak, and the memory gaps seemed real, but..."

"But what?" Bella asked as I trailed off.

I blew out a breath, weighing my words. All I had at this point in time was conjecture. Besides, Finn's rebuke was still fresh in my mind. Was I being too quick to accuse? Maybe. But if it meant we could clear suspects faster and find the culprit before the storm blew over, did the ends justify the means? Maybe. At least Bella wouldn't judge me too harshly.

"Well, I think Seraphina might be involved," I started.

"No way," Bella gasped. "Finn's ex? A jewel thief? But she seemed so nice."

"I know, she's *so* freaking nice," I said, shaking my head.

"But the facts are stacking up against her?" Bella asked.

"Like motive and opportunity and everything?" Alex interjected, his eyes widening.

"Yes, but I talked to Finn, and he was basically with her the whole time, so I'm not sure about the opportunity to do the actual grabbing," I admitted.

"You talked to Finn about his ex-girlfriend robbing the Silverthornes? How'd that go?" Bella's eyebrows shot up in disbelief.

"Well, to be fair, I talked to Finn about his ex robbing herself, mostly." I sighed and my shoulders slumped. "To say it didn't go well is probably an understatement," I admitted. I paused, thinking through what I'd pieced together. "Unless she developed an enchantment for super speed and/or darkness and kept them hidden from him for the duration of their relationship, I've moved her down my list of suspects. Unfortunately, that list isn't very long."

Bella nodded thoughtfully. "So, she could imbue magical gifts into objects? That means she could technically have an unlimited number of gifts if she used those objects herself, right?"

"Exactly," I said, rubbing my temples. "But that's also why I'm starting to doubt her involvement. She might have the ability, but the motive...I still can't see it. Robbing herself doesn't make sense, especially when she's contemplating relocating the business. Surely, she'd want to give the appearance of strength and stability. Stealing her own jewels makes her look weak precisely when she needs to look strong. It just doesn't add up. However, I don't see a better suspect, do you?"

Bella thought for a moment and then shook her head. "Jasper said he met with a man, right? Wouldn't that negate Seraphina and Mystique?"

"Yeah, unless they were part of a team," Alex said, speaking up.

"Given that we are talking about magic here, I suppose it could've even been a woman in disguise that met Jasper. Or there's always the possibility he's an idiot."

"That one might be the most likely," I said, thinking back on my interactions with the waiter.

I took another bite of sandwich and chewed contemplatively. Finally swallowing, I said, "Well, if we don't think it's Selene or Mystique, and Seraphina was too far away and standing next to Finn and her partner, then who snatched the jewels? We need to look at new suspects. Do you think Jasper was part of a network of thieves that infiltrated the catering staff? Maybe he made up the whole story about meeting someone to throw us off his trail."

Bella didn't look convinced. "This isn't some movie. Waiters generally just want to get in, get paid, make a good enough impression to get another shift at a swanky place like this, and get out. Trust me. I used to pick up the odd job or two in my free time."

"Besides, the guy must be a special kind of stupid to risk the wrath of the Silverthornes for a few hundred dollars," Alex added.

I snapped my fingers as something clicked into place. "You know what else doesn't make sense? Jasper said he was supposed to flicker the lights. That's it. He wouldn't have had any power to blot out the light from the moon or stars."

"And yet that darkness in the ballroom was all-encompassing," Bella said, obviously jumping to the same conclusion I had.

"It had to be magic. The lights were off for at least a couple of minutes, and it took the *Silverthornes* to dispel it. That's heavy," Alex added. "Why didn't we think of this before?"

"Probably because we were all running around trying to stop the thieves from leaving and then trying to find the jewels. But this is another clue, right? Someone who has some sort of power over darkness or light?" I hypothesized.

"Yeah, but why would they need this Jasper guy then?" Alex asked.

Bella tapped a finger against her lips. "What if it's one of those gifts that can manipulate something? You know, like a water mage has to have some water to work with before they can do anything amazing? They can't conjure water out of nothing."

I jumped on the idea. "So, you're thinking the person responsible could manipulate or maybe even extend the darkness, but needed Jasper's, um, raw material, I guess, to work with?"

Alex shrugged. "That makes as more sense than anything I thought up."

"Let's go over the timeline again," I suggested. "Maybe we'll think of something we didn't before."

Bella closed her eyes, focusing. "There was a theft. Jewels were taken from numerous people in a crowd when the lights were out for a span of a few minutes. I'd say more than two and less than ten. Is that about right?"

"Fits with what I remember," I said.

"Not much time," Alex observed.

"But they knew that and capitalized on it, grabbing as many jewels as they could," Bella said.

I held up a finger, adding. "And, if Jasper can be trusted, they might've had inside knowledge about the snake necklace."

"Do you really think we can trust his word?" Alex asked.

I shrugged. "Maybe not, but I don't think we should discount it just yet either."

"The timeline you've recalled seems right," I agreed, though the exact mechanics of it still felt fuzzy.

Alex leaned forward, looking between us. "So, what does that tell us? Put yourself in the thief's place. What do you do?"

I paused, letting the question sink in. My mind raced, trying to piece together the puzzle from the thief's perspective. I took a bite of my food, hoping the sustenance would help clear my thoughts.

Finally, I said, "If I were in their shoes, I'd position myself near the most expensive targets. Steal what I can under cover of darkness and then get out."

"Wait! How do *you* see in the dark?" Bella asked. "I mean, as the hypothetical Harper-thief version of you."

"I guess, my magic would let me? Is there any kind of talent you know of that could do that?"

"Night vision goggles," Bella said instantly.

"Okay, so we're going for the mundane approach," Alex said.

"Hey, if it works, don't knock it," she replied.

I shook my head. "Sorry to burst your bubble, but my dad let me use his night vision goggles a couple of times while we were on base. He had this thing about making sure I was prepared for anything."

"Your dad sounds cool," Alex said, his eyes lighting up.

"Yeah, he is. But the point is mundane night vision goggles won't work without ambient light," I finished.

"What about magically enchanted night vision goggles?" Bella suggested. "Something a certain enchanter elf might be able to easily make?"

"Which leads us back to Seraphina," I said with a sigh. Finn wouldn't like it, but try as I might, all the clues seemed to keep pointing back at his ex. "Fine. I use my magical night vision goggles, grab the jewels, and stash them in time to avoid suspicion before the lights come on."

"But you're in the middle of a crowd," Bella pointed out. "How do you get to your exit point? Better yet, what if the lights came back on too soon, and you were stuck holding the jewels?"

I lifted my voluminous skirts. "In this dress? Nothing is fitting in the bodice except me, so I'd put it under my skirt."

"Okay, now we're getting somewhere!" Bella said, excitement creeping into her tone.

"So, the thief tries to make an escape but pockets the jewels somehow as Vivienne and Lucas combat the blackout magic, beating it back and returning the light before expected," Alex said.

Bella twirled a loose strand of hair distractedly. "Maybe we need to come at this from another angle. What if we try to track everyone's movements from before the lights went out to when they came back on? If I owned this place, I'd put hidden security cameras everywhere. If we can get a look at that footage, we could rule out anyone who stayed mostly in the same place in the ballroom, right? Whoever stole the jewels had to have moved, to collect the jewels from all the victims if nothing else."

"We could also re-examine the footage from Jasper's phone," I suggested.

"Or maybe even look at the pictures that the professional photographer was taking," Alex said. "When he wasn't doing the photo booth, he was taking candid pictures of the crowd."

"Great idea! I didn't even see him," I said.

Alex shrugged nonchalantly. "In a job like his? He's supposed to blend in, be forgettable. Much like a chef is at an event like this. The best people in those jobs are the ones who go unnoticed."

"Wait a second," Bella said. "Why haven't we considered the photographer before? If no one really notices him, could he and possibly his assistant be working this together? With all that photography equipment, there would be plenty of places to hide the jewels. Has anyone talked to either of them?"

Both Alex and I shook our heads. "Not that I know of, but I'll ask Gabriel and Isadora," I added.

"I just thought of another problem," Alex said. "If it was completely dark, the security cameras might not give us anything, unless they have thermal imaging or something, which seems excessive even for people like the Silverthornes."

"Or they could've used magic to make sure the camera couldn't spot them or worse, somehow masked their appearance entirely," I said, thinking of Gabriel's use of magic on me backstage.

Bella frowned. "I hadn't thought of that. Honestly, I just assumed we could operate within the realms of reality in our suppositions."

I chuckled wryly and shook my head. "In Havenwood? Reality has a whole other set of rules, I'm afraid."

"Which means we can't rule out anyone," Bella said with a groan, slumping back.

"Not exactly. I think your idea is a good one. We might be able to catch a glimpse of something, some clue to point us in the right direction. To be honest, I think everyone was so focused on a magical solution to the magical problem, that they forgot about common sense. Which is why we need amazing brains like yours," I said, wrapping my arm around her shoulders and giving her a squeeze.

"So, what do you think our next move should be to find this thief? Find out if there are cameras? Questioning the staff? And who's going to talk to the photographer or search his stuff?" Bella asked, obviously warming to the task.

"Start right here!" a shrill, nasal voice broke into our conversation, drawing the attention of everyone nearby. I looked up in surprise to see Oswald and Hortense Puddleton, their faces flushed with anger as they stormed toward us. Oswald's face was a deep shade of puce, and Hortense's normally sharp features were twisted into an expression of self-righteous fury.

"It's her! She's the one causing all this trouble!" Hortense shouted, his voice quivering with rage. "Arrest her, I say! I saw her with a massive necklace! She's been hiding it and all the rest of the jewels, just waiting to escape with her stolen treasures."

Oswald nodded vigorously, sending his jowls wobbling. His voice rose to match his wife's. "Yes, she had it earlier! I saw it, too. The little thief must have used some magic to hide it again. She's been sneaking around, plotting something. It's always the quiet ones you have to watch."

My heart skipped a beat. The necklace was still safely hidden, wrapped in its illusion spell—there was no way they could have seen it unless they'd been watching Gabriel and me as we used it to search for the jewels earlier. But their accusations were loud and convincing, drawing the attention of everyone around us.

Before I could defend myself, Dominic Umbra stepped forward, flanked by two stern-looking security guards. His expression was calm, almost too calm, as he glanced between the Puddletons and me. "Now, now, let's not jump to conclusions," Dominic said smoothly, his voice carrying an air of reason. "It's important that we handle this situation with care."

Dominic's composed demeanor was in stark contrast to the Puddletons' hysteria, and it seemed to have a calming effect on the growing crowd. He turned to one of the security guards and nodded toward the Puddletons. "Please escort Mr. and Mrs. Puddleton to a quiet place where they can calm down."

The guard moved quickly to usher the protesting Puddletons away. Dominic gave me a measured look, his eyes narrowing slightly as they lingered on my throat, apparently devoid of the necklace the Puddletons had claimed to see.

"Please," he said, his voice lowering as he pulled me aside, away from the remaining onlookers, "it's in everyone's best interest if we resolve this quietly. I'm not here to make accusations, but I believe we need to talk." The security guard behind him folded his arms, the man's massive biceps straining the fabric of his jacket.

Dominic's tone was polite, but there was an undercurrent of something more—an edge that made my skin prickle. I glanced around, noticing the hostile glares from the growing crowd, and their whispered gossip, passing along the Puddleton's accusation to anyone who hadn't witnessed it firsthand. Having so many unfriendly eyes on me made me want to run and hide. I could imagine what they were saying right now.

"They caught the thief!"

"She's the one stupid enough to steal from the Silverthornes?"

"And the reason the ball has been ruined for everyone."

Okay, that last one might've just been in my overactive imagination, but it might not be too far off the truth if the locals of Havenwood really thought I was to blame for tonight's fiasco.

Dominic held out his hand, keeping the crowd back as he gestured with the other towards the nearest door. The contrast between Dominic's composed exterior and the Puddletons' frenzied outburst only added to the surreal nature of the situation. And now, with the accusation about the necklace hanging in the air, I felt the stakes rising even higher. The whispers of the crowd seemed to grow louder, each murmur pressing in on me, heightening my anxiety.

As I tried to keep my focus, Dominic took a step closer, his calm voice cutting through the noise. "Please. There's no need to make a scene. Why don't we step away from all of this and have a quiet word?" he suggested, his eyes meeting mine with a reassuring warmth. "I'm sure we can sort this out without further distress." There wasn't a trace of malice or suspicion in his tone—just a genuine concern for fairness and order. Despite the Puddletons' dramatic accusations, Dominic's reasonable, level-headed approach made me feel slightly more at ease.

Bella rushed forward and grabbed my arm. "She didn't do anything wrong!"

Dominic's calm expression remained unchanged. "I don't doubt that, but I would like to have an...erm...more private conversation. I think it's prudent, don't you?" he asked softly, flicking his eyes towards the increasingly agitated crowd.

I hesitated, glancing around. The crowd's demeanor was changing—subtly, but undeniably. It wasn't just their stares or the murmurs I could half-hear, though both were unsettling. A few people started to push forward, their curiosity turning into something more disconcerting. I realized that staying here was only going to make things worse. The way the crowd was acting... they were getting more aggressive. The atmosphere was thickening with an energy I couldn't quite place, but it was making the hair on the back of my neck stand up.

"Bella, it's okay," I said, forcing a calm I didn't quite feel.

"She'll be safe with me," Dominic said, nodding reassuringly at Bella. "But I think it would be wise to get her out of here now, don't you?"

Bella paused for a moment, looking around before nodding.

The growing clamor from the crowd made me cringe backwards. I hadn't thought that a crowd in tuxes and ball gowns could be so aggressive, but I was wrong. I grabbed her hand. "Take Alex and tell Gabriel where I am."

"Yes, do that," Dominic said, placing a protective hand on my elbow.

Before Bella could respond, a sudden commotion erupted behind us. One of Oswald Puddleton's melodramatic gestures had knocked over a large vase, sending it crashing to the floor. The sound echoed through the hall, drawing gasps from the onlookers. Security rushed in to deal with the mess, creating a brief but chaotic distraction.

In the confusion, Dominic gently guided me away from Bella and Alex, who were caught up in the commotion. "Come with me. We need to get you somewhere safe so everyone can calm down," he said smoothly, leading me down a quieter hallway. I glanced back at my friends, feeling a pang of unease as they were momentarily separated from me by the crowd. But I shook it off. Dominic was right. I needed to get away from all the unwanted attention and the increasingly chaotic atmosphere, but I knew one thing for certain: this conversation was going to be anything but simple.

Spark of Suspicion

THE GUARD AND DOMINIC swiftly escorted me through the swarm of people. Each step I took grew heavier, as though I could sense the rumors and accusations weighing down on me as they spread through the watching crowd. The opulent ballroom, which had once felt warm and inviting, now seemed suffocating, its grandeur mocking the growing pit of dread in my stomach. The faces in the crowd blurred together, their expressions a mix of curiosity and judgment. Whispers seemed to coil around me, tightening with each step, like a noose slowly drawing taut. Every murmur was a stone thrown in my direction, the weight of their collective suspicion pressing down on me, making it hard to breathe. It was as if the air itself had turned against me, thickening with each accusation, leaving me gasping for something that wasn't poisoned by doubt.

Dominic led me into a small room off the foyer, the stark, cold silence unexpected and jarring after the clamor of the ballroom. Logically, I knew it was probably a coat room, but something about it felt more like a holding cell than a sanctuary from the accusatory crowd. The guard followed us inside and closed the heavy wooden door with a dull thud, cutting off the last echoes of the ballroom's noise.

Shut away from the crowd, the reality of my predicament settled heavy on my shoulders. I was alone, the accused thief, with nothing but my wits and a magical necklace that was now a chain of suspicion, binding me tighter than any cell ever could. Even if I could use my magic to escape, I wouldn't get very far. Not with the two men seeming to take up all the oxygen in the small space. I felt a shiver run down my spine as I realized that, in this cold, stark space, I was truly on my own—stripped of any warmth, any comfort, and any hope that this would end well.

Even though I knew I was innocent, the primitive side of my brain was screaming at me I was in danger. To run, to hide, to get away. A smaller, more detached part of me wondered if this is what the thieves were feeling, *had* been feeling all night. If after only a few minutes under this pressure, I was contemplating rushing a guard who could've been on the starting defensive line for any professional football team, how were the thieves coping with the stress? They must be more accustomed to dealing with this type of thing than I was, or they would've cracked by now. So, we probably weren't dealing with a gang of Jaspers. But then again, only a professional or an idiot would willingly antagonize the Silverthornes in their own home. I shook my head, amazed at how my cool, logical side kicked in, even though my emotions were simultaneously roiling out of control.

Dominic jerked a thumb at the guard. "You, wait outside. Make sure no one disturbs us."

Without a word, the guard filed out of the room, shutting the door behind him. I heard the bolt snick into place as Dominic twisted the ornate key in the lock and slipped it into his pocket. He turned to face me, his steps measured and calm, not threatening but assured. His presence filled the room, commanding attention without forcing it. My heart still hammered against my ribs. No one had ever accused me of stealing thousands of dollars worth of jewelry before. Or maybe the value was even more? Was it in the tens of thousands? Hundreds? Surely it couldn't be millions...could it?

"Where is the necklace?" he asked, his voice soft but firm, almost inviting. "It wasn't returned, and you were the last person to have it. Tell me." There was something reassuring in his tone, a sense that he genuinely wanted to help, to resolve this. Like he was a father who noticed an empty cookie jar and his daughter with chocolate crumbs all over her cheeks. He wasn't mad, just disappointed.

"I...I..." I stuttered, caught between conflicting thoughts. The necklace belonged to his company in a way, after all. Should I just tell him everything now that we were alone and there was no chance the thieves might overhear us? But what about Lucas' plan? I hesitated, because I wasn't sure what the right course of action was, and there was limited time before the blizzard blew over, which would allow the thieves to escape.

Dominic leaned in slightly, his voice dropping to a gentle whisper that wrapped around me like a comforting embrace. "Where is the serpent necklace? You can trust me. Tell me now."

His words were a caress, soothing and persuasive, making me want to confide in him, to hand over the burden of the secret I was carrying. There was an edge of urgency in his tone, but it wasn't harsh—it was more like the concern of someone who wanted to protect me. For a moment, a flicker of doubt crossed my mind, but the comforting fog that seemed to settle over me quickly smothered it, a fog that made everything simpler, clearer. All I could see were Dominic's dark eyes, filled with understanding.

"Where is it? You can tell me. You should tell me. You *want* to tell me." Dominic's voice was soft, but insistent.

He was right. I did want to tell him. We were on the same team, after all. I felt my hand twitch toward my neck, toward the invisible weight of the necklace. This was right. He needed to know.

"Harper? Harper!" A voice cut through the fog as someone hammered a fist on the door.

"I...Gabriel?" I murmured, shaking my head. The strange murkiness that had settled over my thoughts seemed to lift momentarily.

"Harper? Let me in this instant! Someone unlock this door immediately!" Gabriel's authoritative command pushed the mental haze back even further. In response to his order, I stretched out a hand, even though I couldn't reach the door. Maybe I could use my magic to—

Dominic grabbed my hand. "Oh no, the door must be stuck. Surely someone will fetch a key. Don't worry. You're perfectly safe. Just tell me where the necklace is while we wait to be let out."

With those words, the fog rolled back in. It wasn't the comforting haze from earlier, but a heavier, more oppressive sensation. I realized it wasn't just Dominic's presence; it was everything—the adrenaline crash, the exhaustion from using my powers earlier, and the gnawing emptiness in my stomach from missing dinner. My body was beginning to shut down under the strain, and my mind felt sluggish, the edges of my thoughts blurring together.

Gabriel hammered on the door once again, jiggling the knob as he forcefully tried to enter the room. "Harper? Open the door!"

I did the only thing I could in the moments before the fog closed in completely. I stretched out with my magic, focusing all my will on manipulating the metal in the door. Never before had I attempted anything from this distance, but I didn't have a choice. The mental haze pressed in around me, a cold sweat breaking out on my brow as I concentrated all my efforts on the slim bar of metal. With the last dregs of my strength, I forced it to slide back into the doorframe.

Nothing happened. Was it not enough? Panic flared, and a wave of dizziness threatened to send me crashing to the ground when the door burst open. Gabriel stormed in, Bella right behind him, their faces a twisted mixture of concern and fury.

"What is happening here?" Gabriel demanded, his angry gaze sliding off Dominic and landing on me. Instantly, it was replaced by one of concern as I wavered, pressing a hand against the wall to keep from falling.

In a moment, Gabriel was across the room, wrapping his muscular arms around me, keeping me upright. It was just in time too, as my knees threatened to give out. I steadied myself against Gabriel's solid shoulder as Dominic moved to the side to give us space. Following in Gabriel's wake, Bella dashed to my side, wrapping an arm around me. Behind her, Vivienne Silverthorne, Lucas, Isadora, Alex, Seraphina, and Finn all crowded into the room, making the small space feel claustrophobically crowded.

The next few minutes were a blur of tense, whispered exchanges as everyone tried to keep their voices from carrying to the curious crowd in the ballroom. It was hard for me to follow everything that was being said. My head felt heavy, blurry, and as light as a helium balloon all at once. It was disorienting, making it almost impossible to focus on what was happening. I wobbled and nearly toppled over. I would've fallen if Gabriel hadn't caught me again. Or was it a third time? Someone brought in a chair, and they helped me sit, which seemed to help ease the dizziness that had set in.

Vivienne's sharp voice cut through the fog. Her eyes narrowed as she took in the scene. "What on earth is going on here?" she demanded, her gaze flicking from Dominic to me, then to Gabriel.

Dominic quickly stepped forward, his demeanor calm and measured. "There was some confusion, Vivienne. The young lady was feeling unwell, and some guests were making a rather undignified scene. A short man and a thin woman? I didn't catch their names, but they were quite aggressive so I thought it best to bring her somewhere quiet to avoid causing a stir," he explained smoothly. "I was simply asking her a few questions to ensure everything was all right."

Vivienne's stern gaze snapped to me, and I nodded weakly in agreement, forcing a small smile. "It's true. I just... I didn't eat much earlier, and with everything that's been happening... I guess it all caught up with me." I said, as the room slowly stopped spinning.

Vivienne's expression softened slightly, her concern clear. "Well, we can't have you overexerting yourself," she said, her tone gentler now. "Dominic, thank you for stepping in, but I think we can handle things from here."

Dominic inclined his head gracefully. "Of course. I'll leave her in your capable hands." He turned to me, offering a polite smile. "Take care, my dear. I'm sure you'll feel better after some rest."

As Dominic exited the room, I felt a wave of relief wash over me, though the lingering fog in my mind made it difficult to fully process everything that had just happened. Gabriel crouched beside me, holding my hand and speaking in a soft, comforting tone that was as grounding as it was soothing. I was grateful for his presence, as it gave me a mental tether to cling to while I fought off the last remnants of dizziness. Slowly, the words around me began to make more sense.

"...unacceptable. Utterly unacceptable! This is beyond the pale!" Vivienne Silverthorne stormed, her voice as sharp as a blade.

"Vivienne, you have every right to be upset, but this might not be the time or place" Elara said, stepping forward with a calm but firm demeanor.

Isadora nodded, looking wide-eyed at her mother and me. "Exactly. After all, the Puddletons were the ones causing the disruption, not Harper."

Bella chimed in, her voice trembling with the emotion she was barely containing. "They were out of line, making wild accusations in the middle of the ball. Completely inappropriate! They've always disliked Harper, I think because they view her as competition, but this was completely beyond petty snipes. They virtually screamed that she was the one responsible for everything tonight."

Vivienne's eyes flashed with fury as she turned her gaze to look around the room. "Is this true? They dared to accuse her without any proof?"

Alex nodded, his expression serious. "It's true. The Puddletons weren't just making a scene, they were doing everything in their power to turn people against Harper."

Gabriel looked up at his mother from where he crouched at my side. "They've always had a reputation of being a little negative, but tonight they crossed a line."

Vivienne's face hardened with resolve. "I agree. They've gone too far this time. I'll have them escorted out to a private room immediately and then off the estate once the storm clears. Make no mistake, they will never be invited back to any of my events. Their behavior was disgraceful, and I won't have it."

Vivienne, in a rare act of kindness, squeezed my shoulder before sweeping out of the room, several of the others following her. Bella and Alex moved to the side to allow her to pass. I was so stunned by the unexpected gesture that my mouth hung open, and all I could do was stare after her as she left. That's when I noticed Finn hovering in the doorway. As soon as our eyes connected, he stepped forward, reaching out to hold my other hand as concern and worry drove out any lingering resentment or frustration he might have held towards me.

"Are you okay?" he asked, crouching next to Gabriel in front of my chair.

Under different circumstances, the attentive concern of two handsome men might have been flattering, but their voices were little more than a distant hum against the relentless drumming in my ears. Questions started spiraling through the chaos of my thoughts: Why did something feel so wrong? The Puddletons claimed they saw me with the necklace, but I didn't remember seeing them at all while Gabriel and I were using it. So how did they know it was still in my possession? And why was everyone so fixated on the serpent necklace, anyway?

The more I thought about it, the more it rankled at the edges of my mind, like a puzzle piece that didn't quite fit. Could the necklace be the key to unraveling this entire mystery? The idea sparked a flicker of suspicion that refused to be extinguished. It was as if the answers were just out of reach, hidden in the shadows, waiting for the right moment to reveal themselves. But one thing was becoming increasingly clear: I couldn't afford to ignore this feeling, not when everything seemed to hinge on one elusive piece of the puzzle.

Open Doors

My thoughts swirled as the fog in my mind dissipated more with every passing moment. Bella leaned in over Finn's shoulder, her dark eyes full of worry. "Harper, are you okay?"

"If you want me to, I'll devise a plan to get back at those nasty Puddletons. Put a porcupine in their bed or dump a pot of honey on their heads and glitter bomb their entire house. You just say the word, and they won't know what hit them," Isadora said, the words flying at rapid fire and her eyes sparking with determination.

"Isa...," Gabriel said softly, his tone gently chiding.

I coughed, barely disguising a surprised snort of laughter. "Umm, no need for glitter bombs. But I do feel a bit dizzy... Maybe some water would help."

"I'm on it!" Bella sprang to her feet, clearly eager to help, and raced out the door, with Alex following close on her heels.

Isadora lingered for a moment; her brow furrowed with concern. "Are you sure you're okay? I'm more than happy to give the Puddletons a piece of my mind. After what they did, they deserve it!"

I managed a faint smile. "I'm okay, really. Thank goodness Dominic was there to keep things from getting out of hand. But I just need a moment to catch my breath.

Isadora nodded, though she still looked unconvinced. "Alright, but if you need anything, just call. I'll be close by."

As she finally left the room, closing the door behind her, I let out a long breath. The dizziness was continuing to fade, but my mind was still a jumble of thoughts. In the relative quiet following her departure, I caught Finn's eyes. His earlier animosity seemed to have dissolved in the gravity of the current crisis, leaving space for a truce.

"Are you sure you're okay?" he asked quietly.

"I think so," I murmured.

He squeezed my fingers and in that moment of shared silence, there was a weight of unspoken apologies on both our parts. A tentative hope flickered to life inside my chest at the possibility of mending the bridge between us.

"What do you need?" Gabriel asked from my other side.

I opened my mouth to answer but hesitated, a new wave of thoughts and emotions rising up. Dominic's fixation on the necklace... Why? He hadn't even mentioned the missing jewels. Not once. Did he really think I was trying to pocket the necklace while everyone else was hunting for the thief? The thought cut deeper than I expected. I had been trying to help, to do the right thing, and yet, he treated me like I was the prime suspect. If he truly believed I was the thief, why didn't he ask where the stash was? Did they find it already? Or was he so fixated on the necklace that everything else fell by the wayside?

The sting of his possible distrust gnawed at me. I couldn't shake the feeling that something wasn't adding up.

Finn squeezed my hand again as Bella returned with a glass of water. "Let's get you out of here. Maybe some fresh air will help," he suggested, interrupting my thoughts.

I sipped from the glass, the cool liquid banishing some of the lingering fog, and nodded mutely. As I allowed them to lead me out of the room, there was a slight kerfuffle as each man attempted to be the one to offer me an arm to lean on. But there was no way all three of us were fitting through the door at once. I caught sight of Alex standing nearby and, with a small smile, decided to take his arm instead. It felt like the neutral choice, and besides, Alex had become a good friend over the past few months—thanks to Bella.

With Alex's steady support, I felt a little more grounded. The stubborn dizziness continued to dissipate as we made our way out of the room, leaving behind the confusion and tension, but not the nagging questions that continued to swirl in my mind.

As soon as we exited the room, Seraphina appeared in the hall, looking flustered and upset. Her eyes softened with concern when she saw me. "Harper, are you okay? You still look so pale," she said, her voice gentle and filled with genuine worry.

I managed a small smile, nodding slightly. "I'm fine, just a little overwhelmed."

Seraphina's concern deepened, and she reached out as if to comfort me but hesitated, glancing at Finn. "I'm so glad to hear that. Please let me know if I can do anything to help, okay?" Then she turned to Finn, her voice tinged with urgency but still kind. "I'm sorry to pull you away, Finn, but I need you," she said, urgently waving him over.

He looked torn, glancing down at me, and was obviously hesitant to leave. "Are you sure you'll be okay?" he asked softly.

"Don't worry, I'm fine," I reassured him.

"Okay. I'll check in on you soon. And please, try not to run headlong into danger like that time at the RV," he warned, a slight twinkle dancing in his eye.

I couldn't help but chuckle, despite everything. "I promise I'm not chasing after anything, not even a lost cat," I shot back.

"Haven't you heard? There's never a cat," Finn said with a wink. The familiar banter seemed to bring a small sense of normalcy to the chaos.

"I know, I know" I sighed, going for flippant, but the recent incident was still too fresh in my mind for me to really pull it off.

Finn nodded, seeming to understand everything I said and everything I left unsaid. He gave my fingers one last encouraging squeeze before heading in the direction Seraphina had beckoned him.

As they left, I noticed Bella's worry gaze, her eyes flicking over me as if assessing for hidden injuries. She opened her mouth, but before she could say anything, Isadora appeared, her own expression tense and urgent.

"Bella, Alex, I need you both for a moment," she said, casting a quick glance around us.

Bella looked torn, her gaze shifting between me and Isadora.

I managed a small nod, doing my best to appear steadier than I felt. "Go on. I'm fine," I said softly, glancing toward Gabriel, who had come to stand beside me with a quiet, grounding presence.

"Are you sure?" Bella asked.

"Yeah. I'll be okay," I said.

With one last concerned look, Bella reluctantly followed Alex and Isadora down the hall, leaving Gabriel and me in the quiet of the corridor. He stepped closer, his hand warm and steady as he took my hand, guiding it to rest on his arm. His grip was protective but not possessive, a comforting presence after my unsettling encounter.

"I'm here, Harper," he said softly, his voice grounding me. The words were simple but carried a quiet promise and a warmth that made me feel safe.

As we stepped back into the ballroom, I found solace in his warm, comforting presence. It wasn't lost on me that Gabriel had given me the space I needed with Finn, stepping back without a hint of jealousy or interference. It was... sweet, really. But it also left me wondering—was he doing this because he genuinely liked me, or was it more about showing the guests that I wasn't a suspect? An attempt at restoring my reputation? Simply being a good host?

Almost immediately, the murmurs started. Eyes went wide and there was subtle pointing in my direction as hands shielded gossiping lips. I froze. These people couldn't really think I was responsible for the thefts. Could they? But they obviously did. The few people I knew here might stick up for me, but that wasn't very many. A realization hit me like a wrecking ball to the core of my dreams. If these people—some of the most influential and wealthy in Havenwood and the surrounding area—thought I was behind the theft, what would that mean for my future running Spellbooks? Would I ever shake off the shroud of suspicion?

When I paused, my feet mounting a rebellion at the thought of proceeding further into the ballroom, Gabriel looked down at me in surprise. Understanding danced through his dark eyes a moment later as I stared out at the whispering crowd.

"Would you like somewhere private to clear your head?" he offered softly, so only I could hear him.

"Yes, please."

Gabriel guided me from the ballroom, but not before shooting a disapproving look over my head at the gossiping crowd. Not that it did very much to halt the rumormongers, but I appreciated the sentiment behind his gesture.

Gabriel led me down a deserted hallway. Voices drifted towards us, growing louder with each step. It didn't take long to realize we'd stumbled upon a heated exchange between Finn and

Seraphina. A cracked door to the room let us hear part of their argument.

"...actions cannot be justified!" Finn's voice was tense, the edge unmistakable.

"I'm not trying to justify them, just asking to understand," Seraphina responded, her tone sharper than I'd ever heard from her. There was a defensiveness in her voice, something almost desperate.

"Understand what? That he's out of control? This is beyond crossing a line, Seraphina," Finn shot back, frustration clear in his every word.

Seraphina hesitated for a fraction of a second, then said quietly, "Dominic has been by my side through everything. This company—our company—means the world to him. With the plans for relocating, he's under immense pressure to protect what we've built. We both are."

"That doesn't make it right." Finn's voice was firm.

Seraphina's eyes flickered with something unreadable, a hint of something more beneath her usually calm exterior. "Finn... you don't understand. He's just... he's trying to keep everything from falling apart."

Gabriel gently led me past the door and out of earshot before they noticed we were eavesdropping. My mind raced. Seraphina said that Dominic was upset by the jewel thieves, but I still couldn't get over the fact that when he'd had me alone, he'd only asked about the serpent necklace. Why? My thoughts churned, trying to piece together what I knew.

Could Dominic and Seraphina have been working together? That would explain a lot. Perhaps they were responsible for all the heists, or maybe they were copy-catting the real thieves, hoping to achieve... what? And how did the Puddletons fit into all this? Maybe if I could figure out the answer to either of those questions, it would crack the case wide open.

"Is something going on? You look worried," Gabriel asked as he led me through the quieter parts of the mansion.

"It's Dominic, and the Puddletons—" I said.

"I could wring their necks for what they did," Gabriel growled, cutting me off. His voice was rough with barely restrained anger, but there was something else too—something that made my pulse quicken.

Before I could respond, his hand lifted to my face, his fingers brushing lightly against my cheek. The touch was tender, as his gaze locked onto mine, making my breath catch. His fingers trailed down, skimming over the tender skin at my throat where the necklace had dug in. His touch was warm, spreading a slow heat through me, and his eyes were filled with a fierce determination that made it hard to look away.

"In my house, too," he murmured, his voice thick with emotion. "I should've been able to keep you safe here. I will keep you safe." The words were a promise, a vow that settled deep in my chest, making my heart race even faster. His fingers lingered for just a moment longer, as if he didn't want to let go, before he finally stepped back, leaving me feeling both more grounded and somehow bereft at the same time.

"Yes. No. I mean, don't. Wring their necks, that is. It might put a damper on the party," I said with a sheepish smile, trying to lighten the mood.

"Maybe, maybe not," Gabriel said. The soft timbre of his voice did nothing to hide the steel in his words.

"The Puddletons don't bother me," I lied. "I've come to accept it's just who and what they are. Just ignore them, and they'll go away. Eventually." Although, it seemed like their sniping at me had escalated quickly over the course of the evening. Full-blown, baseless, public accusations weren't really their usual style.

"So, if it's not them, what's on your mind?" Gabriel asked.

"To be honest? Dominic. It's just that he was laser-focused on the silver serpent necklace. If he is so supremely committed to the company, and he thought I had something to do with the theft, why is he only asking me about one necklace?"

"Because it was the one he thought he saw you with? It was the piece they assigned to you after all," Gabriel said as he opened a side door and ushered me into a small study. The room, draped in dark, masculine navy, had rich leather furnishings and tasteful gold accents. As he stepped in close beside me, the warmth of his presence and the realization that we were truly alone together for the first time sent a flutter through my chest, making my pulse quicken.

I took a step away, trying to focus my thoughts over the rapid pounding of my heart. "Maybe. But then again, maybe it's just like Seraphina said. He cares about the company so much that he's willing to do anything to recover the gems," I said, sinking down on a comfy armchair Gabriel indicated. He flipped a switch, turning on the electric fireplace and chasing out the chill that had settled in the empty room as the blizzard continued to howl outside the

French doors leading out onto a wide balcony covered in snow. Gabriel poured two drinks from a crystal decanter nestled in a convenient side bar, passing me one as he settled in the armchair next to mine.

"That doesn't excuse isolating you and then basically interrogating you." Gabriel's face was a mask of outrage.

"Well, I'm not sure I'd put it like that," I demurred, trying to deescalate the situation. "Although, it wasn't my favorite part of the evening, that's for sure," I said dryly, taking a sip of the amber liquid. It was strong, with a slight smokey aftertaste. The burn of the drink dispelled the last vestiges of my lingering brain fog, but it didn't help me resolve the sense of unsettledness in the pit of my stomach. Something still felt off, but I couldn't quite put my finger on it.

Gabriel cleared his throat, looking at me speculatively over his tumbler. "I feel like I may have lost you again. What were you thinking just now?"

I set my drink on the walnut side table and leaned forward. "It's just weird, right? Dominic being focused only on my necklace? Why? I don't get it."

"He is an intense guy," Gabriel said. "But think about it—you're probably one of the last people who hasn't returned their jewelry. He's likely just trying to secure the final items for his company and close this out. Maybe, given the circumstances, he even suspects you are involved in the theft."

"But it's easy to prove I wasn't involved," I countered. "I was right next to you when the lights went out. I don't have the kind of powers to zip around the room and swipe jewels in the dark. And if anyone needed proof, it's all verifiable."

Gabriel tilted his head slightly, his expression thoughtful. "True but consider this: I couldn't see you until the lights came back on. Based on what I've seen so far, I assume you prefer to keep your powers private, which is just fine by the way. But in this case, no one here really knows what your magic can do, and you have a knack for being at the heart of things when they go wrong."

I blinked, taken aback by the implication. "You think I could have—?"

He shrugged, but his eyes were steady on mine, full of quiet reassurance. "I trust you, Harper. I believe you. But for someone like Dominic? That's not empirical evidence. It's not enough to convince someone who's already looking for a scapegoat."

I took a sip from my glass, giving myself a moment as I weighed Gabriel's words. Finally, I decided to float my theory. "What if he teamed up with Seraphina? He uses his whatever-he's-got magic, and she somehow uses hers to infuse it into an enchanted ring or something?"

Gabriel looked unconvinced. "We're discussing magic, so I wouldn't exactly rule it out, but why would they rob themselves? Despite the jewel thieves targeting high society events, business is good for them. I mean, *really* good. So good that I overheard Dominic bragging about a new car and house he just bought. Even Mother was impressed, which is saying something. She told me she was considering investing, especially since Seraphina was moving back to Havenwood. I encouraged her to. Not only was it a savvy investment, but I know how she likes to support local businesses. Seemed like a win-win."

I pounced on the idea. "Maybe someone wanted Vivienne to distribute her support in other ways. Who else knew about her plans?" I asked, sensing a fresh path to pursue.

"No one that I was aware of," Gabriel said with a shrug.

Although part of me couldn't understand why I felt the urge to help, I didn't think Seraphina should lose out on a potential opportunity because of what happened. If Vivienne was upset with Seraphina, maybe I could talk with the powerful matriarch and smooth things over for the elf. The thought surprised me—was I really considering helping her, knowing she had feelings for Finn? I shook my head, trying to push those thoughts aside and focus on the matter at hand.

"So, we're still looking for someone who had motive, means, and opportunity," I said thoughtfully, trying to piece everything together.

"Sounds about right," Gabriel replied with a wry chuckle. "Although, with the amount those stolen gems could fetch, you could argue that most people had a motive—including me."

"Oh? How much was stolen?" I asked, genuinely curious. I hadn't heard a number yet.

Gabriel wavered a hand back and forth. "Just shy of seven figures is what I heard."

My jaw dropped. "But the lights were only out for a few minutes!"

"Most profitable minutes of the evening, I'd wager," Gabriel said dryly.

"But if they knew they'd only have a few minutes, why target my necklace? If they wanted to make the most money possible, the serpent should've been way down their list of targets. Seraphina told me it wasn't one of the most expensive items here, despite its size."

"And yet, everyone seems obsessed with it," Gabriel mused.

"Someone nearly got it too. Which means the thief must've been close to me, but we knew that already from the spread of stolen jewels and the attempt to snatch the serpent."

"None of the missing jewelry was worn by someone close to Dominic or Seraphina," Gabriel pointed out. He tossed back the rest of his drink, holding his glass up in a silent query to me. I shook my head, and he stood, retreating to the sidebar nestled nearly out of sight behind the corner of a large bookcase.

"So, how does this theft fit with all the others? Is it all about money, or could it be about the magic woven into the jewelry? Either way, the most obvious suspects couldn't have committed the crime. Yet a crime still occurred. What are we missing?" I asked, spinning my tumbler on the table. "Could it be the caterers? Some of them might have been present at the other parties where jewels were stolen."

"No, Lucas cleared them all," Gabriel said.

"Okay, what about other people helping out around the ball?"

"Our staff is completely dependable."

"What about someone who isn't on your staff? Someone like Mystique?" I asked.

"You still think it's her?"

"No, not really, but..." My eyes widened as I recalled my conversation with Bella. "What about the photographer and his assistant? They looked like an efficient team and could easily hide all the jewels in their equipment. Besides, no one ever notices a photographer at events like these."

Gabriel paused, considering it. "They've had access to everything and everyone all night. It's a solid theory."

I paused, considering the theory. I'd suspected the wrong person before. Now, being on the other side of a false accusation made me even more hesitant to point the finger at anyone else. As the silence stretched between us, the fire's crackle seemed to mock my spinning thoughts.

"It's all about magic..." Gabriel mused from the other side of the room, almost to himself. I glanced over at him. His gaze wasn't on me but on something distant, a puzzle piece visible only to him. His eyes snapped to mine, a sudden urgency within them. "Harper, the necklace—" His words cut short, a new realization dawning in his expression. "Come here, I want to see something."

As I stood to move across the room to him, the temperature in the room dropped abruptly as cold air gusted into the study from the open French door. Hadn't it just been closed? I spun around, my hand clutching at my bare shoulders as the blizzard's wrath blew straight into the heart of the Silverthorne manor. The glass doors banging open in the wind was the last thing I saw before the room plunged into darkness.

Shadows Falling

Before I could even think to scream, I felt hands on me, pulling me to the side of the room. As someone yanked me aside, something brushed past me, feeling like cold, wet silk against my bare arm. However, this might have been due to the winter gale gusting into the study. I struggled and opened my lips to scream just as a large, calloused hand clapped over my mouth. I fought for all I was worth, thrashing against the muscular man who now pinned me against the bookshelves, but it was no use. He was so much bigger than I was and had overpowered me in the moment of my surprise. I did the only thing I could. I bit down on the offending hand. Hard.

The man sucked in a pained breath, but instead of letting me go, he leaned close, breathing into my ear. "Harper. It's me. Stop fighting."

Gabriel's warm breath was a stark contrast to the snowstorm blowing in through the curtains, but his calm words and the scent of his cologne, rapidly becoming familiar and comforting, finally broke through the hold my primitive mind had on my response system. I immediately relaxed and nodded slightly, letting him know I'd heard him. Slowly, he peeled his fingers away from my mouth, but kept me pressed against the bookcase in the unnatural darkness. The blackout was so absolute that for a moment, I thought Elara's blizzard creation deserved more credit than we'd originally given her. Had she called up a storm so furious that it blocked out the moon and the stars? It was only then that I realized I couldn't see the light from the fireplace anymore either, which meant...

Which meant this was no normal darkness.

I sucked in a silent breath as I heard someone moving through the study. Had the thief struck again? But we were the only people in the room. Why come after Gabriel and me?

My heart stuttered. *We* didn't attract this attention, but *I* did. The necklace around my throat seemed more like an impossible weight with every passing moment. I heard the floorboards creak in the darkness as the invisible assailant crept through the room. It took only a split second for me to understand what was happening. The thieves must know, or at least suspect, that I still had the necklace. They'd come after me as soon as they thought I was alone, probably the first time I appeared to be by myself all evening. From their angle, it must have looked like Gabriel left the study when he'd just stepped to the bar, which was out of view from the balcony.

Another rustle of clothing and the pad of footsteps broke the silence. Not knowing who or what was out there in the inky blackness was terrifying. We were not alone. I could almost feel the intruder's gaze probing at the cloying shadows, searching for us. Gabriel must've sensed it too, because I felt him tense, readying for whatever was about to happen.

"Where is she?" the harsh whisper surprised me almost as much as a gunshot in the silence.

"I don't know. I'm not the one who can see in the dark without enchanted goggles, am I?" a man's voice hissed through the inky blackness.

"Well, if you had secured the room like you said you would, we wouldn't be chasing after her now," the first voice responded in an irritated whisper. It had a sharper edge, maybe feminine, but it was hard to tell. "The first time she's been on her own all night, and you let her slip through our fingers."

"I don't see why we're even bothering. We've got the jewels. Isn't that enough?"

The first person, definitely a woman, scoffed, her voice drawing closer. "You know we get double if we snag that snake necklace. With this blizzard, we're not getting out of here anytime soon. Might as well make the most of it."

"I still think we should take what we've got and disappear," the man grumbled.

"We aren't going anywhere until the storm lets up. Besides, you know we need that key," the woman said, her voice moving closer.

"The key's nothing. You know I could handle that easily. But staying here? These rich folks must have some way to ride out the storm—snowmobiles or skis or something. Isn't skiing a rich-person thing?"

"Look, as soon as the storm breaks, we'll grab the stash from where we've hidden it, get the key, and disappear. Until then, we keep trying to get our hands on that necklace," the woman said, her voice now sounding like it was circling the room.

"Fine, but I'm holding you to it," the man muttered.

"Let's split up. We have a better chance of finding her that way. You go back the way we came, and I'll head down the hall."

"Why do I have to go back out in the snow?" the man said, a faint whine creeping into his voice.

"Because men's formal wear comes with jackets, and this dress isn't doing a thing for me in that wind. Now go on. Find her," the woman ordered.

Silence descended once more in the darkness, completely blanketing the room like new-fallen snow. Then, just as suddenly as they had descended, the shadows lifted. The fire danced in the electric fireplace as the final blast of winter wind gusted through the room, sending shadows and snowflakes dancing wildly around the empty study. A dark shape dashed past the windows outside, an undefined blur in the snowstorm. Gabriel didn't move an inch, standing in front of me with his arms braced on either side, protecting me from the unseen assailant with his body and, I realized with a start, with his magic.

The door to the study shut with the faint, unmistakable sound of an ominous click as whoever had entered the study rejoined the party in the manor without seeing through Gabriel's illusion spell protecting us both.

He held a finger to his lips as he looked around to make sure the thieves really had left. We stood there motionless in the complete silence as one minute stretched into two. Nothing moved in the study other than the crackling of the fire. Gabriel carefully pushed away from the shelves and waved his hand, dissipating the illusion that had protected us.

The truth of our situation was clear. We were far from safe. The thief—or rather thieves—were still too close for comfort, their plan not yet complete. And since we were without even a glimpse, they could be anyone. We were caught in a web of deception with strands leading to every corner of the Silverthorne manor, and the centerpiece, the serpent necklace, was a beacon calling out to those who dared play this game of greed and shadows.

"We've got to get that necklace off you. As long as you're wearing it, you're a target," Gabriel said urgently.

He waved a hand, dissolving the illusion on the necklace, and reached out to unclasp it. I grabbed his hand, a sudden, crazy idea forming in my head.

"Wait. I have a better plan."

Ingenious or Dangerous?

SIX SETS OF EYES stared at me incredulously as I explained my plan for a second time to the Silverthornes, Bella, and Alex. Well, my plan with Gabriel's tweaks.

"This is too dangerous," Vivienne said as soon as I finished explaining.

"I think it's kind of ingenious," Isadora replied. I shot her a grateful look.

"It's both," Lucas chimed in. "But it beats just sitting around and hoping the thieves will turn themselves in."

Vivienne set her jaw stubbornly. "We're relying on an outsider, a guest to handle something critical and possibly dangerous. I believe we should deal with this internally. Surely someone else can do it. It would be safer and smarter to keep this within the family."

"I had the same thought, Mother," Gabriel said. "But if anyone else stepped into Harper's place, it might arouse suspicion and the plan wouldn't work."

Vivienne didn't look convinced. "Surely there is another way."

Gabriel shook his head and spoke gently. "Nothing as good as this. Even with Elara's magic, the storm has to break eventually."

Alex spoke up. "Based on what I can sense, I'd guess you have somewhere between thirty minutes and an hour before the blizzard blows itself out. You might have a little extra time, depending on the road conditions out there, but..." he trailed off with a shrug.

A tense silence settled over the room as the weight of Alex's words sunk in. There wasn't a lot of time. My heart raced at the thought of what that meant. We were running out of options, and fast. I exchanged a glance with Gabriel, who gave me a small, reassuring nod.

He cleared his throat, his voice steady and filled with resolve. "We haven't been able to find the jewels yet, and this might be our best, no, our only plan to catch the thieves and recover the gems."

I took a deep breath, trying to steady my nerves. There was no room for error now, and despite the risks, I knew I had to see this through.

Vivienne considered her son thoughtfully. "You seem very convinced about this course of action."

"I am," he replied without hesitation, his voice confident.

"Even if it possibly endangers a guest?" she asked sharply.

Gabriel met his mother's gaze head-on, unwavering. "Harper says she can handle it, and I believe her. She's proven herself more than capable tonight."

The room fell silent as Gabriel's words hung in the air. His confidence in me was palpable, and it sent a warm flush through me—part gratitude, part something more. He barely knew me, yet he trusted me. Despite the odds against us, he had faith in my abilities.

I glanced at Gabriel, our eyes meeting for a moment. There was something in his gaze that made my heart skip a beat—a mix of respect, confidence, and maybe even admiration. It was more than just support; it was a kind of quiet, unwavering faith that I could do this, that I could face whatever was coming and come out stronger on the other side.

Vivienne narrowed her eyes, and silence descended on the room, stretching uncomfortably long as she considered first Gabriel and then me.

To my surprise, it was Elara that came to our defense. "Oh, come on, Vivienne. It's a good plan. Stop dragging your heels," the older woman said. I blinked in surprise, but held both my tongue and my breath, waiting for Vivienne's verdict.

Finally, the Silverthorne matriarch sighed and threw up her hands. "Very well, let's put it to a vote. All in favor of this plan?" Six hands rose instantly into the air, Vivienne's being the notable exception. She sighed and closed her eyes. When she opened them, they blazed with determination. "Fine, we're doing this. Now, let's go over the plan again in detail. It must be absolutely perfect. We must be perfect. I will not accept any more risk than absolutely necessary nor am I willing to further sully the Silverthorne reputation by not being able to handle our own affairs."

Gabriel shot me an encouraging look as all eyes turned towards me once more. I cleared my throat, the weight of being the mastermind suddenly falling on my shoulders like an unexpected mantle. When it had just been Gabriel and me, the hypothetical solutions had been a fun brain exercise for an armchair expert, or rather armchair amateur detective with an audacious plan. Now that I was being forced into action, things took a very real turn. But I wasn't about to back out.

I reached toward the heavy necklace, brushing the clasp with a whisper of magic so it fell into my waiting hands. I held it out to Elara. "First, we're going to need you to stop the storm."

Elara shook her head, a small, regretful smile tugging at her lips. "I'm afraid my power doesn't work that way. I can add weather, but I can't take it away once it's in motion."

Disappointment seeped in, making me frown. "So, we don't know when it will stop? We have no control?" My plans could really be in jeopardy if the blizzard ended too early or too late.

"Not entirely," Alex interjected, stepping forward. "I might not be able to change the weather, but I can give you a rough timeline as the weather patterns change.

I glanced at Alex, realizing that his ability to predict the weather could be the key to making the plan work. "Okay, then that's when we need everyone in the right place at exactly the right time."

Gabriel nodded, catching on to the shift in strategy. "We'll have to move quickly and coordinate perfectly. Now, here's the plan..."

The Curtain Rises

I REENTERED THE BALLROOM with Gabriel, the silver serpent necklace once again securely fastened around my neck and fully on display without an obscuring illusion spell.

"Are you sure about this?" Gabriel whispered for my ears only. "You don't have to do it if you're having second thoughts."

I was having way more than second thoughts, but I wasn't about to tell him that. "We've worked out every contingency. And remember, as a last resort, I can always hand over the necklace."

"I still don't like that all of the danger is going to be on your shoulders," Gabriel whispered darkly.

"Nothing is going to happen. You'll be right there the whole time."

"Not close enough," Gabriel muttered.

I patted his hand. "We have to give at least the illusion of distance for the bait to work. I trust you. The plan is solid. We can do this. There's no way they are getting away with all the jewels and the damage this could do to your family. Whoever they are."

Gabriel opened his mouth, but before he could respond, we'd reached our destination. Bella turned away from the buffet, holding a plate with a thick slice of a chocolate Yule Log on it. The sponge cake was rolled around a generous helping of chocolate buttercream and decorated with meringue mushrooms, sugared cranberries, and rosemary sprigs. My stomach growled, reminding me I'd missed dinner, and the sandwich, while delicious, hadn't been enough.

She sidled over to us, forcing a smile. "So, everything's in place? We just have to stand here and look like a target, right? How does one look like a target exactly?" she asked.

I chuckled softly. "Relax, Bella. You're doing great. Just act like we're here to enjoy the party, and everything's fine."

"Easier said than done," she muttered, cutting a bite of cake with her fork and popping it in her mouth.

"See, you're a natural," I said, my stomach growling at the sight of the decadent dessert. "Let's get me some cake and blend in. The more normal we look, the better."

"Now you're talking my language," Bella said, signaling to a nearby server for another slice of the Yule Log.

Gabriel leaned in and brushed a kiss against my cheek. "Be safe. Don't take any unnecessary risks."

"Same to you," I whispered back, a blush creeping up my cheeks at the unexpected gesture of affection. I'd told him to make a scene as he gave the appearance of leaving me alone with Bella, but I hadn't anticipated *that.* Gabriel winked at me and then disappeared into the crowd.

Bella cleared her throat from beside me. "Now what was *that* all about?" she asked with an arched eyebrow.

"Would you believe me if I said it was a distraction?"

"It certainly was distracting. To me."

"Well, hopefully it worked just as well on the thieves," I said, devouring the cake. It was just as delicious as it looked. I sighed in satisfaction, setting the plate on a nearby table. Across the room, Alex gave a subtle thumbs up.

"There's the signal. Now, all we have to do is walk around the ballroom and make a scene? It's like I've been training for this all my life," Bella said, setting down her plate and rubbing her hands together eagerly. "Where do we start?"

"Center of the ballroom, don't you think?" I asked.

"Sounds good to me," Bella said. She glanced over my shoulder, her eyes going wide. "Uh-oh."

"What is it?" I asked, freezing in place.

"Finn. He's on a beeline headed straight for us."

I sighed. This really wasn't the time or place, but I also didn't want to blow him off. "Give me a second, okay?"

"But Gabriel told me to stick by your side," Bella protested.

"I'll be with Finn. It'll be fine. I just need a minute to talk to him. In private." Bella looked back, obviously torn. "Please, Bella. It won't take long, and you can watch me from over by Alex the entire time."

"Fine," Bella reluctantly agreed. I turned as Finn approached. Across the room, I glimpsed Isadora's dress disappearing behind the photographer's backdrop. Neither the photographer nor his assistant was in sight. Perfect—the plan was in motion, and everyone was playing their parts perfectly.

"Hey, is everything okay? How are you feeling?" he asked.

"A-okay," Bella said, shooting him a thumbs up. "I just need you to keep an eye on Harper while I find Alex really quick." I shot her a dirty look.

"Why does Harper need to be watched?" Finn asked curiously.

"Have you met this girl? She seems to attract trouble like a magnet," Bella said.

"I don't disagree," Finn said with a chuckle. This time, my dirty look was aimed in his direction. He held up his hands, palms outward. "Hey, just calling them like I see them. Havenwood was a quiet little town until you moved in."

"Is it really fair that you're ganging up on me right now?"

"Fair has nothing to do with it. Accurate on the other hand..." Bella trailed off as she backed away.

"Bella!"

"Harper! Finn! We're all here," Bella said, pointing at each of us in turn. She waggled her finger at Finn. "Now, don't let her out of your sight. I'll be back in a minute or two, and I don't want another incident this evening."

"Hey!" I protested futilely.

"No problem," Finn said at the same time. Bella winked at me and drifted over towards Alex, leaving me standing awkwardly next to Finn. The silence stretched until we both spoke at once.

"Harper, I—"

"Finn, do you—"

We both laughed, the sound breaking the tension that was lingering between us. I waved at him. "You go first."

He stuck his hands in his pockets and looked out at the crowd. "I want to apologize for my behavior. I was hurt that you didn't invite me to the ball and jealous when I saw you with Gabriel. Even though we never agreed to see each other exclusively, it bothered me to see you with him. More than I expected. To be honest, I was so upset by the whole situation that I couldn't even really hear you when you tried to explain there was nothing between you and him. It took Bella sitting me down and giving me a proverbial smack upside the head to get me to pay attention."

I shot a look to where my best friend stood, watching us intently from across the room. She always had my best interests at heart but didn't always succeed at keeping her nose out of other people's business. Especially mine. I didn't know if it was a small-town thing or a Bella thing, but either way, in this case, I was grateful.

"I felt the same way when Seraphina said she'd see you later for a date or something. Honestly, I thought things were rekindling between you two," I said softly.

Finn sighed. "I can see why you'd think that, but nothing could be further from the truth. She wanted to meet up for breakfast and have a talk. She suggested we go to our favorite diner, and I agreed. It was better than having a private conversation that had every possibility of becoming emotionally charged in the middle of the sidewalk or, worse, in my shop during working hours when a customer could've walked in at any time."

A blush crept up my cheeks. "If only I'd just talked to you, none of this would've happened."

"And I could've talked to you just as easily," Finn said, reassuringly. "I guess things aren't always what they seem at first glance, are they? Me and Seraphina. You and Gabriel."

I smiled softly, the last vestiges of the hurt I'd been feeling crumbling away. But as I did, a flicker of guilt surfaced, mingling with the confusion still lingering from Gabriel's unexpected kiss on the cheek. "I think that about sums it up," I said, though I wasn't entirely sure it did.

Finn reached out and brushed a loose strand of hair away from my forehead. "I'd really like to give this another try, if you're up for it. But this time with open lines of communication."

"I—"

Bella appeared at that moment with Alex in tow, cutting off whatever I was about to say, which was good because I hadn't quite figured it out yet.

"Alex says the wind is dying down. The blizzard should end soon," Bella said, in a rush.

"Maybe that means we can finally get out of here or the police can get in and sort this out," Finn responded, glancing toward the windows with a mix of hope and concern.

Bella and I shared a quick look, but I shook my head. We didn't have time to explain everything to Finn. It was better to keep the rest of the plan under wraps for now.

Before anyone could say more, Vivienne stepped up onto the small stage, her voice commanding attention. I pressed a finger to my lips and gave Bella a brief nod before hurrying to join Gabriel.

It was showtime.

The Stage is Set

I FIDGETED NEXT TO Gabriel beside the stage as Vivienne caught the attention of the crowd. Isadora and Lucas stood by us, smiling at the crowd and playing their roles as the dutiful Silverthorne siblings perfectly.

"Any luck?" I whispered to Gabriel. He shook his head slightly. I sighed. It had been too much to hope for that they would've uncovered the jewels. "Okay then, on to the next part of the plan."

Gabriel squeezed my hand. "Show time," he whispered to me. "Are you ready?"

I drew in a deep breath and nodded. "Let's catch some thieves."

Vivienne spoke loudly from the stage. "Good evening, ladies and gentlemen. I know this evening hasn't gone the way any of us had planned, but we have just been informed that the party responsible for tonight's theft has been apprehended." A cheer and a smattering of applause met her words. She held up a hand for quiet before continuing. "The good news doesn't end there. According to my sources, the tempest outside is nearing its end, and soon, we shall bid it adieu!"

A louder cheer met these words, and Vivienne had to wait longer for the crowd to quiet this time. I fidgeted with my necklace, feeling as if my smile was turning more forced and plastic by the moment.

"My staff is busy clearing the drive as we speak, and I've already been in touch with the town authorities who assure me snowplows are on the way. Thank you all for your resilience and grace this evening. If I had to be unexpectedly snowbound, I couldn't think of a more charming group of people with whom to be trapped." A chuckle rolled around the room. "While we wait for the last of the snow to clear, it is my pleasure to welcome back to the stage, the enchanting Mystique!"

Vivienne led the round of applause as Mystique strode out onto the stage, her smile as bright as the sparkling sequins on her costume. She looked much better than the last time I'd seen her. I was glad her recovery had been relatively quick.

"Thank you for that kind reintroduction, Vivienne, and, although we have nothing left to fear from the thief who hijacked my show, I promise not to turn off the lights," Mystique said with a grin and wink towards the audience. She raised her arms and the lights suddenly got brighter.

Everyone laughed and whispered to their neighbors. Not me. I toyed with my necklace as I smiled out at the crowd. Partly, it was a nervous fidget. The other part was intentionally trying to draw attention to the now visible necklace. If the thieves were out there in the crowd, they'd have to be blind to not notice the stunning necklace now on full display. After all, it was the only piece of jewelry in the room at the moment.

Mystique stepped forward, easily commanding the attention of the guests with the seasoned skill of a professional performer. Her face was still a little pale, but she didn't let the earlier events of the evening affect her performance. "Now, ladies and gentlemen, please join me in showing some gratitude for the Silverthorne family's warmth and generosity this evening. I've never been better taken care of during a snowstorm in all my days. As a little 'thank you,' I've set up special front row seats for you. I hope you enjoy the show," Mystique said, gesturing towards some chairs set up to the side of the stage.

I moved with the Silverthornes towards the indicated seats, but out of the corner of my eye, I saw Gabriel slip out of the ballroom. So far, my plan was going perfectly.

As the audience began to settle, Mystique's gaze swept the room theatrically. "But before we begin, I think we need a volunteer," she announced. She made a show of scanning the crowd, her eyes appearing to land on me at random. "Ah, the lovely young lady in the front, why don't you join me up here on stage?" I pretended to hesitate, glancing around as if shy. "It looks as if she needs some encouragement. Come on, ladies and gentlemen, let's give her a round of applause!"

Mystique's smile widened as I joined her on stage. "Ladies and gentlemen, watch closely, for this trick is all about precision and timing," she announced, raising an eyebrow at me. I smiled nervously, playing along.

She pulled out a deck of cards, shuffling them with impressive speed before holding them out to me. "Pick a card, any card," she said with a flourish. I hesitated before drawing a card from the middle of the deck. Mystique nodded approvingly.

"Now, don't show it to me, but hold it up for everyone else to see," she instructed. I turned the card to the audience, who murmured in approval. Mystique then produced a small, golden silk pouch from her sleeve.

"Place your card inside the pouch," she said, holding it open. I slid the card into the pouch, and she gave it a quick shake. "And now, for the magic touch..." She paused dramatically before tapping the pouch three times.

When she opened it again, a cloud of glittery dust exploded from the pouch, surrounding us in a sparkling mist. I instinctively coughed and blinked, trying to clear the glitter from my face and hair.

Mystique gasped, feigning surprise. "Oh dear, it seems the magic was a little too strong!" She glanced at me with a sheepish smile. "Let's give our brave volunteer a round of applause while she freshens up!"

The audience laughed and clapped as I waved, still brushing glitter off my clothes. With a smile, I took the opportunity to step off the stage, glittering slightly, but with the perfect excuse to slip away alone. Which was exactly what I wanted. My exit couldn't have been any more public. Now to see if the thieves would take the bait.

The lighting in the hall seemed dim to my eyes after the brightness of the ballroom. So much so that I nearly missed Bella completely. She silently waved from behind a large potted plant and shot me a thumbs up. I nodded tightly back at her just before Gabriel appeared and wove an illusion spell over her hiding place, obscuring her from sight.

Together, we turned and glided the opposite way down the hall to where Alex hid in an alcove behind a large, carved statue. Gabriel did the same illusion trick, rendering him basically invisible to any thieves who might be pursuing us.

With the next part of our plan firmly in place, Gabriel leaned down, his breath warm against my ear. "You've got a little glitter just here," he murmured, brushing his fingers against my cheek. The warmth of his touch made my heart flutter like a humming-bird, despite my best efforts to concentrate.

Focus, Harper! I mentally chastised myself. "Umm, yeah. A magic trick went haywire. Is there anywhere I could freshen up?" Was it just me, or did my voice sound too loud in the empty hall? Lying really wasn't my strong suit. My dad always said honesty was the best policy, but right now, all I wanted was the ability to act convincingly—or at least not blush every time Gabriel so much as looked at me.

"I'd be happy to assist," Gabriel said smoothly, leading me down the hall towards the library.

We stopped outside the library doors, and Gabriel turned to me, concern softening his usual sharp expression. "You okay?" he asked softly, his eyes scanning my face. "That glitter explosion didn't hurt you, did it?"

I shook my head, trying to ignore the way his proximity made it hard to think straight. "No, I'm fine. Just... a little sparkly."

He chuckled, a low sound that sent another shiver down my spine. "More than a little. Here," he said, reaching up to brush more glitter from my collarbone gently. His touch lingered for just a moment too long, and I felt my cheeks heat up again.

"Thanks," I muttered, looking away to hide my embarrassment. But when I glanced back, Gabriel was still watching me, a small, knowing smile playing on his lips.

"Anytime," he said softly.

"Think we gave them enough time to notice where we went?"

"I believe so," Gabriel murmured before stepping back and pushing open the library doors.

As we stepped into the grand library, I turned to take in the floor to ceiling bookshelves. This was exactly the type of room I'd love to have in my own home someday. I guess, in a way, I did already, what with living above Spellbooks.

Gabriel quirked an eyebrow, a smirk playing on his lips. "You're still sparkling," he noted, a shower of glitter falling from my skirts as I turned.

I laughed softly, looking down at the shimmering specks on the floor. "Occupational hazard of being a magician's assistant, I guess."

"Wait here," he said, his eyes twinkling. "Let me find something to help you clean up." He disappeared through a side door, leaving me alone amidst towering bookshelves and antique furnishings. The room was bathed in a warm, golden light, the scent of aged paper and polished wood filling the air.

My gaze was immediately drawn to the large shield adorning one wall. At its heart was a silver thorn bush set against a field of deep green. Above the bush, a golden crown glittered, while two fierce wolves stood sentinel on either side. Below, a banner carried the family motto in elegant script: Strength in Unity. Intricate details wove through the crest, subtle symbols hinting at the family's magical heritage. I couldn't help but marvel at the craftsmanship, each element likely laden with history and meaning.

Lost in contemplation, I almost didn't hear Gabriel's footsteps as he returned, a soft towel and a bowl of water in his hands. "Find something interesting?" he asked, following my gaze.

"If I haven't said it before, this room is incredible," I replied.

Gabriel smiled in acknowledgement. "It's one of my favorite rooms in the entire manor," he said, setting the bowl of water on a nearby table before handing me the towel. "Here, you might want to start getting some of that glitter off. Though I should warn you, I don't think it's going to come out of your hair without some dedicated scrubbing."

I took the towel with a grateful smile, dabbing it in the water before starting to wipe away the glitter clinging to my face and arms. "Great," I sighed dramatically. "Glitter is like the gift that keeps on giving. I should've thought about that before volunteering."

He chuckled, watching me with a glint of amusement in his eyes. "Something tells me that wouldn't have stopped you." He pulled a small tin from his pocket. "Here, I thought this might help," he said, opening it to reveal a soothing salve. "For your neck."

Surprised, I paused in my cleaning to glance at him. "Thanks," I whispered as he dipped his fingers into the salve. He gently applied it to the tender skin on my neck, the salve cool and soothing. The warmth of his fingers on my throat sent a shiver through me, and I found myself leaning into his hand.

"You don't have to do this, you know. We can just take whoever walks through that door next into custody," he murmured as he carefully applied the soothing salve.

"And tip our hand by arresting a book lover? No one should be detained because they enjoy a library," I whispered back.

"I'm just saying, it's an option. I don't want to see anything bad happen to you," Gabriel said, his voice going a little husky at the end.

"It won't. Not with you around," I responded before I really thought about the words coming out of my mouth. But there they were, hovering in the air between us.

His gaze softened as he met my eyes, something unspoken passing between us. Slowly, he leaned in and pressed a gentle kiss just below my ear, where the bruise ended. His lips were warm and soft, and the kiss was light, almost a question.

My breath caught as his hand slid to the small of my back, drawing me a fraction closer. "You know," he murmured against my skin, "I'd never let anything happen to you."

I nodded, unable to find my voice as his lips brushed my cheek, then hovered near mine. A faint buzzing noise broke the moment. Gabriel leaned his forehead against mine, a regretful smile tugging at his lips. "That's the signal," he breathed. "Are you ready?"

I nodded, my heart still fluttering, but now with a sense of determination. The next part of the plan relied solely on me. It was time to see if I could outsmart a thief.

A man in a dark jacket stumbled into the library, an empty champagne flute in his hand, humming a pitchy rendition of "Jingle Bells." We looked up from our private moment in feigned astonishment.

The man looked around in surprise, swaying slightly at the movement. Other than the slightly too big tux, which was likely a rental, nothing about him stood out, except perhaps the fact that he seemed to have overindulged in the Silverthorne's liquid hospitality if the empty champagne glass in his hand was any indication.

"Oh. Pardon me," the man said, slurring slightly. He raised a hand in apology as he looked around the room seemingly in shock. "I don't think this is where I'm meant to be. Could you point me in the restroom of the direction?"

I felt Gabriel sigh in frustration. Not a thief, just an inebriated guest needing to relieve himself. But this man stumbling into the middle of our plan could scare the thief away. We needed to get rid of him. Fast.

Gabriel must've come to the same conclusion. "Of course," he said smoothly, brushing past the man and heading toward the door. "An easy mistake to make. It's just at the end of the hall—"

As Gabriel laid his hand on the door, the other man spun, balling up a fist and swinging at Gabriel's unprotected back.

"Gabriel!" I shouted, barely getting the word out before the man's fist hit home. The last thing I saw was Gabriel crumpling to the floor of the library. Then everything went black.

Lights Out

BEFORE I COULD MAKE my body follow what my mind was screaming at it to do, there was a rustle in the shadows, and something yanked forcefully on the necklace around my throat, dragging me to the side like a dog on a leash.

"Take. It. Off!" a woman's voice grunted. I recognized it as the same voice I'd heard in the study. So, the thieves *had* taken the bait after all. But now the situation was spiraling out of control. I couldn't let them take the necklace. Especially without catching a glimpse of both the woman and her accomplice who'd attacked Gabriel. Gabriel! Was he okay? How—

The woman wrenched the necklace to the side, throwing me off balance and bruising my already tender throat.

"Oy! Get over here and help me already!" the woman hissed.

I scrabbled at the silver collar that was now strangling me. There was no way I was letting them get away with this. But what could I do? I had only one option. I clamped down hard with my magic on the clasp of the serpent necklace.

Just as I did so, I felt another presence approach out of the darkness, and someone else jerked at the necklace. I tried to tug the silver noose, which was cutting off my air supply, away from my throat and to suck in a breath around the new bruising pain as the man fought with the clasp. Unsurprisingly, it didn't open.

He grunted in frustration and shoved me to the floor. "Leave her. You heard the old bird. The snow is breaking. Let's get the jewels and get out of here." I pulled the necklace away from my abused throat, gasping in great, unobstructed breaths of sweet air.

"I'm not leaving without that necklace," the woman growled softly. "We double our money if we can get that thing off her."

"It isn't coming off. I say we cut our losses and run before we get caught," the man argued.

I inched away from the angry voices, doing my best to stay silent but move swiftly. Both of which were hard to do in a ball-gown.

"And this is why you aren't the brains of the operation. Grab her. We can figure out how to get the necklace off later," the woman snarled.

"You're talking kidnapping? Stealing jewels from rich snobs is one thing, but taking a girl?"

"It's not the girl, it's the necklace. And think of the money! Grab her, and let's get out of here," the woman commanded shrilly.

The next thing I knew, powerful arms were lifting me up, cradling me like I was a baby. I struggled, fighting for all I was worth, but the skirts of the gown tangled around my legs, and my fists seemed to bounce off pure muscle with little to no effect. I screamed, hoping someone would hear me and come to my rescue.

"Shut her up!" the woman hissed.

I opened my mouth to scream again, only to have some sort of fabric stuffed between my lips before I could utter another sound. Maybe it was his pocket square or a handkerchief. Perhaps it was standard operating procedure for thieves to come equipped with a gag. I didn't know. That hadn't ever been part of my educational background. As I struggled silently, the man pinned my arms to my sides and tossed me over his shoulder as easily as if I'd been a sack full of feathers, muttering all the while about how this was a stupid idea.

I finally worked the gag free, spitting it out to the side and drawing a deep breath to scream my head off when a blast of freezing wind hit me, robbing me of any air and turning my scream into a whimper that blew away in a swirl of snow. Goosebumps prickled all over my exposed skin as the man dashed outside, bouncing me on his shoulder as he ran. I fought the cold and the abuse to my diaphragm to let loose another shriek. Just before I did, I heard the door to the library's balcony slam shut. My cry for help was lost in the howling wind of the dying blizzard.

That didn't stop me. I screamed again and again, my throat raw inside and out, but I knew it was futile. No one would hear me. I was on my own against two thieves set on larceny, kidnapping, and who knew what else.

Where were Bella and Alex? They should've checked in by now. The thought that they might be caught too twisted my gut. I had to hope they were still out there, helping Gabriel.

But I couldn't wait. I needed to act—before it was too late.

The inky blackness surrounding us didn't fade one iota as I was carried kicking and screaming out of the Silverthorne manor. For all I knew, the shadows of the night helped the thief's magic. After what seemed like an eternity of being exposed to the frigid cold, but was probably less than two minutes, the wind cut off abruptly. I heard a door shut behind me, and I was unceremoniously dumped to the floor. The cold, concrete floor, by the feel of it. Where were we?

As if in answer to my unspoken question, the shadows surrounding us flickered and dropped. I blinked at the sudden bright light, everything momentarily fuzzy as my eyes struggled to adjust to the abrupt change. The surrounding shapes slowly coalesced into a recognizable scene. We were in a garage. A large one full of expensive-looking vehicles. And unheated, based on the chill. We might be out of the winter wind, but my gown was no match for the freezing temperatures. If I didn't warm up soon, the attempted kidnapping might turn into a successful murder by hypothermia.

The man in the dark suit from the library shot a surprised glare at the woman, who was hidden from my view behind a sleek, black sedan. "What are you doing?" he hissed.

"You try blacking out entire rooms three times in one evening! I'm exhausted!" she retorted, stepping into view. My breath caught—not just because I recognized her as the woman in the high-necked green dress I'd bumped into while dancing with Gabriel earlier, but because of the gun she pulled from a thigh holster and now held steadily in one hand.

And it was pointed directly at me.

The woman's eyes locked onto mine, and panic seized me. My vision tunneled on the barrel of the gun, my breath coming in short, ragged gasps. I was frozen, heart pounding so hard it drowned out everything else. Sweat prickled my skin, and for a moment, I thought I might faint. Somehow, my dad's commands during our self-defense training penetrated my rising terror, his words echoing in my mind.

"Panic is your worst enemy."

With a sharp breath, I forced myself to focus. I had to think, to act, to not let the fear take over completely. I focused, analyzing the situation the way my dad had taught me. The gun she held wasn't big—a small pistol, the kind my dad would call a Saturday night special. It was the sort of weapon meant to be easily concealed, light enough to hide under her dress without drawing attention. It was small caliber, but deadly at this close range. Her grip was steady with her finger resting on the trigger, I knew she didn't have proper training, the kind my dad had relentlessly drilled into me. One slip, one sudden movement, and she could fire by accident.

Panic tried to claw its way to the surface, but I pushed it down. I couldn't afford to lose focus now. Every muscle in my body tensed, ready to react, but I had to be careful—one wrong move, and this could all end very badly.

"Where are the jewels?" the woman in green snapped at her compatriot without looking away from me. I noticed she stopped well out of reach. She was giving me too much credit. Not only would I not make a move towards an armed aggressor, but the ballgown I wore would likely trip me long before I could lay hands on her or the gun. No, if I was going to try something, I needed to be patient, to wait for the perfect moment, just like my dad had trained me. But first, I needed to get to my feet without her thinking I was making a break for it.

"What do you mean, 'where are the jewels?' You told me to get the girl. I got the girl!" the man exclaimed, thrusting his arms towards me.

"You're supposed to be the strong one. Super-human muscles, that's your schtick, right? Surely you can manage one slip of a girl *and* the jewels," the woman sneered.

"You try rooting around under that bush one-handed while holding a girl in a ballgown, and then we'll talk. Whoever decided skirts should be that big should be shot," the man grumbled.

"Hey now, let's all calm down," I said, holding up my hands in protest.

"You, shut up," the woman said, jabbing the gun in my direction. She flicked the weapon at her partner. "You, go get the jewels. We need to get out of here before anyone notices she's gone."

"Or the police show up," the man said, heading for the door. He pulled it open, letting in another blast of freezing cold.

The woman's eyes didn't leave mine for a moment. "Stay right where you are, and don't get any ideas."

I held my hands up. "You have the gun. You're the boss. But could I please get up off the floor? This gown might look like a lot of fabric, but it's not doing much against the cold." I was proud of how calm I sounded, especially in the face of danger.

The woman's eyes narrowed, and she gestured with the gun while she took a few careful steps back, leaning her free hand against a nearby car. "Slowly. And don't make any sudden moves."

I kept my hands raised and carefully got to my feet. It was difficult to not tread on my skirts without the use of my hands, but I didn't want her to think I had a weapon somehow concealed in the voluminous dress. By the time I made it upright, my legs were thanking me for getting off the freezing floor, but my fingers were going numb.

The cold metal of the gun seemed to gleam even in the lights of the garage as the woman in green fixed her gaze on me, her voice sharp as the edge of a knife. "Enough stalling. The snake necklace — hand it over now."

Swallowing hard, I clutched at the intricate piece of jewelry at my throat, feigning struggle. Her words had given me an idea. Maybe I could stall her long enough and help would arrive. It might be a slim hope given the snow and the cold, but wasting time was the only weapon currently at my disposal. When faced with a gun, it seemed like a poor match up.

I tugged at the necklace, putting on a show. "I can't," I said, my voice laced with a concocted panic. "It's not just any necklace. It's...enchanted. A sort of Cinderella deal, you know? It won't come off until midnight, tied to my..." I hesitated, not wanting to say my magic.

"To your what?" the woman snapped.

"To my final dance. You know, just like in the story. She dances with the prince and at the stroke of midnight—"

"Her fairytale is ruined. Yeah, yeah. I know the story," she said, shaking her head. "You have *got* to be kidding me right now."

I shrugged helplessly, trying to look as sincere as possible. "I wish I were, but apparently the enchantment on this necklace is quirky but no less binding. Until the clock strikes twelve, this snake and I are inseparable."

The woman's eyes narrowed as she considered my words. I could almost see the gears turning in her mind, trying to weigh the truth of what I said. After all, they'd tried to remove the necklace twice, and each time it had stubbornly stayed in place. Now, I was the only one in the entire party left with any jewelry. I hoped she bought my story and jumped to the conclusion that I clearly had been unable to turn it back in.

Her lips curled into a mirthless smile, but I could tell she was still uncertain, not entirely convinced but unable to fully dismiss the possible truth of my story, either. "Fine. If the jewels won't come to us, we'll take the entire package. Unfortunately for you, your fairytale is ending a little sooner than you expected," she said, raising the gun.

I flinched, squeezing my eyes shut, every muscle in my body tensing as I braced for the deafening bang of the gun. My heart pounded wildly, the thought that this was it, the end, flooding my mind. An icy dread settled in my chest, paralyzing me with the realization that my clever ploy had backfired. This was it—my one-way ticket, and it was about to get punched.

Seconds ticked by, each one stretching into an eternity. The silence was unbearable, every heartbeat a reminder that I was still here, still alive.

"What are you doing?" The woman's voice cut through the suffocating fear.

I cracked one eye open, confused and still trembling, to see her looking at me with frustration, not the deadly intent I'd imagined.

"Get over here," she ordered, jerking the gun to the right. I took a couple of quick steps in her direction, just happy I didn't have any extra holes in my body. "Slowly!" she ordered.

I slowed my pace and kept my hands up as she pointed me towards a cabinet near the door. "Stand over there," the woman ordered, waving me towards the boxy Jeep. "Put your hands on the side of the car."

I did as instructed, knowing she probably wouldn't hurt me right now unless I gave her a reason to. Still, the weight of the gun aimed at me was impossible to ignore. My dad had drilled gun safety and awareness into me from a young age, and I knew one thing for certain: I didn't want to be any closer to that gun than I had to be.

I needed to lull her into a false sense of security, bide my time, and then launch a brilliant counter move—just as soon as I could think of one that wouldn't get me killed.

With one hand pointing the gun at me, she used the other to open the cabinet and rummage around in the keys neatly hanging in rows inside. With a triumphant smile, she selected a set and held them up, pressing a button. Near the end of the row of cars, one flashed and beeped. The sound echoed in the vast garage, making me jump slightly.

"There you go, Cinderella. Your pumpkin awaits," the woman said, waving the gun at me. "Move. Slowly."

I forced myself to keep walking along the line of expensive cars as a bead of cold sweat trickled down my spine, my mind racing to find a way out of this alive.

What could I use to my advantage? Was there anything I could throw at her or dodge behind? Anything that might buy me a few precious moments for help to arrive. Unfortunately, the Silverthorne's garage was too large and too well organized. Nothing useful was within reach. I blew out a short breath. What I wouldn't give for a little mess right now!

Under the sterile glow of the garage's fluorescent lights, my heart pounded like a drumbeat, each step echoing on the polished concrete floor. With ruthless efficiency, the woman guided me unerringly toward a Mercedes-Benz sedan at gunpoint. Its black paint shimmered ominously under the artificial light, a stark contrast against the white snow visible through the garage windows.

"Get in," she commanded, the edge in her voice as sharp as the winter chill outside.

I inched closer to the vehicle, my mind whirring with the possibility of escape. She beeped the fob in her hand, and the trunk gaped open like a dark maw, ready to swallow me whole.

"Really? The trunk?" I said, forcing a chuckle, trying to sound amused rather than terrified.

The woman's gaze flicked to the side door as it groaned in the wind. The brief lapse of attention gave me hope. Maybe she'd make a mistake I could capitalize on.

"In. Now," she insisted, her attention snapping back with dangerous focus. "My partner will be back any moment, and then we can get out of here. Since your necklace won't come off, you're coming with us."

As I moved, my eyes caught sight of the gun pointed at me, and a chill ran down my spine. The safety was off. That realization hit me like a punch to the gut—one careless move, and she could fire without even meaning to.

My gaze flicked toward a heavy-duty workbench just to my left. There were several tools that I could use as an impromptu weapon if only I could lay hands on one of them. But before I could act, the woman tutted, "Uh, uh, uh. Don't be an idiot. We just want the necklace. As soon as we have it, we'll set you free."

Somehow, I doubted that. I'd seen their faces and could identify them. Although, if they didn't want to add murder to their rap sheets, they could always abandon me at the side of a deserted country lane. I hesitated, my mind racing. She wanted me to believe that if I handed over the necklace, I'd walk away. But if she put me in the trunk of one of these cars, what were the chances I'd ever see the light of day again?

I glanced back at the woman. I found her unwavering gaze upon me, not a single crack in her cold demeanor as she held the gun aimed steadily at my torso. At this range, she couldn't miss.

"Get. In. The. Car." She over enunciated each word.

"Shouldn't we wait for—"

"Now. Or I'll shoot you in the leg. I don't need you mobile to get the necklace off you at midnight."

"Okay, okay. I'm getting in," I said, sitting on the edge of the empty trunk and fighting with my dress to swing my legs in. "But I'm going to freeze back here. I don't think you want my death on your head, do you?"

"Keep talking and you might convince me that I do," she growled.

I kept my hands up even as I tucked myself back into the trunk of the car. The interior smelled like rubber and new carpet, but at least it was spacious enough to hold both me and my dress. "A blanket. A jacket. Something to keep me from freezing, that's all I'm asking. Look there. Behind you. There's a jacket hanging right on the wall," I said, keeping my voice calm even while my stomach churned and my mind whirled. How was I going to get out of this one?

"Get in the car," the woman said, taking a couple of steps backwards and patting blindly at the wall as she kept her eyes on me until she found the jacket.

She was careful. Too careful. And her partner was coming back at any minute. I had to act. Now. But what could I do against a gun? A sudden thought occurred to me. I'd have to act fast when the time came, but it might be my only chance.

The woman tugged the jacket free of its hook and tossed it at me. I used the movement to quickly shift my position in the trunk, putting my hand against the exposed metal and channeling my magic with the extra boost from the serpent necklace. Under the force of my magic, the hinges on the trunk essentially froze in place. She'd be hard pressed to keep me in here and drive the car at the same time.

"There. Now keep your head down and shut up," the woman said, moving forward to slam the trunk closed. Except it didn't move, causing her to lean forward and lose her balance. She shouted as her arm jarred painfully against the unexpectedly rigid trunk lid.

The trunk lid refused to budge. I knew this was my moment. My heart hammered against my ribcage, and I was ready. The second the woman stepped back, lowering the gun even slightly, I lunged, my cumbersome dress slowing me down but not enough to stop me.

The gun swung towards me, her finger tightening on the trigger. An icy wave of terror washed over me, but I shoved it to the side, focusing everything on what I had to do. In the blink of an eye, I thrust my hand forward, instincts and training guiding my magic. A rush of energy flowed from me, merging seamlessly with the magic of the serpent necklace.

I visualized the safety on the gun, knowing exactly where it was, and with a surge of my will, the safety clicked into place. The firing mechanism froze, rendering the gun useless just as her finger pulled the trigger.

The woman's eyes widened in shock, but she didn't have time to react. Using my magic, now effortlessly enhanced by the necklace, I yanked the gun from her grasp. Her mouth gaped open as the gun trembled, then jerked towards me, sliding out of her hand as easily as pearls dripping off a broken chain. I caught it.

The grip of the gun hit my palm with a satisfactory slap, the weight of it solid and reassuring in my hand. Now the tables had turned. I pointed it at the thief. "My turn. Back up," I said.

Her eyes went wide in surprise and then a sneer contorted her face as she took a couple of steps back to allow me to get out of the trunk. I kicked my legs free of my skirts and swung them back over the edge without taking the gun off her.

"Nice trick," she spat, her eyes glinting with malice. "But you can't bluff your way out of this."

With that, she spun on her heel, her dress flaring out in a swirl of green silk. Her intentions were clear as she dashed for the workbench and the heavy wrenches, mirroring my previous idea of escape.

But I knew something she didn't, and I wasn't done yet. The magic still hummed through my veins, potent and responsive. I concentrated, releasing the enchantment on the gun's safety and switching it back to the firing position. The satisfying click of the safety disengaging was almost lost in the echo of her frantic search for another weapon and my hammering heartbeat.

The woman's hand was inches from the nearest wrench when the sharp crack of the gun echoed off the high ceilings. I hadn't aimed to hit, just to halt. The bullet buried itself into the wall above her head with a shower of plaster and paint. She froze, her hand hovering over the cold metal of the tool.

"That was a warning. The next one will go in your leg," I said.

"You wouldn't," the woman said, turning her head slightly over her shoulder.

"My dad is a master sergeant in the United States Army. He trained me to shoot. Believe me when I say not only *could* I shoot you right now, but I *will* if you give me reason. I'll also probably enjoy it after what you just tried to pull," I said, finally working my way completely out of the trunk and bracing my grip with my other hand.

"Okay. No need to be feisty. Tell you what, why don't we cut you in on a share of the jewels. Call this all a misunderstanding. You let us go, and you get paid. Handsomely," the woman said, carefully turning to face me with her hands raised.

"How about this instead? You get in the trunk, and I don't shoot. That sounds fair to me."

"You won't—"

I aimed over her head and pulled the trigger again. She flinched and covered her ears.

"Now," I said, as the echoes from the gunshot died away.

The woman's face was stark white as she nodded, and the cold dullness of defeat was in her eyes as she shuffled past me. I backed up to give her plenty of room, keeping my two-handed grip on the gun rock steady. Her previous determination seeped out of her with every step towards the trunk. Without a word, she clambered awkwardly inside, the long fabric of her dress whispering against the car's luxurious interior. I watched, the gun still in my hand, an anchor grounding me in the reality of the danger just narrowly averted. If I got out of this, I needed to call my dad and thank him for the endless self-defense drills he made me do on base when I was growing up.

But for now, I had to focus on the thief in the trunk.

I stepped to the side of the car, keeping the gun trained on the woman as I dissolved the spell I'd laid on the hinges. Under my direction, the trunk closed slowly and seemingly of its own accord, capturing the woman who had threatened to shoot me mere moments ago. With an extra surge of power, I froze up the mechanisms inside the emergency release, effectively locking her inside. A deep, shaky breath escaped me, and I allowed myself a sigh of relief. It hung visibly in the frigid air of the garage, a misty testament that I was not out of danger yet. Her partner could return at any moment and, despite everything else, I still needed to ward off the cold before I froze. My metal magic wouldn't help me with that.

The snick of a doorknob turning, and a latch releasing caught my attention. My head snapped up, and I crouched by the side of the car in a rustle of fabric. My heart hammered in my chest, and my hands felt sweaty on the gun's grip as the door swung open, revealing a man's silhouette in the entrance. Her partner! I set my feet like my dad had trained me and lifted the gun, preparing to summon my magic once more if necessary. I just hoped that luck was still on my side.

Twists in the Thicket

Gabriel burst into the garage, his suit coat flapping wildly as he ran, a mix of fear and determination etched on his face. His eyes swept the brightly lit garage urgently. As soon as I saw it was him, I rose from my crouch.

"Over here!" I called, flipping the safety on and lowering the gun while waving with my free hand.

He was at my side in an instant, his hands frantically searching for injuries that weren't there. Relief flooded his features when he found none. Without warning, he pulled me close and kissed me. It was fierce, a silent promise mixed with dread for what might have been. I'd wondered if the moment we shared in the library had been mere pretense. This one kiss chased away any doubts. His arms enveloped me, a protective shield against the chaos of the night, as we both trembled with the aftershock of fear and adrenaline.

"How did you know where to find me?" I finally asked, my voice muffled against the warmth of his coat.

"When that goon hit me, I was down, but not out," Gabriel explained, pulling back to look into my eyes. "At least, not totally. I came to as he re-entered the library, but the thug didn't expect me to fight back. Lucas showed up as soon as he heard me shout for help, and together we took care of the thief before he could cause more trouble."

"Where is he now? Is everyone else safe?" I asked in a rush.

"Don't worry. Between Lucas and my mother, things are firmly under control. Bella wanted to come out here with me, and I had to convince her I was better equipped to handle this. She'll be glad to know you're safe. Oh, and Sheriff Jackson is on the way."

"That's good," I said with a sigh, a shiver rippling through me at just how close things had come for all of us. I asked again. "How did you know where to find me?"

His lips curled into a wry smile. "They might have been able to black out the lights, but hubris was their downfall. The snow's letting up, and the winds are calming."

"And it's cold," I said, with a shiver. "What's that got to do with anything?" Gabriel shrugged out of his coat and wrapped it around my bare shoulders. I smiled up at him, grateful for the warmth.

"They couldn't shadow magic their way out of leaving footprints. Once the guy who ambushed me was tied up, I just followed his trail back here. Then I heard the gunshots." His eyes darkened with the gravity of what he'd thought those sounds had signified. "I'm just glad I got here when I did. Where's the other one?"

With a flourish, I used the gun to gesture towards the Mercedes trunk. "All packed and ready for travel," I said, a hint of pride in my voice. "Straight to jail."

With practiced ease, I dropped the magazine, letting it clatter onto the work bench. I pulled back the slide, ejecting the round from the chamber, and caught it in midair before placing it next to the magazine. My hands moved swiftly, almost automatically, as I field stripped the gun in a matter of seconds, laying out each piece in a neat row. Satisfied, I scooped up the magazine and rounds, planning to hand them over to the police later, but for now, the gun was nothing more than a harmless collection of parts.

Gabriel's astonished gaze followed my hands, and a low whistle escaped him, an unspoken compliment. I couldn't resist a small smile as he nodded at me, his expression a mixture of awe and approval. In that moment, I felt a sense of triumph that I hadn't expected, especially considering my uncertainty when the evening started. It felt...good. Surprisingly so.

My relief ebbed as I remembered the reason for the evening's turmoil. "What about the jewels? Did you get them?" I asked.

He shook his head, a furrow forming on his brow. "What are you talking about? There were no jewels. That guy, he came back to finish what he started with me."

"No, you don't understand," I countered quickly. "He returned to grab the jewels, then they were planning to take both the gems and me in hopes of getting the serpent necklace and doubling their score."

Gabriel's eyes darkened as the implication settled in, but before he could speak, a sudden shout rang out.

"Police! Drop your weapons!"

The command echoed through the garage, sending a jolt of panic through me. Two familiar officers burst into the space; their service weapons aimed at us. Instinctively, Gabriel and I raised our hands, fear tightening my chest.

"Johanna! Reggie!" I recognized them, but their focus was razor sharp as they swept the room for threats.

"Hands where we can see them!" Reggie ordered, his gaze darting around. The normally affable officer looked almost fierce.

"It's us!" I called out, voice trembling. "Harper Sullivan and Gabriel Silverthorne!"

Their eyes locked on us, recognition flashing as they rushed over, still cautious but lowering their weapons when they realized we were alone.

"Where's the suspect?" Johanna demanded.

"She's in the trunk of the Mercedes. We got her. Or rather, Harper did," Gabriel's voice was steady despite the adrenaline undoubtedly coursing through him at the sight of armed police.

Officer Johanna immediately took control, waving us back as she moved to confiscate the thief's weapon. Her eyes flicked to the expertly disassembled gun on the workbench, and she gave me a subtle nod of appreciation.

"Your work?" she asked.

"Yeah."

"No lost cats this time?" she said, a hint of a smile playing on her lips.

"Haven't you heard? There's never a cat," I replied, matching her grin.

She nodded approvingly, then moved to the side, ordering Officer Reggie to open the trunk while she kept her own gun steadily aimed at it. I surreptitiously removed the magical freeze I'd placed on the release so Reggie could open it.

The following minutes unfolded with chaotic precision under the direction of a competent police force. Well, an adept police force and Officer Reggie would probably be more accurate. He was a kind soul, known for his genial demeanor and sometimes scatterbrained approach to law enforcement. The friendly police officer looked distinctly out of place in the middle of the crisis and was more than happy when first Officer Johanna and then Sheriff Jackson took the lead. I got the feeling Reggie was probably more comfortable with parade duty than apprehending criminals, the former probably being ninety percent of his job in Havenwood with the other tenth focused on writing parking tickets.

The chaos of the scene blurred together and faded into the background as Gabriel and I were led out of the garage, the biting cold a sharp contrast to the adrenaline still coursing through my veins. The snow had slowed to a gentle fall, but it was thick enough that the world around us felt muted, almost surreal.

Outside, the atmosphere around me was overwhelming—flashing lights, the shouts of officers and paramedics, and the distant hum of a gathering crowd. My ears buzzed with the overlapping voices—the low rumble of Johanna's commands as she cuffed the thief, the sharp snap of Reggie's radio as he secured the area. A nearby paramedic spoke to Gabriel and me, his words almost lost in the din as he guided us toward the manor.

The paramedics had set up shop in a small building adjacent to the main house and connected by a single long corridor. This guest house was elegantly furnished but cold, the chill of the night seeping through its walls. Gabriel and I were ushered into the main room and guided to a pair of plush chairs. I shivered, huddling deeper into Gabriel's coat. It was better than my ballgown, but still couldn't combat the freezing weather. Gabriel noticed and immediately grabbed a thick, soft blanket from the back of the couch, wrapping it around my shoulders. I managed a brief smile of thanks as warmth slowly worked its way back into my body.

The care givers worked quickly, checking our vitals and asking routine questions, though my mind struggled to focus on their words. Through an open door, I could see Sheriff Jackson overseeing the two suspects being similarly examined in another room, both handcuffed. I was relieved the competent and unflappable sheriff was here. He was exactly the person you wanted in charge during a crisis. With him on the case, I felt a little more assured that justice would be served.

But even as the adrenaline ebbed, a gnawing feeling settled in my gut. This wasn't over. Not yet. Where were the jewels? Had someone found them?

Driven by the need for answers, I stood suddenly, moving towards the open door. "Sheriff, have you found the jewels?" I asked, my voice betraying the urgency I felt.

Sheriff Jackson glanced at me, his expression serious. "No, not yet," he replied, his tone steady but clearly not wanting to continue the discussion.

Ignoring the subtle cue, I pressed on, desperate for more information. "What about—"

Before I could finish, Sheriff Jackson gently but firmly cut me off. "I know this must all be a terrible end to your evening, but we need an official statement. I'll send Officer Reggie over right away," he said. His eyes softened minutely, but his message was clear as he closed the door, effectively shutting down the conversation.

Just before the door clicked shut, I caught sight of the woman in the green dress. She was looking directly at me, a smirk playing on her lips—an open challenge. She might have been caught, but the defiance in her eyes was unmistakable. Why did she look so confident?

That unsettling question lingered in my mind as I returned to Gabriel. He took my hand, squeezing it gently and offering silent support while we waited for Officer Reggie. It didn't take long. The friendly policeman hurried over, giving us both a sheepish grin as he entered the guesthouse.

"Hi Harper, good to see you again," Reggie said, shaking my hand. "Awful circumstances though. I'm so sorry you had to go through that. And during your first Silverthorne Ball, too! You really aren't having the best luck settling into Havenwood."

Gabriel shot me a questioning look, but I didn't want to get sidetracked by either my first few days in Havenwood or by what had happened over Halloween. Besides, I was pretty sure Officer Reggie only knew the details about the former, and I'd prefer to keep it that way. Instead, I explained what had happened tonight as clearly and succinctly as possible. As I spoke, I noticed Gabriel watching me closely, his gaze filled with a mix of admiration and respect. It was clear he was impressed by how I handled everything, but even as I recounted the events, a nagging feeling persisted—like there was something crucial I was overlooking.

Reggie interrupted occasionally, asking questions for clarification as he furiously scribbled in his notebook. I answered all of them, but that feeling of something missing kept gnawing at me. Finally, I ended with some questions of my own.

"What happens now? Have they confessed? Admitted where the jewels are?"

Reggie opened his mouth, but it was clear he hadn't really thought the answer through. "Well, uh, we're, you know, still working on it... still piecing things together," he stammered, his eyes flicking nervously to Gabriel and then back to me. "These things, they take time... you know, standard procedure..."

I could tell he was stalling, trying to come up with something that sounded official. But his hesitance only made that nagging doubt in my mind sharper, more urgent. There was something I was missing. I just knew it.

I stood up abruptly, cutting off whatever half-formed excuse Reggie was about to offer. Both he and Gabriel looked startled, though Gabriel recovered quickly.

"Harper?" Gabriel's concern flickered, but he didn't try to stop me. Instead, he simply stood as well, his presence solid and reassuring. "What is it?"

"There's something I'm missing," I murmured, more to myself than to them. "I need to retrace my steps."

Without hesitation, Gabriel nodded. "Let's go."

I shot him a grateful smile and wrapped the blanket more tightly around my shoulders to brave the winter chill once more.

My resolve hardened as I turned and headed across the freshly fallen snow toward the garage, a sense of urgency propelling me forward. Gabriel immediately fell in step beside me, his presence reassuring and steady. Behind us, I could hear Reggie's nervous voice.

"Uh, Harper... Maybe we should wait for the sheriff?" Reggie suggested, wringing his hands. "We really shouldn't go back in the garage without him or Officer Johanna, you know... protocol? Securing the crime scene is what we official police call it."

I didn't break stride, my focus unwavering. "Reggie, I need to see something. I promise we won't mess with anything."

Officer Reggie hesitated, glancing back at the guesthouse where Sheriff Jackson and Johanna were likely still dealing with the jewel thieves. I could tell he was weighing his options. If either of them were here, there's no way he'd bend the rules. But they weren't, and my determination must have been undisputable.

Finally, with a resigned sigh, he gave in. "Okay, okay... but just a quick look, alright?"

The three of us slipped back into the garage, the cold air inside a stark reminder of what had happened here so recently. Gabriel stayed close to me, his support unspoken but undeniable. I was thankful he was there, and an unexpected swell of emotion hit me upon re-entering the garage. I'd gotten lucky to escape relatively unharmed, there was no doubt.

"What do you need?" Gabriel asked gently, his voice low and calming.

I closed my eyes, taking a deep breath as I tried to replay everything in my mind. Opening my eyes, I pointed. "He carried me in and dumped me on the floor... over there." I walked over to the spot, my memory guiding my steps. "The woman pulled the gun... they talked... she wasn't very nice to him. She said he should've been able to manage both me and the jewels because he was super strong."

At those words, I heard Reggie's breath catch. "Super strong? As in magic?" he echoed, his voice barely a whisper.

I nodded. "He didn't have any difficulty hauling me around against my will."

"We didn't know he was a paranormal..." Officer Reggie trailed off as he glanced around the garage, his expression shifting to something far more serious. "Don't touch anything!" he warned, before rushing off, no doubt to inform the sheriff of this new revelation.

Gabriel gently touched my arm, bringing me back to the present. "What else, Harper? Walk me through it. What happened next?"

I furrowed my brow, trying to concentrate and figure out what was niggling at me. "He said he couldn't carry me and root around under a bush at the same time..." My eyes widened as the pieces clicked into place. "Bushes! They must've hidden the jewels under the bushes!"

Without another word, we rushed outside, the excitement between us palpable. The cold barely registered as we searched the area around the garage, our breath clouding in the frosty air. Gabriel and I worked together, our hands brushing against icy branches as we scoured the bushes for anything out of place.

We had no luck with the bushes here, so we rounded the corner, hoping to find something—anything—on the other side.

As we continued our search, I heard Reggie approach us again, his expression a mix of relief and concern.

"They've got him in magically enhanced restraints now," the officer said, slightly out of breath. "He didn't look too pleased about that... But, uh, what are you two doing out here?"

I glanced up from where I was inspecting a dense shrubbery. "I thought the jewels might be under a bush. The man mentioned something about not being able to root around under a bush while carrying me."

Officer Reggie looked around nervously, his eyes darting from the bushes to the trampled snow beneath our feet. "I'm worried you might cover up a clue with all these footprints," he said, his voice rising slightly. "I mean, what if we miss something important?"

Gabriel stepped back, surveying the area with a thoughtful expression. "You're right to be concerned about the footprints, Reggie," he said. "But that's the thing—there aren't any footprints by the bushes. If someone had buried something here recently, we should see signs of it in the snow. But there's nothing."

Reggie scratched his head, clearly puzzled. "Yeah, that's true... And I don't get how anyone would bury anything out here anyway. The ground's probably been frozen solid for weeks."

I frowned, processing the information. They were both right—the lack of footprints and the frozen ground didn't make this a logical hiding place, but I knew what I'd heard. If the jewels weren't under a bush, then where could they be? The initial excitement of our anticipated discovery waned, replaced by a renewed sense of urgency. There had to be another clue, something we were missing.

Gabriel noticed my hesitation and gave me a reassuring nod. "We'll figure it out, Harper. There's got to be something we're overlooking."

Reggie looked between us, pushing his hat back and scratching his head. "So, if they didn't bury the jewels... then where are they?"

My mind raced, trying to connect the dots. There had to be an answer, something we hadn't considered yet. I was determined to find it before the trail went cold—literally and figuratively. But the words kept echoing in my mind like they were on a loop. "He said something about a bush," I muttered, frustration creeping into my voice. "I know it."

Reggie glanced around, frowning. "Could you have misheard? Maybe it wasn't a bush at all. Maybe it was push or, ooh! I know! How about a tush? Wait, that doesn't make sense, that would mean the jewels are in..." he trailed off.

I shook my head firmly. "No way. He definitely said bush."

Gabriel's brow furrowed in thought. "Well, what if it's not a real bush? Or what if it is, but it's inside, and maybe he's not exactly a plant expert? Some of those big potted plants could easily pass for bushes to someone who's not well-versed in the art of horticulture."

I looked at him, a spark of hope lighting in my chest. "We should go search those."

We immediately started tramping through the snow towards the manor, the friendly police officer trailing along behind us. Reggie piped up suddenly. "You know, if it were me, I'd definitely choose an inside hiding place over outside, especially in this weather. And I'd want something to protect the stolen jewels. A bush isn't very safe, but if it was the only thing, I'd make sure it had thorns or was a Venus flytrap or something." He sucked in a breath. "Or maybe it was on fire? Or what if it was guarded by a dragon?"

Gabriel and I exchanged an amused glance. "I hate to break it to you, but we don't have any pet dragons," Gabriel said kindly.

Reggie continued, clearly caught up in his own musings. "And a burning bush would likely draw all sorts of attention, wouldn't it?"

"Yeah, Reggie, it would," Gabriel said.

"Wait a second," I said as we neared the manor. "They wouldn't have just stuck it in any old potted plant. Reggie is right. They'd need something distinctive enough to recognize it, but with a certain level of protection, wouldn't they?"

"And why was he heading back into the library? I thought he was coming back to finish me, but if you say he was looking for the jewels..." Gabriel trailed off.

Gabriel and I both gasped, our eyes locking in sudden understanding. The next words tumbled out of our mouths in excited unison.

"I know where the treasure is!"

Clutching the blanket tightly around my shoulders, I dashed for the manor with Gabriel hot on my heels, and the confused Officer Reggie trailing behind us both.

Initial Suspects

I RACED DOWN THE hall past Lucas and Isadora, who were chatting nervously. Their questions followed me, but I let Gabriel respond to them. I was focused on one thing—the answer. By the time I pushed open the library door, Bella and Alex had somehow joined the others trailing in my wake. Their curiosity swirled behind me as my eyes locked on the large metal shield painted with the Silverthorne crest hanging on the wall.

I spun around, skirts flaring dramatically and pointed up at the ornate symbol. "The jewels are hidden behind the crest!"

Understanding dawned on Officer Reggie's face. "The bush! It was a symbol, not a real shrubbery. You think the jewels are really there?"

I nodded emphatically. Bella and Alex exchanged glances, shrugged, and nodded. "Let's look!" Alex said, moving forward, something crunching under his feet. I glanced down, noticing the bits of something white scattered under the shield.

Lucas looked confused, shaking his head. "I've seen behind that crest. I swear to you, there's nothing back there but a solid wall."

"But it all fits," Gabriel said, quickly catching his brother up on the broad strokes of the past few minutes.

While they talked, I moved closer, trying to figure out how to check without damaging the crest. There was even more of the dust and debris pushed next to the floorboard. Was it poor cleaning on the part of the Silverthornes' household staff or a hasty cover up job from a thief under pressure? Based on the immaculate state of the rest of the manor, I was willing to bet on the latter.

Bella called out. "Hey, Harper, come look at this!"

I rushed over to a nearby pedestal holding an ornate vase. Bella pointed inside, and I went up on my tiptoes to take a peek. Sure enough, there were handfuls of plaster and stone—the same that had been on the floor. My excitement peaked.

"This has to be it," I said, waving everyone else over, pointing out the hiding place and the bits of debris under the shield.

I turned to Lucas. "This has got to be it. Please. Help us."

"C'mon Lucas, give us a hand," Isadora implored.

Gabriel nudged his brother. "What have we got to lose?"

"A couple of toes if that thing comes crashing down," Lucas muttered. He glanced between the vase and me, weighing his options. With the promise of finding the missing jewels, it didn't take him long to agree. Without further hesitation, Gabriel and Lucas pushed against the heavy metal crest. It groaned in protest, but slowly swung to the side, revealing a shallow alcove behind it. A collective gasp filled the room.

Nestled inside the broken wall was a metal box.

"He made a makeshift vault," Isadora murmured.

"Smart. No one would've been able to move this by themselves," Lucas grunted, awe softening his earlier skepticism.

"Unless the person had super strength," I said, glancing at Gabriel.

He tipped his head towards the alcove. "It was you who figured this all out. You deserve to finish the treasure hunt."

My heart pounded as I reached for the box, the thrill of discovery coursing through me. We had found it—hidden in the heart of the Silverthorne estate.

Alex and I wrestled the box out of the makeshift vault while the others held the crest aside. Once free, we set the small but heavy metal box on the floor, and the men readjusted the crest. Being uniquely attuned to metal my entire life, I automatically scanned the box with my magic. It was ornately decorated, the aged bronze patina of the swirling etchings emphasizing the intricate design. I caught my breath, momentarily stunned by the beauty of the box. It displayed the kind of singular craftsmanship that demanded the utmost attention from a master metalworker. While I was distracted by the box itself, it was the locking mechanism that caught everyone else's attention.

"Three keyholes," Lucas muttered, crouching to get a better look. "Where are we going to find the keys?"

"They must've hidden them nearby," Gabriel cut in, his tone urgent. "They wouldn't have gone far with the blizzard."

"Maybe they're in the garage," Alex suggested. "Or what if they're hidden in plain sight?"

"No, no," Isadora interjected, "if I were them, I'd have stashed them somewhere completely unrelated. Somewhere no one would think to look."

Suddenly, everyone was talking at once, their voices overlapping as they threw out theories and debated possibilities. The room buzzed with frantic energy, and I realized this was the perfect opportunity. With everyone distracted, maybe I could unlock the box with my magic. I caught Bella's eye and gave her a small, silent signal. Without missing a beat, she sidled over, subtly blocking me from view with her skirt as I knelt beside the box. My fingers traced the cold metal, and I focused on the locks, trying to use my magic to manipulate the tumblers. Three was an odd number of locks for a box so small, but that didn't faze me. With my affinity for metal and the amplified magic from the serpent necklace, three locks seemed a trivial obstacle.

But something was wrong. The locks felt impenetrable, like they were forged from another world. Frustration simmered as I tried again, pushing harder with my magic, but it was like trying to whisper against a hurricane.

Bella murmured out of the corner of her mouth, "Any luck?"

I shook my head, frustration and confusion swirling inside me. Just then, Isadora noticed us. "Did you find anything?" she asked excitedly.

I straightened up quickly, covering my failed attempt. "Not yet. Just checking out the keyholes. It looks like the box has a really complex mechanism. Also, based on the design, I'd guess the keys are likely bronze as well. Probably pretty intricate too."

Officer Reggie spoke up, his voice filled with that familiar, almost sheepish enthusiasm. "Wait a minute! This might help." He fumbled with his phone, pulling up some photos. "These are the keys we found on the thieves. Each of them had one. Based on your description of the locks, maybe they're a match?"

He handed the phone over, and everyone crowded around, passing it from one to another, examining the photos of the keys. Lucas squinted at the screen, then looked at Reggie with a raised eyebrow. "Why didn't you mention this before?"

Reggie blushed, scratching the back of his head. "Well, there were only two keys, not three... so I didn't think they were the right ones."

"They definitely look like a match to me," Gabriel said, passing the phone to me.

"Now that you mention it, I think I see it," Officer Reggie said. "And, uh, could you all maybe not mention this to the Sheriff? I'm not really supposed to take photos of evidence, but sometimes I forget the details, you know? Helps me keep track of things, you know."

I shot a quick look at Gabriel, who instantly understood. He smoothly stepped between us, clapping a hand to the police officer's shoulder. "Don't worry. We're all on the same team here. You were just being thorough, right?"

Bella jumped in. "Absolutely! We're all friends here. We promise not to say anything."

Gabriel nodded instantly, miming zipping his lips. "Mum's the word."

While they kept Reggie distracted, I swiftly swiped through the rest of the recent photos on his phone, my pulse quickening as I searched for any additional clues the well-meaning but often forgetful officer might have overlooked.

Most of the items in the photographed evidence bags looked mundane—just a green clutch, a tube of lipstick, a compact mirror, and a pocket square. Not exactly the breakthrough I was hoping for. I swiped back to the keys, zooming in on one. The ornate, aged bronze key caught my eye. It was intricately designed, with delicate filigree twisting around the shaft and an asymmetrical bow engraved with what looked like an elegant script. The teeth of the key were unusual, clearly made for a specific and complex lock. The way it caught the light in the photo gave it an almost otherworldly glow.

"What are you doing?" Reggie asked, noticing that I had lingered on his phone a little too long.

I quickly zoomed in on the second key and flashed him a wide-eyed, innocent look. "Just looking at the key," I said, pointing out the intricate details.

That's when I saw it—a small inscription at the top of the key. "What does 'SE' mean?" I asked, trying to keep my voice casual.

Reggie shrugged. "We're not quite sure. Could be a place or someone's initials. I don't think it's a direction, but I haven't ruled it out," he added with a firm nod.

"Initials?" I repeated, glancing at Gabriel. He met my gaze, his expression serious. Clearly, he had made the same connection.

"No," I whispered, the realization hitting me hard. "Not...Seraphina Everbright?"

Family History

IN HIS HASTE TO tell the sheriff about Seraphina, Officer Reggie nearly forgot his phone. While the excited police officer said hasty goodbyes and hurried out of the study, I'd had time to contemplate the situation, and something felt off about it. The evidence seemed to be piling up against Seraphina—she was an enchanter elf, skilled with creating incredibly powerful enchantments like the one on the locks. Her initials were engraved on the thieves' keys, and she stood to benefit from the thefts, not just through the sale of stolen goods, but also in manipulating her business in order to move back to Havenwood.

Lucas quickly stepped up, taking charge. "We need to keep this contained," he said, his tone authoritative. "Isadora, can you go inform the guests that everything's under control? They need to stay calm and remain inside. Harper, Bella, and Alex, you should probably go with her. Gabriel, I need you to stay here and guard the box while I find Mother."

Isadora nodded and quickly made her way toward the grand hall. "I'll take care of it," she said, determination in her voice. She followed Lucas out of the room, Bella and Alex close on her heels. I moved to exit as well, but the box caught my eye, and I lingered.

There was something that still bothered me, like an itch I couldn't quite scratch.

Gabriel noticed the pensive look on my face and caught my hand, stopping me in my tracks. "What's wrong?" he inquired, a note of concern threading through his voice.

Bella said from the doorway. "Harper, are you coming?"

"Be there in a sec!" I called back, shooting her a thumbs up.

Bella hesitated for a moment, taking in the sight of Gabriel holding my hand, and then returned the gesture. "We'll be in the ballroom with everyone else if you need us," she said before disappearing.

Gabriel lifted an eyebrow. "I'm starting to learn your expressions and that one says you're onto something. What is it?"

"We have three keyholes, but only two keys, and we're assuming that Seraphina has the last one, that she's somehow involved in all this." I shook my head, the pieces of the puzzle still refusing to fit together. Gabriel waited patiently for me to continue. "Evidence says it's Seraphina. I just don't see the logic," I finally said, the concept of a jewel heist mastermind meshing with the friendly elf seeming to be at diametric odds in my head. "Why would she do this? She talked about moving back to Havenwood, and now she's implicated in robbing the jewelers she collaborates with and potential customers, right under the noses of the most influential family here? It doesn't add up."

Gabriel pondered for a moment, his gaze distant. "Maybe the whole 'moving back' story was just an elaborate con," he suggested, but even as he said it, he didn't sound convinced.

"No," I said, more to myself than to him. "I've seen her, *talked* to her. She seemed genuine about wanting to change her life. Her business was flourishing, and it wasn't the money that motivated her. She wanted..."

I caught myself just before I could say too much, before mentioning Finn and the possibility that Seraphina wanted to rekindle her relationship with him. That might lead to questions I wasn't ready to answer. The words died in my throat, and I suddenly felt exposed. My cheeks flushed with heat, and I instinctively looked down, avoiding Gabriel's eyes.

There was a pause, just long enough for my thoughts to scatter and nerves to tangle. Gabriel's voice, when it came, was quiet, but probing, "What did she want, Harper?"

I hesitated, feeling cornered by the simple question. My mind raced, searching for an answer that wouldn't reveal too much.

"I don't know... Maybe she just wanted something different," I offered weakly, peering up at Gabriel through my lashes, knowing it wasn't the whole truth.

Gabriel took a step closer, his gaze steady on me. "I can empathize. I wanted something different tonight too," he murmured. "A lot different."

The intensity in his eyes sent a shiver through me, the connection between us suddenly crackling with everything we left unspoken. My heart skipped, and I felt an almost overwhelming need to redirect the conversation.

"If she's not guilty, Reggie might push the sheriff to accuse an innocent woman," I said, my voice a little too rushed.

"And let the real culprit slip away," Gabriel finished, his tone still laced with the undercurrent of what was left unsaid between us.

Before I could respond, a sharp knock sounded at the door. It swung open to reveal Vivienne Silverthorne, her presence commanding the room with an air of unyielding authority. Lucas stood just behind her, his expression unreadable but grave.

"There you are," Vivienne said, her voice cool and precise. "The police need to speak with us all. Now."

My pulse quickened. The stern Silverthorne matriarch had always made me uneasy, but this was something more. Whatever the police wanted, my gut told me it wasn't good. And with Vivienne herself delivering the message, the stakes felt impossibly high.

The Key to the Case

THE WEIGHT OF THE bronze box slowed us down as we made our way through the grand halls of the Silverthorne estate. Just as we rounded a corner near the entrance to the ballroom, we nearly collided with Bella, who was returning from the restroom. She stopped abruptly, her eyes widening at the sight of the box we were carrying.

"What's going on?" Bella asked, her curiosity clear as she glanced between the box and our tense faces.

I quickly explained, as Bella walked beside me behind the Silverthornes. "We're on our way to see the sheriff. All the evidence is pointing towards Seraphina, but I'm still not entirely convinced she's to blame. I can't figure out a logical motive for her doing all of this."

Bella bit her lip and then shrugged. "Does it matter? If the evidence says she's guilty, then she probably is. The motive can come later. Some people just do terrible things for no reason whatsoever."

"That's what doesn't sit right with me," I said, lowering my voice. "Does she really strike you as the person who does terrible things? Every interaction I've had with her, she seems like a genuinely nice person."

"Maybe too nice," Bella said.

"Perhaps," I allowed. "Or maybe we're missing something bigger."

Bella gave me a sidelong glance, half-smiling despite the tension. "So, what's your plan? Catch the real culprit by surprise? It's not like they'll jump out and confess, 'I would've gotten away with it if it weren't for you meddling kids.'"

I couldn't help a wry smile at Bella's cartoon reference, a momentary lightness in the heavy atmosphere. "I can hope it's that easy," I replied.

"Or," Bella added with a playful glint in her eye, "gather everyone in a room, accuse all the innocent people, luring the actual bad guy into a false sense of security before revealing that you've known it was him for quite some time?"

I laughed softly. "We're not in an Agatha Christie novel, Bella."

"Maybe not," she shot back, "but if the shoe fits..."

"This isn't a scene from a childhood TV show. It's real life, and the stakes are far higher. I still can't help but feel that we're missing something."

Vivienne opened a door leading to a short hallway and the guesthouse beyond, signaling the end of our whispered conversation. As we entered, the tension was almost strangling, like a thread pulled too taut. Sheriff Jackson and Officer Reggie stood close together, their conversation a murmured undercurrent beneath the strained silence that filled the space. While they spoke, the sheriff kept a careful eye on the couple across the room.

Seraphina was a picture of distress, seated with her posture deflated, the tracks of tears on her cheeks glistening in the soft light. Finn was beside her, his hand enveloping hers, his expression a complex tapestry of anger and bewilderment. The scene struck a discordant note within me—something didn't add up.

I pushed aside the tangle of my own emotions, the sting of seeing Finn so devoted when he hadn't even checked on me since I was attacked. Now wasn't the time for me to deal with the complexity of my emotions. Instead, I focused on Seraphina. This tableau of vulnerability and support clashed with the narrative of her as a mastermind.

Sheriff Jackson turned as we entered. "Ah, good. You're here. I just wanted...wait. What's that? Is that the chest of jewels?" he asked, pointing at the metal box the men set on the carpet. He shot a questioning glance at Officer Reggie, who nodded.

"At least we think they're inside," Gabriel added. quickly "We haven't been able to get the box open."

Sheriff Jackson's attention was unwavering as he approached the ornate box. His fingers traced the contours of the box, its intricate design seeming to fascinate the sheriff. "Just like you said, Reggie. Three keyholes. Interesting," he mused. I imagined he'd made the same leap that I had about the two keys that had already been confiscated from the thieves, but the sheriff said nothing. I didn't want to get Officer Reggie in trouble by admitting I knew of the keys' existence too."The box is enchanted shut. We haven't been able to get it open," Lucas said.

"Enchanted, you say? Perhaps by an enchanter elf?" The sheriff stroked his moustache, considering the box. When he turned to Seraphina, his voice was firm. "Ms. Everbright, I'm afraid you need to come down to the station."

Seraphina's protest was immediate, her voice a mix of indignation and fear. "I didn't do anything! I'm not responsible for any of this!"

"Then break the enchantment," Sheriff Jackson said, pointing at the ornate box.

Her face drained of all color. "I can't," she whispered.

"Why not?" the sheriff demanded.

Seraphina's shoulders slumped. "Because I designed that enchantment to be unbreakable without the keys. Those boxes are how my company transports valuable items without fear. It will only open with all three keys."

Sheriff Jackson's expression hardened. "I've heard enough. You're coming with me to the station."

"Wait!" The word erupted from me before I could catch it, halting the unfolding scene. Flushed with the sudden attention, I struggled to articulate the conviction that was so clear in my gut, yet so nebulous in my mind. "Umm, you can't take her," I said, my voice softer than I intended.

The sheriff's brow furrowed, his gaze settling on me. "Why not? There's substantial evidence that links her to the theft."

My mind raced, the earlier conversation with Bella echoing in the back of my mind. Seraphina didn't fit the mold of a thief. The more I thought about it, the more certain I was. Something was amiss, and I needed to make them see it.

"Because it doesn't make sense," I finally said, my voice gaining strength. "Seraphina had no reason to steal, especially not in such a convoluted way. This isn't about opportunity; it's about motive, and hers doesn't align with the crime. The..." I caught myself before I could say the evidence didn't line up. "It just doesn't fit," I finished lamely.

Sheriff Jackson shook his head. "Be that as it may, there is enough evidence here that I still need to take her in for questioning." He turned to Seraphina. "Ms. Everbright, I'd like you to willingly come with me."

"To the station?" Seraphina's voice quavered.

"Don't make a fuss, and I won't cuff you and make a public display of this," the sheriff said, softening as Seraphina turned her beautiful, tear-stained face to him.

The room erupted into a maelstrom of protest and emotion. Seraphina's voice cracked as she pleaded her innocence, with Finn's firm yet comforting words backing her up. Vivienne stepped forward, her tone sharp and controlled, questioning the sheriff about the need for such drastic measures and whether the mansion could finally be released back to them. Lucas added his voice, concerned about the impact on their guests and the reputation of the Silverthorne family.

Meanwhile, Bella, Gabriel, and Officer Reggie were engaged in a heated debate off to the side, hypothesizing on where the third key could be. The cacophony of voices and emotions clashed, threatening to drown out any semblance of order.

I stood silently to one side, feeling like I was in the eye of this storm, my thoughts a tempest unto themselves. Then, like a lighthouse piercing through fog, a realization dawned on me. The solution had been with me all along, hanging rather conspicuously around my neck—the serpent necklace. It enhanced my power before, turning me into a human metal detector who could sense metal through the walls. Possibly the only reason I hadn't sensed the box of jewels in the first place was because it was hidden behind a giant metal shield. I already knew the necklace could amplify my powers. What if I could extend my magical senses to seek out the metal of the missing key? The Christmas ball had been a jewelry-free event to prevent just such a magical interference, so the field was clear save for the smallest bits of incidental metal in clothing or maybe a belt buckle. Those should be easy to identify and ignore.

Closing my eyes, I reached for the magic within. The silver serpent seemed to come alive, its energy intertwining with my own as I extended my senses outwards. It was like the room lit up with a veritable array of colors only I could see. A symphony of metallic whispers returned to me—buckles, cufflinks, hidden zippers. None had the distinct, unmistakable signature I sought. I was looking for a key, a shape both precise and utterly unique. With a clear picture of the key in mind and my magic-enhanced senses, it would stand out against the mundane murmurs of incidental metal like a star in the night sky.

I moved methodically as voices rose and fell around me, discreetly directing my focus toward each person in the room. The commotion swelled as the sheriff ushered Seraphina out, her fate hanging in the balance of evidence and law. The Silverthorne family's voices melded into a tapestry of discontent. Their frustration was palpable—whether aimed at the disruption of their evening or at Seraphina herself, I couldn't quite tell. The tension clung to the air, sharp and cold, as we followed the sheriff out into the snowy expanse beyond. Waiting police cars lined the driveway, their lights reflecting off the freshly fallen snow. Emergency responders milled about, while curious guests watched from the windows, their faces shadowed with a mix of concern and intrigue.

Gabriel's hand was firm on my arm as he pulled me aside and jarred me out of my magical focus, a questioning look creasing his brow. "Harper, what's going on? You looked like you were about ready to launch yourself at Seraphina. Or the sheriff," his voice cutting through the sea of chaos.

I met his gaze, urgency sharp in my own. "I was using my magic, trying to locate the third key," I confessed. "But I've looked. Seraphina doesn't have it. I'm certain."

His suggestion came quickly, a logical solution for the absent key. "She could have stashed it before all this."

Shaking my head, I couldn't accept that. "Maybe, maybe not."

Time was precious, and I didn't want to spend it arguing with Gabriel. The necklace's power seemed to hum at my throat as I tapped into it with my own magic, scanning the people around me and sifting through the myriad of slight metallic signatures that thrummed back to me. But as the seconds ticked by, a realization struck—I wouldn't find anything here. Most of the people outside hadn't even been on the scene at the time of the theft.

I skidded to a stop, frustration bubbling up inside me. Gabriel nearly collided with me; his eyes filled with questions. But there was no time to explain. I spun on my heel, my resolve hardening. "The ballroom," I muttered, more to myself than him. And then I was off again.

I wove through the throng, my senses stretched to their limits, the serpent's magic acting as an arcane beacon. The gathered responders, abuzz with speculation as Sheriff Jackson lead Seraphina towards his cruiser, parted around us, unaware of the invisible tendrils of my power that touched each of them, seeking the shape and feel of the third key, but there was nothing in the crowd that I could sense.

Time was running out.

Out of the corner of my eye, I saw the sheriff, his grip firm on Seraphina's elbow. She looked dazed, her steps unsteady, as he led her toward the waiting squad car. Officer Reggie stepped forward to assist, his expression a mix of concern and determination.

A knot tightened in my stomach, doubt creeping in. What if Seraphina wasn't the mastermind? If I didn't know for sure, how could I let this happen?

"It just doesn't feel right," I whispered to Gabriel, my voice trembling with uncertainty. "What if she didn't do it?"

Gabriel's gaze flicked to mine, a shadow of doubt crossing his features. "But all the evidence points to her," he said softly, though his tone wasn't as firm as before. "We've got the keys with her initials, the enchanted box, everything."

"I just...I need to know for sure, Gabriel. I need to be certain before we let them take her away."

He hesitated, clearly torn. The rest of his family might be upset about the scene, the ruined ball, but I could see the conflict in his eyes. He hesitated and then said, "I think in this case, we're going to have to trust the professionals. The sheriff is good at his job. If he thinks there's reason to take her in, we shouldn't try to stop him."

His words were meant to console, but they felt like a weight, anchoring me to a reality I wasn't ready to accept. Especially because I knew from personal experience, the sheriff wasn't always right, even if he was good at his job.

Before I could respond, Dominic appeared beside us, his expression calm and measured, completely at odds with the tension in the air. "Please, if I may," he interrupted smoothly, then turned to me, his tone polite but carrying an air of authority. "Could someone tell me what is going on? Why is my business partner being escorted to a police cruiser? What is happening? No one has told me anything."

Gabriel glanced at me, and I could see him weighing the options in his mind. What could either of us say to Dominic to explain everything that had recently happened?

Suddenly Vivienne called out, her voice urgent. "Gabriel, I need your assistance!" She was standing a several feet away, her expression strained as she spoke in low tones to one of the officers.

Gabriel squeezed my hand briefly. "I'll be right back," he said, his voice low with reassurance, though I could see the hesitation in his eyes.

I nodded, watching as he reluctantly walked away. Dominic turned back to me, his smile friendly, although there seemed to be more than a hint of frustration in his eyes. "It looks as though I will have to wait a while longer for my answers. It's freezing out here. Why don't we head inside while we wait?"

I shivered, not having realized in all the excitement that my fingers were already numb with cold. "That's probably a good idea," I agreed, falling into step beside him and blowing into my cupped hands to warm my icy fingers.

As we walked, Dominic's tone was light, almost conversational. "This whole situation is a mess, isn't it? Seraphina being implicated like this in the theft...I have to admit, it's really thrown me for a loop. Could she be involved in all the recent jewel thefts? Or is there something else going on? What are your thoughts on it?"

I hesitated, recalling the unsettling incident in the closet earlier. But Dominic's question seemed genuine, and his concern for his business made sense. With the police nearby and plenty of people around, I gave him the benefit of the doubt. If anyone could help me understand the situation with Seraphina, it would be her business partner. Taking a deep breath, I replied, "Honestly, I'm not convinced she's guilty. It doesn't make sense—why would she risk everything she's worked for?"

Dominic nodded thoughtfully, his expression serious. "I agree. I've known Seraphina for years, and to commit a robbery seems wildly out of character for her. That's why I wanted to understand the situation more completely before I get our company lawyer involved. I want to make sure we're doing the right thing, protecting our interests, but also not throwing an innocent person under the bus."

His words made sense, and the more he spoke, the more I felt my initial hesitation about him ebb away. It felt good to be heard, to have someone genuinely consider my concerns. I became absorbed in our conversation, laying out my doubts and theories as we entered through a side door of the mansion. My fingers tingled as the warmth replaced the cold, but I was too caught up in our discussion to notice. It wasn't until we were deep in a secluded part of the house, far from the bustle of the main event, that the unnerving quiet made me realize just how far we had wandered.

I paused, suddenly aware of the surrounding stillness. "Where are we?" I asked, glancing around.

Dominic smiled, a little too smoothly. "Just a quieter place where we can discuss things without interruptions. Don't worry, Harper. I just want to make sure we're on the same page before we take any action."

Something about his tone made my earlier apprehension resurface, but before I could react, he continued, "You were saying something about being unsure of Seraphina's guilt?"

I nodded slowly, feeling a sudden chill that had nothing to do with the cold. "Yes, but... I think we should head back. I need to talk to Gabriel—"

"Oh, I'm sure Gabriel will understand," Dominic cut in smoothly, taking a step closer. "But before you go, let's finish our conversation. After all, you wouldn't want an innocent woman to go to jail, would you?"

"No, but I really should go—"

"Stop!" The command halted me in my tracks.

I tried to move, to step back, but it was like wading through molasses. My brain screamed at my body to move, but the connection was sluggish, my limbs heavy and unresponsive.

Dominic's gaze hardened, his genial façade slipping as he stepped closer, crowding me against the wall. "I need that necklace, Harper," he hissed, desperation creeping into his voice. "I'm running out of time."

A chill of realization crept up my spine. "You... it was you all along," I whispered, the words barely audible as the truth slammed into me.

The pieces fell into place with horrifying clarity. Dominic wasn't just involved—he was the mastermind behind everything. The theft, the framing of Seraphina. It was all him. And he wasn't just a good salesman. He was compelling me to bend to his will. With magic. My mind flashed back to the theories Gabriel had put forth about the spell worked on Mystique. Could Dominic have whisper magic? Was he going to take the necklace from me and then cast the same spell that had left Mystique's memory in shambles?

With my feet frozen to the floor by his compulsion, there was little I could do except scream. I opened my mouth to do just that, but Dominic was faster.

"Don't make a sound!" His voice cracked like a whip, and the weight of his magic smothered me, pressing down on my chest like a heavy blanket, stifling my breath and any hope of resistance. I realized now that he'd been subtly using his magic all along, but this was different—this was a raw, overpowering force, suffocating any hope of resistance.

The scream that had bubbled up inside me slipped out as a mere puff of air. Dominic's eyes gleamed with satisfaction.

"Good," he purred, his voice a twisted mockery of gentleness. "Now, shut your mouth and give me the necklace."

My teeth snapped shut with an audible click. Panic swelled in my chest as I looked up at the man who had so completely rendered me helpless with mere words. I fought against his pull, my mind racing. If I gave him the necklace, he'd disappear, leaving Seraphina to take the blame, and no one would ever know the truth.

Dominic's patience snapped. His hand shot out, grabbing my arm with bruising force as he leaned in, his face contorted with a mix of fury and desperation. "You're going to give me that necklace, Harper. Now," he snarled, his compulsion magic wrapping around my mind like a vise.

Fear tightened my chest, but something inside me refused to surrender even as my hands drifted towards the back of my neck. I fought against his whispered commands with everything I had. My fingers hesitated between us in a battle of wills.

"Give me the necklace, then go hide somewhere in the house where no one will find you. Stay there for an hour, and don't make a sound," Dominic snarled. "Do it now or I'll compel you to do something truly awful. Like stop breathing."

His magic snaked through my mind, trying to override my will. I felt my muscles twitch in betrayal, my hands moving to obey his command as they hovered over the clasp of the serpent necklace. But the defiance within me grew stronger. I pushed back against Dominic's coercion, every ounce of resolve fueling my resistance. I'd been trained for physical self-defense, but this was different—this was a battle for my very mind. Even as I struggled,

I could feel his will crushing down on mine, trying to force me into submission.

My fingers brushed the cool scales of the serpent, and I drew on its power, not just to strengthen my magic but to anchor my will. The necklace had become a symbol of my power, my identity, a testament to the strength that had seen me through the night.

I wasn't about to let it go. Not to him. Not like this.

Dominic's whispered compulsions coiled tighter around my mind, squeezing out my remaining resistance. My fingers fumbled with the clasp, betraying my last shred of defiance. The chain slackened, the serpent's head dipping toward his waiting grasp. I was losing—losing the necklace, losing exposing him, losing everything.

His eyes gleamed with triumph as he reached out, the serpent's metallic scales catching the light in a final, mocking flash. I had no choice. The necklace was slipping away, and with it, any hope of stopping him.

meddling Kids

THE SHARP CLICK OF heels on the marble floor reverberated through the empty hall.

"Harper? Where are you?" Bella called, her voice echoing slightly off the marble

The moment Bella's voice unexpectedly sliced through the air, Dominic's concentration wavered, his magical hold momentarily faltering. It was the moment I needed, the split second of freedom from his coercive whispers. With a surge of willpower fueled by desperation, I snatched the necklace back from the precipice of his grasp and took several steps away from him, shouting, "Help!" My voice, freed from his magic's silencing by Bella's distraction, echoed through the halls, a clarion call that shattered the night's unnatural quiet.

"Freeze! Silence!" Dominic roared, thrusting a hand forward. I froze, as did Bella. But this time, his hold over me wasn't as complete.

"Help." The single strangled syllable escaped my lips.

Bella echoed me, but being closer to the crowd, her voice carried further. "Help us!"

Dominic glared and snatched at the necklace in my hands. Stubbornness welled within me. I might not be able to break his whispered orders, but the serpent was metal. It was my element. There was no way he was getting it out of my hands if I didn't want him to.

Dominic tugged futilely, grunting with the effort. He yanked me off balance and, without the ability to break my fall, I crashed to the marble floor. Hard. But I retained my grip on the necklace. I reached out with my magic, finding the item I was now sure was in his possession. A uniquely engraved bronze key. It was there, in his jacket pocket. I could sense it clearly with my magic, confirming my suspicions.

The pain from my fall cut through the fog of his magical compulsions. "It's him! He did it!" I said, pointing a finger at Dominic as I tried to scoot away across the cold marble floor.

Dominic's face twisted with fury, and his eyes flared with madness as he lunged at me, hands reaching for my throat, his control slipping entirely. Bella, showing no fear, threw herself between us, her fists swinging wildly. Dominic dodged easily, snarling as he did so. With a sharp command, he barked, "Freeze!" His voice lashed out like a whip, and Bella's body jerked to a halt, immobilized by his compulsion.

In that brief moment, while Dominic was focused on Bella, I scrambled to my feet. Panic surged, but I knew I had to act quickly. His power was in his voice—if I could stop him from speaking, maybe we could get away.

Dominic spun toward me, his expression ferocious, his eyes blazing with anger. There was no time to hesitate. My dad's self-defense lessons flashed in my mind, and I acted on instinct. I drove my knee up hard into his stomach, catching him off guard. The air whooshed out of him in a painful gasp, his body folding forward as he clutched at his midsection.

Seizing the opportunity, I chopped at his throat with my bare hand in a swift, brutal motion. The blow connected, cutting off any words he might have been about to utter. Dominic staggered, choking, his hands now scrambling to soothe the pain at his throat.

But I wasn't done. As he bent forward in agony, I snapped the heel of my hand up into his face. The impact with his nose produced a sickening crack, and his head jerked back as blood spurted from the break. Tears of pain welled up in his eyes, and for the first time, I saw genuine fear in his gaze.

Dominic crumpled to his knees, gasping and wheezing, his power over us broken. Footsteps echoed down the hallway, and

Gabriel skidded around the corner. Gabriel's eyes widened as he took in the scene. Without hesitation, he withdrew a gun from behind his back, leveling it at Dominic. "Don't move," he commanded, his voice cold and steady.

Dominic's face twisted with pain and fury, but he wasn't foolish enough to resist. His hands trembled as he slowly raised them in a gesture of surrender, his defiance now smothered by the torment of his injuries and the threat of Gabriel's gun.

The sheriff appeared a moment later. "Put that gun away!" he ordered, holding his own ready, but aimed at the floor.

"With pleasure," Gabriel said, waving his hand. The gun vanished in a whiff of smoke.

"An illusion!" Dominic wheezed through the blood dripping down his face.

Sheriff Jackson stepped past us, his own weapon drawn, the air around him crackling with authority. "Yes, but this one is not. Face down on the ground. Now," he thundered, his voice carrying the weight of an unyielding command.

Dominic, still clutching his nose and struggling for breath, glanced around frantically, his eyes darting from Gabriel to the sheriff's imposing presence. Panic flickered in his eyes, and he hesitated for a fraction of a second, weighing his nonexistent options. The sheriff actually growled, a low rumble that seemed to shake the very air. Despair contorted Dominic's features. I guessed he knew even if he could speak there was no way he could control this many people's wills at once, especially not a strong werewolf like the sheriff. His voice gone, his shoulders sagged in defeat, and with a pained groan, he slowly lowered himself to the cold marble floor, lying face down. His last vestiges of defiance crushed under the sheriff's unrelenting command.

I immediately ran to Bella, wrapping her in a tight hug while clutching the serpent necklace fiercely in my hand. Gabriel approached. His concern was palpable, and his presence was a comforting warmth amidst the chill of unfolding events. He put his hand on my shoulder, and I turned into his warm embrace gratefully. "We've got to stop meeting like this," he murmured into my hair. "Are you okay?" His voice was soft yet filled with an earnest care that made my heart flutter.

"Yes. I am now," I replied.

Maybe it was my adrenaline spiking or my low blood sugar, but the scene seemed to blur around me as Bella, Gabriel, and I followed Sheriff Jackson and the handcuffed Dominic back towards the guesthouse and the waiting police cars beyond.

Gabriel stopped us just inside the door. "Wait here. There's no need for you to risk frostbite," he said before hurrying over to his mother and siblings. A quick, whispered conversation ensued as the sheriff guided Dominic towards an empty cruiser. Vivienne stepping forward with a commanding presence, and Lucas and Isadora rushed off towards the ballroom, I assumed to manage the remaining guests.

What surprised me most was the approving nod Vivienne gave Gabriel, and then, astonishingly, one directed at me. There wasn't time to dwell on it, though, as Gabriel quickly returned and whisked us away to a quieter part of the mansion.

Gabriel guided Bella and me into a sitting room, a warm, inviting space filled with the soft glow of lamplight reflecting off polished wood and richly colored rugs. The quiet room was a sanctuary compared to the chaos outside. As we sank into the overstuffed chairs, a staff member discreetly appeared with a tea tray, setting it down with a gentle clink of porcelain. The fragrant aroma of freshly brewed tea filled the air, and as I took my first sip, the warmth of the chai started to calm my racing heart. The store-bought ginger snap cookies were a small comfort, but they did wonders in helping the world to stop spinning.

Slowly, the tension in my muscles began to unwind, and the adrenaline that had been coursing through my veins finally started to ebb. I was almost feeling normal again when Vivienne swept in with her usual composed grace. She was followed closely by Officer Reggie, who was escorting a slightly disheveled Seraphina, Finn trailing behind all of them.

"Please, sit," Vivienne said, gesturing to the remaining chairs as she took her place by the fire.

Seraphina, looking relieved yet cautious, took a seat beside Finn. Officer Reggie, always eager to help but not exactly subtle, filled the silence with his usual enthusiasm, his voice a little too loud in the otherwise quiet room. "Good news! The sheriff barely made it off the estate before those two thieves, Esmerelda and Aiden Jacoby, cracked. They saw Mr. Umbra being arrested and spilled everything, hoping to get a deal before he could. Apparently, his greed got the better of him, and even though business at Starlight Treasures was doing well, his debts were piling up. After several competitors had been hit by the thieves, Ms. Everbright here asked him to investigate and make sure their business was secure."

All eyes turned to Seraphina, who nodded silently, confirming Reggie's account.

The officer continued. "Apparently, he's a pretty decent detective because he figured out the Jacobys' identities rather quickly. If it weren't for the fact Mr. Umbra had just attempted grand larceny and is complicit in an attempted kidnapping, I'd consider working with him as a detective."

"I must say, that is one town appointment I would not approve," Vivienne said dryly.

The statement hung in the air, and I felt a chill run down my spine. I'd always known Vivienne Silverthorne wielded influence in Havenwood but hearing her speak so casually about the power she held—it was unsettling.

The realization hit me: being on good terms with her children didn't mean I was safe from her scrutiny. If anything, it put me more in the spotlight. I forced a smile, hoping it didn't betray my unease. Vivienne's attention flicked briefly to me, her gaze sharp, as if she could see through the layers of my thoughts. Then, just as quickly, she turned back to the conversation at hand.

"There's also the whole soon-to-be-convicted-criminal thing," Officer Reggie said with a nervous chuckle. "Anyway, when he discovered who they were, he realized he knew Esmerelda. Apparently, they both went to the same shadow magic academy as Mr. Umbra back in the day. The same one as your illusionist, Mystique, in fact. So, rather than turning them in, he partnered with them. First, it was for the money. He'd get them access to the events, they'd split the profit from the stolen jewels, and he'd protect his company from getting hit by thieves."

"Is that how he got the box Seraphina made? From the company?" Gabriel asked curiously.

"Exactly," Reggie said, snapping his fingers. "He borrowed it from work, knowing it would keep the Jacobys honest since there was no way to break the enchantment without all three keys. But when Ms. Everbright started talking about moving out of the city, Mr. Umbra panicked. He was scared that if she left, his scheme wouldn't continue to work, the business would slow down, and his debts would catch up with him. So, he concocted a plan to keep her around—without her even realizing it."

"The silver serpent," Seraphina gasped.

"Yep," Officer Reggie said, snapping his fingers. "His plan was to use the necklace to enhance his compulsion magic—his 'enigmatic whispers' as it's officially called—and convince Seraphina to stay in the city. Then, he'd use his magic again to make her forget all about it, including the necklace."

Finn frowned and put a protective hand on Seraphina's shoulder. "If he'd pulled it off, he could have controlled her with no one being the wiser." Seraphina shuddered at the thought.

"It's a good thing he didn't succeed then," Vivienne said sternly. "Although I am not at all pleased that he came as close as he did, especially under my roof."

I lifted the serpent necklace from my lap, turning it over in my hands. Its intricate scales glinted in the light, a symbol of power and a connection to a world I'd barely begun to understand. It had saved my life, made me feel like I belonged, like I was part of something bigger. Gabriel had trusted me with it, and in doing so, made me feel valuable and competent in ways I hadn't expected.

But as I stared at the necklace, a sudden realization hit me—it was dangerous. Although it was beautiful, this lovely piece of jewelry could so easily and disastrously be misused. In the wrong hands, it could be a weapon to manipulate and control, just as Dominic had tried to do. The thought sent a chill through me. I didn't want to become someone who clung to power or relentlessly chased money. I wanted to be someone who valued doing what was right and enjoying the small treasures of life, not hurting my neighbors. I thought of Spellbooks — I wanted to be like a good book, filled with warmth, wisdom, and a little bit of magic, leaving others better for having crossed its pages.

"I think this is safer with you," I said, handing the heavy necklace back to Seraphina. "You were right, though—it did lead to a pretty unforgettable night," I said with a small smile.

Lucas frowned, his voice cautious as he interrupted. "Are you sure that's a good idea? No offense, but she's been involved with some pretty shady characters. Can we trust her judgement?"

I felt a twinge of uncertainty, but Seraphina's expression was resolute as she cradled the necklace. "I understand your concern, and I don't blame you. Yes, I made mistakes, and trusted the wrong people. I see that now. But this...this is my chance to make things right."

She glanced down at the necklace. "I'm going to undo the enchantment," she declared, her voice steady. "Life isn't just about chasing wealth or status. I've been doing that for too long and look where it's gotten me. It's time for a new start." Her emerald eyes flicked up to Finn with a softness that belied the strength of her words.

My heart felt surprisingly light as I followed Seraphina's gaze to Finn. The expected pang of jealousy or loss was absent. Perhaps it was the chaos of the night that lent perspective, or maybe the silver serpent wasn't just a symbol for transformation, but a catalyst for it. My gaze found Gabriel across the room. In his eyes, I saw not just the reflection of the night's dark turmoil, but the promise of a dawn yet to come.

Perhaps I wasn't the only one who'd undergone a transformation this evening.

...And a Broom

COMPARED TO THE EVENTS of the Silverthorne Ball, Christmas Day felt remarkably peaceful. I woke up late to a crisp, clear morning with the sun sparkling off the drifted snow outside. The calmness of the day was like a gift the universe had designed just for me. I called my parents to wish them a merry Christmas and ended up spending much longer on the phone than I'd expected, catching them up on all the events of the night before. When we finally hung up, I contemplated lying in my cozy bed and either dozing some more or starting a new book. But there was coffee to drink and presents to give. Most importantly, the presents.

I slipped my feet into my fuzzy slippers and padded across the apartment to start the morning ritual of caffeination. As the rich, enticing scent of freshly brewed coffee filled the air, I grabbed a gingerbread man from the tray Honey had sent over earlier in the week. Since it was Christmas, eating cookies for breakfast was not only acceptable but also encouraged. At least, that's what I told myself as I grabbed another one before filling my mug and heading downstairs.

"About time you got up!" Luna harrumphed when she saw me. "How was the ball?"

"Well, in some ways, I'm envious of Cinderella. At least she was home by midnight or shortly thereafter," I said, a yawn cracking my jaw. Mr. Wigglesworth padded over, twining around my legs in a surprising display of affection. I crouched down to pet him.

"Danced the night away, did you? Don't tell me you lost a shoe," Luna said.

"No, not a shoe," I said with a rueful shake of my head as Mr. Wigglesworth left to stand by his conspicuously empty food bowl and gaze up at me with sorrowful eyes. I chuckled at his antics before filling up his bowl.

Luna's gaze sharpened. Nothing got by that rabbit. "If not your shoe, what happened? Are those bruises I see on your neck? Why do I feel like there's more to this story?"

"Because there is." I filled her in, stealing sips of the richly brewed cup of caffeinated joy in between sentences. By the time I finished, Luna's jaw was nearly on the floor, and my cup was empty.

"By the hoppy haunches of Thumper the Loud!" Luna exclaimed when I finished. "So, what happens now?"

"Well, I assume they're going to charge Dominic and his cronies, but I'm going to leave that up to the sheriff."

"Smart choice. That Jackson boy will show those fluffernutters what's what," Luna said with a derisive sniff.

I chuckled at Luna calling the sheriff a boy and set my empty coffee cup down on the counter. "Now that you know all the news and I've had time to recover from last night, I think we should do presents."

"That's the best idea you've had all week," Luna said, her whiskers twitching.

I hurried back upstairs and returned with an armful of gifts. A luxurious cat bed for Mr. Wigglesworth, which he promptly put to its intended use, having already scarfed down his breakfast. I'd asked Grimgor, my handyman-turned-friend, to help craft a perch upgrade for Gideon, the shop's guardian gargoyle. He dropped it off a couple of days ago, but I'd install it later. Gideon wouldn't wake up until the sun went down anyway, and it would be a pleasant surprise for him.

For Luna, I'd opted for a spellbound booklet I'd found in one of the local shops. It generated new puzzles daily, challenging her sharp mind and providing endless entertainment. I'd even gotten Spellbooks a gift. Most people might think it was silly to buy a shop a present, but, then again, most shops weren't sentient. The shop gave a little rumble of pleasure as I explained that I'd purchased a high-quality feather duster with an extendable handle, perfect for gently dusting the bookshop's delicate books and tall shelves to help keep the store in pristine condition.

Luna hopped over to her hutch and dragged out two small parcels. "Spellbooks and I chipped in for these together," she said, pulling the rectangular packages out.

"Aw, thank you. That's very kind," I said, unwrapping the first one.

"That one is from Spellbooks," Luna said.

It was a small book on the history of Havenwood that looked interesting. "This is very thoughtful of you, thank you," I said, placing my hand on the wall. The wood warmed beneath my fingers as the shop vibrated with happiness.

"Open mine next," Luna said, nudging it closer.

This package appeared larger and heavier than the one from Spellbooks. I unwrapped it to discover a cookbook with easy but delicious-looking recipes.

"Because you can't survive on coffee and cookies," Luna said with a sniff that sent her whiskers twitching. "I don't know what you're talking about," I said innocently and then grinned unrepentantly. Luna might not approve, but I thought my breakfast of gingerbread men was the perfect start to this or any other day. "Thanks Luna. I appreciate it."

Later in the day, Luna and I headed over to the Enchanted Oasis. The DeLucas had invited us for a Christmas day lunch, and I wasn't about to miss Honey's cooking for the world. Even with my new cookbook, it would be a long time before I could rival Bella's mom for culinary delights. Okay, I probably would *never* be able to cook like her, but I was more than happy to sample everything she made.

Antonio and Honey welcomed me with all the warmth and love of family. Bella and Alex had told them most of what had happened at the Silverthorne estate last night, but I filled in a few details as we feasted on Honey's delicious lunch spread.

The table was a masterpiece of culinary delights, groaning under the weight of roasted meats, fragrant pies, and an array of sides and sweets that could feed the town twice over. Laughter and the crinkling of paper accompanied the unwrapping of gifts, adding to the tapestry of festive joy as we exchanged them.

The walk home was a necessity both for returning to Spellbooks and working off some of the decadence of Honey's cooking. The crisp evening air helped to dissipate the warmth of overindulgence and ease my full belly. It also carried the clear voices of carolers performing somewhere nearby.

As fun as the ball was, nothing quite compared to sweatpants and a good book. I'd just settled into the armchair with my new history of Havenwood when I heard a knock at the door. Thinking it was carolers coming to spread some festive joy, I opened it wide. To my surprise, Finn stood on the other side.

"Merry Christmas, Harper," he said, holding out a small square box.

"Merry Christmas, Finn. Come in, won't you? I have your present inside," I said, waving him in out of the cold. Weeks ago, I'd gotten Finn a book on Celtic mythology that I thought he might enjoy because of his druidic roots. However, given the events of yesterday, I wasn't sure he'd want it. Part of me was very happy I still got to share it with him. We exchanged gifts, and I was delighted to unwrap a silver charm bracelet, complete with a delicate silver book charm.

"It's from Elowen Wispdale's shop. No enchantments. I promise," Finn said with a rueful grin.

"That's good to know. Here, help me put it on?" I asked, holding out my wrist. He snapped the clasp into place on the second try. I lifted my arm and admired the delicate jewelry glittering in the twinkle of the Christmas lights. "It's beautiful. Thank you, Finn."

"I have something else for you," he said, looking a little nervous. He pulled out a second flat box, this one emblazoned with a swirling gold logo. "Seraphina had to head back to the city to handle the fallout from Dominic's arrest, but she said she wanted you to have this."

I opened the box. Nestled inside was a necklace. The pendant was a silver disk surrounded in a rim of gold. Carved into the middle of the disk was a serpent coiled on top of a book. It was much more my style than the ornate, enchanted necklace.

"She said to tell you she selected it especially for you, as a 'thank you' for all you did for her. And she promises this one isn't enchanted with anything other than a tarnish-repelling spell."

I chuckled softly and shook my head. "She really is too kind. Please tell her thank you for me."

"You can tell her yourself. She's officially relocating back to Havenwood permanently. It might take her a couple of months to sort out the details of the business, especially without Dominic there to help. But she said that you and your friends were very kind to her, and that's one of the reasons she wants to move back here. For the more genuine people rather than the fakes she usually deals with in her job."

"I imagine finding out her partner was plotting to betray her doesn't help her good feelings towards the business or the city."

"Probably not," Finn admitted.

A pause of silence stretched awkwardly between us. I fidgeted with my new charm bracelet, and Finn shifted from foot to foot.

"So, what—" I started.

"Are you—" he said at the same time. We shared a smile, and he gestured towards me. "Ladies first."

"I was going to ask what your plans were with Seraphina? With her moving back here I mean," I rushed to add at the end.

Finn lifted a shoulder. "She and I have history, that's no secret. I think she's also interested in seeing if there is still something between us, but with the whole mess with Dominic, her business, and the big move, she's got a lot on her plate. I don't think that immediately jumping back into an old relationship when we've both grown as people is the best choice. For either of us."

"I see," I said, mostly to fill the silence.

Finn tapped his new book against his leg. "What about you and Gabriel?" he asked. "It seemed like something might have been happening between the two of you at the ball?"

I fiddled with the charm on my bracelet. "Not intentionally, but then there was the jewel heist, and I think everyone got swept away in the excitement." I knew I was dodging the truth, but I didn't know how I felt about Gabriel. It had only been a day, after all.

"I see," Finn said, echoing my words from a moment before.

"What does that all mean? For us, I mean?" I asked softly.

Finn sighed and ran his hand through his hair. "It means I like having you in my life. Seraphina is moving back to Havenwood eventually, which makes things challenging and confusing for me. But I'm not the kind of guy to lead you on."

"And I don't want to lead you on either," I said instantly.

Finn's smile was warm and genuine, cracking the ice that had been forming around my heart. "Well then, until we figure our lives and feelings out, how about we take a step back from any romance but keep doing what we've been doing? Hanging out, eating too much pizza, and enjoying sharing books? But with more open and honest communication than has happened in the past week?"

"I'd like that," I said softly. And I meant it. I didn't want to be a placeholder in Finn's life, but at the same time, he was one of the first friends I'd made in Havenwood. For an army brat who didn't have many long-lasting friendships, it was important to me to keep the ones I did have.

Finn's gaze carried a gentle understanding that seemed to smooth over any awkwardness. "Merry Christmas, Harper," he said, his voice carrying a warmth that matched the sentiment. He leaned forward, placing a soft kiss on my cheek, a chaste but meaningful gesture that spoke volumes of our intertwined past and the tenuous threads of the future.

In the wake of his departure, I stood for a moment, the ghost of his kiss lingering, a silent acknowledgment of the unexpected directions my life had taken since I moved to Havenwood. Once upon a time, I would have wanted all the answers immediately to what was going on between us, but for the moment, I was content to let things unfold as they may.

Shaking off the quiet reflection, I switched on some upbeat Christmas songs and set about tidying up the shop, the festive music lending a springy beat to my steps. With the handle of the broom as my microphone, I let loose a rollicking chorus of "Jingle Bell Rock" that woke Mr. Wigglesworth from his fourteenth nap of the day and set Luna's paws to tapping. Another knock on the door interrupted my grand finale. Curiosity piqued; I opened the door to find Gabriel.

He stepped inside, brushing a flurry of snowflakes from his shoulders. "Merry Christmas, Harper," he said with a shy smile.

"Gabriel! What are you doing here? I mean, Merry Christmas. But why aren't you celebrating with your family? Not that I'm unhappy to see you, of course, I just..." I felt myself tripping over my words and trailed off awkwardly.

Gabriel smiled and loosened his scarf. "I was. Celebrating with my family, that is. But I wanted to say I'm sorry about what happened at the ball. The heist, the danger...it's not the impression of Havenwood I want anyone to have. Especially you."

My heart skipped a beat at the look in his eyes. "Just Havenwood?" I teased lightly, trying to appear easy-breezy.

He met my gaze, earnest and a little intense. "No. Not just Havenwood. I especially didn't want you to get the wrong idea about my family or me, in particular. I know my mother can come across as a bit…well, intense. But I didn't want that to cloud your view of us." He paused, a slight smile playing on his lips. "Anyway, I wanted to make sure your Christmas was sweeter than your Christmas Eve. Here, this is for you." As he spoke, he extended a beautifully wrapped gift towards me.

I took the box, already curious, and carefully unwrapped it. Inside, nestled in tissue paper, was a selection of gourmet ice creams—perhaps the very ones he'd promised if the ball became too much. It was a thoughtful gesture that warmed my heart, and I couldn't help but smile up at him.

"I wanted you to know I'm a man of my word," he added, his tone soft, yet sincere. "And also," he continued, shifting slightly from one foot to the other, "I was hoping to make last night up to you—take you out for dinner since you missed most of the meal at the ball."

Glancing down at my less-than-glamorous ensemble, I raised an eyebrow. "Now? I'm hardly dressed for a night out."

Gabriel chuckled, his eyes twinkling with mirth. "Oh no, I wouldn't dream of missing out on broom-karaoke at Christmas. This looks far more entertaining than anything happening at home. In fact," he said, looking around at the scattered decorations and my impromptu microphone, "it looks like exactly my type of party."

For a moment, I felt a flicker of insecurity. Last night had been all glitz and glamour, a world of powerful magic where I didn't quite feel I belonged, especially without the serpent necklace. But as Gabriel stepped closer, his smile warm and genuine, I realized he wasn't just here out of obligation or to humor me. He truly wanted to be here, in this cozy, chaotic space, with me.

He brushed a strand of hair back from my eyes, his touch light and gentle. "Mind if I join in?" he asked, his tone easy and unpretentious. At that moment, I realized he wasn't trying to pull me into his world. Instead, he was happily stepping into mine. My earlier worries dissolved, replaced by a sense of ease and a smile. I nodded shyly.

With a sweep of his hand, he conjured a broom for himself, joining in on my makeshift concert as the instantly recognizable opening of "All I Want for Christmas is You" poured out of the speakers. The music swelled, and the snow painted the world outside in hues of silence and peace as we danced and sang, our laughter echoing through the empty shop.

As it turns out, I didn't need a fancy silver serpent to make my first Christmas in Havenwood unforgettable. All I needed was good friends, great music, and a broom.

Thank you

Thank you for making it this far. I hope you enjoyed the story. Now, I'd like to share another, albeit much shorter one with you, along with a piece of my heart.

Once upon a time, I was a kid with mountains of notebooks, each one bursting with stories and dreams. Writing was my sanctuary, my escape from the world. But as I grew older, reality knocked on my door and whispered, "Writing won't pay the bills." So, I did the "sensible" thing and focused on the real world. For a while, at least.

Then came 2020, a year that turned many of our lives upside down. As an athlete and musician, I suddenly found myself unable to do the things I loved most. In a desperate bid to fight against depression, I turned back to writing. It was like finding a long-lost friend. The stories poured out of me, and I started to feel alive again.

Not that it has been without struggle. Trying to fit writing in around work, kids, and life is like juggling flaming torches while riding a unicycle. But I've kept at it. Since then, I've written and published over 20 books, each one a labor of love and infused with a piece of my heart. I'm not an overnight sensation or a best-selling author, nor do I have a stack of rejection letters from traditional publishers. Instead, I've taken a different path, connecting with incredible readers like you who cherish a good story and a touch of magic.

This is where you come in. Your review is more than just words on a screen—it's a lifeline, a beacon that helps me reach new readers and continue this incredible journey. If you could take just a few minutes to share your thoughts, I would be deeply, deeply grateful. I read every single review, and they touch my heart in ways you can't imagine.

So, if my stories have made you smile, laugh, or brought a little magic into your life, please let me know. Your support and feedback mean everything to me, and they help keep the dream alive.

Thank you for being a part of my story, for believing in my characters, and for sharing this journey with me.

With all my gratitude and a heart full of hope,

Want a free book?

Of course you do, what madness could possess someone to **not** want free books?
There's no catch - you do sign-up for my mailing list but you can unsubscribe at any time.
There's also no spam.
Ever.
Sign up here to get your free book!
https://www.subscribepage.io/havenwood

Also By

Havenwood Paranormal Cozy Mysteries

The Mystery in the Margins
The Chaos in the Chronicles (exclusive novella)
The Puzzle in the Pumpkin Patch
The Secret of the Silver Serpent
The Riddle at the Revelry
The Heist of the Hidden Heart
The Mayhem in the Masquerade
The Legend of the Leaf

Smoke and Shadows Series

Shadows and Relics
Pixie Pranks (exclusive novella)
Felons and Fangs
Bones and Blades
Tempest and Treason
Daggers and Deception
Sleuths and Scoundrels
Legacy and Lies
Crossroads and Curses

Children's Books

The Secret About Mistakes
Corner of the Sky
To Mom. Love, Me
To Dad. Love, Me

To Grandma. Love, Me
To Grandpa. Love, Me

About the Author

L.L. Gray writes fast-paced, captivating fantasy full of wit, warmth, and magic. Her books whisk readers into charming, cozy worlds filled with lovable characters and whimsical adventures. A lifelong enthusiast of fantasy and myths, she weaves humor and heart into her stories, inviting readers to escape into tales that feel like home—cozy, magical, and hard to put down. When she's not writing, you'll find her on magical adventures with her children, battling make-believe elves or outwitting those mischievous gnomes next door.

Psst, it's me—L.L. Gray!

I love connecting with fellow story lovers and adventure seekers. If that sounds like your cup of tea (or coffee, or whatever magical potion you prefer), come say hello! Visit my website www.llgray.com to join my newsletter, where you'll find exclusive goodies, or join us in my Facebook readers group. And if email is more your style, feel free to drop me a line anytime at info@llgray.com.

I hope you stay in touch!

Acknowledgments

To my fabulous ARC and Street teams: you've become like a second family to me, cheering me on through every twist, turn, and chapter. Your unwavering support, encouragement, and excitement fuel my creative fire—I truly couldn't do this without each of you. Thank you for believing in these stories as much as I do.

To you, the reader: thank you for stepping into this world with me. I hope you felt the magic, warmth, and wonder woven into these pages. If you'd like to stay up to date with new releases and special content, head over to my website. And if you're looking to connect with a welcoming, book-loving community, join us on Facebook—there's always room for another story lover.

Lastly, to my wonderful husband: your support is the foundation of every story I write. Thank you for believing in me, for being my rock, and for making all of this possible. I'm endlessly grateful to have you by my side.